'As uplifting as summer sunshine'

Sarah Morgan

'A lovely story of families,
love and loyalty'

Milly Johnson

'A gorgeous read'

About
VERONICA HENRY

Veronica Henry is the *Sunday Times* bestselling author of twenty-one novels. She was a scriptwriter for some of our best-loved dramas such as *The Archers*, *Heartbeat* and *Holby City* before she turned to fiction. She lives in North Devon with three sons who come and go with the tide, and she flips between walking on the beach, swimming in the sea and mixing killer Negronis.

Find out more at www.veronicahenry.co.uk

Sign up to her Facebook page
www.facebook.com/veronicahenryauthor

Or follow her on Twitter @veronica_henry
and Instagram @veronicahenryauthor

First published in Great Britain in 2020 by Orion Fiction,
an imprint of The Orion Publishing Group Ltd
Carmelite House, 50 Victoria Embankment,
London EC4Y ODZ

An Hachette UK company

3 5 7 9 10 8 6 4

A CIP catalogue record for this book is
available from the British Library.

ISBN (Mass Market Paperback) 978 1 4091 8355 6
ISBN (eBook) 978 1 4091 8356 3

Typeset at The Spartan Press Ltd,
Lymington, Hants

Printed and bound in Great Britain by Clays Ltd,
Elcograf S.p.A.

www.orionbooks.co.uk

A Wedding at the Beach Hut

Veronica Henry

ORION

My dear,

I can't tell you what it means to be writing this to you. I have dreamed of this moment for so long. Thank you, for being brave. I know it must have taken a lot of courage, and I'm so grateful.

I wrote down our story some years ago, both for me and for you, on the advice of someone very wise, because I didn't want to forget a single detail if ever you were to ask. And it has helped me, to put everything down in black and white, because it made me realise that it wasn't black and white. That there were no victims and no villains, just a lot of people who were very afraid. And that what is right for one person is wrong for another, and how do you decide whose future is the most important?

Of course yours was the most important. I have spent the whole of my life praying that what happened in the end was the best thing for you, and now I know my prayers were answered.

Please read this with forgiveness in your heart and know that I have never forgotten, or stopped loving, you.

Emily

I

The first orange-tipped butterfly to appear in Everdene that year was spotted by Robyn Moss. She had no idea it was the first, but was delighted by the sight of it dancing across the dunes, skittering above the marram grass as if leading the way for her through the spikes, for it meant winter was firmly behind them and bright days were ahead.

She tried to keep up with it as she ran from the track at the top of the dunes, where her truck was parked, down towards the beach, but eventually she had to accept that she couldn't. She paused to kick off her flip-flops, which were always a hindrance as the sand got deeper. It was cold, icy cold on the soles of her feet, as the early morning April sun was not yet strong enough to heat the ground. She stuffed the shoes into her straw holdall on top of her towel and two warm pains au chocolat in a paper bag that she'd picked up on her way through.

The shop in Everdene sold everything you might need for a trip to the beach, from body boards to sunscreen to sticks of rock, and it had a hot oven that served up temptation throughout the day: French sticks, fat pasties, roast chickens. Her mouth watered at the thought of the sweet, melting pastries, the perfect reward for the ordeal she was about to face. Though on days like this, she didn't mind that their resolution this year had been to start each day with a swim in the sea unless the waves were really treacherous. She wasn't so keen when it was dreary and wet and the whole world seemed grey – the dunes, the sand, the sea, the sky all blurring into one.

Today, though, the colours were clearly demarcated. The grassy dunes were sage, the sand pale gold, the sea turquoise and the sky powdery blue studded with white clouds. And in between the dunes and the sea ran a meandering row of beach huts set out like a watercolour palette: blue, red, yellow, pink, green. They were all slightly faded after a long winter of assault from the sea spray; and they were all different sizes and shapes and ages. Some were immaculate, some battered and well worn, and it was inevitably the latter, the huts that had been in the same family for years, that held the most interesting people.

It was one of these huts that Robyn was heading to as she ran down the steep slope; one of the very first to have been put up on this stretch of beach in the sixties, when summers seemed longer and sunnier and more innocent, and ice cream didn't melt so quickly. When people knew how to change a bicycle tyre and recognised the chirrup of a stone chat, and were happy to eat potatoes from a tin. When there were three television channels and the *Radio Times* only told you what was on the BBC.

Being only just thirty, Robyn had no memory of this decade, but she loved the fact that her boyfriend's family had kept their hut almost frozen in time. Fondly known as the Shedquarters, it had bright floral curtains and Formica kitchen units and cracked old leather chairs and a record player, together with a stack of retro LPs: the Beach Boys, Joni Mitchell, Neil Young. She and Jake often picked things up in charity shops to bring back there. It was a nostalgic hug of a place, somewhere to leave your troubles behind, pour a beer or a coffee and switch off. Jake, his dad and his brother Ethan were all crazy surfers, and one wall was stacked with surfboards and wetsuits, the air heavy with the coconutty scent of board wax. Robyn surfed too but it was out of the question at the moment. She wasn't taking any risks.

She arrived at the front of the Shedquarters to find Jake still asleep in the single bunk at the back in a tangle of blankets and pillows. She knew how warm and cosy it must be in there and was tempted to clamber in and fall back to sleep in his arms. She'd made a decision not to shack up in the Shedquarters with him when he moved out of his rented flat to save money, preferring to stay in the relative comfort of her parents' farm. But she still felt a pang at the sight of his little nest, and her heart melted at how cute he looked first thing in the morning, all stubble and sleepiness and messed-up hair.

'Hey!' Jake reached a burly arm around her and pulled her in towards him. How easy it would be, she thought, as they kissed as if they hadn't only seen each other ten hours ago.

'Mmmmmm.' Jake pulled her in closer. She laughed, knowing what he had in mind. But a resolution was a resolution.

'Come on. Our appointment's at nine thirty. We better get going,' she said, rolling off him and prodding him. 'I'll make you a coffee. Which is pretty noble of me.'

Going off coffee had been one of the first signs. She'd

taken one sip of her morning latte and thrown up, and hadn't touched one since. She flicked the kettle on as Jake headed to the bathroom, made him a coffee, then grabbed her wetsuit from a hook. The water was still pretty nippy in April and she didn't want to get a chill.

She inserted one leg into her wetsuit and tugged on the neoprene in an attempt to get it on in one go. It was always a struggle. It was going to become even more of a battle before long. She pulled the rest of the rubbery fabric over her hips and turned for Jake to pull up her zip as he emerged minty fresh from the bathroom.

Once she was done up, she turned to one side, automatically breathing in. 'What do you think? Does it show yet?'

He smiled quizzically. 'Isn't it only the size of a chickpea?'

She counted on her fingers.

'Blueberry, raspberry, green olive, prune, strawberry – lime. I think we're on lime.'

Jake circled his fingers into a lime size. 'Wow.'

'Anyway, they'll measure it later. To work out the exact due date.'

She made an excited-but-scared face.

'Are you worried?' he asked, concerned.

'Of course I am. Aren't you?'

Jake looked again at the imaginary lime baby contained within his fingers.

'A bit, I suppose. But I know that whatever happens, we'll get through it.'

Robyn gazed at him. That was why she loved him. Jake was as solid as the rocks jutting out into the bay. Always there. Always the same. He never panicked or catastrophised. Was that what had drawn her to him? A contrast to the emotional rollercoaster of life at Hawksworthy Farm, always rife with drama and crises? Not conflict, for her parents adored each other. But there was often something thrumming in the air that made her careful and wary. Maybe that was farm life? You were always at the mercy of Mother Nature; never fully in control. They'd learned that, to their cost.

Yep, she thought. That was what had drawn her to him. That and the fact he looked super-hot in his board shorts – no wetsuit for him. She looked admiringly at him as he sipped his coffee. Broad shoulders, flat stomach, strong legs, shaggy dark hair. He was solid, in both senses of the word.

'Come on,' she said. 'Let's get going or we'll be late for our appointment.'

They set off across the beach, their fingers entwined. The tide was out, and it was a good few hundred yards across the damp sand, scarred with ridges from the pounding of the waves. The air here was forever filled with their noise: they were rarely silent, only in the highest pressure at the height of summer when the water was unusually flat, like a sheet of glass, and the surfers complained and looked on their apps for somewhere else along the coast to take their boards. A lone runner plodded along the shoreline; in a little while, the dog-walkers would start to appear. They had come to recognise the regulars: a frenetic Dalmatian, a pair of rescue greyhounds, an ancient basset whose ears dragged along the sand.

Robyn wondered if now was the time to mention what was on her mind? Probably not. Best to take it one thing at a time. Anxiety about the scan was making her thoughts whirl, and they would settle once it was over, she felt sure. It was weird, she thought, how one small change of circumstance could make something you thought you'd made peace with start to press on your conscience.

Ten feet from the water she stopped dead.

'It looks cold today.' The sea always looked more glacial with the sun on it. As bright and clear as arctic ice.

Suddenly, she found her legs going from underneath her as Jake scooped her up in his arms and started running towards the water's edge.

'You can't do that to me!' she shrieked, laughing as he surged through the first of the waves. 'I'm carrying precious cargo!'

He looked down at her lovingly. 'Oh, yes,' he said. 'So you are.'

He bent his head to kiss her and just as she shut her eyes to kiss him back he dropped her into the water, prompting a squeal of outrage.

They frolicked for about quarter of an hour. After two minutes, the water always felt warmer, and Robyn floated on her back, watching the sun rise higher over the dunes and letting her thoughts and worries drift away. It was all good, she reminded herself. The Linhay was coming along faster now. It was impossible to tell how much longer it was going to take, because you could never tell, with building projects, especially if you were doing them in your spare time. Even with professional help from Jake's dad, it had seemed to be taking for ever. But in the past month, the plastering and wiring had been done, the kitchen and bathrooms were being installed, and although the outside was a quagmire, all churned up with mud, their little house was starting to move on after all the seemingly endless, back-breaking, bank-account-draining hard work.

It was Jake who'd pushed the boundaries. Who'd fought for the plate glass wall in the bedroom that took advantage of the view over the wild ocean, and then found a Japanese soaking tub to go in front of it. And who'd suggested the oxide-red corrugated-iron roof instead of tiles, as a nod to the building's agricultural heritage. As soon as Robyn had seen it go on, she realised he was right. It had transformed it from a derelict cattle-shed into what would become a proper home. Their home. Their *family* home, all being well.

He'd consistently pushed the project a little further to tie it in with the natural world around it and make the most of its breathtaking location. He had a quiet vision and an eye for quirky design that Robyn found inspiring after being brought up by farmers who appreciated the practicality and longevity of UPVC. She looked at him now, powering out towards the horizon with his crawl. In a moment, he would turn back and swim to her and they would walk back up to the hut together and get dressed, eat their breakfast. And then it would be time.

She felt a little flutter inside her. It must be nerves, for it was too early for it to be anything else. All being well, this morning would be a turning point. They could tell everyone their good news. Start making preparations. The room at the Linhay that was next to the master bedroom would officially become the nursery.

It was all the architect's fault. She had pushed them to put extra bedrooms on the plans.

'This is going to be your for ever house. You don't want to wish you'd made it bigger in five years' time. You don't want to go through the stress of building an extension. And you might not get permission. Much better to think big now and factor in everything you might need.'

And once the rooms had been there on the drawings, they seemed to be crying out to be filled. Robyn had half-joked to Jake that they might as well start trying for a family straight away. They'd been together four years, after all, and were both keen on the idea of children, and agreed they wanted them sooner rather than later as Everdene was such a wonderful place to bring up kids.

'We might as well crack on now. We're both the wrong side of thirty,' she pointed out.

'Only just!' protested Jake, vainer than she, but he'd agreed.

And boom! Two months later, she was pregnant. They were shocked, delighted and alarmed in equal measure. Now they really did have to get cracking with the house. The idea had taken some getting used to at first, and Robyn had felt a bit off-colour, made worse by the strain of keeping it quiet. But not for much longer.

Robyn sculled herself around in the water for a few more minutes, wondering if this was how the baby inside her felt, weightless and floating and free, like a little astronaut in space. And no matter how hard she tried, another image kept coming back to her: a young girl, panicking, worrying, wondering what to do for the best. The image had been haunting her over the past few nights, waking her several times, along with the need to pee, both impossible to ignore.

Suddenly, Jake's head popped up beside her like a friendly seal.

'Will you stop doing that?' she laughed.

He always took her by surprise, gliding underneath the water and bobbing up when she least expected it, making her jump.

'You OK? You look miles away.'

'Fine. Just anxious about the scan, that's all.' She didn't tell him the truth. It was a quandary she didn't want to share with him. Not yet. 'Come on. Let's go.'

She swam back towards the shore, Jake following behind her.

In the hut, she jumped under the lukewarm trickle that passed as a shower – another reason she wasn't shacking up with Jake while they waited for the Linhay to be finished – then fell upon her pain au chocolat. The morning swim always sharpened her appetite, and the nausea she'd felt in the early weeks of pregnancy was thankfully fading.

She pulled on her clothes, trying not to think too much. In two hours' time, she thought, I'll know if everything is OK. And if it was, then she could decide what to do.

2

'This is surreal,' said Jake as they walked through the hospital car park half an hour later. 'The last time I was here was when Ethan broke his collarbone at the skate park. Me and Dad sat with him for five hours in A and E before he got a scan.'

'Last time I was here was when I broke my nose.' Robyn touched the slight kink left when a horse threw up his head just as she was leaning forward to take a jump. 'Ruined my modelling career.'

Jake grinned. 'I'm glad. Can you imagine how high maintenance you would have been? Impossible.'

Robyn rolled her eyes but she was smiling. She could never be accused of being high maintenance in her Breton shirt and dungarees, her curls still damp with seawater.

They walked in the entrance through the automatic doors. By reception, Robyn scanned the list of departments until she found the maternity unit.

'Second floor,' she said, and they headed off along a long corridor with grey flooring marked out with yellow arrows. There were red double doors. A cavernous lift. More red double doors. And eventually, a waiting room with blue plastic chairs, piles of old magazines and anxious couples pretending to be blasé.

'I hope we don't have to wait long,' whispered Robyn. 'I'm dying for the loo already.'

She'd drunk a bottle of water in the car, following the midwife's advice. 'It makes it easier to see the baby,' she'd explained. Which was all very well, thought Robyn, trying not to think about it all sloshing about inside her. They sat in silence, because it seemed wrong to make idle chatter or speculate about the scan in front of other people when you didn't know their circumstances. Eventually, they were summoned into a dimly lit room by the sonographer.

Robyn lay on the examining bed. 'I've just realised this wasn't the most sensible choice of outfit,' she said, rolling down her dungarees and pulling up her top so her tummy was exposed. The sonographer tucked a paper towel into her knickers, then squirted a clear, cold gel onto her stomach.

Robyn made a face at Jake, who was sitting on a nearby chair, feeling slightly superfluous.

'I won't show you anything until I've found the heartbeat,' said the sonographer, the screen tilted away from them. She ran the probe over Robyn's tummy, rolling and re-rolling while looking at the screen intently. Robyn concentrated on breathing and tried not to panic. Jake held his breath completely, hating the feeling of being out of control of the situation.

It felt like hours, but it was probably only half a minute until the sonographer smiled.

'Perfect,' she said. 'Take a look. Here's your baby.'

There was a grey blur on the screen, indecipherable at first, but gradually an image became clearer. A little head on top of a body, lying at the bottom of the screen as if it was lolling in an invisible hammock.

'Oh,' said Robyn softly.

Jake said nothing. He just stared, his eyes like saucers.

'Here's the head and the spine.' The sonographer pointed them out with a little white arrow. 'This is quite a good view. Sometimes they try and hide everything but look – there's a hand.'

'Look at those little fingers!' breathed Robyn.

Jake couldn't speak.

'I thought it would just be a blob,' he managed eventually.

'It's got everything,' said the sonographer. 'It's all there. I just need to get some measurements done and then we can confirm your due date.'

'I reckon it should be about the fifth of November,' said Robyn.

'So we'll have to call it Guy,' said Jake. 'Or Catherine.'

'Or Roman.'

Nerves were making them banter while the sonographer clicked away on her keyboard.

'Yes, I reckon you'll be setting off fireworks about then,' she laughed. 'Fifth of November it is.'

'Bloody hell,' said Jake. 'Who's going to light the village bonfire? That's my job.'

'It'll probably be late,' said Robyn. 'First babies usually are.'

'Everything looks absolutely just as it should,' the sonographer smiled. 'We'll see you again at twenty weeks.'

Afterwards, Robyn shot to the loo before they made their way back along the corridors to the exit.

'Fifth of November,' Jake kept saying, and wiped a tear away with his sleeve.

'You softy,' Robyn teased.

'That was our baby we just saw,' he said. 'A real baby.'

'I know,' she said.

Just as he was about to pull himself together he burst into proper tears, putting his arms around her neck. She patted him on the back, still laughing.

'I didn't know I'd be like this,' he said. 'I didn't know I cared this much.'

'Well,' said Robyn. 'I'm glad you do.'

'We'll tell everyone tonight, right?'

'Yes. I think we should tell them all together. It seems fairest. You can ring your mum afterwards.'

'I'll probably cry again.'

'We could just show them this.' Robyn held up the photograph the sonographer had given them to take away as a memento.

Jake took it off her and stared again at the little figure. 'You beauty,' he said.

Robyn traced her fingers over the limbs. 'Hello, little one.' Her voice quavered. 'Oh, dear. It's my turn now. Hormones. Sorry.'

She laughed through her tears.

'Well,' said Jake. 'At least we've got the perfect name. Whether it's a boy or a girl.'

'What?' She looked at him, puzzled.

'Sandy,' he laughed, and she gave him a nudge on the arm, blushing at the memory of a crisp cold night on the beach staring at the stars under a fleecy blanket, one too many shots of Baileys in their flask of hot chocolate. And sand everywhere. The two of them were still laughing when they reached the truck, earning smiles from passersby, for who couldn't smile at two young people in love?

3

The recreation area at the Mariscombe Hotel was a scene of organised chaos, workmen running hither and thither in a choreographed dance of wheelbarrows, a radio blaring as they dug and tiled and laid bricks. Getting the contract to do the renovation had been a massive achievement for Jake and Robyn. All the painstaking hard work they'd put into smaller projects had paid off, and their reputation was going before them. The hotel was in the next bay along from Everdene and was the biggest in the area: once a rundown family hotel, it was now a glamorous seaside playground that provided a lot of local employment.

The brief from the owner, Bruno Thorne, had been to create an Ibiza vibe around the hotel's outdoor swimming pool. White concrete and turquoise tiles, teak sunbeds and parasols, built-in cocktail bars and a row of thatched cabanas for changing; everything interspersed with sculptural palms and tropical plants. It was a challenging project but hugely exciting. They'd won the bid despite stiff competition from other much bigger companies, and it was a real step forward.

Robyn and Jake had joined forces after bumping into each other on several jobs a few years ago. They were both freelance landscape gardeners, but Jake was the 'hard' side – digging, slabbing, fencing, decking – while Robyn was the 'soft' side, the plantswoman, and gradually people started recommending them as a pair.

'You two should go into business together,' a client told them after inviting them round for a drink to admire their joint effort. 'You'd be unstoppable.'

As they'd looked out over the tiered terrace, planted up with drifts of lavender that scented the evening air, they had to admit it made sense. They could coordinate projects more cost-effectively and share expenses. Jake was always behind on admin and didn't get around to chasing-up enquiries; Robyn often needed to hire in an extra pair of hands for the heavier jobs. They went on for a drink at the Ship Aground afterwards and sealed the deal over a plate of loaded chips – thick and triple-cooked then smothered in melted cheddar, sour cream, spring onions, jalapeños and salty lardons. It was the pub's signature dish and no one could eat a portion on their own.

At first, they were just business partners, and they made the perfect team, gradually learning from each other: Robyn taking on board the practical implications of what was possible and how to make it cost-effective, and Jake beginning to be more understanding of plants and flowers and how they could be integrated at the planning stage rather than plonked in afterwards.

Now they were hugely in demand. More and more people in the area were taking on renovation projects, and hotels and restaurants were having to keep up with the Instagram age. Raised beds stuffed with alliums and aga-panthus; fairy-lit pergolas; zen-like water features; playful topiary; outdoor kitchens with fire-pits ablaze – whatever your garden dream, they could bring it to life.

Jake was brilliant at translating what people had in their heads – or had seen on Pinterest – into something achievable, and had the practical skills to copy anything clients showed him; and Robyn was a genius at creating drama and atmosphere with plants. They were good at pricing, too – they brought the jobs in on budget but with plenty of profit for themselves by doing most of the work between them and taking on a couple of youngsters they were training up. They worked hard, kept the lines of communication open between themselves and their clients, and were quick to make suggestions that would expedite the project.

At first, they had both been seeing other people, but as the weeks turned into months, they found they were spending more and more time together outside work: a quick six o'clock drink, a couple of working lunches to brainstorm. Robyn invited Jake and his girlfriend to dinner at her flat in Tawcombe, and her own date had been sulky at the end of the evening.

'You two did nothing but talk shop,' he complained, and after that he dialled it down before telling her it wasn't working. She didn't protest. Then Jake told her his girlfriend was moving up country and he didn't think they were going to carry on seeing each other.

Once they were both unencumbered, they felt slightly awkward. Robyn suspected that had they not been business partners, it would have been easy for them to express their attraction, but instead they were rather coy, both scuttling away at the end of the day, scared of making the first move in case it ruined their working relationship.

To hell with it, she thought the day she had found herself gazing at the strip of brown skin between the top of his cargo pants and the bottom of his polo shirt as he bent over. I'm going to have to take things up a gear.

And she'd asked him over for dinner. On his own.

'I've been wanting to kiss you,' said Jake later that evening, 'since you strode onto my site in your shorts and wellies and told me I was laying the path all wrong.'

'You were,' she said. 'It was supposed to be herring-bone.'

He lifted his hands and buried his fingers in her hair either side of her neck, his strong fingers caressing the back of her scalp. Robyn tipped back her head and shut her eyes. She'd been longing to be touched by him for so long.

That had been nearly four years ago. We've come a long way since then, thought Robyn, as their pick-up swept in through the hotel gates and rumbled through the grounds to the pool. She looked at their sign perched at the site entrance – The Moss Partnership. Jake hadn't minded them using just her surname. It was perfect, and he had no ego.

Robyn picked up the bag containing her work gear – boots and gloves and a hard hat.

'I'll see you in about an hour,' said Jake. 'I'm going to the builder's merchant to pick up some gabions.'

Robyn frowned. 'Won't they deliver?'

'I need them today. I want to get started putting them in. If I can get them in place by the middle of next week, we're nearly done.'

'Except for the planting and the painting and the snag-ging and getting all the furniture in.'

He grinned. 'Like I said, nearly done.'

'Two weeks, do you reckon?'

'Yep.'

Robyn clenched her fists in triumph. Then they could take pictures for their website and hopefully more contracts would come in off the back of it. And they'd get paid, which meant they could move the Linhay on. The baby had given them something of a deadline, after all.

She scrambled out of the truck and slammed the door, banging her goodbye on the window.

Jake watched her go for a moment, a lump in his throat. He couldn't remember the last time he'd cried, but he'd done it three times today. He turned the truck round and drove out of the grounds. He wasn't going to collect gabions at all. Not yet, anyway. He needed to clear his head. He felt overwhelmed. Until today he'd only had Robyn's word for it that they were having a baby. Not that he disbelieved her but it had been a bit theoretical. A blue line on a white stick meant nothing to him, but a collection of limbs on a screen were living proof. It crystallised so many things for him. How much he loved Robyn. How excited he was about the house they were building together. How happy he was about everything they had in Everdene, not least their two families. They were going to tell them all tonight.

Every Friday once the weather got finer they all gathered at the Shedquarters in the late afternoon. Jake's dad Rocky got the barbecue going early on and everyone brought along contributions. It was a great way to start the weekend, everyone talking over what they'd got up to during the week, getting a chance to unwind, have something to eat and drink together. And if anyone wanted to carry on and go out afterwards they were usually all done by eight o'clock. Robyn's younger sister Clover and his brother Ethan would go off to the Ship Aground, where there was usually a band on.

There was only one slight problem. Tina. His mum. She was miles away, up in Enfield. She'd gone back there after she and their dad had split when he and his brother were teenagers. Should he tell her before or after his dad that she was going to be a grandmother? She was his mum, after all, even if she had abandoned them, though strictly speaking it had been him and Ethan who had chosen not to go back with her. It was still hard, even now, being the child of divorced parents, trying to keep everyone happy and do the right thing. Sometimes it seemed impossible.

He wasn't going to let anxiety about his mother ruin the day.

He had something else to do first. Something had hit him inside that darkened room, and he was going to do something about it straight away. And he knew just the person who could help him.

He headed off into Tawcombe, the small town just a few miles from Everdene. It was a town of many sides. Its harbour was small and buzzy and had undergone a renaissance in the past few years, lined with bijoux restaurants and boutiques and gift shops that had once lain empty. Further into the town were the tacky tourist shops selling keyrings and postcards and paninis and ice cream, interspersed with arcades and pottery-painting cafés for rainy days. And right in the heart of the town were the greengrocers and the key-cutters and the sprawling old pubs that served the residents: the people who were still here out of season and struggled to make a living when the tourists vanished.

He wound his way through the back streets just off the harbour to Artist's Row, where there was a wiggly line of picture galleries and workshops. He pulled up outside a small shop painted dusky blue with gold writing. Inside he could see just the person he wanted. He pushed open the door and stepped inside.

'Marley!' He greeted his old friend. 'I need your help.'

She turned to him. She looked as beautiful as ever, with her trailing white-gold hair and pale-green eyes. She smelled of tangerines and salt. She'd smelled the same as long as he'd known her, the first person who had spoken to him when he'd arrived at the sixth-form college in Tawcombe, an uncertain boy with a London accent, though he had soon realised he was never going to be of interest to her.

'It's about time.' She looked at him archly, her eyebrows raised. 'It's taken you long enough. I was starting to think you might have gone to someone else.'

4

Plump local mackerel slashed and coated in rose harissa. Chunks of Exmoor lamb skewered with red onion and peppers and button mushrooms. Slices of aubergine and courgette cut lengthways, marinating in sesame oil and garlic and ginger. And some halloumi and baby new potatoes in their skins.

It was all laid out neatly in tins, ready to be put over the flames.

Rocky Young took his barbecuing very seriously. He tried not to be a control freak, because he knew that was unattractive. But he loved the preparations and the careful timing, the science of it all. And because he was always the first one there on a Friday night, and the Shedquarters belonged to him, and therefore so did the barbecue, he thought he got away with it.

Today, he had gone for easy options because his concentration was slightly off, even though he was trying to play it cool. Nevertheless, every now and then he had a moment of panic. There was still time to cancel. People must get cold feet all the time. He could easily make up an excuse. But that was the coward's way out. How would he know, if he didn't try?

He hadn't told anyone yet about his date later that

evening. If there was one thing he hated, it was gossip. People had stopped asking, but not wondering, why Rocky Young was still single after his divorce fifteen years ago. It was one of Everdene's greatest mysteries. There were rumours of older married mistresses and girls too young for him, and even men.

None of the rumours was true. He'd had the odd fling, usually when he was off his home turf, but Rocky simply hadn't had the heart for another relationship after the breakdown of his marriage. He blamed himself, and it had shaken him. When you married your childhood sweetheart, and did everything you could to keep her and your resulting family happy, it was a kick in the teeth when it all went wrong.

Being single had just seemed easier. You couldn't let anyone down then.

He didn't know what had made him feel now was the right time. Perhaps he was feeling his empty nest more keenly than he realised? After being pretty much a single dad to the two boys for so long, his younger son Ethan had moved out a couple of months ago to a houseshare. It was about time, as Ethan was twenty-six, and nothing would have made Rocky stop him, but it was odd to have the house entirely to himself. Jake had moved out five years before, and Rocky had felt a leap of hope when he'd left his rented flat recently, but Jake had opted to camp out at the Shedquarters.

'It just feels wrong, moving back in with your dad at thirty,' he explained, and Rocky had to stop himself from begging.

Small and snug though his coastguard's cottage was, it now felt cavernous. He could feel its emptiness when he woke up in the morning. No sound of someone else in the shower. No one else's shoes to trip over, or their music pounding up through the floorboards – what had once been an annoyance was now an echoing silence. Even though he had a job that brought him into contact with people all day long, even though he was a fixture at the Ship Aground and had endless mates to go surfing and fishing with, he felt lost.

He needed a partner in crime. Someone to discuss the weather with when he got up – as a builder, it was key to his day. Someone to debate what to do with the leftovers in the fridge: chuck them, or liven them up with a bit of chilli and some garlic? Someone to confess his dread of an upcoming dentist appointment. Someone to bring him a beer when he'd mowed the lawn. Someone he could ask to pick up a spare loo roll on their way home.

It wasn't the big things. It was the tiny ones. The ones that reminded you that you mattered.

He picked up his phone again and flicked through to the app. Seaside Singles – for people who lived on or loved the coast. It was a little bit niche, but he felt more comfortable with parameters than having the entire universe at his disposal.

Writing his profile had been agony. How did you describe yourself without coming across as either boring or big-headed? You had to strike the right tone. And have a sense of humour about it; not take yourself too seriously. He had spent night after night re-writing.

A little bit Hemingway with a splash of Anthony
Bourdain and a hint of Guy Ritchie. My perfect
Saturday would be an early morning surf, good

coffee and the newspapers, down to the harbour to
get some fish, chuck it on the barbecue, watch the
sunset and listen to some Sufjan Stevens or play my
guitar (badly!). I'm a builder by trade but I'm looking
to wind down over the next few years and maybe
have some adventures. Costa Rica? Comporta? I
love the sea but I come from London, so quite at
home in the big smoke – but only for a short while.
Looking for a chilled-out companion with a sense
of fun who will push me out of my comfort zone.
Oh, and I have a Hungarian Vizsla called Lara so it's
probably best if you're a dog lover.

That was as much as he wanted to say. It made him cringe
every time he read it, but he had to take the plunge.

He'd received a lot of likes, but he knew he probably
would: he was a good-looking man, with his thick salt
and pepper hair cut close and his denim-coloured eyes.
He'd chosen a picture of him sitting on the steps of the
Shedquarters in his jeans and a roll-neck jumper, his feet
bare. A little bit Paul Newman; a little bit James Dean,
but not showy-offy like some of the gym bodies displayed
online. He looked after himself but of course there was
a touch of softness about his belly now, a slackening of
the arm muscles. He was over fifty, so he thought that
was allowed.

Eventually, he had struck up a dialogue with a woman
who described herself as a 'successful entrepreneur/
wannabe mermaid'. He wasn't too sure about the whimsical description, and she looked a bit twee in her picture:
there was a lot of long hair, and she was lying in a hammock, wearing silky harem pants and an off-the-shoulder

sweater. He supposed she was going for a hint of sexy, though thankfully not pornographic and pouty like so many of the profiles he saw and instantly rejected.

> I work hard and play hard (don't we all!). I'm a
> physiotherapist with a successful practice but I live
> for the sea – stand-up paddle-boarding, kayaking,
> swimming. I have a healthy lifestyle but like to
> let my hair down at the weekends. Looking for
> a playmate to discover everything this beautiful
> coastline has to offer.

Rocky wasn't convinced she had the potential to be his soulmate, but perhaps she was a good person to test the water with. It was so hard to read between the lines, even harder to tell if the photographs on display were recent or touched up.

After a few evenings of polite online chat, they had agreed to meet for a drink. And you just never knew. Maybe she would turn out to be the love of his life? Maybe they would grow old together in utter bliss?

Oh God, he was getting carried away and romanticising. But the fact that he was made him realise that he *did* want someone to be with. And what was the worst that could happen?

Lara bounded up to him and nudged his calf, looking for attention.

'Hey, girl.' He fondled her smooth, tawny head and felt a surge of gratitude towards her. A dog went a long way to filling any hole in your life, he thought. They brimmed over with unconditional love and kept the other side of the bed warm. And gave you a reason to get up in the morning if you didn't feel too chipper. Many a time he had been tempted to stay under the duvet but had forced himself up and out with her.

He hadn't been out on a proper date since he'd asked Tina out in 1986. Though actually, she'd asked him. She'd been a Saturday girl at the salon where he was having Paul Weller spikes and pointy sideboards, and she'd swept up the remnants of his hair and caught his eye in the mirror. He'd winked at her and she'd come and leaned on the counter while he paid.

'You a Paul Weller fan, then?' she'd asked. 'Only my brother can get tickets to the Style Council, if you want to go.'

He'd been blown away by her boldness and her peroxide bouffant hair and her red pout. She had sass and style. He was already working as a hoddie, carrying bricks on a building site, and had a pocketful of pound notes. They were golden. They were young and beautiful and ambitious—

He couldn't look backwards. Regret got you nowhere. It was his time now. His second time, maybe. There was no reason he couldn't find someone who dazzled him, challenged him, drove him, like Tina had.

He looked back at the picture on his phone. Chances were that the first person he met wouldn't tick all those boxes, but he had to start somewhere.

'Hey, Dad!'

He turned to see his younger son bounding down the dunes, cradling a box of beer in his arms. Ethan was Everdene's poster boy – six foot of toned golden flesh topped with tousled sun-streaked curls and a dazzling smile. Jake had never seen Ethan unhappy. He'd got life worked out. Work and chill. He spent the summers teaching surfing, taking people coasteering and swimming with seals, fulfilling their outward-bound fantasies. In the winter he helped Rocky with whatever building project he had on the go. He was a good labourer and took the pressure off Rocky in the inclement months when the work felt more intense.

Ethan wasn't interested in money, and Rocky couldn't ever see him on the housing ladder without a hefty contribution from the bank of mum and dad – or probably the bank of just dad. Rocky hadn't given Jake any money towards the Linhay per se, but he was helping him out with the build, and of course he would do the same for Ethan – come the day.

'Hey!' Rocky said. The two men embraced, clapping each other on the back. 'Has one of those beers got my name on?'

Ethan opened the box and flipped open two bottles, handing one to his dad as he hovered over the food.

'Wow, this looks good enough to eat.'

Rocky was filling the tray of the barbecue with coals, spreading them evenly.

'Just about ready to fire her up.'

He took a slug of his beer, looking out at the sea gleaming in the later afternoon sun. This was when he was happiest. The prospect of his family and friends around him, fresh air, sunshine, good food. Maybe life didn't get better than this and he shouldn't try to change things by dipping his toe in the murky water of dating?

He hadn't told either of his sons yet about his upcoming date but he suddenly felt the need for reassurance. He knew there were rules these days. And dating could be brutal. If you could even call it that. He didn't like the term 'hooking up'. It seemed so bloodless and unromantic.

'OK, so – I need your advice,' he said to Ethan as casually as he could. Ethan was play-fighting with Lara, ruffling her ears and pretending to pounce on her. He looked up.

'That's a first.'

'I've got a date. Later on tonight.'

For some reason, Rocky found himself blushing. He was a fifty-something-year-old man, not a teenager. What was the matter with him? But Ethan didn't bat an eyelid.

'That's cool, Dad. It's about time. And you don't need my advice.' Ethan sat back on his heels and took a sip of beer. 'You know all my female friends fancy you more than they fancy me.' This was true. They always went a bit giggly when they met Rocky. 'I'm sure that's why everyone always wanted to come back to ours.'

'Ha ha.' Rocky squirmed. He didn't like being the centre of attention.

His little cottage had always been where everyone headed after hours. And Rocky missed the energy and vibrancy it had brought to the house now Jake and Ethan had both gone, even if it had been noisy and messy at times. Stepping over bodies on his way to the kitchen on a Sunday morning had once been the norm. Now it was like the grave. Spick and span and silent. He longed for the throb of dubstep and a sticky floor.

'So who is she? Can I have a look?'

Rocky hesitated. He suddenly felt protective of his upcoming date. He didn't think it was fair for her to be under scrutiny. But it was only Ethan, and he trusted his son's opinion, so he took out his phone and showed him.

Ethan nodded his approval. 'Looks fit. But you never know until you meet her. You'll know in the first five minutes.'

'What if she's a bunny boiler?' Rocky made a face.

'Pre-write me an emergency text. If it all goes wrong, ping it to me. Then I'll call you and pretend to have broken down and you make a sharp exit.'

Rocky laughed. 'That's horrible.'

'That's dating, mate.'

Rocky thought about the logic. It made sense. No doubt his date would have a similar arrangement with a friend.

'OK. I'll send you a bunny emoji if I want to do a runner.'

Rocky smiled and turned back to his barbecue. Now he had a fool-proof exit strategy, he could relax and enjoy the evening ahead.

Ethan gave him the double thumbs-up, just as Mick and Sheila, Robyn's parents, hove into view carrying a big hamper between them. Clover trailed along behind them in minuscule shorts, a cropped leopard-skin fleece and chunky neon trainers, looking like an Ibiza holiday rep. She always brought a party vibe with her.

'Hello!' called Sheila. 'We come bearing gifts. Coleslaw and potato salad. Not very exciting.'

'Your coleslaw is legendary,' said Rocky. 'And no barbecue is complete without potato salad.'

'I've made mojitos,' said Clover. 'Ginger ones.'

'And there's a load of sausages from the freezer – they

should have thawed by now.' Mick put them down next to the barbecue. 'Lovely evening for it.'

'It is,' agreed Rocky, shifting a few coals about, then striking a match and holding it against a firelighter. The two men watched in satisfaction as it caught light, the flames beginning to flicker and spread.

Rocky looked up and saw Jake and Robyn appear at the top of the dunes. Everyone was nearly here. A perfect Friday evening was about to begin.

5

Half an hour later, everyone had arrived and clustered around the front of the Shedquarters, laying out blankets and unfolding deckchairs and wind breaks. The beach was still quiet at this time of year: there were a few people taking advantage of a sunny April evening to fly a kite or stroll along the water's edge and some intrepid surfers bobbed around further out to sea. A light breeze flipped up the edges of the waves into a gentle froth, the air smelt brackish and bracing with a hint of smoke from the barbecue, and while there was still a hint of gentle warmth in the air, the temperature would soon drop as the sun went down.

Clover was sloshing out glasses of ginger mojito and passing them round.

'Not for me,' said Robyn. 'I'm driving.'

'You can have one,' protested Clover. 'It's got fresh ginger in it. And mint from the garden.'

Robyn took one without further demur. She knew her sister wouldn't take no for an answer and didn't want to arouse suspicion yet. She caught Jake's eye and he gave her a Secret Squirrel grin.

She wandered over to greet her parents. Sheila was laying out bowls of coleslaw and potato salad and garlic bread wrapped in foil that could be reheated on the barbecue at the last minute. Her food offering didn't have the zing of Rocky's but she was used to catering for large numbers. Good plain farm cooking was her expertise.

'I didn't think I'd get away,' said Sheila as Robyn appeared at her shoulder. 'I had a nightmare client who won't listen or do any of the exercises I set her and thinks her precious pooch is beyond reproach. Which it is, because it's all her fault!'

'Mum. If people knew how to discipline their dogs you'd be out of a job.'

Robyn tried to soothe her. Sheila had no patience with her clients when they didn't cooperate. She was known to be strict and no-nonsense, but it got results.

'Yes, but it's a bad advert for me when they don't get them under control.'

'You'll get there. You know you will. You always do.'

Sheila harrumphed. 'I didn't even have time to get changed or put on a face.'

'Mum. It's Friday night at the beach. You don't need to put on a face.'

'Yes, but sometimes I like to make an effort. I spend my whole life looking an absolute heap.' She pulled at her unkempt hair, disgruntled.

Robyn put her arm around her. 'No, you don't.'

Mick rolled his eyes at Robyn.

'She's got herself all aerated,' he said. 'I told her, it's Friday. Relaaax.'

He put his fingers up in a double peace sign to imitate a hippy. Robyn laughed because this was so not her dad, who was a typical Devon farmer. She was surprised he

34

wasn't on the beach in his wellies. Sheila raised her eyebrows but she was smiling.

'Yeah. TGIF. Give me one of those mojitos, Clo.'

'This will make you forget all your woes,' grinned Clover, filling a glass for her mother. 'Anyone coming for a swim first?'

She looked hopefully over at Ethan, who was sprawled in a deckchair with his shades on.

'Not me,' he said. 'I've been in the sea all day teaching. I've practically got gills.'

'Spoilsport.'

Ethan and Clover were partners-in-crime a lot of the time, although it was no secret that Clover had a crush on him. She flirted with him outrageously, but he was aware of their considerable age gap and treated her like a little sister. Much to her annoyance.

She poured herself a large mojito instead.

'Steady,' warned her mother, who knew what Clover was like after a few drinks.

'I've been revising all day! This is my reward.'

She raised her glass and did an Instagram pose, pouting with one hand on her hip. No one would have guessed she had a place to study law at King's College London. The pressure was on, though, as she needed straight As in her upcoming exams. Clover veered between breathtaking overconfidence and utter despair. And studying never seemed to come before partying. Sheila fretted she would burn herself out.

Mick, conversely, had no doubt that his daughter would achieve her goals. She was whip-smart with a photographic memory. She was too clever to jeopardise her future, and had enough energy to burn the candle at both ends. He was proud of her. Proud of both his daughters and what they had achieved. Although their achievements put a fresh perspective on his own predicament.

Mick went back over to the barbecue where Rocky was turning over the grilling basket he'd put the mackerel in.

'Those look handsome,' said Mick.

'Just another couple of minutes. You only need to show them the flames. All good with you?'

Mick shrugged. 'Just done the farm accounts. Pretty bleak reading.'

'It's that time of year, isn't it?'

Mick nodded. 'Something's got to happen. Sheila's working all hours. It was all I could do to get her out tonight. I feel like a spare part, but what can I do? I've got no cash to invest in anything.'

Rocky was about the only person Mick ever confided in about his situation. He'd opened up to him one night when Jake and Robyn had approached him about buying the Linhay. Rocky had helped him put everything into perspective and made a lot of helpful suggestions about the best way to make it tax efficient. Admittedly over a half bottle of rum, but most of the best conversations come about after a few glasses.

Mick admired Rocky, too. He'd brought up Ethan and Jake with no help and turned his business around. That took some doing. Mick knew he'd never be able to cope on his own. Sheila was his wingman. What she had done to keep Hawksworthy afloat was beyond the call of duty. He would never be able to repay her.

The horror of it still stayed with him as if it was yesterday, but it was over ten years now. If he shut his eyes, he could remember every awful moment. The cattle being herded into their pens. The vet pinching the skin on each neck and jabbing them with a needle. The agonising week's wait until the vet returned with his assistant and examined the site of the injection. If it was raised or swollen, the cow's ear would be tagged and they would be put into isolation. A victim of bovine tuberculosis, to be quarantined until slaughter.

He would never know what had brought the infection to Hawksworthy, but it was most likely badgers. There had been signs of them on the edge of the wood. And 80 per cent of his herd had been infected. The vet had barely been able to look him in the eye as he put a hand on his shoulder and told him the news.

That was the moment he had died inside. He'd had to walk away. He didn't want anyone seeing him cry, even though he thought he had caught a tear in the vet's own eye. It was the moment vets dreaded, giving the death sentence.

The infected cows had all been carted away to be slaughtered, some of them descendants of the herd his own father had tended. They were more than just cattle. They were history. They were his legacy. They were gone, except for a lucky few, but they were no use to him in such a small number. He'd sent the rest to market.

He knew of men who'd shot themselves in similar circumstances. And he couldn't say his mind hadn't strayed once or twice to the gun cabinet when the anger had bubbled up, though it was the badgers he wanted to turn on, not himself. And those men who'd buckled under the strain hadn't had a wife like Sheila. A wife who wasn't going to let a case of bovine TB bring them down.

Sheila had been magnificent. Hawksworthy Boarding Kennels and Training School was up and running within six months. An old tractor and trailer had been done up to take tourists across the fields and along the coast path to see the seals in the summer months, along with picnics prepared by Sheila. And they did equestrian bed and breakfast for people wanting to bring their horses on holiday, to ride across the moors and along the beaches. It was all frantic work in the summer months, and quieter in the winter, but that was the way of life down here. It was all about making hay.

So they had just about managed to survive, financially. But it was hard work on Sheila, who dealt with the clients: Mick was a man of few words and didn't have the patience to deal with a lot of them. He stayed behind the scenes, doing maintenance and running repairs.

And keeping the farm shipshape was expensive. There were hedges and fences and walls to be maintained. The potholes in the drive to be tarmac-ed. The kennel maids' wages to be paid. Insurance. Public liability. They had barely broken even the past few years. If they hadn't sold the Linhay to Robyn and Jake, they'd be in serious trouble, and that money was running out now, as he had seen when he'd been through the accounts. It made him feel sick.

There was one obvious solution, but he wasn't sure if he was brave enough. Or if he had the right. There had been a Moss at Hawksworthy for four generations. But one thing was becoming clear to him: neither Robyn nor Clover would want to take over the farm.

Now probably wasn't the time to discuss it. Not with everyone milling about and Mick trying not to singe the mackerel. He'd take him for a quiet pint. Maybe next week—

'Hey, everyone – can I have your attention for a second?'

Mick looked over to see Jake standing on the steps of the Shedquarters, holding up a glass of Clover's mojito and tinging his fork against the rim. He felt a needle of anxiety. Ever since the cows, he tended to fear the worst.

Gradually the chatter stopped and everyone looked over at Jake. Robyn glided over and stood at the bottom of the steps underneath him. In a floral playsuit and her hair in plaits, she looked no older than her sister.

'Um . . . me and Robyn have got a little bit of news for you.' Jake looked sheepish.

'Very little,' added Robyn.

'About this size, in fact.' Jake circled his thumb and middle finger. 'We kept it quiet until we were sure everything was OK this morning. At our twelve-week scan.'

Robyn held up the photograph. 'And if you want evidence, here it is.'

'Oh my God,' said Sheila. 'She's having a baby.'

'Get on!' said Mick, flooded with relief.

'Shit!' said Clover. 'I'm going to be an aunt.' She banged Ethan on the back. 'Hey, you're going to be an uncle.'

Rocky stood stock still with a beer in one hand and a fish slice in the other. A grandfather. He was going to be a grandfather.

Sheila ran over to her daughter and folded her in her arms.

'Oh, my lovely girl. Oh, congratulations.' She hugged

her tight, her eyes closed. 'Have you been all right? Why didn't you say anything?'

'I'm fine,' Robyn smiled. 'I didn't want to jinx it. Or worry you.'

'Worry me?' Sheila laughed. 'I'm not going to let you out of my sight.' She shook her head. 'I can't believe it. I've never really thought about being a granny.'

'You're not too shocked, are you?'

'I'm thrilled to bloody bits.' Sheila looked proud.

'That's why you haven't drunk any of my mojito! I thought it was weird.' Clover was staring at her sister, fascinated. 'Can I see the picture? Do you know what it is yet?'

Robyn handed her the scan photo. 'It's too early to know.'

Mick hovered on the sidelines until Robyn noticed him and caught his eye. She wriggled past Clover and slid into her dad's arms.

'I'm proud of you, girl,' he said, gruffly. 'You'll be a good mother.'

'I still can't believe it.'

'Well, you know we're here. We'll do what we can.'

He never said much, her dad, but she knew there was a lot of emotion underlying his words.

'I know, Dad. And thank you. You've already done so much, with the Linhay.'

'Ah, you bought that fair and square.'

'I know. But no way would we be able to afford somewhere like that otherwise.'

Mick put his hand on her back and patted her to indicate she didn't need to say any more. He couldn't, because he could feel tears clogging up his throat. And he wasn't a man who cried in public.

*

'I think they're happy,' said Jake to Robyn a little later, when everyone had time to digest the news and was sitting down to eat. 'Don't you?'

'Definitely,' said Robyn. 'And so am I. Aren't you?'

Jake put his hand in his pocket and felt for the little box. Now wasn't the moment. He'd wait until everyone had gone.

'Of course I am,' he replied. 'This is the best thing that's ever happened to me.'

6

'Well, I didn't see that coming,' said Sheila on the drive home. 'I can usually spot the signs a mile off.'

Sheila had midwifed quite a few litters of puppies over the years at Hawksworthy Farm. She could tell if a bitch was in kindle or not early on, so she was puzzled not to have seen the signs in Robyn.

'Yeah, but Robyn's not a dog, is she?' pointed out Mick, quite reasonably. 'And I guess she was trying to keep it quiet.'

'I still don't understand why, though.' She opened the glove compartment and pulled out a packet of butter mints, unwrapping two and handing one to Mick. 'I am her mum.'

She put the other mint in her own mouth.

'I expect she just didn't want to worry you until she knew it was all OK,' Mick told her. 'She knows how busy you are.' And how much you worry, he added in his head.

'Do you think it'll get her thinking?' Sheila leaned forward to turn the heating up.

Mick didn't answer for a moment. Sheila was agitated. He could tell by her fiddling. Although he had wondered the same. But he wanted to reassure her.

'It's lovely news. Don't spoil it.'

'Oh, I'm not going to let it spoil anything,' said Sheila quickly. 'I'm thrilled to bits. Of course I am.'

'Yep. It's good they're cracking on with it. I don't hold with this waiting-till-you're-forty lark.'

'You can't say that kind of thing, Mick.' Sheila teased, nudging him with her elbow.

Mick shrugged. He knew his views weren't modern, but they were his.

'I just wish I wasn't so busy,' sighed Sheila. 'I'm not going to be much help. Their business is just getting off the ground. She can't afford to take a back seat.'

'You worry too much. She'll sort it out. She knows what she's doing.'

Sheila was quiet for a moment.

'I don't like the thought of her baby having to go to a nursery.'

'Most kids do these days.'

'I want to be there for her.'

'We will be.'

'I want the baby to have the best start in life. After what happened to Robyn.'

Mick kept his eyes on the road ahead, but he reached over and squeezed her hand.

'Of course you do.' He could never, ever reassure her enough.

She took in a breath to dislodge the panic that was squeezing itself up. She hadn't thought about it for a long time. But this changed things.

'I just hope . . . You don't think—'

'Look,' said Mick as they turned the corner. 'The Pink Moon.'

There it was, hanging over them in the black velvet sky. The April full moon, called pink in the farmer's almanac, though it wasn't quite pink tonight, just a shimmering pale silver grey, as perfectly round as a dinner plate.

'Yes,' sighed Sheila, though she wasn't fooled by his distraction technique. Mick didn't want to talk about it. He never did. And maybe he was right. Maybe she needn't worry. But she couldn't help it. It was her darkest fear.

7

Rocky pulled into the car park of the Mariscombe Hotel and slid into an empty space. He'd suggested the bar here because no way was he going to go on a date in the Ship Aground for everyone's entertainment. There wouldn't be many locals in here because the prices were quite high, and as it was still early in the season it would be relatively quiet.

He looked in the rear-view mirror, ruffling up his hair a tiny bit and making sure his eyebrows were in order and he had nothing in his teeth. He'd changed into jeans and a white linen shirt in the Shedquarters before he left.

He headed inside. The interior was designed to resemble a yacht, done out in sleek wood and chrome and white leather banquettes, with a beautifully curved bar jutting out into the room like the prow of a Sunseeker. Carly Simon ran through his head as Rocky walked in, though he didn't think he was all that vain. Just nervous.

He saw Melisaa straight away, sitting at the far end on a high stool with what looked like a gin and tonic in front of her. There were a few couples sitting at tables, but otherwise it was fairly quiet for a Friday night.

'Melissa?' He put a hand on her arm and gave her a tentative smile as she turned.

Her face lit up when she saw him. 'Hi. Rocky, I'm guessing?' She slid off her stool and shook his hand. 'I was here early. I'm always early. So I got myself a drink. But what would you like?'

Her voice was low; she seemed very composed and in control. He was impressed with her manners and her confidence. And she looked better than her picture, if anything, in cropped white jeans and a grey linen jacket and espadrilles. She smelled good too, a light citrusy scent filling his head.

'I'll just have a small glass of Merlot,' he said to the hovering barman. 'This place looks great. I haven't been here since it reopened. I hope it was the right choice?'

'Perfect.' She smiled, her light brown eyes twinkling with warmth. 'Are we OK at the bar or do you want to go to a table?'

'The bar's fine,' he said, sliding onto the stool next to hers.

'So, do you come here often?' she laughed. 'As they say?'

'Every now and then. I live just round the bay, in Everdene, so we sometimes come here for a bar snack. But not since they've done it out.'

'They've spent some money, that's for sure.' She looked round in approval. Rocky could see she had an eye for expensive things. She had a fine gold chain around her neck with a semi-precious stone hanging from it, and a cluster of tiny diamonds up the side of her ear.

'Actually, my son's doing the landscaping for the pool area,' he told her. 'It's going to look pretty amazing. Like you're in Ibiza.' He smiled. 'Although the weather might not be as reliable.'

'Sounds like what we need round here.' She pointed at him. 'You have two sons, right?'

They'd exchanged a few personal details online during their exchange. Nothing too intimate. Facts rather than feelings.

'Jake and Ethan.' He nodded. 'And you've got a daughter?'

'Isabelle. She's been at uni in Newcastle for a year. I can't wait for her to come back this summer.'

'Empty nest, eh?'

'It's been really tough.' She wrinkled her nose. 'All those times when they're young and you think you need space? When you get it, you don't want it.'

'Tell me about it. My younger son's just moved out. I don't know what to do with myself.'

They both laughed at the same time.

'Is that why you went on the app?'

Rocky took his glass of wine from the barman, nodding his thanks.

'I guess so. It felt like the right time.'

He was surprised how easily the conversation was flowing. Melissa seemed very relaxed. She leaned her elbow on the bar and rested her head in her hand, looking over at him, smiling. Her eyes were dancing. Was she flirting with him already?

'So – have you got the emergency exit text thing set up?'

He couldn't help but look shamefaced. 'Well, I wouldn't have known about it until my son told me. But I don't think I'm going to need it.'

She laughed and put a hand on his arm. 'Nor me. But I have done in the past, I can tell you.'

'So you're an old hand at this?'

'Oh gosh, no, I didn't mean to make it sound like that. I've been on a few dates. But there aren't many single people our age down here.'

'Full disclosure,' said Rocky. 'But I think I'm quite a bit older than you. I'm well over fifty.'

She looked at him thoughtfully. 'Well, I'm forty-six. I don't think that's cradle-snatching. Do you?'

'No.' He took a sip of wine. He felt his shoulders relax. This was fun. Why had it taken him so long to pluck up the courage?

'So shall we get the baggage out of the way?' she asked. 'I'll go first. Husband a pilot; serially unfaithful. Utterly charming and a great dad but I couldn't take the humiliation any longer.' She made a tentative face. '*Kind* of an amicable split.' She shrugged. 'I moved down to this area for a fresh start two years ago. I wanted to get my business up and running before I started dating.' She did jazz hands. 'So here I am.'

'And you're a physio?'

'Yeah. And it's going great. Turns out there's a lot of sporty people round here who injure themselves. Surfers, climbers, cyclists. Even walkers. Kerching!'

Rocky was surprised. Most women weren't so open about their success but Melissa seemed to be revelling in it.

'Good on you.'

'I've had to work really hard at it. I still work hard. So when I play, I play.' She opened her eyes a little wider.

'Um . . .' Rocky wasn't sure exactly what she meant, but he felt sure she had moved in a little closer to him. 'Yes, well, we all need a bit of down time.'

There was a pause. She straightened herself up, moving herself away from him slightly, sensing his discomfort.

'So. Your baggage?'

She was very direct. Very much taking control of the situation. Not that he minded, but he wasn't used to such frankness. He thought carefully for a moment, choosing what to say and what to leave out. Melissa was beguiling, but he wasn't going to fall into any traps.

'I made the big mistake of thinking my dream was my wife's dream. We'd always come on holiday here with the kids and loved it. I worked out we could sell our house and get something for half the money down here, and invest the rest in setting up on my own. It went OK for about six months, but Tina hated it down here. It was too quiet. She missed her friends and family. To cut a long story short, she left us.'

Melissa's eyebrows shot up. 'Wow. She left you and your kids? That's unusual.'

Rocky took another sip of wine. He never liked talking about it. He felt ashamed. Ashamed that what he had done had broken up their family. There were details he'd left out, of course. Things he'd never told anyone, because it was too awful to admit. And it felt disloyal to Tina, despite her being the transgressor.

'These things happen.' He kept his tone light, even though it had been an absolute nightmare. Guilt, recrimination, blame, more guilt. 'And the boys ended up having a great life. They were teenagers by the time they moved here. They lived for surfing and girls. What's not to like?'

'So you brought them up?'

'Hey, I soon taught them how to cook and wash up

49

and use the washing machine. I wasn't going to run round after them. So they can both look after themselves.'

She looked at him. 'What a great dad.'

He sighed. 'I don't know. Maybe if I hadn't forced my dream on everyone . . . ?'

How many times had he asked himself that?

He saw she had finished her gin and tonic. He pointed at it.

'Can I get you another?'

She looked at her watch. She seemed to be debating whether to stay.

'I shouldn't. I've got parkrun tomorrow. I'm a little bit obsessed. I absolutely have to beat my personal best.'

'Ahhh, the tyranny of parkrun.' Sometimes he saw them running along the beach on a Saturday morning if he got up early to surf.

'You don't do it?'

He shook his head. 'Plantar fasciitis.'

'I could sort that out for you.'

'It's on the mend. But thank you.'

She stared at him for a moment, thoughtful, as if assessing him. Then she slid off her seat and bent down to pick up her bag.

'Anyway, I must go. It was lovely to meet you, Rocky.'

She leaned in and kissed him on the cheek. Her scent swirled around him for a moment and then followed her as she sashayed across the bar and out of the door.

He was stunned. What had he said or done to deserve her walking out after barely fifteen minutes? Was it a game? Was he supposed to run after her? Was he way too old to be dating and making a fool of himself, thinking he looked all right? He felt a little bit crushed. She wasn't obliged to like him, of course she wasn't.

He took a look at himself in the mirrored wall behind the bar. Was he deluding himself that he looked OK for his age? Did he have jowls, or a surfeit of frown lines? Did his close-cut hair make him look more convict than Clooney?

The barman came along to clear away Melissa's glass. He raised an eyebrow; Rocky shrugged.

'Must have been something I said.'

'The trick is not to take it personally,' said the barman, knowingly.

That was all very well, thought Rocky, but how else was he supposed to take it?

8

Darkness had fallen over the Shedquarters. There were only a handful of huts with a welcoming light on as the waves inched up the beach to high tide, murmuring a gentle lullaby. Jake piled more logs onto the fire-pit he'd lit earlier and draped a blanket around Robyn, tucking it in even though she protested.

'I don't need wrapping up in cotton wool.'

He pointed a warning finger at her. 'Don't argue. It's properly cold.'

She snuggled underneath the fleece. He was right. With the sun completely gone, there was an icy frisson to the air. Frost was still possible at this time of year, as she knew only too well, thinking about her seedlings in her mini-polytunnel and hoping they were safe.

She gazed up at the sky. It was as black as squid ink, the Big Dipper poised like a ladle above them. From there it was a straight line to the North Star, the brightest star of all, a comforting, anchoring presence for everyone on land or at sea. If you could find that, you knew where you were.

'I'm just going to grab another blanket.'

Jake disappeared back into the Shedquarters. She wondered if this was the right time to talk to him about the impact the scan had had on her. Of course, her primary emotion was relief that everything was just as it should be. But alongside that was the realisation that the heartbeat on the screen belonged to the first person she knew in her life to be actually related to her. The heartbeat of a blood relative. It was almost overwhelming, and she hadn't expected to feel so rocked by it.

But she didn't want to make today's adventure about her and her feelings. It was momentous for Jake, too, of course, and she was mindful of overshadowing his experience. So she wanted to make sure the time was right before explaining.

He wandered back over to her. He had something in his hand.

'I found this today,' he said. 'It jumped out at me. I had to get it.'

'What?' Robyn frowned, peering at his outstretched palm.

It was difficult to see at first, for there was only the faint light that spilled from the doorway behind them to see by. She looked more closely. It was a ring, in a little box, sitting on black velvet. A slender band of twisted matte gold, topped with a tiny starfish. It was exquisite. Delicate and different and beautifully crafted.

'Oh!' Robyn was nonplussed. They didn't have the kind of relationship where they lavished extravagant gifts on each other out of the blue. Especially at the moment. Lately, all their money was going on horribly expensive things you couldn't actually see, like RSJs and chimney flues and a future-proof cable network. 'It's gorgeous.'

'I wanted to give you something. To mark the import-ance of today. A starfish represents infinite divine love,' Jake told her. 'And that's an aquamarine. Seawater.'

'It's gorgeous.' Robyn looked more closely at the stone, a pale greeny-blue. But she still wasn't sure why he was giving it to her.

'Robyn?' He was looking at her with a funny expression.

'Yes?'

'You know I've always said I didn't want to get married? That I thought marriage was an outdated institution, and pointless, and that weddings were a complete waste of time and money and I'd rather have a new pick-up truck?'

'Yeah. It's kind of why I've never asked you to marry me,' Robyn joked. She knew Jake was touchy about marriage, because of his parents' divorce. It had coloured his vision and made him wary. Why get embroiled in something that went on to cause bitterness and anguish and, not least, financial hardship, when you could just muddle along?

And Robyn had always gone along with him. She didn't want to put their relationship under any pressure when they were in business together. Life was sweet, and if marriage turned out to be the right thing, it would happen in good time. She knew his aversion wasn't because of her.

'I think I might have changed my mind.'

Robyn stared at him. 'What?'

'Seeing that little being on the screen makes it seem like the right thing to do. I need to get over my prejudice. History doesn't have to repeat itself. We owe it to him – her – to make a real solid commitment to each other.' He paused, then swallowed. 'Give me your hand. Your left hand.'

She held it out to him. He straightened her fingers.

'They say this finger has a vein that leads straight to

your heart.' He stroked the third one in. 'Will you marry me?'

For a few moments, there was no sound but the crashing of the waves on the beach. The tide was out, but the sound of the water hurling itself onto the sand had a comforting and familiar rhythm. Boom. Boom. Boom. The thud was in time with Robyn's heart as she tried to find the words to reply.

'Oh God,' said Jake, looking crestfallen. 'Forget I said anything. I'm an idiot. Of course you don't want to marry me. What was I even thinking? I got carried away.'

He gazed at her. Her eyes were grey; her face long and thin, with sharp cheekbones and that slightly wonky broken nose.

She stared back at him, burly and scruffy, with his wiry dark hair that never did what it was told, his six o'clock shadow that started at about two o'clock, his thick brows over eyes that were as confusing as the sea, sometimes green, sometimes blue.

'Oh Jake, you know what the answer is,' she said.

'I don't.' He shook his head, not taking his eyes off her.

She smiled at him.

'Yes! Yes, of course I will.'

They gazed at each other for a moment, taken by surprise by the turn of events. The night breeze danced around them, gleeful at the evening's outcome, and the sea edged in even closer for a look, not wanting to be left out, and the stars glowed just a little brighter as the two of them leaned into each other, and their kiss almost had the wonder of a first kiss.

Eventually, they broke apart, laughing at the magic of it all. Jake reached out for Robyn's left hand again.

'I'd better do this properly.'

They both watched as he took the ring out of the box and slid it onto her finger.

'There,' he said. 'And do you know what? Marley had put this aside for me specially. As soon as she saw it, she knew it had your name on it. It's been waiting in her shop, under the counter. She knew.'

'I guess sometimes your friends know you better than you know yourself.' Robyn took his hand and put it on her tummy. 'I think this little one is going to be responsible for a lot of changes.'

'Not too many changes, I hope.' Jake looked anxious. 'I want things to stay just as they are.'

Robyn laughed. 'I think expecting things to stay the same is a bit optimistic.'

'You know what I mean. You and me, the Linhay, our families . . . We're so lucky, Robyn. We're safe and secure and we've got everyone we love around us.'

'We're *very* lucky. And don't worry. Nothing needs to change.'

Jake sighed. 'I just wish my mum and dad were . . . at least amicable.'

He looked troubled. His parents' split had affected him deeply. He was usually very matter of fact about it, but there had been a lot of hurt and bitterness and sometimes it leaked out. Robyn didn't know the full details of the split, and there were always two sides to every story, but it seemed the move to Everdene had been to blame. A dream that had gone sour.

She was determined it wasn't going to affect their future, though.

'Hey,' she said. 'We can't have everything. We'll do the

best with what we've got.' She held out her hand at arm's length. She was surprised how at home the ring looked on her finger, despite her reddened, chapped skin and her ragged nails. 'And you do realise what else this means?' she said with a grin, hoping to change the reflective mood.

'What?'

'We actually have to have a wedding now.'

'We do?' Jake did his best startled Gromit face.

'Oh yes.'

'We can't just sneak off to the registry office and do it quietly?'

'You really think we could get away with that?'

'I don't see why not. It's about us, isn't it?'

'Yes, but...' She went quiet for a moment.

'Oh,' said Jake. 'Oh, hang on. I get it. You *want* a big wedding.'

'No!' She paused. 'Not *big* big...'

One caterpillar eyebrow went up. 'What's not *big* big, exactly? Because it doesn't sound small.'

'Well, we'd have to have family. And our mates. And it all has a knock-on. You know, if you invite blah then you have to invite blah.'

'We can't just have close family and a couple of friends?'

'Maybe. But it's very hard to know where to stop. Especially when you live in a small community. I mean, we won't be able to keep it quiet.'

'Well, I don't mind. Whatever you think works.' Jake sat down in the deckchair next to her and stretched out his legs. 'Though I don't want to spend a fortune. I'd rather spend it on the house.'

Robyn thought about what he was saying. He was right. There were bound to be more hidden expenses at the Linhay, especially as they now had a deadline. It was far more sensible to save their money for unexpected emergencies.

'You're right. We'll keep it small. Family and close friends. And we'll keep it simple.'

'Definitely.'

'No horse and carriage or ring-bearers or endless photographs or seating plans.'

'Or boring speeches or cringy first dances. Please don't make me dance in front of everyone.'

Robyn laughed. Jake's dancing prowess amounted to vigorous stomping to 'I Would Walk 500 Miles' and even then he couldn't keep time.

'And no weird net bags with sugared almonds. I've never understood those.'

'No stag night.' Jake shuddered at the memory of the ones he'd been subjected to. Images of Amsterdam and Dublin and Alicante clicked through his brain, all sweat and alcohol and lost passports.

'Definitely no hen night either.' Robyn was emphatic. 'So we're agreed, then. Simple, and small. The bigger it gets, the more expectations people will have.'

'We can always have a party when we finish the Linhay.'

'A house-warming/wedding reception/baby shower?' Robyn laughed.

'Do you think we've bitten off more than we can chew?' Jake looked a bit daunted for a moment.

'No,' said Robyn, ever the optimist. 'We'll take each thing as it comes.' She counted on her fingers. 'Wedding, house move, baby. What could possibly go wrong?'

9

A little while later, Robyn drove back home along the coast road, the Pink Moon guiding her anxiously as if she needed a chaperone, but of course she didn't because she had driven this road a million times; the road that led from Everdene to the other side of the headland and along the half-mile track to Hawksworthy Farm. It would be too wild and remote for some, stuck out on the edge of the moors, but to Robyn it was where she belonged.

She had sold her flat in Tawcombe and moved back in with her parents when she and Jake bought the tumble-down Linhay off them. Once used to shelter the flocks of sheep that grazed the moors during the bleak winter, it had lain empty for years. Selling it had been a timely solution: Hawksworthy Farm had been running at a loss for the third year in a row, and there was nothing much left in the coffers to prop it up. The Linhay was at the edge of the farm's eastern boundary, with a dirt track running to it from the main road, which meant it could be neatly sliced off without affecting the farm, along with an acre of ground.

It was Jake who'd suggested the two of them buy it to keep it in the family. They had scraped enough money together for the deposit, managed to raise a mortgage, and were using the proceeds from Robyn's flat sale for the renovations, as well as some of the profits from The Moss Partnership. She'd secretly been glad to leave her flat behind, even though it had glorious harbour views, for she had never been a town person, and it felt good to be close to home.

There were times when Robyn had despaired, wondering if they had overstretched themselves, practically and financially and emotionally. It had tested them to the limits, and there were moments when she couldn't imagine the crumbling stone walls becoming remotely habitable. It often felt as if they were throwing money over the precipitous cliff on which the Linhay was perched. She had fretted endlessly, both in front of Jake and in secret in her own bed, when she had been overwhelmed by misgivings that sometimes morphed into pure panic and sometimes tears. Renovation really was like living in a reality TV show.

But now, there it was with a new roof, small but theirs, snug but perfect. She felt safer now the house was almost habitable and their investment was secure, and they'd somehow managed it without bankrupting themselves.

And the twist in tonight's tale made her feel safer still.

She smiled as the tiny road wriggled up over the hill, lit by the beams of her truck headlights, picking out the stone banks and twisted tree trunks. She took her left hand off the steering wheel for a moment, rubbing the ring with her thumb as if to check it was real. Everything was falling into place, she thought. She had been surprised by Jake's proposal, but as soon as the words had popped out, it had seemed so logical, so right, for them to get married, and not least because their accountant had strongly recommended it now they owned a property together.

As she reached the crest of the hill at the top of the downs and began the descent down into the valley, the disquiet that had become so familiar of late began to creep over her. It was slithering to the surface, the issue she had been determined to ignore for so many years, because confronting it brought too many problems. Sometimes, she could forget about it altogether. It came to her in waves of differing strengths, like the sets of waves on the shore: sometimes gently lapping, sometimes almost knocking her off her feet with the force.

It had gone from a seemingly inconsequential detail she ignored to a burning curiosity. From the moment she had realised she was expecting a baby, images flashed through her head and a voice called out to her. The one she usually silenced.

Maybe, she thought, as she dropped down a gear, the voice shouldn't be silenced this time. Maybe it needed to be heard. Maybe it was time for her to listen?

She negotiated the steep descent through the oak-clad ravine that was as old as time. The Pink Moon still appeared sporadically through the gaps in the bare branches, but she could have done this part of the journey blindfolded, even the final hairpin bend that tourists found so alarming.

It is your right, she told herself. It had been ever since the day she had turned eighteen. But it was more complicated than that. There was no guarantee that what she wanted to do wouldn't lead to distress or even heartbreak, and not just hers. After all, she could look after herself.

It was everyone else she was worried about. The impact it might have on those she loved, and the woman she didn't know.

Her birth mother.

Hawksworthy Farm was in darkness by the time she bounced along the driveway, over the cattle grid and into the yard. The security light came on with a click as she scurried to the back door, breathing in the icy air. It was always a few degrees colder here, exposed as they were on the rocky promontory, and the wind off the Atlantic was sharp and unforgiving in the dead of night. She slipped into the kitchen, kicked off her shoes, relishing the last of the warmth from the inglenook fire, and quickly made herself a hot water bottle. Clutching it to her chest, she went through into the hall and crept up two flights of wooden stairs into the attic. She flicked a glance underneath her sister's door but there was no light on. Clover wasn't back yet. She was probably still in the Ship Aground with Ethan, necking sambucas.

The walls of her tiny attic room were sloping with only a five-foot strip down the middle having full head height. Her bed was at one end, covered in woollen blankets and satin eiderdowns. At the other end was a cast-iron rail where all her clothes were hung, a big chest of drawers painted blue and a wooden desk with a captain's chair.

There wasn't room to swing a cat. It was certainly too small to accommodate both her and Jake, but it was comforting and familiar and it was hers, and it had grown with her. She knew every damp patch on the plaster, every threadbare hole in the carpet, every squeaky floorboard.

She flicked on the fan heater and flopped down on her bed. There was no central heating up here, but she was used to it. She slid the hot water bottle in between the sheets then lay for a few moments while the warm air from the heater took the edge off the cold, wishing she had the solid warmth of Jake next to her. She breathed deeply, trying to focus, trying to slow her heartbeat. It was beating too fast, for she knew what she had to do.

She had to make a choice. It was now, or never.

She went over to the desk under the window. She sat in the chair for a moment, swinging it round from side to side, running her hands over the wood of the desk where she had sat revising for her exams. Even though she'd failed most of them, Sheila and Mick had been kind and supportive, helping her to find the horticultural course that had set her on her career path.

They'd always been the most wonderful parents. Attentive, loving, thoughtful. She told herself that what she was about to do didn't diminish her love for them in any way. It wasn't a rejection. She wasn't looking to replace them.

Nevertheless, her mouth felt dry as she bent down and slid open the bottom drawer of the desk.

There it was.

She lifted it out, her heart beating faster. The box that contained her identity, her origins – all the things she didn't know about herself. The box Sheila had given her on her eighteenth birthday. The box she had never opened, until tonight.

10

12 years earlier

Robyn was standing in front of the mirror, putting the finishing touches to her outfit, not sure how comfortable she felt in a denim waistcoat, black suede chaps and a pink Stetson. It was way more daring than her usual dress code, but it fitted the Country and Western theme of tonight's party, a joint celebration of her eighteenth and her mum's fiftieth. The theme had been Sheila's suggestion, and Robyn had gone along with it happily as it was the perfect way to bridge two generations and easy for most people – all you needed was jeans and a checked shirt. They were having a big hog roast in the Dutch barn, with hay bales to sit on and dancing until the small hours.

'Mum! You look fantastic!' Robyn laughed when her mum knocked on her open door. 'Shania Twain, eat your heart out.'

Sheila posed in the doorway, in a plaid shirt knotted at the waist, a denim miniskirt and cowboy boots. She'd put her hair in curlers and it was spectacularly bouffant, and she had on false eyelashes and red lipstick. She looked so much younger than she usually did, but Robyn knew that from tomorrow onwards both of them would be back to fleeces, wellies and ponytails.

Sheila was smiling but she looked nervous.

'I've got something to give you.'

She was holding a box. Robyn frowned, confused.

'But you've already given me my present.' Her parents had bought her a new surfboard. She'd taken it to the beach in Everdene that morning, catching wave after wave before dragging herself out and coming home to help with the party preparations.

Sheila walked across the room and sat on Robyn's bed. Her face was serious. She was drumming her fingers on the lid, riddled with nerves.

'I've been plucking up the courage all day to bring you this. I've even had a swig of Jack Daniels.'

'Mum! I don't understand. What is it?' Robyn had never seen Sheila so agitated. It was odd, looking at this dolled-up version of her mother, and Robyn felt unsettled. She could smell the Jack Daniels, too. Sheila and Mick weren't great drinkers. It didn't fit with the lifestyle. The early mornings.

'I know we don't talk about it very often,' Sheila began, hesitantly. 'But it's not because we want to hide anything from you. And we'd always talk about it if you wanted to. It's just . . . difficult.'

She looked down at the box.

'Oh,' said Robyn, finally understanding. 'You mean my adoption.'

Robyn knew her mother had been very young when she had her – still at school – and unable to look after a baby, and Sheila and Mick had adopted her when she was just three months old.

Sheila nodded. She ran her fingers across the wrapping paper covering the box. It was a musical manuscript, hundreds of black notes dancing across black lines.

'I know we've always been open about adopting you. But I've never told you much about why. Before... you... I had three miscarriages. Late ones. The last one... was very late. I had to deliver him. A little baby boy. Tiny. Perfect.'

'Oh, Mum.' Robyn had always guessed that there must have been problems, but not that her mother had had to go through such an ordeal.

'It was awful. Of course it was. I found it very traumatic. But your father found it even more difficult than I did. I didn't think he would ever get over it. He didn't speak for weeks. He wouldn't talk about it. I was beside myself with worry. And I had no one to turn to. People didn't talk about things in those days. You just got on with it. Or in Dad's case, shut down.'

'Couldn't the doctor help?'

'Your dad wouldn't see anyone. You know what he's like. How he goes in on himself.'

Robyn knew only too well. It was a year since the cows had gone and Mick's livelihood had been snatched away. It was only in the past couple of months that he had emerged from his introspection and become himself again. It was hard for him, but it was hard for everyone else too. Especially Sheila.

'You were like the sun coming out when you arrived. He became a different person. He doted on you from the moment he saw you.'

Tears welled up in Robyn's eyes. She had been too tiny then to remember it now, but she could imagine Mick picking her up with his big hands, his eyes twinkling with kindness, his gentle voice.

'And please don't see it as a fault, but your dad doesn't deal with the memories very well. Talking about your adoption makes him remember everything that happened before.' Sheila sighed. 'It's part of my job to protect him. He's strong in so many ways – there's no one else I'd ever want on my side – but sometimes he doesn't cope very well.'

'I understand that, Mum. And you don't need to talk about it. It's in the past. I don't need to know anything, really.'

'We didn't know much about you ourselves. Just how young she was. We knew she came from a good family from up country. But as of today, you have the right to search for her.' Sheila swallowed. She obviously found the words difficult. 'Your birth mother.'

'I know,' said Robyn. 'But—'

'Which is why I'm giving you this.' Sheila rushed on, patting the box. 'She sent it with you, the day you came to us. I've kept it safe for you. Now you're eighteen it's for you to keep.'

Robyn bit her lip and nodded, staring at the box as she handed it over. She took it. It felt very light. What other secrets were in here?

Sheila smiled at her daughter. She looked relieved but exhausted by the exchange. Giving Robyn the box was the right thing to do, but she probably also feared the consequences of handing it over. She couldn't help wondering about that other woman, somewhere, who knew the significance of today, and was probably thinking about the daughter she had given up, and whether she would now try to find her.

It was up to Robyn. From today, she was officially an adult, responsible for her own future. But also her past.

'All I ask,' Sheila said finally. 'All I ask is that you tread carefully, if you do ever want to find out more.'

'I'm not going to open it,' Robyn told her. 'Not now. I'll keep it safe, and if I ever feel the need, I will open it. But right now . . . I'm happy with who I am. I don't need to know anything.'

She put the box down on her desk and put her arms around her mother, pulling her close.

'Oh dear,' Sheila half-laughed through tears. 'I'm going to have to do my make-up again.'

'Come here,' said Robyn, wiping the black streaks from under her mother's eyes. 'There. That's better.'

When her mother had gone, Robyn picked up the box again. She shook it and could feel a few items sliding about inside. Outside, she could hear a couple of cars arriving – probably the hog-roast man, or the DJ. She should go and help. Now wasn't the time for emotional upheaval.

So she put the box in the bottom right-hand drawer of her desk and pushed it firmly shut.

II

And there it still was. Robyn lifted it out. It was a lever-arch box file of the kind found in an accountant's office stuffed with receipts. To disguise the dreary grey of the cardboard, it had been covered in wrapping paper made to look like a music manuscript, with rows and rows of minims and crotchets and quavers punctuated by flourishes. The paper was a little faded now, the yellowed sticky tape lifting, but she ran her fingers over the notes, imagining her mother wrapping it carefully, wondering what she was feeling. Relief? Despair? Grief?

She lifted the lid.

Inside was a scroll of paper rolled up and tied with a red ribbon, a Maxell C60 cassette tape and a faded velvet toy piglet. And at the very bottom, a photograph with rounded edges, the colours faded now. It was of a baby in a white romper suit with a scalloped collar, lying on a yellow furry rug, looking up with the faint half-smile of someone who has just discovered the joy of recognising someone they know.

That must be me, thought Robyn. That must be me, smiling up at my mum. She wondered who else had been there when the photo was taken, and if the circumstances that had led to her adoption had already unfurled. Or was this a happy moment before things went wrong?

She certainly didn't look like a baby who wasn't being looked after or who was in any kind of danger. She looked content, well fed and well dressed.

Just holding the photo made her feel a step closer to her mother. Knowing that perhaps she had taken the photo and had sent off the film to be developed. Had she rifled through a selection and picked this out as the best one to give to the baby she was giving away?

Or who was being taken away from her?

The thought was unbearable. Even at this early stage, the thought of her own child being put into someone else's care was too painful to imagine. It was primal, the need to protect.

She picked up the tape. The writing on the label had faded into nothing and she couldn't decipher the words. She turned it over to see if there was a clue on the other side, but that was blank. There wasn't a cassette player in the house any more. Her pick-up had one, though. She shivered at the thought of going outside again, but her curiosity burned brighter than her desire to keep warm.

It was funny, she thought, how she had kept the box unopened for so long yet now she couldn't wait another moment to examine everything in detail, to find out as much about what had happened as she could.

She pulled on her Uggs and a fleece and crept back downstairs. Thank goodness Clover still wasn't back. If she saw her, she wouldn't rest until she knew what she was doing. Twelve years younger than Robyn, Clover had been something of a surprise to her parents, and now her mother had told her about the miscarriages, Robyn understood why the pregnancy had been such a stressful time for them. She remembered her dad being anxious and overprotective, and her usually energetic mother spending a lot of time in bed. She must have been terrified of losing the baby. But by some miracle, Clover had made her way into their world, exuberant and noisy from day one.

There had never been any favouritism between them. No implication that Clover was properly 'theirs'. They hadn't been treated in the same way because they were so different and so far apart in age, but they'd had the same opportunities, the same attention, the same unconditional love.

Inside the car, she made sure the headlights were off and switched on the engine so the cassette player would work. Her hands were shaking slightly as she pushed the tape in. She didn't know what to expect. A recorded message? Or worse, nothing? Might the recording have faded over the years? How long did sound last?

There was silence for a few seconds, and then she detected the sound of an expectant audience. The occasional cough. Then a round of polite applause. Whoever was about to perform must have appeared on the stage.

There was a moment's silence, then the music began. It sounded more like a harp than a piano, the notes rippled so fast up and down the keyboard. And then a dreamy melody emerged, fragile yet insistent. It was spine-tingling, each individual note so delicate and yet when combined the music pulled you in with surprising strength, at some moments alluring, at others menacing and at the end, achingly sad. It built to a climax, and then drifted away.

Robyn felt a lump in her throat as the final traces faded, the melody becoming almost a ghost of itself. What was this piece of music, and what did it mean? She found it profoundly affecting, even without taking into consideration that it was something that held significance for her mother.

Was it her favourite piece of music? Was she the one playing it?

She listened to the rest of the tape, in case there was anything else on it, but it spooled through to the end in silence. She rewound it and listened again, and by the end she had tears pouring down her cheeks. That was the kind of music it was.

Afterwards, she sat for a while in the darkness and the silence. She knew that now she had to undo the ribbon on the last thing in the box.

She went back upstairs, putting the tape back and lifting out the velvet piglet, a soft squashy toy perfect for little hands to clutch. She held it to her face and breathed it in, but apart from smelling a little musty there was no scent that she recognised. Then she lifted up the scroll of paper and pulled on the ribbon. It came away easily, and she unrolled the thick green paper. It was her original birth certificate. She'd been issued with a fresh one when she'd been adopted, with her adoptive surname: Moss. But here were the details she had never known.

Her birthplace: Ronkswood Hospital, Worcester.

Her own name: Robyn Amanda. She had always known her parents hadn't changed her Christian names, but seeing them there made her feel a surge of love for them and their respect for who she was.

And there was her mother's name: Emily Anne Silver. Born in 1972.

Her father was Unknown.

She felt overwhelmed. Each of the words that were new to her were written in thick black fountain pen, as if to drive their importance home.

Silver. What a beautiful surname.

And Emily. She tried to picture her. Did her own dark hair come from her, or did it come from Unknown? And what of her bone structure, her stature, her grey eyes? Her soft voice; her lack of fear when it came to water and horses and heights? Her disinterest in fashion and her love of plants?

Emily Silver. Seventeen years old when she'd become a mother. Younger than Clover was now. She wouldn't even be fifty yet.

Hello, Emily Silver, whispered Robyn. *Our story starts again here.*

12

1986

When she was sixteen, Emily Silver pushed a girl down the stairs at school. Backwards. She could have killed her.

It was the first thing in her life that was in any way out of the ordinary. And it had a massive effect on what happened later, because it proved, to the people who had the power to decide her future, that she was unstable.

But she wasn't. Any sane person would have cracked under the pressure. If anything, it was proof that she was normal. But records are subject to context, and if people want to rewrite history, or use evidence against you, it can be difficult to prove them wrong, especially if you are vulnerable.

Everything up until the incident had been quite dull. Emily's parents, Vivian and Neal, were older than her friends'. Her mum had her when she was nearly forty and her dad was forty-five. This made them both overprotective but slightly detached, as they didn't really remember being young themselves by the time she came along. Her father worked in the planning department, enforcing building regulations and issuing completion certificates. His job meant they had the best house in the close they lived in, tucked away at the end with the biggest garden, because he'd been given first refusal when they were built – the only time he'd taken advantage of his position.

It was the kind of road where everyone washed their car on a Sunday. And if one person got something new, everyone copied. Like bay trees. There was a craze for bay trees in big pots outside the front door; a craze that Vivian started. The weekend after she put hers out, the local garden centre ran out. It had given her a little boost, to think that she had some influence in the close.

Vivian was just a wife and mother, which was OK in those days. She always looked worried, as if she knew she was getting things wrong. She fussed a lot over Emily's father, and she didn't have many friends of her own. She didn't really socialise with the other mums in the close, being that much older. She would watch them come out in their fitness gear, off to the gym. Secretly, she wished she could prance about in Lycra and go for coffee with them afterwards. She knew they didn't invite her to their little evening get-togethers, when they sold cookware or skincare or sometimes something much naughtier – she'd heard on the grapevine what they were selling: skimpy nighties and fluffy handcuffs – and although she didn't really approve, she would have liked to have been asked.

Perhaps if she'd been friendlier with all the other mums in the close, she'd have handled things with Emily differently.

Emily was about to sit her GCSEs at Wormestall High when it all started to go wrong. After primary school, her parents had wanted her to go to St Anne's, the girls' convent on the other side of town, with its hideous purple uniform that made its pupils a laughing stock. They thought she had a good chance of a scholarship because she was studious and she played the cello. She'd passed her grade five with distinction by the age of eleven, not because she was a musical prodigy, but because she practised doggedly for at least an hour a day, every day.

Emily didn't want to go to St Anne's. She was afraid the other girls would be too posh and glamorous, when she was just ordinary. So she used every trick in the book to persuade her parents that Wormestall High was the right school for her. Rhetoric and tears, mostly.

'I don't see the point of paying to go to school,' she said, 'when I can get a perfectly good free education and stay with my friends.'

'But St Anne's has so many more opportunities. And facilities,' argued Vivian.

'They both have the same cello teacher. Miss Bembridge is peripatetic. And that's all I care about.'

'We should let her go where she wants, Vivian,' said Neal. 'There's no point in her being unhappy.'

'I think it's a mistake,' said Vivian. 'But whatever you think is best.'

Emily suspected her father was rather relieved not to have the pressure of school fees, but she was hugely relieved to have won the debate, despite her mother's disappointment. She knew her mum just wanted the best for her, but the thought of St Anne's terrified her. All those girls with long blond hair and endless legs.

She could disappear into the background easily at Wormestall High, because it was so big. Emily never wanted to be noticed, or be the centre of attention. Most of her friends from primary school were there, and everyone else soon got used to her being a little odd. Not a total freak, but she was a bit of a swot – she found work easy and didn't mind doing homework. And she was useless at fashion.

She had hair she could sit on, and she wore long ethnic skirts and baggy jumpers and Doc Marten boots. Basically anything that would cover her up from head to toe and not draw any attention to her body or the fact she was a female. She shied away from anything that was 'trendy'; she loved Tolkien and Dungeons and Dragons and chess and Led Zeppelin and Fleetwood Mac (although her first loves were Bach and Beethoven and Brahms, but she didn't mention that for fear of mockery).

By the time she was sixteen, the thought of putting on a skimpy dress and heels and make-up and going out to a pub or club, like all her friends were starting to do, terrified her.

What she was, though, was funny. She had a sharp eye and an even sharper tongue, and she was a brilliant mimic. So although she wasn't like all the others, wasn't into raunchy vampy singers like Madonna and Transvision Vamp and Shakespears Sister, she was quite popular with all the different subsets – the cool girls and the sporty girls and the arty girls – who were amused by her.

There was, however, one person who didn't like her one bit.

Corinna was everything Emily was not. She was wild and rebellious and always in trouble. She lived in a rough part of town and went to nightclubs in Birmingham with her cousin in his clapped-out Ford Fiesta. She loved dance music and had taken ecstasy. She wore neon and fishnet and crop-tops and ripped jeans – daringly outrageous clothes Emily couldn't imagine wearing. There were rumours that she as good as lived on her own. Her parents were hardly ever around. And she had a reputation for being a bit easy.

Emily couldn't understand why Corinna felt the need to bully her when she was hardly a threat, and they were so different. Polar opposites, almost. But something in her thrived on making Emily suffer. She seemed to get high on her fear. She seemed to relish asking her personal questions that would make Emily blush and everyone else laugh. Crude questions about her sex life designed to make her squirm with embarrassment. Or personal comments.

'Do you spit or swallow, Emily?'

'Oh, look, Emily's off to the toilet. Cystitis again, I'll bet.'

'Watch out, lads, here comes the Worcester bike.'

Emily was mortified. Corinna was everything she loathed. Crass, insensitive, cruel. What had happened to her to make her like that?

'Don't pay any attention to her,' the others would say. 'She's a cow. She's jealous because you're clever.'

At first, she tried to ignore her, but it seemed to make Corinna worse. One weekend she saw Corinna with a bloke, in the video shop, and Corinna nudged him and pointed at Emily.

'Wanna come back for a threesome?' Corinna cornered her by the comedy section. 'Watch some porn?'

Emily had fled, their laughs ringing in her ears.

Corinna carried on, honing in on all the things that Emily was self-conscious about but wasn't sure how to change: her shyness, her lack of fashion sense, her obvious chastity. It made her withdraw even further, her clothes getting longer and baggier. She'd go over to the music block and practise her cello, hiding away for the whole of the lunch hour, eating the ham sandwich and prawn cocktail crisps and the two Jaffa cakes wrapped up in foil that her mum gave her every day.

'Are you eating enough?' her mum asked. 'You look awfully pale. Are you sure you're not anaemic?'

'I'm fine,' Emily insisted, but noticed that her mother kept adding extra things to her lunch box. Little squares of cheese and bunches of grapes.

She knew what her mother would say if she told her about Corinna. 'Sticks and stones, darling. Just ignore her.'

Her cello teacher, Olivia Bembridge, was the only person who sensed how much the bullying was affecting her. She tried to get her to talk about it, and even said she would speak to the head.

'I should notify him, really. If you think you're being bullied.'

This suggestion filled Emily with horror.

'Please, please don't. If Corinna gets any idea that I've squealed on her, I'll be dead. It'll make her worse. Forget I said anything. If you tell anyone, I'll deny it.'

'OK,' agreed Miss Bembridge, but she was very unhappy about it. 'Why don't you take an earlier bus to school, to avoid her? And leave a bit later. And you can stay in the music block whenever you like.'

It wasn't that easy, but Emily appreciated her support. Miss Bembridge was her refuge, the one person who understood what she was going through, and it inspired her to practise even harder for her Grade 8, which was looming. She set herself demanding challenges – Elgar's Cello Concerto in E Minor, Shostakovich's Cello Concerto Number 2 – losing herself in the impossibility of the task. The music was the only thing that drowned out the taunts in her head. And playing the cello was the only time she didn't mind being the centre of attention. She could play in front of an audience as long as her cello was between them and her. It was both a shield and a comfort.

In the meantime, Emily tried her hardest not to react to Corinna, remaining stony-faced when she taunted her, because, she thought, eventually – surely – she would get bored? But with every encounter her stomach would be churning and her pulse racing. The flush on her face would give her fear away. She was terrified because she didn't know what Corinna wanted. She came to the conclusion that she was simply evil. A dark shadow flittering along the school corridors, lying in wait.

Eventually, Corinna teased and needled and humiliated her once too often. Emily was tired of turning the other cheek. It never had the desired effect. And she was only human. She had a breaking point.

One lunch hour, when Emily had been so absorbed in her cello practice that she was late back to lessons, Corinna and her friend Lisa were coming up the stairs to the music block as she was on her way down.

'Do you walk like that because you play the cello,' asked Corinna. 'Or because you take it up the backside?'

Lisa snorted, and Corinna fell against her laughing.

Today, Emily drew herself up, like the caterpillar in *Alice in Wonderland*, and looked Corinna in the eye.

'What did you say?'

Corinna blinked in surprise. Emily hadn't ever reacted

to her, let alone confronted her. And Emily could see that in that moment she wasn't so sure of herself after all. She could smell her perfume, strong and sickly – a knock-off designer scent that her cousin sold on his market stall. It turned her stomach.

Then Corinna recovered her composure and repeated her question, smirking.

Next to her, Lisa gave a twisted smile that could have been interpreted as appreciation of Corinna's wit or sympathy for Emily, her eyes flicking back and forth between the two girls. How gutless, thought Emily, to try and please us both.

A mist of blood shimmered behind her eyelids. She was so angry. All the months of needling crowded into her mind at once.

She reached out and pushed her.

It was so sudden. She didn't even need to push that hard. She took her completely by surprise. Corinna fell backwards down the stone steps, tumbling in slow motion, her long legs in their black tights flailing desperately for purchase, like a spider thrown from a window. Emily stood there, impassive, until she landed at the bottom. She didn't move.

'You've killed her!' screamed Lisa. Emily crossed her arms. She felt almost nothing, except a mild curiosity as to what would happen next.

There was chaos as staff and students came running and gathered around Corinna's body. The deputy head came to the top of the steps, her face creased with anxiety.

'Did you see what happened?'

'I pushed her,' Emily said calmly. 'It wasn't an accident.' She wasn't going to pretend it was, because then she couldn't explain what had driven her to it, and she was ready to reveal the truth.

The headmaster listened with an impassive expression in his office when she outlined, calmly and clearly, the vile invective Corinna had levelled at her over the past year. Her parents arrived halfway through her evidence. Her mother gasped in horror and her father looked distressed.

'How do we know you're not just saying this?' the headmaster asked. He knew she was clever. Emily could see he wouldn't put it past her to make it all up to save her skin.

She shrugged. 'You can ask Miss Bembridge. I told her everything.'

Miss Bembridge was duly summoned and corroborated her evidence.

'Why didn't you come forward before?' demanded her mother.

'Emily begged me not to. I was keeping her confidence.' Miss Bembridge looked defiant. 'The bullying affected her deeply. I can vouch for that. I've seen her in tears on numerous occasions. Too frightened to go back to class. I've been very concerned about her indeed.'

But somehow, a physical assault was perceived as more serious than verbal bullying.

Corinna wasn't dead. She had slight concussion and a broken wrist where she put her hand out to break her fall. Nevertheless, the incident was every school's worst nightmare. Corinna's mother, suddenly on the scene, was talking about a lawsuit, no doubt seeing the opportunity for a lucrative pay-out. That was the kind of people they were. And although lots of people came forward to back

Emily up, it was too little too late. She was asked to leave the school after her GCSEs.

Her parents did as much as they could to comfort her, but they were rather bewildered.

'Darling, I wish you'd told us,' said her mother. 'I can't bear to think of you being bullied.'

Of course she'd said nothing to them. Her parents would have gone straight to the school if she'd told them about Corinna. And that would have been disastrous.

At least by pushing her down the stairs, it was now over. Even if it was Emily who was being punished, not Corinna.

Somehow, her parents managed to broker a scholarship based on her GCSE predictions and her musical talent and got her into St Anne's. And when she finished her exams, they bought her a new cello.

'We're not waiting for your results to reward you,' said her mother. 'We know you will have done your best.'

Emily was overjoyed. She poured all her pent-up emotions into her music. She loved her cello. When her arms were around it, it was like holding a living, breathing being. It spoke to her in a way that nothing else did. She could feel it in her heart. It understood her.

Luckily, she loved St Anne's. Her original prejudice proved to be unfounded. The girls there were lovely – by and large, their parents were working their fingers to the bone to send them there, so none of them seemed to take it for granted. Mostly they were hard-working, kind and generous. It was heaven, after Corinna's reign of terror, for Emily to come out of her shell. She felt confident again, and was even a bit more adventurous on the clothing front. She wasn't an extravert or a trendsetter or about to go charging off to Cheltenham or Birmingham to hang out in nightclubs, but she did buy some jeans and a red plaid shirt – a massive change from her shapeless baggy black – and chopped six inches off her hair because it was getting ridiculous.

She thrived. Her parents were hugely relieved, glad that the horror of what had happened had had no lasting effect on their daughter, and were bursting with pride when the headmistress suggested she might be good enough for Oxbridge.

'You wouldn't have been pushed at Wormestall,' Vivian said. 'I'm so thrilled for you, darling. You've got a bright, bright future.'

'And,' grinned Emily, 'I look better in the purple uniform. It suits my inner Goth.'

Emily started going to parties, bought a Maybelline eyeliner and felt generally optimistic about the world after all the trauma. Especially when she learned that Corinna had moved up to Birmingham to go to sixth-form college, so she wasn't in danger of bumping into her in Worcester any time soon. She was still a bit of an oddball, but never made to feel like one by her new classmates. They quickly became fond of her, and any teasing was good-natured, never malevolent. It seemed as if her turbulent past was behind her and she was on her way to becoming an ordinary teenage girl.

If she had known what was around the corner, would she have done things differently?

13

'They've had a cancellation,' said Robyn on Monday morning, putting her phone on mute while she consulted Jake. 'The first Saturday in May. If we don't say yes now, there won't be time to give the official notice. Otherwise we'll have to wait till autumn. They're fully booked all summer.'

Jake counted on his fingers and looked alarmed. 'But that's only a month away.'

They were holed up inside the bar at the Mariscombe Hotel. The weekend's gorgeous weather had vanished, and the rain was pouring down on their site. It looked terrible, covered in muddy puddles, like a building site abandoned by cowboys. Jake was anxious to get back on track. Bruno had offered them a bonus if they finished the project by the end of April. Only a couple of thousand, but it would go a long way. Experience had told them the rain would pass if they were patient, and they could be back on site by the time they'd drunk an Americano. Or a hot chocolate in Robyn's case, while she tried to book the registry office for their wedding ceremony.

'I know. But think about it. It gives us the perfect excuse to keep it small. And I don't want to wait until autumn. I'll be out here.' Robyn put her hand in front of her stomach.

Jake thought for a moment. He thought of his friends who had got married, and all the build-up and the stress and the tension leading up to their big day. All the things they'd had to deal with that they didn't realise could be such a massive issue: choosing a wedding cake flavour or working out a seating plan. And it seemed leaving it to the bride wasn't an option as then you were accused of not being interested. So maybe having it sooner rather than later was the best way of stopping the plans getting out of control? But was it wise to schedule it in between finishing the Linhay and the pool project? His head was already full of timetables and deliveries and orders. He didn't want the pressure to spoil what should be a special day.

But Robyn's eyes were shining. He could see this was what she wanted. And because she was the least likely person to become a nightmare over the arrangements – what did they call them? Bridezillas? – he relented straight away.

'Go on, then. Why not?'

Robyn went back to the phone. 'We'd love that date. Thank you. It's obviously meant to be.'

She finished off her conversation by agreeing that they'd come in and do the paperwork at the first opportunity so the notices could be put up in time. She rang off and looked at Jake, her eyes sparkling.

'I can't believe it,' she said. 'We've got a wedding date.'

'I can't believe it either,' he said, then laughed. 'No pressure. Isn't that what they say?'

'We love pressure, remember?' Robyn prodded him with her foot. 'We work best under pressure.'

'Of course we do,' said Jake as their drinks arrived, tearing open a packet of sugar and letting the contents trickle into his mug. 'I guess I ought to ask for your dad's permission to marry you. I can ask him tonight.'

They were going to Hawksworthy Farm for shepherd's pie made with the remains of the Sunday roast.

'What?' said Robyn, open-mouthed. 'Don't be daft. That's like something out of Jane Austen.'

'Isn't it polite, though?'

Robyn crossed her arms. 'Only if I get to ask *your* dad's permission.'

Jake laughed. 'OK. Now you put it like that.'

'At least we can tell everyone now.' They'd kept the news to themselves over the weekend, wallowing in the novelty while everyone absorbed the baby news.

'I really must phone Mum. I've been putting it off. I just hope she's not going to be tricky about the wedding.'

'I'm sure she won't be,' Robyn reassured him. 'She won't want to spoil it for you, surely?'

'She won't *mean* to,' said Jake. 'But she can't help herself, sometimes. I know she'll be pleased about the baby, though.'

'Good!' said Robyn, who sometimes thought the Youngs worried too much about Tina's feelings. She wasn't sure how any woman could walk out on their husband and family, even if she was unhappy. She'd met her a couple of times, but usually Jake and Ethan went up to Enfield for the weekend to see her on their own. Robyn had liked her – Tina was fun and friendly and obviously very successful – but she was a little wary of her. She hoped she wouldn't cause problems.

She sipped at the last of her hot chocolate, thinking that now Jake had brought up Tina, it was the perfect time to mention that she had opened her box of secrets. After all, if they were getting married they shouldn't keep things from each other. They'd had a conversation about looking for her birth mother once, a few months after they'd first met, when Robyn had told him she was adopted.

'I've always been too scared to find out anything more about her,' she explained. 'Some adopted people are obsessed with finding out, but I worry that it will cause more problems than it's worth. And I don't know what would be worse. Finding out your real mum was some amazing beautiful princess, like in a Hollywood movie. Or that she was a total loser. Someone you wouldn't give the time of day.'

'Probably something in between,' said Jake, reasonably. 'Someone who was a victim of circumstance.'

'Yes. Probably. But it's still a risk. And I've not quite had the courage to take it.'

The more Robyn thought about it, the more she realised Jake was right. Her mother was probably an ordinary girl who'd been dealt the wrong card early in life. Her curiosity about her began to grow along with the baby inside her, as if motherhood was the bond between them.

Now she'd opened the box, and her mother had a name, she had become a real person in Robyn's mind, not just a vague shadowy concept. The few things Emily Silver had put in the box had personalised her. She was a mystery Robyn wanted to solve. Who was the person who had chosen the velvet piglet, and placed it in the box? Who had taken the photograph, and where? And who was playing the piano on the tape? What did that haunting music mean?

She'd dreamed about her mother all night, a blurry figure on the edge of her line of vision, reaching out her hands as the tune played itself over and over. Robyn had woken at four o'clock with tears streaming down her face, convinced her mother was in the room with her.

She went back to sleep eventually, but the emotions lingered. She felt reluctant to tell Jake, though. She knew he would worry about the effect all this would have on her. And the baby, of course. He would be anxious that she might be upset by what she discovered. It was lovely to think he cared about her so much, but this was a very personal undertaking, and it had taken her a long time to take the plunge: years of agonising and indecision.

And now she had finally taken the first step, she felt a peculiar loyalty to her birth mother; an urge to keep everything confidential until they had decided between them what their future might hold.

If they found each other, that is.

Besides, Jake had enough to worry about, trying to smooth things between Tina and Rocky. He was protective of his father, but mindful of his mother. It was a precarious, fragile relationship they all had, even fifteen years on, and she knew it weighed heavily on Jake. He had strong shoulders, but she didn't need to burden him further, especially when they were under pressure to finish the pool on time.

So she said nothing for the time being. She decided she would take advice from someone older and wiser. Her friend Gwen had been her rock, her confidante and her advisor for over five years now. She would understand the nuances. She would know the right thing to do.

She changed the subject.

'We need to think about where to have the reception.' She put her empty cup on the table. 'Maybe Bruno would give us a deal here?'

'It would still be expensive. And it's all so slick now. Not like when Dad used to take us here for scampi and chips as a treat.' Jake looked around the bar. It was stunning, but probably a bit formal for what they had in mind.

'I suppose the tradition is to have it at home. But Mum will go into overdrive if we have it at Hawksworthy. You know what she's like.'

Sheila had the biggest heart in Everdene. She personified the saying that if you want something done, ask a busy person. She ran two businesses, helped at the food bank in Tawcombe and was treasurer of the Everdene WI. She did more before breakfast than most people did in a day and was always the first to put her hand up. But she had a tendency to take over and she could get a little worked up as she overthought things and micromanaged.

Robyn suspected that if the wedding was at Hawksworthy, it would run away with itself and be the exact opposite of what she and Jake wanted. She sighed.

'What about having it at the Shedquarters?' suggested Jake. 'Like one of our Friday nights, but with a bit more effort?'

Robyn's eyes lit up. 'Would your dad let us do that?'

'Of course he would! He'd love it.'

Robyn began to laugh. 'You're a genius. You know that, right?'

'Yep, yep. I do.' Jake nodded his agreement, trying to look modest.

'It's the perfect way of keeping numbers down. We could have, what, twenty? Thirty max?' She began to count on her fingers. 'That really does keep it to family and a few close friends.'

'Sounds good to me.'

'And no one has to get too dressed up if they don't want to.' She grinned. 'Even me. I'm not a meringue sort of person. I'd be happy going up the aisle barefoot.'

'We need to check the tide times.'

'Oh God, yes. Can you imagine? Everything floating away? The cake heading out to sea.'

'Hang on. What if it rains? Like it is now.'

'It wouldn't dare. But we can put up gazebos.' She held up her ring finger. 'It ties in with where you proposed. We can have a starfish theme.'

'Whoa – let me talk to Dad first.' Jake laughed at her getting carried away. 'Though I know he'll be cool with it.'

Robyn was delighted. Everything was falling into place, and all her other worries began to fade. She gave a little clap.

'A wedding at the beach hut, Jake. It's going to be perfect.'

14

A grandmother.

She was going to be a grandmother.

That was quite a lot to take in on a Monday morning.

Tina Young sidled over to the nearest mirror to check her reflection. There were enough of them in the salon, and she'd chosen them very carefully to take at least five years off anyone who looked into them, for she wanted all her clients to be pleased with what they saw.

As a result, they took five years off her too. She definitely didn't look like a traditional 'nan', she reassured herself, in her sleek white trouser suit and high-heeled boots, her hair in a long bob that managed to be both sleek and tousled from expert blow-drying. Good cheekbones, strong eyebrows, full lips. She nodded in approval.

Tina had always been fixated on her appearance, but that was the job she was in. When you gave people the hairstyle of their dreams and made them look like a million dollars, you had to look good too.

'All right, babe?' Tomas, her top stylist glided past her, scissors at the ready. He knew she had been suffering of late – years of hairdressing had resulted in RSI in her right hand, and of course the answer was to step back a bit, but how could she?

'Fine,' she responded automatically, but she was still in shock.

Of course, she was delighted with the news. But she hadn't been prepared for it at all. Jake hadn't given her any indication that he and Robyn were trying for a family when she last saw him at Christmas. The boys always came up to her in Enfield, to see their London relatives and do the things they used to do when they all lived here.

Before everything went wrong.

She appreciated them keeping up the tradition. They were grown-ups now, and they could do whatever they wanted at Christmas, but they loved going down the pub with their old friends and going into the West End to finish their shopping. Every year she was convinced this would be the year they would tell her they were staying in Devon, but it hadn't happened so far. They knew she was tied to the salon and only had a few days off. She worked right up to Christmas Eve, and was open again less than a week later for New Year's Eve hair-dos.

A baby meant that would all change, she realised. For Jake, at least. She didn't resent it, but her eyes filled with tears. The end of an era. And where was she going to fit into the picture? She was so far away. She was surprised to feel a tug deep inside her. Something similar to a maternal urge, but deeper and richer. She laughed at her image in the mirror. For all her obsession with looking young for her age, she couldn't fight nature. Or deny the fact that she was going to be a grandmother – and she was chuffed to bits about it.

She knew, as the mother of the baby's father, she was in the second division. Robyn's mother would get first dibs. That was the unspoken rule of grandmothering, unless things were out of the ordinary. And she knew Robyn was close to her parents. Tina had a vague idea that she was adopted, but it didn't matter a jot. They were a tightly knit farming family. Jake and Robyn were going to be moving in right next door. Mick and Sheila would be on hand for babysitting and cuddles and emergency cover and farmhouse tea and Sunday lunch and nursery drop off and school pick-up . . .

Tina sighed. She would have to be a different kind of granny. Glamorous granny. The one who whisked them off on holiday, perhaps, or took them to the pantomime at Christmas and sent down big shiny parcels wrapped in proper ribbon.

It wouldn't be a fight, she reminded herself. There was room for all of them in the baby's life. And it was very early days yet.

'We had our twelve-week scan on Friday,' Jake told her. 'Everything's good. Due on the fifth of November, so keep your diary clear.'

She felt a thrill go through her. She almost laughed out loud. She had no idea she'd be so excited. She wanted to tell someone, but not yet. She didn't want everyone in the salon speculating about whether it was a boy or a girl and what it would be called. It was her own secret, something to keep to herself and mull over. Something lovely to think about when she woke up in the morning.

His other piece of news she wasn't so thrilled about. For him and Robyn, yes. It was wonderful that they were getting married. But she was shocked that the wedding was only a month away. That wasn't long enough for her to prepare herself.

Not practically. She had a million outfits she could choose from. Emotionally.

It was over ten years since she had seen him. She could call his face to mind even now. The most handsome man in Enfield. North London. The country! And his looks weren't even his best quality. Rocky Young was the kindest, most dependable, hardest working man she'd ever come across. Why hadn't she recognised the importance of that? Why had she been so caught up in herself that she'd lost sight of what mattered?

She'd lost everything. Again, not materially – it was a fifty/fifty split. Instead, she'd lost her heart, her mind, her soul; her place in the family; her reason to get up in the morning. Her confidence and self-belief. All through selfishness and an inability to compromise. Her stomach curdled with anxiety as it always did when she thought about it, even now.

When you put yourself first, before everyone you supposedly loved, you ended up at the bottom. No one looking at her today would suspect the truth. She looked like the woman who had it all: the looks, the glamour, the successful business, the flashy car. But it was a glossy veneer: despite her success, she knew she had failed at the most important thing in her life.

Would she have the courage? Could she find the mettle to turn up to the wedding and see it all unfold around her, smiling graciously, as if it wasn't tearing her apart? She had to, for Jake. He would want her there. She was still his mum, after everything that had happened. Her sons had never held it against her. Though if they had known the truth, maybe they might have felt differently.

Honourable, selfless Rocky had made sure Jake and Ethan never found out what she had done.

She caught sight of the clock and realised she needed to get going.

'I'm off now for the rest of the day,' she told the receptionist, and headed to the staffroom to get changed. There, she took off her suit and high heels and slipped into jeans and a hoody and trainers. She picked up a large bag full of hair products, dryers and brushes and headed out to her car.

Every other Monday afternoon, she went to the refuge. She never talked about it to anyone. Even her staff didn't know she went there. The location was a secret, for the women there were in hiding, most of them in danger from abusive ex-partners. Going there had saved Tina from herself. It had given her a reason to climb out of her misery. She arrived at the refuge twice a month with her bag of tricks and spent the afternoon washing, conditioning, snipping and drying. Some of the women hadn't been to the hairdresser for as long as they could remember, and most of them certainly hadn't been pampered for a long time. She did some of the children as well, teasing out tangles, cutting too-long fringes and straggly pigtails. For some, the intimacy was an ordeal, but Tina was kind and gentle. Sometimes, the gratitude affected her so much she had to rush to the cloakroom and shed a few tears.

She loved it a million times more than tending to the clients who paid her over a hundred pounds for her services. She was the best hairdresser for miles around and she knew her handiwork went on to attend the most glamorous places, to glitzy parties and premieres and on cruises. But nothing meant more to her than a woman staring at herself in the mirror and seeing a transformation. She hoped it went some way to rebuilding their confidence and empowering them. Even if it just made them feel like someone else for a moment, she had done some good.

Half an hour later she was spreading all her kit out on a table in the refuge while an orderly queue formed outside the door. For the next four hours she worked without a break. She chatted while she worked, for sometimes the women would open up to her. She never gave them her opinion or told them what to do, just let them say whatever was on their minds. She saw fear and hopelessness and exhaustion. And she did her absolute best to alleviate it for the short time she was there.

Today, she had done a wash and blow dry for a woman her own age whose face still bore the yellowing traces of bruising. The woman could barely look at herself in the mirror, her confidence was so low. She had almost refused the offer of a hairdo, but somehow Tina had persuaded her.

'Let me do your make-up,' said Tina when she'd finished the blow-dry, and with the lightest of touches she'd applied a bit of her own foundation and mascara and a hint of lipstick.

'I can't remember the last time I put make-up on,' said the woman, looking in the mirror. Her eyes looked slightly less dead and it took years off her.

'Have that little lot,' said Tina. 'I've got loads more. I get samples at the salon.'

She might as well have given the woman the moon.

It always made her feel guilty when she heard their stories, and realised how hard-done-by she had once thought herself. How little effort she had put in to rescuing her marriage. She could have done more – found premises to open her own salon like she was supposed to, instead of sulking.

And she could definitely have ignored the advances of the smooth-talking chancer she had met when she was back in Enfield one weekend. It had only been once, but once was all it took to lose Rocky for good. It made her feel sick when she remembered. At the time, she'd given herself a million reasons to justify it, but now there wasn't one that stuck.

The refuge wasn't all doom and gloom. There was humour and camaraderie too, and they loved a bit of gossip.

'I'm going to be a grandmother,' she told them while she sat drinking tea after she'd finished. It felt so good to say it and she knew her news would be safe here. All secrets stayed inside these walls. 'My son phoned me this morning. The baby's due on Bonfire Night.'

The baby. Now she had spoken about it, it became more real.

'No way!' They were all amazed. 'You're not old enough. Everyone will think it's yours.'

For a moment, Tina imagined pushing her grandchild along in a pushchair. It gave her a funny warm feeling. Maybe she would buy one of those four-wheel-drive strollers you could take on the beach?

'And my son's getting married. In four weeks.'

'Oh, that's nice. What are you going to wear?'

A big smile, thought Tina. That's what I'm going to wear. A big smile to cover up the broken heart I stupidly smashed into tiny pieces. And it was nobody's fault but mine.

15

'Congratulations, son.' Rocky clapped his hand on Jake's knee. 'I'm really pleased. For you and Robyn. And the baby. Not that it matters,' he added hastily. 'I would never put you under pressure to get married. But I'm glad you are.'

'Yeah. Me too. The more I think about it, the happier I am.' Jake appreciated his dad's words. They were from the heart.

They were parked up in Rocky's truck at the top of the dunes. The rain from earlier had stepped aside and the sea looked inviting, the sun shining through the tops of the waves. They were good and clean and pretty irresistible to a pair of seasoned surfers. The two of them tried to get in for a surf together as often as they could. They'd both assumed that today's weather meant they wouldn't have a chance to get in the water but it had cleared up just in time for a late-afternoon dip before they headed up to Hawksworthy Farm to toast the wedding news with Mick and Sheila.

'Robyn and I wondered if we could use the Shed-quarters for the reception.'

'Course you can.' Rocky looked at him, pleased. 'You're not going for a marquee job, then? Or a hotel?'

'We want small and simple – no fuss.'

Rocky raised an eyebrow and grinned. 'Good luck with that.'

'Yeah, I know. I've phoned Mum and told her, by the way. She was chuffed to bits about the baby. Much more than I thought she would be. Positively gooey, which isn't like her.'

'That's good.' Maybe, thought Rocky a little uncharitably, Tina would pull it out of the bag on the grandmother front.

'I told her about the wedding, too. Obviously she needs to sort things out at the salon but I think she'll be coming.'

'Of course. She's your mum.'

'It'll be cool, won't it?' Jake looked worried.

'Jake, it's been a long time, we're both grown-ups, and it's your wedding. Of course it will.' It better be, he added to himself.

'She can stay at the Mariscombe Hotel. She can get ready there, and go back when she wants.'

'Good idea. We can arrange cabs so she can do her thing.' Rocky wasn't going to let their situation spoil their son's day. The guilt still gnawed at him. He honestly hadn't expected things to still be difficult. It was over fifteen years, yet every family event seemed to bring stress and tension. They didn't bother getting together any more just to pretend they had once been a unit. It was his biggest sadness that they couldn't be amicable.

The boys always spent Christmas with Tina back in Enfield, because Rocky didn't feel that strongly about it, and if it made Tina happy, it was worth waking up on his own. He knew the boys felt bad for him, but he assured them it was fine, and they always had a bash on New Year's Day instead. No matter what the weather was, they did a big barbecue at the beach hut and went swimming in the sea. There was nothing like starting the year with a challenge. They had steak sandwiches with fried onions and a crate of beer and they all discussed their resolutions. Rocky had made a rule: the resolutions had to be positive rather than negative, no giving things up; it had to be about *doing* things.

He looked over the dunes and along the beach, along the sand that shimmered pink or cream or grey, depending on the weather, at the vast blue sea butted up against the vast blue sky, constant companions watched over day and night by the sun and the moon. And he saw the grey felt roof of the beach hut, and the bleached-out peeling paint and he felt proud. It would be the perfect wedding venue.

He'd seen the advert for the hut in the post office in Everdene when they were on holiday, over twenty-five years ago now, before beach huts became all the rage and wildly overpriced. It was the best ten grand he'd ever spent. He could still remember getting the key, running across the sand with Ethan and Jake beside him. Opening the door, hearing the creak of the hinge and smelling damp wood, and thinking that this was the best den in the world, somewhere to hide, somewhere to hang out, somewhere his boys would never forget. He couldn't believe their luck. They went there every summer and every half term, until he'd finally hit upon the idea of them moving to Everdene for good.

He should have realised that the move was the wrong thing for Tina, but she'd bought into it at the time. They'd sold their house in Enfield and bought one overlooking the headland. He'd set up in business doing plastering and renovations and had a full diary. He couldn't just turn his back on the work.

And it had been all right at first. They'd moved down in the summer, and she seemed to embrace the beach life. But then the weather had got colder and the days got shorter and the wind and the rain blew in. He and Jake and Ethan didn't care. They went in the water whatever the weather brought.

He remembered Tina shivering, her goose-bumped flesh blue-white, sitting miserably on a rug while Rocky and Ethan and Jake frolicked in the waves, having the time of their lives.

Rocky was frustrated. She didn't have to get in the water, of course she didn't, but she could have made some attempt to integrate and make a new life for herself. But she didn't value the calmer pace of life by the sea, the beauty of nature. She was homesick, horribly homesick, for Enfield and her friends and her family and the cama- raderie of the salon she'd sold, the one she'd had since she was twenty-four.

She was supposed to be looking for somewhere to open a new one.

'There's no point. No one ever has their hair done down here!' she protested.

'Yes, they do,' said Rocky.

'Not often enough to make it worthwhile.' She slumped, despondent, which worried him because if Tina had anything it was fight.

He tried to figure out a way to placate her. He was baffled that she seemed to take no pleasure from the fact the boys were as happy as clams. And riddled with guilt that they all seemed to be living the dream but her.

He was working on a compromise when she did the unforgivable and cheated on him. Just a one night stand, but he should have seen it coming. Maybe it was inevitable? Two unhappy people: one too busy, one bored. He shuddered at the memory of the hurt it had caused. It had been so much more painful than it had needed to be, and he blamed himself. Of course he did. But now, it was time to put it all behind them. He wanted his son's wedding day to be unblemished. Nothing was going to stop it being perfect.

'Hey,' said Jake, breaking into his thoughts. 'Ethan said you had a date.'

'Can a man have no secrets?' Rocky laughed.

'It's cool, Dad. You need to get back on the horse. How did it go?'

'Well,' said Rocky, remembering Melissa. He was still puzzled. 'It was going really well. And then she just left.' He clicked his fingers. 'Just like that. I don't know what I said.'

'You can't take it personally.'

'That's what the barman said!'

'Seriously. You don't know what people have got going on. Maybe she was nervous. Or married. Or she thought she was punching above her weight.'

'Above her weight?' laughed Rocky.

'Yeah, Dad. You're a good catch. Any woman would be lucky to have you.'

Rocky was quiet for a moment. It was funny, taking dating advice from your own son. By rights, he should be giving Jake marriage advice, but he didn't feel equipped. 'Thanks. That means a lot.'

Jake punched his arm playfully. 'Come on. Last one in the ocean buys a round at the Ship Aground.'

They jumped out of his truck, ran down the dunes and unlocked the door of the beach hut, racing to get into their wetsuits that were hanging by the door. They couldn't stop laughing, because getting into a wetsuit quickly was almost impossible. They were both ready at about the same time and shot out of the door with their boards under their arms.

This was the kind of thing that made him happy, thought Rocky. Racing to get into an ice-cold sea with his son. He shouldn't have regrets. If he'd stayed in his marriage, gone back to Enfield, he wouldn't be doing this now.

At the last moment he slowed down to allow Jake to be the first into the waves. As if his son was still five years old. Jake put his arm in the air in a gesture of triumph, threw his board down and climbed on.

Drinks are on me, then, Rocky grinned to himself, and followed his son into the water.

16

Later that afternoon, when Jake headed off surfing with his dad, Robyn made her way to see the one person in the world she felt safe sharing her secret with, even if she was more than twice her age. How old, she couldn't be sure, but she'd mentioned seeing the Rolling Stones before they were famous. So much older than she looked. Or behaved.

Gwen Chadwick lived in the flat beneath Robyn's old flat in Tawcombe, taking up the whole of the first floor, her drawing room vast with floor-to-ceiling windows and a wrought-iron balcony. Gwen was the one thing Robyn missed about living in the town, and she made sure to see her at least once a fortnight, either for coffee or tea or cocktails or a curry in the high street. There wasn't a person in the world less like Robyn than Gwen, but she adored her all the more for it.

In all the time Robyn had lived in the flat above, she had never seen Gwen without make-up, or known her not to smell utterly delicious, a mixture of powdered sugar, smoky cinnamon and crushed peppercorns. While Robyn strode, Gwen drifted. She did exactly what she wanted whenever she wanted. She cooked like a dream, drove like a demon, and cut her own hair with the kitchen scissors into her trademark pixie crop, kept platinum white with peroxide and coconut oil.

Gwen filled her home and her life with treasures. She had a nose for a bargain, and people phoned her when they found something of interest and off she would zoom, in her powder-blue 1970s Mercedes convertible. Somehow, she seemed to make a living, picking things up and passing them on. House sales, charity shops, flea markets, car boots: Gwen would haunt them with her beady eye, seeing beauty – and profit – where others would see unwanted tat. She had a string of connections she had built up over the years. When she lit on something, she knew exactly where it was destined. Sometimes the item would need repair or renovation, and she had endless skill and patience. A small armchair would be reupholstered in bright silk velvet stripes. A lamp would be re-wired and given a new shade trimmed with beads or feathers. A painting would be carefully lifted from its heavy gilt frame, cleaned and re-mounted while the frame was given a wash in a contrasting colour and lo – now the painting would jump out, transformed. She was a magpie and a magician.

She could make you pale green macarons at the drop of a hat, or plant you up a tub of flowers that come spring would greet you with a cluster of crocuses and narcissi and tulips that would make your heart sing. She lived in Tawcombe because she had to breathe the sea air. But she loved the city too, and would disappear for weeks on end to Paris or Vienna or Istanbul – she had more friends than anyone Robyn had ever met.

Robyn didn't really know much about Gwen's past. She seemed reluctant to share any details, and the fact she'd remained resolutely single all her life suggested a broken heart. Robyn had never intruded: Gwen was one of those people who made it easy for you to spill your own beans but never shared her own private life.

And this afternoon, Robyn was preparing to take Gwen into her confidence about what she was about to do. She was still a little unsure, but she didn't want to talk to either her parents, or to Jake quite yet. And Robyn thought Gwen might know what the piece of music was. Gwen was an encyclopaedia, cultured and well read. She absorbed and memorised information, drank in music and literature and art, frequented Glyndebourne and Covent Garden and the Royal Academy, mostly courtesy of friends who had boxes or tickets to opening nights and private views.

'You have to keep your eyes and ears open,' she often told Robyn. 'And your heart. Always your heart.'

And so she'd decided to call in on Gwen after she and Jake had done their best to salvage a day's work after the deluge. Robyn parked in the car park at the end of the harbour, squeezing her truck into a space, remembering how people in Tawcombe didn't seem to be able to park properly and how aggravating she'd found it. In the harbour, the tide was out and the boats were sunk into the grey damp sand. A few hours later they would be bobbing about on the water, the vista completely transformed. Sometimes, when it was sunny, you could think yourself in the South of France, with the striped awnings and the sun throwing glitter on the waves.

She walked towards the row of shops and houses that lined the harbour front, and noticed that the flat underneath Gwen's had a 'sold' sign in the window. It had lain empty for nearly two years now. That was the problem with Tawcombe: even though it was on the up, if a property didn't move straight away it got stuck. Someone had obviously seen the potential and was brave enough to overlook the fact it had been on the market for ages.

She looked up and could see Gwen on her balcony. If it was fine, her French windows were inevitably flung open so she could breathe in gusts of fresh air.

'Have you got time for a coffee?' called up Robyn.

'Always!' came the reply. 'Come on up. I'll buzz you in.'

Robyn pushed the front door open, ran up the stairs and through Gwen's open door.

'How lovely,' said Gwen. 'I was thinking about you yesterday. I don't know why.'

Sometimes, there was something a little bit mystic about Gwen.

'Well,' said Robyn. 'I do have news.'

Gwen's eyes widened with excitement. She was wearing a grey silk blouse with tiny covered buttons, flowery culottes and staggeringly high heels. She ushered Robyn in, led her to the chesterfield sofa in front of the French windows and sat her down. Robyn found herself drowning in a sea of cushions and bolsters in a multitude of colours – burnt orange, hot pink, emerald green – and fringed with tassels. She picked one up and hugged it to herself. She saw Gwen's eyes narrow as she surveyed first her left hand and then her stomach.

'Stop scrutinising me!' laughed Robyn.

'Well, it's either wedding bells or a baby because you know jolly well nothing else would be of interest to me.'

'I might have won the lottery.'

Gwen gave a dismissive snort. Money matters were of

no interest to her. Robyn had no idea how she survived, yet she seemed to. She was a shrewd businesswoman, certainly, but she never discussed her income. She could be as rich as Croesus or as poor as a church mouse; Robyn had no idea.

'Well, come on. Don't tease.'

'It's both.'

'Both?'

'I'm three months' pregnant.'

'Darling!'

'We didn't want to say anything until we had our twelve-week scan, but it's all good.'

'I can't think of nicer news. Congratulations. You will be the sweetest parents.'

'And.' Robyn burrowed in her pocket. She'd taken off her ring while she worked. 'Jake asked me to marry him. Ta da!'

She held up the ring.

Gwen's eyes lit up as she took it from her. 'I knew it!' She scrutinised it closely. 'Aquamarine. Very pretty.'

'I know it's not a diamond or a sapphire but I wouldn't want that.'

'Quite. You're not a rock sort of a girl. It would be wasted on you. And I don't mean that as an insult. This is perfect. He's very clever, your boy.'

'He is.' Robyn took the ring from Gwen and slipped it back on her finger, admiring it once again. The little starfish filled her heart with joy.

'Well, I think that calls for a *coupe de champagne*,' Gwen went to stand up. 'Can you have the tiniest drop or is that frowned upon?' Gwen moved over to her cocktail cabinet and removed two glasses.

'Just give me a tiny splash and I can pretend to drink it.'

'Good idea.' She went into the kitchen and came back with a mini bottle of Moët. 'We can split this.' She always kept one or two of the little bottles in her fridge. You never knew when you might need one, as Robyn's announcement had just proved.

'There's something else I want to show you.'

Robyn pulled a padded envelope out of her bag and took out the cassette.

'This tape was in a box,' Robyn told her. 'The box my birth mother made for me. Mum gave it to me on my eighteenth birthday, but I never opened it. I thought if I opened it, something would come out that could never be put back, like Pandora's box. While the box was shut, I was safe. I belonged to Sheila and Mick Moss, at Hawksworthy Farm, and that was that. I was always happy. I never felt the need to dig into my past.'

'No, of course not,' said Gwen. 'Your parents are wonderful. But...' she nodded at Robyn's ringed finger. 'Has this changed how you feel?'

'Yes. As soon as I realised I was pregnant, I felt as if I needed to know exactly who my mother was. As if it was important to know the truth about my background, not just for me, but for Jake. And the baby...'

'I understand that.' Gwen nodded. 'It seems logical to me. Our identity is crucial to us. To know whose blood runs through our veins.'

'But I don't want to upset Mum and Dad. I know they went through a lot before they had me. Mum lost three babies.' Her eyes filled with tears. 'I always felt as if it might bring back the memories, if I went digging.

I didn't want to remind them of what they'd lost. Even though they've had Clover since. And I know if I went to them they'd say go ahead. Which almost makes it worse.'

'Your mum kept the box for you. She needn't have. She could have kept it hidden, or even thrown it away. She must have wanted to leave the line of enquiry open for you.'

'I know. That's what I keep telling myself. But it's hard.'

'This is your story, Robyn. Giving you the box was your mum's way of saying it's OK.' Gwen smiled at her, and Robyn felt comforted. Gwen always put things into perspective.

'I guess so. Anyway, now I've opened it. And my birth certificate was in there, with my mum's name on it. Emily Silver. And there was a photo of me, probably about a month old, and a cuddly little piglet.'

Robyn faltered. For a moment she imagined her mother putting the piglet in the box, knowing that was the last she would see of her baby.

Gwen put a hand on her arm. She understood how momentous this was.

'And this cassette.' Robyn handed it over. 'It's someone playing the piano, but I've no idea who it is. Or what the music is. I thought you might be able to help.'

'Well, let's see, shall we?' Gwen took the tape and went over to her hi-fi, an ancient Grundig that would have cost a fortune in its day. When the applause started, Robyn jumped: it sounded as if they were in a concert hall. And then the music began.

After only a few bars, a smile of recognition spread itself across Gwen's face. But she said nothing, just leaned back in her chair and shut her eyes as the music spilled its way into the room, drifting into every corner and up to the ceiling and out of the window. Hearing it on a quality sound system made it even more eerie and magical. Almost haunting, thought Robyn. For the full six minutes, they sat and listened, until the last notes faded away.

Gwen opened her eyes at the end and Robyn looked at her.

'"Ondine",' said Gwen with a sigh. 'From *Gaspard de la Nuit*. By Ravel.' She smiled. 'People used to dismiss Ravel as mediocre, but this is one of the most difficult piano pieces ever written. Most players would quail at performing this in public.' She pressed the tape deck to rewind it. 'Ondine was a water nymph. She tried to seduce a mortal man into coming down to her kingdom beneath the lake. But he refused. He was betrothed to someone on earth. And she was furious.'

'Oh!' Robyn shivered.

'Ravel is especially good at musical narrative. He constructs this dark, watery, magical world and you just get drawn in. Didn't you feel as if you were underwater?'

'Yes! Now you say it. Absolutely,' said Robyn, utterly fixated by the explanation. 'It's beautiful, but very sad.'

'The question is why your mother gave this to you. It seems to be a live recording.'

'That's the puzzle.' She looked at Gwen. 'Do you think this could be my mother playing? My real mother, I mean?'

'If it is, she's a pretty marvellous player.'

'Well, I certainly didn't inherit her musical talent.' Robyn managed a laugh. 'Could we listen to it again? It sounds so different in here.'

She shivered as Gwen pressed play again. The notes

were like droplets, ripples, cascades, tumbling waterfalls. The emotion of it ran through her and by the end, Robyn had tears in her eyes.

She had made up her mind. She needed to know the answer to the riddle.

'I need to know who she is,' she told Gwen. 'I need to know what this means. You see, I should never have opened the box.'

'So what will you do? How do you go about finding her?'

Robyn had gone online first thing that morning before she'd even got dressed. She'd woken at six and crept out of bed in the chill morning air, turning on her laptop and typing *find your birth mother* into the search engine with frozen fingers.

'There's a special register for adopted people who want to trace their parents. If Emily wants me to get in touch, she'll have put her name on it. All I have to do is contact them, and they'll give me her details. It's that easy. Or it seems to be.'

Robyn still couldn't believe it was so simple. Emily Silver could be just an email away. It made her nervous, but excited too.

'Oh,' said Gwen, turning this information over in her mind. 'But what if she hasn't registered? Or doesn't want to be contacted?'

'If she's not on the register, I'd have to think carefully about whether to pursue it. I could go to an agency who could try and trace her for me. But I don't want to upset her, or cause trouble. I mean, she might have married and not told her husband or her children about me. Nobody wants a stranger turning up on the doorstep claiming to be a long-lost daughter.'

'I guess not,' said Gwen.

'What do you think I should do?' asked Robyn.

Gwen was silent for a moment.

'I think, if your mother has registered and wants to make contact, that it would be a wonderful thing. For her to see you after all this time, and know you are all right. I imagine she's thought about you every day since she gave you up.'

'She was only seventeen when she got pregnant. That's really all I know about her.'

'Only a baby herself,' said Gwen.

'I feel so close and yet so far away,' said Robyn. 'And I'm afraid.' She tried to smile. 'I watch those programmes on the telly about reunions, and sometimes it's wonderful. But sometimes, it's awful.' She sighed. 'It can mean the world, for a mother to make contact with her child. But not always. How am I supposed to know which ending I'll get?'

'It's a risk, I suppose,' said Gwen. 'But all the important things in life are, Robyn. You don't lead a rich and full life by taking the safe path.'

Robyn looked at her, wide-eyed, nodding at her wisdom.

'But tell me about the wedding,' said Gwen, changing the subject, for Robyn needed to go away and think. 'That's the important bit. When's the big day, my darling girl?'

'I booked it this afternoon. For the first Saturday in May.'

Gwen's eyes widened. 'That's only a month away.'

'Exactly. We thought if we had it sooner rather than later, we can keep it really simple.'

'Mmmm,' said Gwen, doubtful.

'What do you mean, "mmmm"?' asked Robyn with a grin.

'In my experience, there's no such thing as a simple wedding. Even with the best will in the world.'

'Well, we're going to try. And Jake's had a brainwave. We don't have time to arrange anything extravagant – work's mad, and we can't afford it while we're trying to finish the Linhay. So we're going to have it at the Shed-quarters. What do you think?'

'Well, that sounds perfect.'

'We'll do a big picnic. Clover can do some wedding cocktails. Really simple but fun. We can put on some music at sunset. Dance the night away.'

'Let me organise it for you.' Gwen leaned forward, her eyes shining. 'I'll run everything past you first. And I won't make it expensive. That is my forte, after all. Making things look good without spending a fortune.'

'Would you really?'

'It could be my wedding present to you both.'

Robyn looked thrilled. Gwen had the magic touch. She would make it the most beautiful wedding in the world. She'd think of all the little details that would make it memorable.

'I can't think of anyone I'd rather have in charge. I haven't a clue about organising a wedding. And Mum definitely doesn't have time.'

'Well, I'd love to do it. It'll keep me out of trouble for at least a month. And there'll be no balloon arches or fake red carpets.'

Robyn laughed. That was exactly the sort of thing she didn't want, and she knew she was in safe hands with Gwen. 'Phew. As long as we're clear on that.'

'Just give me numbers and a budget. It will all be done in the best possible taste.'

Afterwards, Gwen watched out of the window as Robyn made her way back to her truck. She was delighted with her news. Jake was solid and kind and good fun, which in Gwen's opinion were pretty much the three requisites you needed in a man if you wanted to be happy. She had been through enough to know kindness was particularly key, and that money and looks counted for nothing without it.

She knew that better than anyone.

17

The kitchen at Hawksworthy Farm was typical for a Devon longhouse, with three outside walls and a flagstone floor, which would be chilly but for the inglenook fireplace kept fed with logs, and the ancient range, where Sheila was putting the finishing touches to the gravy.

The kitchen served as an office too. There were piles of paperwork on top of the units, a huge whiteboard at one end with bookings for the kennels scrawled all over it, biscuit tins and Tupperware pots, an ancient black-and-white telly, and a rack with fleecy dog blankets drying on it.

Mouse, the Moss family's wire-haired lurcher, was padding around waiting for scraps to fall onto the floor. Occasionally he would get bored and flump into his basket, but his eyebrows and ears would twitch constantly, ever vigilant.

'A month gives me just enough time to get the hut into some sort of shape.' Rocky was saying as he put a dollop of shepherd's pie on his plate. 'It's been needing an overhaul for a while.'

'But the whole point of having the wedding so soon is so no one makes a fuss. The hut's fine as it is.' Jake brought a big dish of peas over to the kitchen table.

Rocky shook his head. 'It's been the shabbiest hut on the beach for ages. But you know what they say: cobblers' children have no shoes.'

'That's why we like it!' protested Robyn. 'It's a beach hut. It's supposed to be all faded and weather-beaten. Some of the huts on the beach now are like show homes. Not that there's anything wrong with show homes,' she added hastily, for Rocky took pride in his work. His last development had sold before he'd even printed the brochure.

But Robyn was right. The beach huts at Everdene were becoming more and more elaborate with owners trying to outdo each other. The Shedquarters definitely erred on the side of rustic.

'I'll spend the next couple of weekends doing it up.' Rocky wasn't going to take no for an answer. 'We need the toilet working properly for a start. It's a bit temperamental at the moment. And what's your colour scheme? I can paint the hut to match.'

'We don't have a colour scheme.' Jake looked at Robyn. 'Do we?'

'Blue and white stripes might be nice,' said Robyn. 'A turquoisey blue. Not navy.'

'Oh. So we do have a colour scheme?'

Robyn looked sheepish.

'No. I just think that if Rocky really insists on painting it, blue and white would look nice in the photos.'

Jake put his hands up, laughing. 'It's getting out of control already.'

'I can give you a hand, Rocky. Just say the word.' Mick took the dish from Rocky and started to serve himself.

'And we're chuffed to bits, Jake. We couldn't ask for a better son-in-law.'

'Hear, hear,' said Sheila, waving her wooden spoon in agreement.

'Thank you,' said Jake. 'And I'm very proud to be marrying Robyn.'

Robyn smiled and fiddled with her ring. She felt a bit self-conscious, but it was lovely that everyone seemed so delighted.

'And we'll do whatever we're asked, but we won't interfere. Will we, Mick?' Sheila said, undoing her apron and slinging it on the rail over the range then bringing a Pyrex jug over to the table. 'Everyone help themselves to gravy.' She pushed back her hair and re-tied it in a scrunchie she kept on her wrist. She was almost ready to sit down. Although Sheila didn't really do sitting down. She was always on the go. 'And if you want a hand with the catering. Or flowers.'

'Actually,' said Robyn. 'Gwen's offered to do the organising for me. It's her present to us.'

'Oh?' Sheila looked taken aback. 'So you've told Gwen already? Before you told us?'

Robyn realised she'd made a tactical error. 'Only because I wanted her advice, and before I knew it she'd offered to take it all off my hands.'

'I see,' said Sheila, in a tone of voice that suggested she didn't see at all.

Robyn panicked that she'd already offended her mum.

'The things is, Mum, I want you to enjoy the day. I don't want you to be running around. You're a guest. A guest of honour.'

'Cake. What about the cake? I can do you a nice fruit cake, but I need to do it now because it needs to mature.'

Robyn could already see her mother calculating ingredients and wondering if she had the right tin.

'I'd love a cake, Mum. But probably not fruit cake. No one likes fruit cake.'

'Chocolate? That'll be messy if it's hot. It'll melt.'

'I don't know yet, Mum. Just chill.'

As soon as the words were out of her mouth, Robyn worried that she'd been a bit harsh. It was obvious Sheila was going to need to be given something to do to make her feel useful. She felt a squiggle of panic. She had thought delegating the organisation would take the stress out of it, but it seemed everyone had bigger expectations than she did. She caught Jake's eye and he lifted his shoulders a little in solidarity.

Sheila was staring at the whiteboard. 'Well, I won't take any more bookings at the kennels, so we're not having to rush back. Though that is always a busy weekend...'

She jumped up and put a red line through the wedding date with a Sharpie.

Robyn felt even more anxious. If they didn't take any more bookings for that weekend, they'd be losing quite a bit of money.

Rocky gave her a sympathetic smile across the table. He couldn't be much younger than her dad. They were both wearing a jumper and jeans, but while Rocky's were smart and close-fitting, Mick's were baggy and misshapen and had probably been bought at the farmers market when he went to get his shears sharpened. And it was almost impossible to get him to cut his hair, which straggled over his ears. He was a Devon farmer through and through, she thought fondly, but maybe they'd be able to get him to a barber before the wedding.

It was funny, she thought, how Rocky was single. In all the time she'd been going out with Jake, she hadn't known Rocky go on a date with anyone. He worked hard, of course, and loved his surfing and went to the gym a lot, but he didn't seem interested in romance. Maybe he didn't need anyone else? He certainly seemed happy enough.

The door opened and her sister Clover bounded in from off the bus. She looked as if she'd just come back from a week at Glastonbury rather than college: pink streaks in her hair, feathers and bangles and nose-rings and a tiny dress with combat boots. The complete antithesis of a straight-A student.

'Hey, dudes. What's going on?' She smelled of chewing gum and sweet perfume.

'Robyn and Jake are getting married,' said Sheila. 'He proposed to her on Friday night.'

'No way!' Clover looked between the two of them, then glared accusingly at Robyn. 'You could have said. I saw you this morning before I left for college and you didn't say a word!'

'We wanted to get it booked in before we told everyone.'

'Do I get to be bridesmaid?' Clover plonked herself down next to Rocky and reached for the serving spoon.

Robyn realised she hadn't even thought about bridesmaids.

'It's not that kind of a wedding.'

'What do you mean, "not that kind of a wedding"?' Clover stared at her in horror. 'You've got to have a bridesmaid. To look after you. Hold your veil. And your bouquet. Organise your hen night.'

'I don't think I'm having any of those things. Definitely no hen night, anyway.' Robyn felt slightly uneasy at the mention of veils and bouquets, neither of which had crossed her mind until Clover mentioned them.

'Oh.' Clover looked a bit crushed. Her eyes slid across to Jake. 'You're having a stag night, right?'

'Maybe.' Jake was floundering, not sure of the right answer.

'So can I crash the stag do? If Robyn's not having a hen night. And anyway, it's sexist to keep them separate. You can't discriminate.' Clover's ability to argue boded well for her legal career.

'Me, Dad and Ethan might go for a quiet pint. And Mick as well. If you want to come.' Jake was diplomatic. He knew what Clover was like when she got the bit between her teeth.

'Paintballing. You should go paintballing.'

'Clo,' Robyn gave her a warning look.

'Sorry. I'm just excited.' Clover picked up her fork then looked pleadingly at Robyn. 'At least let me take you shopping for the dress.'

'Dress.' Robyn said the word as if it was strange and unpronounceable, like *hygge*. She couldn't remember the last time she'd worn a dress.

'It's non-negotiable,' said Clover. 'I'm not having you turn up in dungarees and wellies.'

'I can't spend a fortune, though.'

'That's cool. We can do vintage.'

'I'd really love that, Clo,' Robyn smiled. Clover would be the perfect person to advise her, as long as she didn't get too carried away. 'But just so you know, we're keeping everything super simple. Me and Jake at the registry office, with parents and you and Ethan. Then we're having a party at the beach hut. Thirty people, tops. And Gwen's pulling it all together for me.'

Clover raised her eyebrows. 'Nice one.' Even Clover couldn't deny that Gwen had impeccable taste and great style.

Robyn had to smile at her spirited little sister. It was funny. Clover was loud and extrovert and very unlike her parents. Whereas Robyn was so unassuming and low key, like Mick and Sheila, that people found it hard to believe that she was the adopted one.

Who were the people who had made her the person she was? Who was she part of?

She looked around the kitchen, the very one she'd been brought to when she was barely three months old, and Mick had put her proudly on the kitchen table in her Carry Tot. The photo was still in the photograph album her mum had bought: Baby's First Year, the pictures carefully stuck in and captions put in underneath with Sheila's best calligraphy pen, along with records of Robyn's weight gain, the food she liked (*Robyn loves parsnips but hates raisins*) and her favourite nursery rhymes.

She wanted to know more, about what happened before that day. She wanted to know who she was.

18

Later, up in the eaves of the farmhouse, Robyn lay down on her bed to let everything digest. Not just the shepherd's pie. It had been the perfect family get-together: nourishing food, banter, laughter, hugs, a few tears. Rocky had proposed a toast to her and Jake, and Sheila had got a bit emotional.

And now, here she was, about to do something that might throw everything into chaos. She felt as if she didn't have a choice. She had stared at her birth certificate long enough. It was almost as if she could feel an umbilical cord between her and Emily. If she wanted more answers, she had to take the next step.

She couldn't stop thinking about the young woman wondering about the baby she had given up. She wanted to tell her how happy she had always been, and what a good life she'd had, and how wonderful her parents had been, and still were.

Although would that be what Emily wanted to hear? Or would that be confirmation that she had not been important to her own child? How would you ever recover from that, knowing you weren't fit for the most natural role in the world? The one thing every woman was supposed to be good at.

She decided, if they ever did connect, or speak, or meet, she would take her lead from Emily. She wouldn't volunteer information unless she was asked for it. She wouldn't grill Emily either – she would let her tell her the truth in her own time.

She longed for every tiny detail about how she'd found her way into this world.

Robyn stared at the contact form on the screen in front of her. She'd filled out all the information. She had ticked the box to say she wanted contact, should her mother be on the register. She just needed to print it out and post it off.

Robyn jumped as someone knocked on the door. She realised how tense she was; how she was holding her breath.

'Hello?'

The door opened and Clover put her head around the door, tentative. 'Can I come in?'

This was unusual. Her sister usually wandered in without asking.

Robyn shut her eyes, pressed save then quickly exited the website and closed the lid of her laptop.

'Course!'

Her mouth felt dry as Clover came over and flopped down on the bed next to her. It was a long time since this had happened. Clover used to climb into bed with her when she was much younger, and Robyn would read to her. *Famous Five*, usually. And her own favourite, *The Secret Garden*. But then Robyn moved to her own flat, and now she'd moved back Clover was far too old for bedtime stories.

But perhaps not.

Clover tucked herself under her older sister's arm, and rested a hand on her tummy. Robyn twiddled Clover's hair like she used to. They lay there for a while, so comfortable with each other they didn't need to say anything, on top of the old silken eiderdown with faded roses that had belonged to Mick's grandmother.

Robyn's heart was still hammering from what she had just done. She felt guilty and secretive, and was scared of being found out, of a drama unfolding before she had even started.

Then Clover broke the silence. 'I'm so proud of you. You know that, right?'

'What?' Robyn turned to look at her, bemused. 'Why?'

'You're only thirty and you've got it all sorted.'

'Have I?' Robyn looked puzzled. 'Not really.'

'You so have.' Clover's tone was adamant. 'You're doing a job you love. You're building an amazing house. You're marrying the man of your dreams. And you're having a baby...' Clover was staring up at the ceiling. She looked distressed. 'I don't know how I'm ever going to get any of that.'

'Of course you will. Clo, when I was your age I'd just failed my A levels. I didn't have a clue what was going to happen.'

'But you knew you loved gardening. It was your passion.'

'I suppose so. Though passion is going a bit far. It was what I decided to do because I didn't have many choices. You'll have loads, because you've got all the smarts.'

'The smarts.' Clover rolled her eyes. 'What if I fail my exams, though? Sometimes I panic that I'm going to mess it all up.'

'You won't. But if you do, you can retake them. What's got into you? It's not like you to have a wobble.'

Clover didn't answer. Robyn frowned. Her fearless little sister let nothing stand in her way.

'Baby, has something happened?'

'I'm just scared. I'm scared of going to uni. Of leaving Hawksworthy, and Mum and Dad, and you. And not being here when the baby comes. I've just got this awful feeling.' She made a fist and pressed it against her tummy. 'This awful feeling nothing is ever going to be the same after this summer.'

Robyn pulled her little sister in closer. It was rare to see Clover vulnerable or having a moment of doubt. It was unsettling. But it was also nice, having this moment of closeness, and being able to reassure her.

She supposed this was what being a mum felt like.

'The thing is, Clo, things don't stay the same. Of course they don't. But it doesn't mean they're going to be bad. Just different. We will all be here for you. Always. You know that. And you've got to go out into the world and do your thing. You're Clover Moss. You are going to be awesome.' Robyn laughed. 'If anyone should be worried, it's everyone else. You're a force to be reckoned with. You're going to do great things.'

Clover didn't say anything for a moment. She lay there, thoughtful, patting Robyn's tummy. Then she sat up and grabbed Robyn's laptop.

'Hey!' said Robyn, panicking, praying she'd closed the window properly.

'Let's look at dresses,' said Clover, opening the navigation bar.

Robyn felt giddy with relief to see there was no sign

of the form. 'OK,' she said, marvelling at how Clover's moods and needs could switch in a nanosecond.

'What kind of thing are you thinking?' Clover started typing into the browser. 'Long? Short? What colour?'

'I've literally got no idea. And don't forget I might have a bit of a bump by then.'

'How big?' Clover stared at her stomach.

'I don't know. I'll be nearly seventeen weeks. Depends how much weight I put on. I'm not going to try and stay thin for the wedding, though.'

'No!' said Clover. 'The baby is way more important. But you still need something wow. It can be done.'

Robyn was trying to concentrate.

'Ugh,' said Clover. 'These beach wedding ideas are really tacky. I can't see you in any of them.'

Robyn glanced at the screen. Image after image of white, flowing dresses marched across the screen: acres of lace and net and tulle on over-made-up-women displaying their toned tanned flesh.

'No,' she agreed. 'They're horrible.'

'You want something simple but pretty. And practical. If we're going to be on the beach.' Clover frowned, typing in to the browser again.

For a moment Robyn wished she could take her sister into her confidence, but she wasn't sure now was the right time to broach the subject, especially when Clover was supposed to be revising for her exams. And Robyn couldn't gauge what her reaction might be. Would Clover think it was Robyn's right to trace Emily and contact her, or would she think it was a betrayal of Mick and Sheila? Clover was very protective of her mum and dad. She'd been very mindful of Mick's fragility, after the TB episode.

Clover had been the most visibly upset of all of them when the cows had gone, and although she was only tiny, she'd followed her father like a little shadow for months afterwards. She had been the one thing that had made his face light up in those dark days.

Oh God, thought Robyn, overwhelmed. Might this tip her father back into gloom again? She was being selfish. What did it matter who her birth mother was? It was of no consequence. Surely all that mattered was they all loved each other. She could see the wretched box sitting on her desk. The box that had started it all.

She was playing with people's hearts.

Clover was burbling on. 'You could wear this with some beaded flip-flops. I know I'll never get you into high heels, and they'd be useless on the beach anyway...'

For a moment, Robyn thought she might be sick from the stress. But there was nothing she could do. So she sat and listened with a fixed smile on her face while Clover went through the rest of her outfit, oblivious to Robyn's dilemma.

Later on, Robyn took her laptop down to the farm office to print out the form. She'd decided to send it off. If she got a letter back saying Emily was on the register, she would think again. If she didn't, no one need ever know she'd been thinking about it.

'Hello, love,' said Sheila, coming in pink-cheeked from the evening feed at the kennels. Robyn had heard the barks of excitement.

'Just printing out a quote,' she said, pulling the last page of the form out of the printer and folding it in half.

'You don't want to be doing too much, love,' said Sheila. 'It's still early days.'

'It's cool. Jake and I have worked out how we're going to manage over the next few months.'

Of course her mother was cautious, after what she'd been through herself.

'It's a special time, though. Try and enjoy it. I wish I'd enjoyed Clover more, but I was so worried the same thing would happen.'

'Oh Mum. I'm sorry it was so hard for you.'

'That's life, isn't it? And she turned out to be all right in the end.'

'She sure did.'

'Take it easy, though. When you can. I'm worried it'll all be a bit much, with the wedding.'

'Honestly, Mum. That's why we're keeping it low key.'

She should tell her. She should tell her right now. Show her the form. Explain what she wanted to do and why.

'It's very exciting. It's everything I've ever wanted for you. A lovely man. A lovely home. A baby.'

Sheila's eyes were shining. Robyn thought she even detected a tiny tear, which was so unlike her mother. She couldn't ruin the moment and bring her crashing down. She just couldn't.

Afterwards, she had to go and lie down again. She wasn't sure which was the more exhausting, pregnancy or deception.

Or the stress of waiting to hear if Emily Silver wanted to be found.

19

1987

The summer after Lower Sixth, Emily went to a music school for a month, recommended by Miss Bembridge.

'You'll absolutely love it. You'll be immersed in gorgeous music all day long, and your playing will come on leaps and bounds,' Olivia enthused.

Emily's parents had willingly agreed to pay the considerable fee, grateful that their daughter seemed to be back on her feet after last year's incident, and what could possibly go wrong at a music summer school? It fitted in perfectly with their idea of what a nice girl should be doing and stopped them worrying about her skulking around Worcester during the holidays.

It was held in the depths of the Shropshire countryside in a rambling private school that rented itself out over the summer. There was one-to-one tuition with top music teachers and workshops and ensembles and there was going to be a big concert at the end. Each pupil had their own room and they all ate together and had activities in the evening. They were expected to work hard and practise in between sessions and it was quite competitive – the really good musicians were particularly intense. Emily wasn't nearly as good as most of them but she didn't mind; it was fun to be immersed with like-minded people who didn't think you were weird for liking Elgar or thinking Jacqueline du Pré was a goddess instead of Madonna.

She arrived earlier than most people. Vivian was an anxious driver so had left about two hours longer than she needed for the journey, so she dropped Emily and shot off back to Worcester straight away, to be home before dark. Emily found the room she'd been allocated, then wandered down to the main auditorium, lured by the sound of piano music.

There was a boy at the piano playing Chopin – Étude Op 10 Number 4. It was a tricky piece of music, very fast and very complicated and she didn't much care for it, as it was very jumpy and not particularly melodic or emotional. But she couldn't help but be impressed by his playing.

Towards the end, he tripped over his own fingers and made a mistake, swearing profusely and bashing down on the keys in frustration.

Emily burst out laughing and he turned around.

He was tall and broad and slightly awkward, as if he wasn't quite sure what to do with his long limbs. His hair was wild and curly and almost to his shoulders, and he had the kindest face with a lopsided grin and wire-rimmed glasses.

'Shit. Sorry. I really shouldn't swear.' He stood up, looming over her. He was wearing a baggy blue coat over jeans and a checked shirt – it made him seem larger than he really was. Behind his glasses she could see eyes the colour of a calm sea on a winter's day: a soft blue-grey that would twinkle when the sun came out.

'I'm sorry if I distracted you.'

'No. I always get it wrong at that bit.'

'I've never heard anyone play that in real life.'

He looked sheepish. 'It's a bugger, that's for sure.' He frowned. 'I thought people weren't getting here till four? I got here yesterday – I live in York so it's a bit of a hike.'

She could hear it now, in his voice, a trace of Yorkshire. She liked it. It was warm and comforting, like a toasted teacake or a slab of gingerbread.

'My mum dropped me off early.'

'You're a student, then?'

'Yes. Are you?'

'I'm accompanying. I do it every summer. I'm Jonathan.'

He held out his hand and Emily took it. Warmth travelled up her arm and straight into her heart. She blinked in surprise and wasn't sure what to do.

'I'm Emily,' she said eventually. 'Would you play something else?'

She longed to hear what else he could do.

He smiled and turned back to the keys. He began to play. She recognised *Liebestraum*. Love Dream. By Lizst. She could hardly breathe while he was playing. It was as if he was testing her heart and seeing how much it could bear. The notes swirled around them, dreamy, magical, enchanting. Emily wanted to cry. That wasn't unusual. Music often made her want to cry. But she only ever did it in the privacy of her own room. This was something else.

The notes faded away and he turned around. She

couldn't speak, overwhelmed with emotion she wasn't used to showing in public.

'Are you OK?' He stood up and came and put a hand on her shoulder. She wanted to lean against him, curl up against his broad chest, but of course she didn't.

'You're very good.' Her voice was a small squeak she managed to squeeze out through her tears.

He laughed. 'Oh. Well. Thanks. I've got a great teacher. And I practise my arse off.'

'Well, it shows.'

He shifted about a bit. He didn't look as if he liked praise. 'This your first time here?'

'Yes.'

He nodded in approval. 'You'll enjoy it. It's good fun. I've been coming for the past five years.'

'So are you doing A levels?' His face was boyish but he had an air of assuredness that made it hard to tell how old he was.

'Yeah. History. Music. French. You?'

They were at that time of life, when they were defined by their A-level subjects. And where they were hoping to study.

'English. Music. French. Where are you applying?'

'Royal College. You?'

'Durham. Maybe Cambridge.'

He nodded his approval. 'Do you want a cup of tea? There's a kitchenette just through there?'

Emily hesitated. Was he sending her away, or was it an invitation?

'That sounds good.'

'Come on, then.' He stuffed his hands in his pockets and ambled towards the door. 'I've got a secret stash of chocolate Hobnobs too. They only do custard creams and Bourbons here and I'm not a fan of either.'

By the time they got to the kitchenette, she was smitten. She'd never felt like this before. She'd never had a crush on any of the boys she'd met in Worcester. She joked with them and talked music, sometimes, but they didn't interest her in the least. She didn't think she was better than them – if anything, Emily was self-deprecating – but they held no thrall for her. They were just mates.

Later, when everyone else had arrived and they'd all registered and been given a talk about what to expect from the week, then been divided into their ensembles, she lost him. She'd observed from afar that he seemed to know almost everyone, all the teachers, certainly, and the pupils who'd been before. He treated everyone with the same scrupulously polite kindness he had her, which sent a boiling shoot of envy through her veins. She could feel it, sharp in her stomach, as they trooped into the dining room for dinner, her eyes raking about for him.

He was there, a plate piled high with food, gesticulating, smiling, chatting. She lined up to fill her own plate with the lasagne and jacket potato on offer, and tried to work out how she could sit next to him.

Dinner was at three long tables with everyone sitting where they liked, shuffling around to get a place near to whoever they wanted. The arrangement was particular torture for Emily as she always felt shy among new people and didn't have the confidence to sit at the next available space in case she got a glare or caught an exchange of glances. Though here everyone seemed very open and there didn't seem to be cliques. But she felt awkward nevertheless. Her heart was pounding while she waited for Jonathan to sit at one of the tables, then wandered over oh-so-casually to sit next to him.

'Is this place taken?'

'Be my guest.'

'This whole sitting-next-to-strangers at dinner is a bit...' She made a face.

'You're best not to think about it. Everyone's as nervous as you are.'

'They can't be. They all seem totally confident.'

Jonathan looked around the table and shook his head. 'They're all bricking it.' He leaned forward. His eyes were gleaming with mischief behind his glasses. 'Who's your money on, then?'

'For what?'

'You know.' He waggled his eyebrows. 'Getting it on by the end of the week.'

She looked around the table. There was a very prim viola player who kept looking hungrily at a violinist with jet-black hair. It was obvious he thought he was the bee's knees. He would only have to click his fingers and she would come running.

She realised Jonathan was waiting for a reply.

'I don't know,' she said, and blushed.

He didn't press her, and thankfully they moved on to less stressful topics. By the time they had moved on to their jam and coconut sponge pudding, they were arguing about the best Led Zeppelin track. Emily had never met anyone who had a more encyclopaedic knowledge than she did.

'Just don't say "Stairway to Heaven" or we can't be friends,' he said, shovelling in a spoonful of sponge.

She snorted. 'Everyone knows it's "Whole Lotta Love".'

He shook his head, clearly outraged but his mouth too full to contradict.

'Just kidding!' She said. 'It's "Kashmir".'

He stared at her, swallowing. 'Do you really think so?'

'It's so intense. So dramatic.' She tapped out the staccato intro with her spoon on the side of her plate. 'It's genius.'

'It's all genius.' He put his spoon down.

'But,' Emily held up her finger. She rarely got a chance to have this discussion. She was in full flow. 'For pure emotion – "Since I've Been Loving You".'

She sang a couple of bars of the chorus, to prove her point.

He nodded, not taking his eyes off her for a second.

'Eat your heart out, Robert Plant,' he said. 'Can I demonstrate the reasons that it is, in fact, "Immigrant Song"? I mean, it would be a tragedy if you came away from this labouring under an illusion.'

Emily burst out laughing. 'Definitely,' she said, realising this meant she was going to go to his room. This was new territory for her. But she wasn't nervous. She felt so at home with him.

They dumped their plates and left the dining hall, not caring if anyone was watching them go. They were in a little bubble, delighted with each other. Emily followed him up the red-carpeted stairs to his room. He'd brought a ghetto blaster with him, a big shiny portable cassette player that was his pride and joy, along with a case full of tapes, everything from Gershwin to Genesis, Brahms to Black Sabbath.

They sang and argued their way through *Led Zeppelin 1*, *Houses of the Holy* and *Physical Graffiti* before Emily realised they'd missed the bell for lights out and it was midnight

'I should go.'

He looked at her. There was silence for a moment as he seemed to contemplate something. Then he smiled.

'Yes. They get pretty irate if you're late for rehearsals. I don't want you getting into trouble.'

He turned to put away the cassettes that were strewn around the room. Emily slipped away. And all night she dreamed of him, accompanied by a Led Zeppelin soundtrack, and she woke the next morning feeling quite exhausted. And longing to see him again.

There he was. At breakfast. Eating fried tomatoes on toast. She decided to play it cool while she queued up for scrambled eggs. She'd sit next to someone else. But he waved his fork at her and nodded to the space next to him. Casually. And she sat next to him and they almost didn't need to speak, just sat next to each other in companionable silence eating their breakfast. She couldn't believe how easy it felt, being his friend.

They were inseparable for the rest of the week. After tea she would go to his room and they'd play tapes. There was a whole stack of home-recorded ones that he'd put to one side.

'What are these?'

'Oh, my mum records me playing. So I can listen to myself and see where I've gone wrong.'

'Oh.'

He made a face. 'What you must understand,' he said in a Joyce Grenfell voice. 'Is I'm a prodigy. My talent mustn't be wasted.'

And although he was trying to make a joke of it, Emily

didn't think he thought it was all that funny. There was a tension underlying his jocularity. His mother was very ambitious for him. He'd told her his dad had died a few years ago, so it was just the two of them.

'Can I have one?'

'Sure. I'm probably not going to listen to them, to be honest. Help yourself.'

It would be a little bit of him to take home with her. To play in her room. It would be like having him there. She took two. The *Liebestraum* she'd heard him play on the first night. And *Gaspard de la Nuit*. Ravel.

A week later he played her 'Ne Me Quitte Pas' by Jacques Brel. They sat in silence, taking in the plink of the piano, the heart-rending strings, the mournful lyrics, the emotion in his voice, when Emily saw a tear on Jonathan's cheek. She froze for a moment. Did the song remind him of a lost love?

Then he sniffed, and another tear followed the first, and he started to cry properly.

'Sorry,' he choked. 'This was my dad's favourite song.'

'Hey. It's OK.' Emily scooted over and put her arms around him without even thinking about it. For a moment he leaned into her.

'I'm all right, usually,' he gulped. 'I'm used to him not being here any more. But sometimes it hits me. It comes out of nowhere. I'm sorry.'

'Don't be sorry. It must be awful. *I'm* sorry.' She hugged him as tightly as she could, and before she could help herself she had kissed him on the side of his head. A consoling, reassuring, kiss-it-better kind of a kiss, but a kiss nevertheless.

He turned and gazed straight into her eyes. He took her face in his hands.

'This has never happened to me,' he said. 'I've never felt like this with anyone. As if I can say anything I like. And you'll get it. And you won't just agree with me for the sake of it.'

She put her hand up to touch his hair. She'd never touched anyone's hair. She put her finger inside a curl and twizzled it.

'I know,' she whispered. 'It's the same for me.'

He shivered slightly at the contact and moved forward until their foreheads were touching.

And then their lips.

What happened next was the easiest, most natural and most wonderful thing to happen to either of them. Neither of them was experienced, but it turned out not to matter one jot. Emily didn't go back to her room.

They couldn't stop laughing the next morning. She clambered out of his bed and got dressed to sneak back before anyone saw her.

'See you at breakfast,' she whispered, and he waved at her from under the duvet, then did a comedic shrug as if to say, 'What on earth happened last night?' He looked sweet without his glasses on, blinking like a little owl. Her heart twisted with adoration, and she fought the urge to rush back over and kiss him again.

She skipped down the stairs and along the corridor to her room on the other side of the building. She looked in the mirror and couldn't stop laughing at her reflection: her sparkling eyes and the slight rash on her face where his midnight stubble had scraped her tender skin.

She jumped in the shower and changed into fresh

clothes. She couldn't wait for the day ahead. It seemed to have an extra dimension. *She* seemed to have an extra dimension. She felt at long last as if she meant something. As if she wasn't just inconsequential funny little Emily Silver, but the living, breathing object of someone's desire. She felt as if she'd been rolled in glitter. If you touched her, her skin would give off sparks, like an electric fence.

'Jonathan.' She spoke his name out loud, then gave it a different intonation. 'Jonathan. Jonathan and Emily. Emily and Jonathan.'

She couldn't believe how natural it sounded. How believable.

She laughed again. This was not normal behaviour for her. She was the least romantic person she knew. Although that couldn't really be true, or why did certain pieces of music move her to tears? Give her Mimi and *La Bohème* and she'd be on her knees, sobbing. Or Mozart's *Req*. Or a soaring bit of Elgar, especially if was played by Jacqueline du Pré. So she knew there was a passionate heart beating inside her somewhere.

It had taken Jonathan to find it.

The month passed in a blissful swirl of discovering each other. Their favourite food, their hopes and dreams, what made them laugh – each other, it turned out. The laughter was joyous and never-ending. They even laughed in bed, wrapped up in each other's arms. Emily thought it was heaven. She never wanted to leave. The end of summer school was getting nearer and nearer and she dreaded the final day. She didn't dare ask what was going to happen to them afterwards, for she was afraid of breaking the spell. But something inside her told her they would be together forever.

There was only one bad thing that happened to mar the magic. One evening she was on her way to the dining room when the viola player she'd spotted on the first night fell into step beside her.

'You've been Jonathaned, then?' she said.

'What?'

'Jonathaned.' She repeated it as if Emily must know what it meant. 'It happens to the best of us.'

'What do you mean?'

She gave her a knowing smile. Emily's stomach clenched.

'Don't be taken in by that shambling friendly bear act.' She suddenly looked very uptight and disapproving. 'He goes for the innocent ones. The ones who don't have a bloody clue. Don't be surprised if he drops you like a stone.'

She swished off down the corridor and Emily stared after her. Whatever she was implying was rubbish. It might have taken her a long time to fall in love, but she knew it was real when she found it.

She mentioned the exchange to Jonathan that evening. She wanted to be open with him.

'Ruth said that?' he said, and gave a bark of laughter.

'She told me not to be fooled by your shambling friendly bear act.'

'Well, don't be fooled by her uptight virginal nun act.' He rolled his eyes. 'She made a pass at me last year on the last night, when she'd had a few too many ciders, and was livid when I turned her down. Hell hath no fury and all that.'

He took his glasses off and cleaned them, which he did

when he was agitated. Emily looked at him, longing for his words to be true.

'Em,' he laughed, seeing her look miserable. He put his glasses back on and pulled her to him, kissing her, and she knew he was telling the truth. What a spiteful girl Ruth was.

On the last afternoon there was a concert for all the parents. It was all quite formal. Everyone dressed as if it was a proper affair: bow ties for the boys; black dresses for the girls. Someone had photocopied a programme, and there was wine at the interval. The atmosphere was buzzy and everyone was rushing around, full of adrenalin, like a scene from a film.

Jonathan introduced Emily to his mother. She was a tiny round woman in a shiny red dress and a helmet perm. Emily could see she only had eyes for her son, following him around the room with a loving gaze.

'Mum, this is Emily.'

'Oh, hello, love.' She gave her a tight smile. 'Oh dear, I get so nervous before he plays.' Her cheeks were pink with panic. 'More nervous than if I was going on. More nervous than him! He never gets nervous. Are your parents here?'

'Not yet.' Her parents hadn't said if they were coming. Her dad probably couldn't get the afternoon off and Mum didn't want to drive all this way on her own again. She was supposed to be getting a lift back with another pupil of Miss Bembridge.

'Mum, just sit down and enjoy the concert,' Jonathan told her. He was obviously used to fielding her anxiety and blocking out her chatter. 'I've got to go and copy some sheet music for the finale. The double bass player's lost his.'

He steered her towards the chairs and found her a good spot near the front.

'Honestly,' he said to Emily. 'You'd think this was Wigmore Hall.'

'At least she cares,' she sighed.

Jonathan frowned, looking at Emily in concern. She was in a black velvet skirt she'd bought in a charity shop the week before she left home, knowing they had to dress up. She'd even put some lipstick on and done her hair in a bun. She felt elegant and sophisticated. Almost – almost! – like a woman rather than a funny little girl who hid herself away.

'I care. And you look fantastic,' Jonathan said, and something in his eyes made her ripple and shimmer. All at once she felt taller and stronger.

And then she saw her parents. They'd made it. She couldn't believe it. She was pleased, because she'd been worried about being the only person there with no one in the audience. They walked straight past her.

'Mum!' She said, and her mother turned. And when their eyes met she frowned, not recognising the assured young woman before her at first.

'Emily?' Her face lit up. 'Emily, look at you. You look wonderful.'

Jonathan patted her on the shoulder. 'You see,' he whispered. 'They do care.'

Her heart gave a little flip.

Her mother looked up at him.

'Mum,' I said. 'This is Jonathan.'

She felt so proud of him. Of knowing him.

'Hello.' Her mother's smile was warm, and her father shook his hand. 'Where should we sit, darling?'

'My mother's just over here,' said Jonathan. 'I'm sure she won't mind you sitting next to her.'

Emily watched in a daze as he settled the parents in next to each other and left them to chat. It felt like a big step for her, and she wondered if her parents could see how happy he had made her. It felt like a turning point, as if her life had new meaning and she could see the future. She put her heart and soul into her playing, pouring all the emotion she'd felt over the past few weeks into every note. She felt uplifted as it all came to an end. Slightly euphoric.

And then Jonathan played the Ravel at the end. *Gaspard de la Nuit*. The piece of music on one of the tapes she had taken. Everyone was spellbound. His mother sat bolt upright; her hands clasped as if she was praying. The applause went on and on.

Emily felt so proud of him as he turned to bow to the audience. He looked for her, and his second bow was just for her, she was sure.

But after the concert, they didn't get to say goodbye. Emily's parents were hustling her to leave, worried about the Friday night traffic. They had swapped addresses the night before, promising to write to each other and make arrangements to meet. Emily wanted to say goodbye properly, feel his arms around her one more time, but he was nowhere to be found. She felt panicky, especially when Ruth gave her a knowing look as she walked past as if to say, 'I told you so.' Emily had more faith in Jonathan than she did. He wouldn't just abandon her.

Nevertheless, she got into her parents' car with the most awful hollow feeling inside.

'Well, that was very good,' said her mother. 'Did you enjoy your month away? We missed you.'

She couldn't answer. She wanted to cry. Her throat was tight with tears.

'Emily?' asked her mother as her father reversed out of the parking space. She caught sight of Jonathan coming out of the entrance, his mother beside him.

'Stop,' she said, pulling at her seat belt.

'Don't stop.' Her mother put her hand on her father's arm. 'We need to get to the M5 before five o'clock or we'll be caught up.'

Of course her father obeyed her mother. Of course he did. Emily turned and looked at Jonathan as he ambled over to where his mother had parked, wishing that she knew when she was going to see him again, wondering if he was thinking about her too.

'The pianist was very good,' said her father. 'Very talented.'

'He's going to the Royal College,' she said sadly. 'Hopefully.'

She wanted to tell them everything about him. She talked about him nearly all the way to the motorway. She was already composing her first letter to him in her head. Eventually, she put her head back and shut her eyes, dreaming all the way back to Worcester.

There were two weeks left of the summer holidays before she had to go back to school. She walked to the train station at Shrub Hill to pick up the timetable and see how long it would take to get to where he lived. It would be impossible to get there and back in one day by train. Maybe they could meet halfway? She wished she could drive, but she hadn't started lessons yet, even though she'd got her provisional licence. She wondered if her mother would drive her. Probably not.

She decided she would send him a postcard, but she'd put it inside an envelope. She went into Worcester and spent hours choosing the right one. In the end she found one of the Malvern Hills, which were nearby.

> *Dear J – This is the view that inspired Elgar.*
> *Maybe we could go one day? How are you? How is*
> *the practising? I can't believe it's only a fortnight*
> *till school starts again – groan. No more lie-ins.*
> *Summer school seems a million years ago, not just*
> *yesterday. I thought we could meet halfway one*
> *day? I miss you. Emily xx*

She couldn't write what she really wanted to, in case he left it lying around. She couldn't tell him that she thought about his hands, and how they had touched her as gently as he touched the piano keys. She thought about how he had wrapped himself around her as they slept. She was tiny inside his embrace, tucked up like a koala.

Three days went by and there was no reply. He must have lost her address. She should have put it on the post-card, or on the back of the envelope. She decided to send another one. She sent a Peanuts card this time: Woodstock standing on Snoopy's tummy, which gave her the same happy feeling she got when she was in Jonathan's arms. And she put her address on it, and her phone number.

A whole other week went by. She didn't know where to put herself. She couldn't eat, sleep, read, speak. Every time she put on Led Zeppelin she fell into a reverie, each beat of the music pounding in time to her heart.

She phoned Directory Enquiries to get his phone number, but there was no Hudson listed at the address he'd given. She started to panic. Had she imagined it all? Was he ill, or worse? Had his mother locked him in his room? She wouldn't have put it past her. She had a funny look about her.

Or had he just had second thoughts? Was Ruth right after all? Had she been Jonathaned?

No, she told herself. It was real, what they'd had. She hadn't imagined it. It was impossible to imagine that kind of closeness.

Her mother could sense her misery. When the postman pushed an electricity bill and a copy of the *Radio Times* through the letter box, Emily sank onto the bottom step of the staircase with a moan of despair.

'I understand how you feel,' her mother said, looking at her in sympathy.

Emily picked at the frayed edge of her jumper sleeve. How ludicrous. How could she understand.

Her mum sat on the step next to her.

'It's like something eating at your insides, isn't it?' She held a fist over her stomach and Emily looked at her, surprised, because that is just what it felt like. 'And you think you'll never be happy again. And every now and then you hear something that reminds you, and it's almost unbearable. Or you smell something...'

She seemed to drift away. Emily suspected she wasn't talking about her father. She'd never thought of her mother falling in love, or having feelings for someone. Or having sex, which obviously she had.

Her mum put her arm around her.

'There'll be other boys. Wait until you get to university. You'll be spoilt for choice. And they'll be lucky to have you.'

She was trying to be kind, but she was making her feel worse. She wanted her brain to stop, wanted the constant whirl to end, that toxic mix of panic and longing and something deeper and sweeter that kept curdling. Part of her wanted to believe her mother and be comforted by her, but she knew there was only one person who could stop the torture.

One word from him would have been enough. A funny postcard on the doorstep would have meant the world.

And then the longed-for day arrived. A letter. A brown envelope with black scrawly biro on the front and a stamp that was tilted at thirty degrees, with a York postmark. Emily took it and ran up to her room. A thrill of excitement zipped through her as she tore open the envelope and took out a sheet of A4 lined paper.

Dearest Em

Thank you for your letter and the card – Snoopy rules!

Meeting you at summer school was one of the nicest things to happen to me. You are an amazing person. But I can't have a relationship at the moment. I've got to focus on my music, and get ready for my auditions. The Royal College is my dream, but there's no guarantee of getting in – as you know, being good isn't enough! – so I can't take any risks by being distracted. I've *got to give myself the best chance. I hope you understand.*

Have fun, amazing Em, and may all your dreams come true too.

Jonathan xxxxxxx

Nothing could have prepared her for the shock. She was devastated. The one person who had made her feel as if she mattered had turned his back on her. Yet again, her exchange with uptight Ruth flashed into her mind – her knowing expression, her arched eyebrow.

Did he have some special power that had made her imagine something between them? She replayed every moment they had spent together, every smile, every kiss, every touch, every word, analysing it and wondering how she could possibly have misjudged it.

He was the first person ever to make her feel as if it was OK to be herself. As if she was enough.

She wasn't angry, like some girls would have been. She didn't tear up the letter and scream. She just crumpled. She shut down. She didn't speak. She didn't eat. She didn't want to get out of bed. She didn't wash, or get dressed.

'You've got to go to school tomorrow,' said her mother, standing in her bedroom doorway the day before term started. She'd been desperately worried about her, trying to coax Emily out of her room, trying to get her to eat.

'I'm ill,' Emily told her. 'I feel sick.'

She'd felt sick the moment she read the letter and it hadn't gone away.

It would be some time before she realised the real reason why.

20

The following Wednesday, Mick slipped out into the yard with Mouse at his heels and headed to his four-wheel drive.

'Hup,' he said to Mouse, who jumped into his place on the back seat and settled down on his blanket. Mick climbed into the driver's seat. He'd told Sheila he was going to pick up his eyedrop prescription, which was only half true. He'd pick it up afterwards so his alibi held water. But he was on an entirely different mission this morning. A fishing expedition.

Though he wasn't going anywhere near the harbour.

He tapped nervously on his steering wheel as he headed west on the main road towards Tawcombe. It was the wedding announcement that had made up his mind and galvanised him into action after months of mulling it over. He was thrilled with the wedding news, of course. Jake was a good lad: a hard worker, not much of a drinker, a good laugh. Exactly what every father would want for his daughter.

He remembered the night they had brought Robyn home. Sheila had been very upset by the thought of the poor girl who had relinquished her baby, even though Robyn had been with a foster carer in the interim.

Nevertheless, Sheila had sobbed all the way back in the car. Mick had felt pity for the girl, of course he had, but they weren't responsible for her grief. He didn't know how to console his wife, but he supposed the whole thing was a bit of an upheaval and maybe a good cry was what she needed.

They still couldn't believe they'd got her, this little creature with the grave grey eyes who watched them intently when she wasn't sleeping. He had carried her car chair into the kitchen and put her on the table, and her gaze had glided around the room, as if checking it over, and then up to him.

'Hello,' he said, holding up a thick finger for her to grab. 'Hello, Robyn.'

At the sound of his voice, she'd given a big smile, a dimple appearing in her cheek, and the smile reached her eyes, making them crinkle up, and Mick and Sheila had visibly melted, leaning against each other for support.

'You're my little maid,' he said to her, in a broad Devon accent, and Robyn's smile had got even wider. 'You're my little maid.'

She was still his maid, thirty years later.

But the wedding announcement had brought home his predicament. He couldn't hide from it any longer.

In Tawcombe, he managed to find a coveted parking spot on the high street. Then he walked with Mouse at his heels, past the greengrocers and the mini-market that housed the post office and the tiny cinema that was, by some miracle, still going, and into the estate agent by the pelican crossing.

'I'd like to see Geoffrey, if that's possible,' he said to the receptionist. 'It's Mick Moss, tell him.'

She asked him to wait for a few moments. He wandered around the office, looking at all the houses for sale, marvelling at the prices of the prime properties. Little cottages you once couldn't give away were going for over a quarter of a million. Penthouse apartments with a sea view were going for even more. In the last decade, the area had gone from a quiet coastal backwater to a playground. And it was going to get even more popular, with people cutting down their carbon footprint by not flying abroad for holidays.

People like him had been cashing in over the past few years. So far, he had managed to resist the temptation.

Geoffrey had once been the only independent estate agent in the area, but now there was stiff competition from chains and online agencies and Geoffrey had to fight to keep up. He kept his ear very close to the ground, and most of the people who were Everdene born-and-bred still went to him if they decided to sell up. Despite his flashy exterior he was old school, and his assistant did a very nice job of showing around prospective purchasers. And he still had the personal touch.

'Mick,' he said cheerily, coming out of his back office. 'Come on in. What can I do for you? Coffee?'

'Tea for me, please. Two sugars,' said Mick, following him into his office and sitting down in front of his desk. After a few minutes of polite chat, while coffee and tea and chocolate digestives were brought in, Mick played his hand.

'I'm thinking about selling Hawksworthy,' he said. 'Can you tell me what it might be worth?'

Geoffrey looked shocked. 'I never thought I'd hear you say that, Mick.'

'Nor me,' said Mick. 'And it's not definite. I just want a ballpark figure. So I can think things over.'

He knew he could trust Geoffrey to keep quiet. Confidentiality was key in this business.

Geoffrey leaned back in his chair and considered his reply. Valuing was a game. You had to get the estimate right, both for the vendor and the buyer. He'd been out to Hawksworthy often enough over the years so he didn't need to view it. He knew every farm along the coast and over the moors. Their acreage; the farmhouse; the outbuildings: his mind was a map.

'Well, there's quite a demand for a place like yours these days. People wanting to live the good life. I've got a film director looking for somewhere. His wife and kids are horse mad. And he's a keen surfer, in his spare time. He wants a nice holiday home for them all. Hawksworthy would do him perfectly.'

'Holiday home?' Mick scoffed. 'He's kidding himself if he thinks it would be a holiday home. Hawksworthy is a full-time job, even when you're not farming it. And a drain on the pocket.'

'Money's not a problem.' Geoffrey took a chocolate digestive from the open packet on the table. 'And he'll be doing a complete re-vamp.'

'Good for him.' Mick tried not to sound bitter, but it had torn him apart, seeing Sheila so despondent in the wake of their financial troubles.

'I know things are tough for you up there.'

'We manage.' Mick tried not to sound defensive, too. Somehow life was grinding him down. He wanted to feel joy again, and he suspected that meant freeing himself up and giving himself some room to breathe.

'I know. You've done a great job. But I know you've found it hard since...' Geoffrey bit into his biscuit. He didn't much want to say the words. No one in the farming community ever liked mentioning it.

'The truth is, Geoffrey, I'm never going to recover from that. Not unless I win the lottery.'

He didn't just mean financially. There'd been compensation, after all. It was the emotional toll. He was still ashamed that it had affected him so badly. He hadn't had the fight to start again and build up a new herd. He couldn't live with the shame or the humiliation or the fear. He felt like a coward. Thank goodness for Sheila. But he didn't want to talk about that.

'So how much?'

Geoffrey puffed out his cheeks. 'Well,' he said. 'It's a unique spot. Ticks a lot of boxes, especially with that view. That's what they all want. A coastal setting commands a premium.'

'So what do you reckon's a reasonable asking price?'

'On a good day?'

Geoffrey named a sum. Mick gave a low whistle.

'You think someone would pay that?'

'If you get the right person. You can always come down on price, but you can't go up,' Geoffrey told him.

'Handsome,' said Mick.

'I'll come and stay on the yacht,' joked Geoffrey. He wasn't going to put pressure on Mick. That didn't work with farmers like him. They had to work through the pros and cons, and there was a lot of emotion tied up in their land. Emotion they didn't always show, but felt deeply.

Though if Mick had made the effort to come and see

him and ask the question, he'd worked through a lot of that already.

'I could put a feeler out to this film chap? Mention you're thinking of selling?'

'Can't hurt to ask. Can it?'

'It can't hurt at all.'

'Right,' said Mick, standing up. 'Thank you.'

'I'd be happy to do business with you, Mick.'

Mick nodded. 'Let me know what he says. And I'll have a think in the meantime.'

The two men shook hands, knowing that if Mick was to sell, the deal was sealed.

When he got back to Hawksworthy, Mick let Mouse out and set off across the land.

He and Sheila could find endless ways to make the farm work. But he didn't see the point of them slaving even harder. They should be winding down. They were both over sixty. Not retirement age, by today's standards, but not a time of life to be embarking on new ventures.

Geoffrey's valuation was circling around Mick's head as he set off across the fields, Mouse leading the way, ears pricked in excitement, bouncing like a deer. The spring grass was coming through now, rich and lush. The hedges were greening up, teeming with wildlife: weasels and voles. Foxes. Shrews. Hedgehogs. There would be deer over the crest of the hill. In the summer, swifts and skylarks; red admirals and painted ladies; shimmering dragonflies and beetles. A hare if you were lucky; perhaps a buzzard.

And any minute now, swathes of bluebells would replace the last of the daffodils he was walking through, a purple carpet that would bring an ache to the throat of any painter.

Sheila had once suggested Bluebell Walks at the farm, followed by cream teas, but he hadn't wanted any old person tramping over his flowers. And that was the crux of it. Even with the promise of big money, he couldn't bear the thought of the bluebells belonging to someone else.

Not just the bluebells, of course. All of it. This was where he had been brought up. The only place he had ever lived. He had been born in the bedroom that was theirs now. His mum had popped him out and gone down to make breakfast for the farm workers, by all accounts. He could believe it. His mum had been capable, hard-working, tireless, and he had found those qualities in the woman he had married. They were women who gave of themselves and didn't ask for much in return, because on a farm like this you were all in it together.

He spoiled Sheila when he could, and made sure she was appreciated. But it was several years since he'd been able to whisk her off to the Scillies for a week of pampering.

The sum of money Geoffrey had mentioned whirled around in his brain. OK, so he might not get that much, but even if it was a hundred grand less . . .

He began to work out what they could do with it.

He'd be able to help Clover out with her university fees and living expenses. She'd been working hard and he didn't want her to have to worry about getting a bar job or going deep into debt. He could get Sheila a new car: the Corsa had only just got through its MOT last time and Lionel at the garage had warned about the crank shaft. He could pay for another polytunnel for The Moss Partnership, which would make their profit margins higher if they could supply plants themselves to their clients. There was plenty of room for another on the piece of ground that had gone with the Linhay.

And if he didn't have the farm round his neck it would free him up to help them with the business. They were talking about taking on a couple of full-time labourers, but he could offer his services as and when – that way they wouldn't have to pay over the odds.

And now Jake and Robyn had announced their plans, he could help out with that too. It would be lovely to slip them a bit of cash to give them the wedding they wanted. He was pretty sure Rocky would. He wouldn't be crass enough to do it in front of Mick and Sheila – he'd be discreet – but no doubt he would take his son to one side at some point. That's what good parents did, after all.

And the baby. Babies were expensive. He eyes went misty as he thought about his two girls. He'd have given them the moon if he could, but they'd done their best with what they had. It would be lovely, he thought, if he could give his grandchild things without a second thought.

He climbed up over the brow of the hill and looked down through the cleft that led down to the sea. It was a unique position, the vertical cliff with its grey face shearing down into the frothing sea – he had never seen it calm and flat, not even in the height of summer when the pressure was high and the sea just around the bay at Everdene was like a millpond. Here, it was always in a torment, raging at the shore for some imagined slight.

It took his breath away every time.

Could he really give it all up, just for the sake of never having to get up at five in the morning again? To take the pressure off him and Sheila? Hawksworthy looked idyllic – at its best, it was paradise – but it came at a price. It was needy, demanding, expensive. Perhaps, when it came down to it, it was a luxury he could no longer afford. No doubt the film director could pay for the hedges to be relaid, the drystone walls to be repaired, the cattle grids with missing bars to be replaced.

Mick still had a dream; a little fantasy he indulged in whenever he walked the land. He longed to buy a small herd of Jersey cows and let them loose on his pasture, using the traditional techniques once used by his grandfather before more intensive farming became necessary. He'd produce beautiful rich, creamy whole milk which he would bottle and hand-deliver to selected suppliers. Mick Moss Milk had a ring to it – or did that sound silly? Either way, he imagined it poured into porridge and creamy rice puddings and splashed onto cornflakes. Small plump hands wrapped around glasses of ice-cold milk; elderly fingers warmed by mugs of cocoa.

But he would never have enough spare cash to buy the beasts he needed. The farm was taking up every last penny. He had to let go of that dream. He would have to find another. It looked as if the answer had been handed to him. But did he have the courage to give up the thing that mattered the most to him, and turn his back on four generations of the Moss family?

21

Like any job that you blithely assumed would only take five minutes and a lick of paint, tarting up the Shedquarters in just less than a month was going to take up far more time than Rocky first thought.

A few days after Jake and Robyn had announced their plans, he came down with a notebook and pencil to make a list of what he needed to order. Half an hour later he had filled two pages. Two different colours of paint, for a start, because Robyn had mentioned stripes and he wanted to give her what she wanted. New felt for the roof – it was torn in several places and they only needed a severe winter and it would peel off. Varnish for the steps. Two new lights for outside the door. He thought some of those industrial fisherman's lamps would look the part. And then perhaps some LED lights for added twinkle. A new sign – he could paint that at home; there was just an old bit of plywood with The Shedquarters daubed on it, but he would do some proper lettering. New door-handle.

This was going to be a total refurb. He'd have to come off-site to get it done. He didn't mind. He had a good gang working for him and they wouldn't miss him for a week or two. He didn't take on skivers or shirkers.

And it was important to him, even though Robyn and Jake had insisted the hut was fine as it was. It was a matter of pride to Rocky, who was a perfectionist. It was fine for the hut to be ragged round the edges while it was a glorified changing room, but if it was going to be the wedding venue for his oldest son, it needed to step up.

He was just pulling at the soffit boards and concluding they could do with replacing too when his phone beeped at him. He pulled it out of his pocket and squinted at it in the April sun.

A WhatsApp message. From Melissa.

They'd moved from the dating site to WhatsApp after they'd matched, because that seemed to be the protocol if you were interested in each other.

He'd taken himself off Seaside Singles straight away after his disastrous date. He wasn't going to put himself through that kind of humiliation ever again. He didn't think he was quite so sensitive, but it had really knocked his confidence. He'd gone over and over the evening in his head, wondering what he had said or done, despite both his sons telling him, 'It's not you, it's her.'

'People have baggage, Dad,' said Ethan. 'Even at my age. So imagine how much they've got at yours.'

'Thanks,' Rocky said wryly. But Ethan was right. You didn't get to middle age unscathed, unless you'd been in a nunnery, and Melissa definitely didn't look as if she'd taken her vows.

Although maybe that was it? Maybe she was a lapsed nun and this had been her first outing and she'd lost her nerve?

Rocky laughed to himself, because you had to. He contemplated Sister Melissa's message. Should he just delete it? He didn't think he was up to reading whatever she had to say after what she had done. Maybe it would be a list of complaints? Was he too old? Too fat? Too rough round the edges?

He frowned. What was the matter with him? Why was he being so paranoid? He was none of those things. His boys were right: if she didn't like him, that was her problem.

It was all so pressurised, this internet dating. If you were single, you felt a duty to be online and looking, offering yourself up to complete strangers whose idea of how to behave could be so different from yours. He longed for the old days, when meeting people was something you did naturally, catching someone's eye, chatting them up if they took your fancy. It had all seemed much simpler then. And it had worked. People had been getting together for centuries without the intervention of an app.

He had decided he was going to take himself out of the game. If something happened naturally, it happened. In the meantime, he wasn't going to put himself under pressure checking for matches, waiting for responses. Wondering whether to meet.

He couldn't quite bring himself to delete Melissa's message, though. He was curious. And he'd quite liked her – for all of the five minutes he'd had to speak to her.

So he opened it.

Hey Rocky. I just want to apologise for my behaviour on Friday. It was my first date and I was so nervous. And you being so gorgeous made me even more nervous. I guess I'm not as tough as I think. Anyway, if you want to meet up for a second attempt,

I promise not to do a runner. Though I totally
understand if you don't want to. Melissa x

Rocky sat on the beach hut steps and read her words
again. He found himself smiling. There wasn't anything
wrong with him. She thought he was gorgeous. And she
must have been tied up in knots to be so worried.

He went to reply and reassure her. But then he imagined Ethan's voice.

'Let her stew a bit, Dad. Give her a taste of her own
medicine. She gave you a bit of a knock. Don't go running. Play it cool.'

They were hardened to it, Ethan and his mates. It was
easy come, easy go. It was a process, not an ordeal. One
strike and you're out.

But Rocky was a gentleman. It must have taken a lot of
courage for Melissa to apologise. She was opening herself
up to possible rejection yet again. He didn't want to make
her suffer. He wasn't that kind of guy.

He wouldn't look too keen, though. He'd play it cool.
Kind but distant. That was the tactic he'd take. A compromise.

Hey Melissa. It's all good. I was nervous too. I'm
tied up at the moment getting ready for my son's
wedding, but maybe we could go for a walk along the
coast sometime. Rocky

He thought that was politely reassuring without being too
eager. He didn't have to wait too long for a reply.

Thank you. That would be lovely. M

He hoped his message had stopped her feeling bad about herself.

He never wanted anyone to feel bad. Even when they did terrible, terrible things, Rocky never wanted anyone to feel bad.

Maybe it was time for him to stop worrying about everyone else and put himself first?

22

Two years ago, Gwen had, after many years of Luddite resistance, finally succumbed to an iPad.

'A diary and a notebook is all I need,' she had protested, but Robyn had taken her to buy one (together with a pistachio-green leather case, which Gwen was far more interested in) and had set everything up. She got her an email address, and then showed her all the different apps that might be useful. And now it was Gwen's right arm. She couldn't believe how much easier life was. She could pay all her bills, order whatever she wanted to come straight to the door. And as for eBay! She was an addict. She could have her eye on several things at once and nip off to put on a bid. And she'd sold a lot of her clutter for good money.

It was going to be her saving grace over the next few weeks, she realised, as she sat down and began to plan Robyn and Jake's wedding, starting a spreadsheet and a Pinterest board.

If there was one thing a wedding should be, it was true to the bride and groom. So many couples booked places that had no real connection to them and were just an attempt to impress: swanky hotels and stately homes that were a façade. But the beach hut was Jake and Robyn through and through. It was nestled at the bottom of the dunes, backed by swathes of marram grass, with the curve of the bay in front of it, sparkling pink sand and, of course, the drama of the waves. As a wedding location, it was a gift. Gwen's fingers twitched with excitement as she began to put down her ideas.

Although the setting would have its own logistical problems. There would be no proper kitchen and not much power, and it was a long way to lug things, along the coast path, down the dunes and over the sand.

So the challenge was to organise something breathtakingly beautiful but simple, with easy food that didn't need tending to. Gwen wanted it to be in keeping with Robyn and Jake's ethos, too – the way they worked with landscape and nature. But it had to be fun. A few witty little touches to make people smile, without being twee.

And all without costing a fortune.

She began a list of ideas to kick-start her inspiration.

Picnic baskets
Stripy rugs/deckchairs
Sea holly/thistles
Upturned boat?!!
Driftwood
Storm lanterns
Hessian

It was all about texture and colour and layering and scent and taste all working together. She would need a couple of gazebos, for extra shade and shelter, and some trestle tables, but she was pretty sure she could get them from a local village hall or scout troop. Gwen wasn't shy about asking for what she wanted. She was adept at begging and borrowing.

She soon found herself down a rabbit hole of seahorses and starfish; anchors and lifebuoys. If she wasn't careful, she was going to get carried away. She smiled to herself, imagining a pirate ship swooping along the bay to take the happy couple off at the end of the evening. She had never lacked imagination, only restraint.

She stopped for a moment, leaned back in her chair, took a sip of wine. She was conscious, though, that the wine might lower her guard. Already the memories were swooping in. It was, she supposed, ironic that she had appointed herself wedding planner, having tried so very hard to avoid weddings most of her adult life. She was a modern-day Miss Havisham.

She could remember it as if it was yesterday. Standing on the stone steps of the Chelsea registry office, scanning the King's Road for his car and shivering in her lace minidress. She was the absolute height of fashion, right down to her floppy hat, gamine crop and false eyelashes. People even stopped to take photographs of the young bride, wondering if it was a magazine shoot. She had to laugh at that.

That was how they'd met. She was modelling for an ice-cream advert, and Terry was the photographer's assistant. He had to bring her ice cream after ice cream from the freezer, as they were melting so quickly under the lights. By the end of the shoot she felt quite sick from licking endless lollies in her bikini, trying to look as if she was having a heavenly day out on the beach.

She remembered Terry wiping a drop of melted ice

cream from her collarbone with his finger, his eyes not leaving hers.

'Oi,' shouted the photographer. 'Stop handling the merchandise.'

He had loitered after the shoot until she'd got dressed, then asked her to the pub. Two weeks later they were in love; two months and they were engaged. She booked the wedding, bought the dress and borrowed a Mini Clubman off a friend so they could drive to Brighton for a quick honeymoon: he could only get a few days off work.

After an hour and a quarter, it had been obvious he wasn't going to turn up. It couldn't just be a hangover or a flat tyre. Beautiful, bad, quixotic Terry must have decided that getting married was not such a good idea.

No one had made her feel like he did since. He had been drunk when he proposed, but then he always was, even when he worked, and it never seemed to stop him doing or getting what he wanted. She had believed the sincerity in his eyes. His declaration of undying love. His insistence that they belonged together, forever.

No doubt some other girl had caught his eye the night before the wedding and reminded him that marriage was a trap. That the pick-and-mix of Chelsea girls would no longer be available for him to choose from. As the clock struck twelve, she went inside to tell the registrar that it wasn't going ahead, and threw her bouquet of white lilies in the bin.

She had been marriage-averse ever since. The dress was still hanging in her wardrobe, reminding her not to be drawn in by bedroom eyes and silver tongues. Not that she had been a nun, but she knew to press the eject button early on in a relationship. She was never going to let someone else take control of her emotions the way Terry had.

And actually, her philosophy had served her well. Her life had been rich and full. Her romantic relationships might have never come to anything, but it was always her choice and by contrast her friendships were deep and enduring and meaningful. And many. In fact, she felt that being unencumbered meant she had more time to devote to her friends. There was no one making demands on her time or questioning her whereabouts. She felt sure she was a nicer person for it. She was free to roam the world, and roam she had.

And Tawcombe was the perfect place to exercise that freedom. There weren't many places she would be able to afford a Georgian flat with floor-to-ceiling windows and a harbour view. And now, with the greatest of ease, thanks to the Airbnb app on her iPad, she could rent it out when she went away, thereby paying for her adventures without having to lift a finger.

She wasn't going to let her aversion to the institution of marriage cast a cloud over Robyn and Jake's wedding, though. It might not be for her, but she knew in her heart and her gut that they were right for each other. They each had strength of character and self-esteem in spades, and the grace to give each other the space to be themselves. Their relationship was balanced. They had strong family behind them. They would have a happy life together, she felt sure.

And she was determined that even though they wanted a low-key wedding, it would be a memorable one.

Her eyes wandered back to the search bar. It was always there, the blank space, the siren call of the search engine, waiting to be filled in. How could his memory still affect her, after more than fifty years? Why hadn't it faded, along with her penchant for pale pink lipstick and white kinky boots?

Thankfully nowadays, it was only ever a fleeting feeling. She could squash it down and make it go away by thinking about other things, other people. She had learned not to use alcohol to suppress it, because that ended in damp pillows and nausea. Drink was much better used for happiness and celebration, or simple relaxation, like today, but you had to be careful not to let the memories winkle their way in.

She stood up and walked over to the window. Looking out at the view always calmed her. It was why she had moved here, for there was always something to look at that gave her hope. After a long winter the harbour was slowly coming to life. The boats were being put back in the water. The gulls were circling, keenly eyeing up the chip shop and the ice-cream parlour.

Beyond the harbour was the ocean, the waves rising and falling in a hypnotic dance, a symphony of blue and grey and green that could change colour and tempo in an instant, on the whim of the weather. It was never the same, not for one moment, and that was what Gwen loved about it. It was as changeable and capricious as her own moods. It was funny, she thought, she loved the sea so much, but she rarely went on it or in it. Was it fear, or respect? Or for the simple, practical reason that she didn't care for getting wet?

She felt the nostalgic needling of earlier fade away as she breathed in the salt coming in gusts off the sea. As she turned to go back inside, she heard music further up the promenade. A battered old Porsche was making its away along the front, Van Morrison blaring. In the driving seat was a man with a head of thick silver hair and Ray-Ban aviators, singing along.

Midlife-crisis car, she thought. Midlife-crisis sunglasses. She watched as he mounted the pavement right underneath her window, completely ignoring the double yellows.

'Hey,' she called down, pointing at the painted lines as he jumped out of his car. 'They'll whack you with a fine.'

She'd seen endless people come back to find a ticket under the windscreen wiper.

He looked up at her, squinting. 'I'm unloading,' he said, just as a transit van rolled up and parked behind him.

'I wouldn't risk it,' murmured Gwen, but she wasn't going to interfere.

The new arrival was in jeans, a crumpled linen jacket and suede brogues. Gwen squinted for a closer look while pretending not to. He had an air of confidence underwritten with the kind of charm that would win over a traffic warden. She leaned further over her balcony and realised, as he approached her own front door with a key, that he was moving into the flat below. A new neighbour. She smiled. The flat had been empty for ages. The bloke in Robyn's old flat above was hardly ever around. A new tenant might liven things up.

She watched for a few minutes as he and the van driver started unloading furniture. There wasn't a great deal. An impressively battered and cracked leather sofa, a dozen cardboard boxes, several large paintings wrapped in brown paper, a desk that looked as if it could be vintage Bauhaus

– Gwen had a very appraising eye and she was optimistic that this was a man of style and taste.

And of course, she was intrigued. How had he washed up here? And was there anyone with him? A wife, or indeed a husband? It was hard to tell.

After just half an hour everything had been unloaded and she watched as he paid the van driver and waved his thanks, then put the hood up on his car and moved it to the car park at the end of the promenade. He wandered back along the harbour wall, hands in his pockets, and stopped to look back out to sea. Perhaps he was wondering if he had made the right decision? Gwen could remember doing the same when she moved here. You got a lot for your money in Tawcombe, and the harbour was the best address in town, but it was a long way from anywhere.

He turned and hurried back over the road to his new front door. Now he had taken his sunglasses off she could see he wasn't midlife at all. Much nearer to her age, probably. Late sixties? He disappeared beneath her. She went back to the iPad and carried on researching ideas.

At six o'clock, she ruffled up her hair, put on some mascara and lipstick and a squirt of Mitsuoko, then headed down the communal stairs leaving her door on the latch. She rapped on the ground-floor flat door.

She smiled as it was flung open.

'Yep?' he said, brusque and unwelcoming. He'd taken off his jacket and the T-shirt underneath showed patches of sweat under the arms. He had a rugged handsomeness: it was clear he had lived. His haircut was good – there were expert layers in that shock of silver. He was stocky, but not overweight – probably not as lean as he had been as a young man, but there was no beer belly overhanging the waistband of his jeans.

All in all, she thought, he had potential, especially as she could hear John Coltrane echoing around the empty walls. Good clothes, good furniture, good music.

She pointed upstairs.

'I'm your upstairs neighbour. Gwen.' She smiled. 'If the sun was out I'm sure it would be over the yard-arm so I wondered if you'd like a drink? To say welcome.'

He frowned. 'Uhhh, thanks, but no,' he said, curt. 'I've got rather a lot of unpacking to do.' He went to shut the door, then seemed to realise how rude he was being. 'I'm Boyd. Thank you for the invitation. Another time, maybe.'

He flashed a smile then shut the door.

'Oh,' said Gwen, nonplussed. She'd known some rude people in her time, but that was spectacular. Quite the brush off.

She shrugged and went back up the stairs. She'd have a gin and tonic on the balcony to make up for the disappointment. For if Gwen was good at anything, it was consoling herself when things didn't go as expected.

23

It was Friday evening and Emily Silver was looking forward to the end of a long week. Back-to-back appointments and a long day at a couple of the schools she taught at and preparation for a weekend workshop she was giving. She was looking forward to the weekend. A takeaway curry tonight, perhaps. She was pretty sure all there was in the fridge was a couple of old parsnips and some Greek yoghurt. They could go to the market tomorrow and stock up. Maybe she'd spend Sunday cooking some things to put in the freezer.

Emily smiled at herself. She always planned to do that but never had. Once, she'd made a double batch of Bolognese and put a portion in the freezer, but that was about two years ago. She wasn't destined to be that organised on the domestic front. There were more interesting things to do with their time at the weekend. Like kite-flying. Or going to see the new Marvel movie. Or riding their bikes along the canal and stopping at the pub for cider.

The hill seemed endless but that was the price of living in Bath. It was worth it for the view from the top of the house. A tiny house, but property was expensive here. Her goal was for them to move to somewhere big enough for her to have a consulting room. What she saved on renting her premises could be put towards the mortgage.

Emily's practice was really taking off now. It had been hard when they first moved to Bath, building up from scratch, but as her reputation spread her appointment book was filling up, and more and more schools were turning to her for help with their performance pupils: actors and musicians. And she'd just agreed to start at a nearby theatre school in the autumn. Her kind calmness was infectious and helped people understand the Alexander technique. She had amazing results and had turned people's lives around. People with chronic pain and stress symptoms. Nothing was more rewarding than making a difference. Every day she thanked Olivia Bembridge for inspiring her to train.

She had a lot to thank Olivia for.

She began to puff for breath as she reached the very top of Lansdown Hill. She could have caught the bus but the walk kept her fit and it was a good chance to mull over the day and unwind. She really only caught the bus if it was pouring with rain. She turned right into the little row of artisan cottages. They used to house the workmen who built the grand crescents but were hot property now. Theirs was in the middle, small but perfectly formed.

She opened the front door, swooped the post off the doormat and smiled as Ron and Hermione, one ginger, one tortoiseshell, bore down on her, conducting an elaborate maypole dance around her legs.

'Hang on, you two. Let me get rid of my coat.'

She hung up her yellow mac on the peg in the hall and walked through into the living/dining room then into the kitchen. She chucked the envelopes on the table and grabbed the box of cat food, shaking the terracotta lumps into two bowls by the back door. Then she flicked on the kettle, sat down at the table and opened the mail.

A reminder for her professional insurance. A quote for the tiny conservatory extension they were considering to increase the house's value: she took one look at the figure, grimaced and pushed it to one side. The third envelope was plain, and she couldn't decipher the postmark.

She unfolded the sheet, her eyes dancing over the words.

She had to read it twice to make sure.

She put her hand to her mouth. 'Oh my God,' she whispered.

Once, she had dreamed nearly every day of getting a letter like this. But as the years slid past, her hope had faded. She told herself that she had no control over when or if it might happen, so there was no point in expending energy wondering and waiting. It had taken all her reserves to come to terms with that realisation and put her longing to one side. She knew it made her vulnerable, to flirt with the past, and it was best laid to rest. But although people were kind about it, they could never fully understand that gaping hole inside her, and the desperation to know the truth. How could you understand, unless it had happened to you?

Thirty years had been a landmark. Thirty years had been a bad day. She had put on a brave face in the morning, not letting on that she'd blocked out her diary and spent the day by the river. She'd written a poem, folded it into a boat and thrown it into the water, watching it float downstream, letting it take her grief and her memories with it. Someone at a support group she'd been to once had taught her the trick and it had helped, a tiny bit. By the time she got home, no one would have known she had spent the day in tears.

But it was here. The letter she had dreamed of had arrived. She read the words over and over again.

Her daughter had contacted the register and wanted to get in touch.

Could Emily confirm she still wanted contact and supply her email address.

Her heart was pounding. She had never felt such an adrenalin rush as joy and fear and doubt welled up inside her. Questions came at her, pounding her brain. Why now? Why now, after all this time? What did she want? What was going to happen? Would they be able to meet?

Her mind tried to conjure up an image, as it had done so many times. A thirty-year-old jigsaw made from pieces of Emily and Jonathan. She remembered how long his curls had been, reaching beyond his collar. And the kindness in his grey eyes that had first drawn her to him so long ago. Time and again she had tried different versions, but it was impossible to know which bits Mother Nature had chosen.

Was the answer within reach? Was this the start of her dream coming true?

With a stab of disappointment she realised it was Friday. She wouldn't be able to contact the office until Monday to get the information to them. A whole weekend of agony. Keeping the secret to herself. This wasn't a secret she was ready to share yet. There was too much at stake. Too many questions. Too many decisions. She needed time to take it in. She had, after all, done this against all advice.

'You must move on, my darling. Lay it to rest.'

She heard a key in the lock. She flicked a glance at the clock. She hadn't expected anyone back this early. Swiftly she folded up the letter, put it back in its envelope and tucked it into her rucksack. For some reason, she smoothed down her hair, as if that would make her look less ruffled, then rushed over to the now-boiled kettle to make a pot of tea, trying to look as if something moment-ous hadn't just happened.

Thirty years. Over half her lifetime.

She could still remember the day she had realised. It felt like yesterday.

24

1987

Of course, Emily didn't work out the real reason she felt sick at first. She thought it was her reaction to Jonathan's letter and so did her mother. Vivian threatened Emily with the doctor, and in the end she decided it was better to be at school than lie in bed moping and be badgered.

She didn't tell anyone at school about Jonathan. Instead, she imagined what it would have been like if things had been different. She could have regaled her friends with stories of their grand passion, like Sandy in *Grease* telling the Pink Ladies about Danny Zuko. She would have chatted to him on the phone in the evening, made plans to meet up, sent him mixtapes and packets of Haribo. She could have walked around the school feeling proud and happy to be loved, confident in her own skin, with that special glow of a teenage girl in love.

Instead, she felt foolish. And ashamed. And heartbroken. Her confidence trickled away to nothing. Her grades slid, and the headmistress told her she could no longer consider Cambridge if they continued to go down. She cut off all her hair, to match the ugliness of how she felt. She looked like a pale-faced, thin little boy, a Dickensian urchin. Every time she thought about Jonathan, which was 99 per cent of the time, she wanted to be sick. Sometimes she was. She lost about half a stone.

Christmas came and went. In the new year, Olivia Bembridge took her to one side before her cello lesson one day.

'I'm very worried about you, Emily. You're looking very tired.'

'I feel sick all the time. I can't eat.'

Olivia frowned. She had been wondering if Emily was anorexic. But something else had occurred to her. 'Emily, you couldn't be pregnant, could you?'

Emily stared at her. Her little face was pinched and pale. She swallowed. 'Maybe,' she said in a very small voice. She'd tried not to think about it, but as each week passed the likelihood had got bigger and bigger. Now she'd been asked the question, she had to admit the possibility.

Olivia chewed on her thumbnail. She felt a ripple of doubt run through her. How should she handle this? She was very fond of Emily. She was probably her favourite pupil, although not her best.

'We better go and get you a test.' They could miss her lesson. She could get to the chemist and back in an hour.

Emily chewed her lip. 'What happens if I am?'

'Well. You'll have to make some choices.' Olivia put a hand on her shoulder. 'Don't worry for now. Wait here and I'll nip and get one. Go and practise your scales.'

Olivia drove to the chemist and back, then waited outside the loo while Emily did the test. She came out of the cubicle five minutes later.

'Positive,' she said, with a wobble in her voice.

'Right.' Olivia tried to think. Emily was over sixteen, so not a child. She could take her to her doctor to discuss the options. 'Do you know when your last period was?'

Emily shut her eyes. 'In the summer. Probably.'

'In the summer?' Olivia's tone sharpened.

'I met a boy. At music school.'

'And you slept with him?'

Emily's voice wobbled. 'We tried to be careful.'

In all the thrill of discovering each other, perhaps once or twice they had not been careful enough.

'Didn't you worry when you missed your period?'

Emily shrugged. 'I've always been a bit irregular.'

'But this means you're over five months. It doesn't leave you with many options.'

Olivia didn't want to spell out that it was too late for an abortion, but Emily knew that's what she meant.

'I couldn't get rid of it,' she burst out. 'I couldn't get rid of his baby.'

And she burst into tears and told Olivia the whole story, how magical and special it had all been and how it had come to an abrupt end.

'Oh, you poor love.' Olivia's heart broke for the girl. And she was furious with this boy Jonathan for luring her in and then being so brutally selfish. She felt a surge of protectiveness towards her, and hoped this wasn't going to disrupt her future.

Emily tried to gather her thoughts. 'My parents are going to go mad.'

'Do you want me to come with you? While you tell them?'

Emily thought for a moment. It seemed cowardly to

hide behind Miss Bembridge. And not really fair on her parents, who would be mortified. She would have to brace herself for their wrath.

'Thank you. But I'll do it by myself.'

Olivia hugged her. 'If you need me, just ring. You've got my home number.'

Emily went home that evening feeling confused. On the one hand, she had living proof of the passion she had shared with Jonathan. A talisman. A little bit of her felt as if the baby was her consolation prize.

On the other hand, she was rigid with terror. Single mothers were less of a scandal than they used to be, but schoolgirl pregnancies were still looked down on. Getting pregnant at her age was seen as a ticket to a free council flat and benefits.

The school wouldn't be happy. And her parents would be devastated.

She didn't have the courage to tell them both together. So she told her mother, in the kitchen over breakfast, after a spoonful of Cheerios had nearly choked her, her mouth was so dry.

'Mum,' she said. 'I need to tell you something. I don't know what to do.'

Vivian frowned. She was in the middle of poaching an egg for Neal, flipping the water over the yolk to seal it.

'What is it, darling?'

Emily put her spoon down. She just had to say it. There was no way of breaking the news gently. 'I'm pregnant.'

'Oh God,' said Vivian. She turned off the pan of water and came to sit down on the stool opposite. She leaned forward, her voice lowered, looking around for Emily's father. 'It's OK. We can sort it out. Your father doesn't need to know. Don't say anything, for God's sake. We can make the arrangements.'

Emily shook her head. 'I don't think we can.'

Vivian shot her a look and leaned even further in, grabbing Emily's hands.

'Emily. This will ruin your life. It's the only solution.'

'It's too late, Mum.' Emily's hand went instinctively to her stomach. How strange. Now she knew, she could sense the little being inside her.

Vivian seemed to crumple as she put two and two together. 'It was that boy. That awful piano boy.'

'He wasn't awful. It wasn't his fault.'

'Of *course* it was.'

Emily opened her mouth to protest further, but then realised that blaming Jonathan was the only way her mother was going to cope with this. And she needed her mum.

'What am I going to do, Mummy?'

'We'll just have to ride it out, together.'

'What about Dad?'

Vivian paused, looking at her daughter. 'Leave your father to me.' She sighed. 'Oh, Em, this isn't what I wanted for you. But don't worry. We can deal with it.'

This wasn't what Emily had expected. She'd thought there would be hysteria, tears, recriminations. She felt grateful. And she felt more love for her mum than she'd ever felt, which was a surprise. She'd thought this might drive them apart.

'We'll speak to the midwife, and the social services,' Vivian went on. 'There's no need to involve anyone else. This is a family matter.'

'Social services?' said Emily.

'You do realise,' said Vivian. 'You'll have to give the baby up?'

Emily put her hand on her tummy again. That primal need to protect. 'What do you mean?'

'Well, you can't *keep* it, darling. I can't see your father allowing you to bring it up here. Can you?'

'No . . .' Emily couldn't imagine it. A tiny baby in the spare room at Manor Close? It was unthinkable.

'What else would you do? Get a council flat? What on earth would you live on? You won't be able to do your A levels, or get any qualifications. And how would you work with a baby in tow? You'd have to live off the dole. That's no life, for you or the baby.'

Of course her mother was right. Emily wasn't sure what she had imagined was going to happen. A schoolgirl mum with a tiny baby had very few options. She wanted to cry, but she felt too numb.

If only Jonathan hadn't cut her off. They might have managed it together. He could have worked. Emily could have looked after him and the house and the baby and maybe gone to college part-time, eventually—

But Jonathan wasn't in the picture. Finally, the tears came as she remembered him, and how close she had felt to him, and how that must have been an illusion.

'I know it's sad, darling.' Vivian's voice was soft. 'Terribly sad. But you'll manage. I've got you.'

She pulled her daughter in tight. Emily felt a huge wave of relief that her mother was standing by her. She'd thought she was going to deal with her predicament on her own. But Vivian had a look of determination about her. She was going to protect her daughter at all costs.

In that moment Emily saw the truth about her mother's

existence. It was almost as if Vivian had waited all Emily's life to rise to the occasion. A respite from making her husband's poached egg and her daughter's packed lunch. A chance to really matter. And she wanted Emily to get more out of life than she had. A baby would take all her opportunities away.

'Thank you, Mum,' she said.

'You're my daughter. It's my job to look after you, whatever happens.'

How those very words were going to ring round Emily's head in the days to come.

'What about the boy?' asked her father, when Vivian had broken the news and told him, in no uncertain terms, that what was done was done and they must be supportive. 'Shouldn't he be told?'

'Absolutely not.' Vivian was adamant. 'What on earth could he do to help?'

'Well, it's his responsibility too.'

Emily didn't want him told either. She wasn't going to use a baby to force him to recognise her. And she knew that by this time Jonathan had probably received his offer for the Royal College. She wasn't going to ruin that for him.

Her own school wouldn't countenance her staying on to do her exams. It didn't send out the right message to the other girls, to have a pregnant pupil. For the second time, she was being edged out of a school when she wasn't really all that rebellious. She'd always been conscientious and hard-working, but somehow events had conspired against her and made her look like some kind of wayward lost cause.

'You can go to the college next September and start

again,' said Vivian. 'You'll only lose a year. It might seem like a long time to you but it's nothing.' Her lips tightened. 'I am not going to let this ruin your life. I want so much for you.'

Emily's friends were shocked when they found out she was pregnant, then thrilled, then secretly admiring. Her pregnancy gave her a certain cachet. She was a novelty. They visited her quite often at first. But gradually the visits tailed off, because she wasn't very exciting company, and they were far too busy getting tans under Jackie's mum's tanning bed and planning where they'd go on holiday after their A levels: a tour of the Greek islands. They told her she could come too, for she'd be a free agent again by then. Emily couldn't imagine it. She was getting bigger and bigger, and the baby was squirming around, becoming a reality.

She received wonderful and kind care, once Vivian had taken her to the doctor. The system took over, and Emily felt comforted by the rhythm of examinations and her little red booklet. A social worker took on her case and talked her through all the options without her parents present.

'This is your decision, Emily. It's important for you to know that.'

She couldn't look after the baby alone. Of that Emily was certain. She had seen other young mums in Worcester, and they seemed to take to it with ease, but they had boyfriends, friends in the same boat, family who mucked in. They knew the rules and all the tricks. Emily wouldn't have a clue where to start.

She asked Olivia if she thought she was making the right decision.

'I think adoption can be beneficial, for both sides,' said Olivia carefully, not wanting to influence Emily unduly, but not wishing to distress her either. 'And perhaps it's the best thing for you.'

Her cello lessons continued, for Emily was able to go to Olivia's house. She loved it there: her house was tiny and messy and smelled of cinnamon. And the music was a huge comfort. She felt it resounding through her, and the baby jumped about in response. It got more difficult as her bump got bigger, but Emily struggled on, her bow almost at arm's length.

Her social worker Deirdre was robustly reassuring. She didn't fuss over her, or use any euphemisms, either in terms of what to expect from the birth or when discussing the adoption. Emily felt reassured that it was the right thing to do, especially when Deidre told her how much joy she would be giving to the couple they had tentatively found for the baby.

Emily read the letter they had written. They sent photographs of the farm they lived on. Rolling fields filled with white fluffy sheep overlooking the sea. They promised a pony and a dog and kittens. Endless adventures and fresh air and farmhouse cooking. It looked like a *Famous Five* adventure come to life.

She knew she could never compete with that. The best she could ever offer her baby was a back-street council flat. Her father had found out from work what accommodation would be available and had driven her past one evening when she'd had a wobble about what she was doing. The block was six storeys high, dilapidated, noisy, not a patch of green. Gangs of youths hung around smoking or riding bikes. One of them had a ghetto blaster blaring out discordant rap music.

'I can pull strings to get you in here now,' her father told her. 'If that's what you want.'

Everyone kept saying it was her choice. But she only had one option that she could see. As the day of the birth came nearer, Emily repeatedly told herself giving the baby up was the right thing to do.

Deirdre helped her to start putting together a little memory box for the baby to take with her. Emily covered it in wrapping paper decorated with musical notes, for it was music that got her through the dark days and she wanted to pass that on. She put in the cassette of Jonathan playing 'Ondine'. She thought it might inspire the baby one day. Or bring comfort.

The tape of *Liebestraum* she kept for herself. Love Dream. For that is what it had been. A dream of love. Nothing more than that.

25

It was nearly a week after his arrival before Gwen had contact again with her new neighbour. She'd heard him moving furniture around, smelt the drift of good coffee from under his door as she passed in the hallway and seen him whizzing up the street in his Porsche, but he seemed to be keeping a low profile. If he didn't want to be neighbourly, that was fine by her. Gwen had never been intrusive and was mildly curious rather than nosy.

She'd just got out of the bath that evening when she heard someone knock on the door of her flat.

'Bugger.' It was bound to be him, because who else could get in to knock directly on her door? She could pretend not to be in but he would know she was. He would have heard the gurgle of her bathwater draining out. She had little choice but to answer.

He was standing on the doormat with his hands in his pockets, looking at the floor, like a small boy who's been told off. He'd obviously just bathed too – his hair was sleek and still damp, and he had a shirt on, untucked, pale violet, slightly creased.

'I've come to apologise for the other day,' he said. 'I was really rude. It was very kind of you to ask me for a drink. But...' he sighed. 'You got me at just the wrong time. I was in the kind of mood where if I'd started drinking I'd never have stopped.'

'Oh no,' said Gwen. 'Oh God, I'm sorry. I didn't even think. I should have offered you tea. I can still offer tea! I have about seven different kinds of tea. Would you like tea?'

'I hate tea.'

'Oh.'

'But,' he said with a winning grin. 'A coffee would be great if you have it?'

'I certainly do.' Gwen opened her door wider to let him in. 'You caught me getting out of the bath. Would you give me two minutes to make myself look human? If I point you towards the kitchen you could put the kettle on.'

'Perfect.' He strolled in past her. 'You got the good flat, then? With the high ceilings and the balcony.'

'I did. Sorry. But yours is nice too. You've got the little garden at the back.' Gwen led him through to her tiny kitchen. 'Kettle on the side, coffee in a tin in the fridge, cafetière in the cupboard.'

She rushed back into her bedroom, grabbed a pair of jeans and a camel-coloured cashmere polo neck and pulled them on. There was no point in making too much effort. He was going to be living underneath her. She wasn't going to spend the rest of her life in full make-up with her hair all done just to impress him. But Gwen was the queen of the speedy makeover. All those years in Paris hadn't gone to waste. A light tinted moisturiser, two coats of mascara, a dot of liquid blusher on the apples of her cheeks and a swipe of nude lipstick: she nodded approvingly. She still had bone structure; her eyes still sparkled. She ruffled some conditioning gel through her hair and popped a pair of diamond studs in her ears.

'You fox,' she told herself, as she always did, then kissed the tip of her finger and touched her reflection with a smile.

When she came back into the living room, he'd made the coffee and laid it out on the small table by the French windows. It was dark outside, but there were lights strung all along the harbour, and it looked twinkly and welcoming.

'Thank you,' she said, taking a cup. 'Boyd, isn't it? Is that your first name or last?'

'Both,' he said. 'Strictly speaking it's my last name, but I ditched Nigel a long time ago. For obvious reasons.'

'If it's any consolation, you don't look like a Nigel.'

'Thank God.' He seemed a little more relaxed. 'And you're Gwen.'

'Chadwick. I've been here about ten years. Didn't have a pension so I cashed in my London flat and bought this.'

'Classic,' he replied. 'Do you like it here? In Tawcombe, I mean. I can see you love the flat. It's wonderful.'

For a moment she saw her flat through his eyes: a light, airy and feminine space, filled with clutter and trinkets, most of which had little use but simply pleased her. Ostrich feathers, an inkwell, a pair of china shepherdesses, leopard candlesticks, antique champagne coupes, a tiny pair of leather gloves with buttons, a Polaroid camera with six portraits pegged below it, friends from another age . . . Her shelves were, she realised, better than a diary. They would mean nothing to anyone else, but to her they meant the world.

She pondered his question.

'It's sweet. Dead in the winter and heaving in the summer and the theatre's more panto than Pinter, but people are kind and...' She gestured towards the window. 'You'll never get tired of the view.'

'That's what I thought.'

He stared out into the blackness for a moment. She could feel his mood drop. He had seemed to rally.

'Are you OK?'

He turned round to face her.

'You'll find out eventually, I suppose,' he said. 'So I'd rather be up front. But I'm warning you. I hate talking about it.'

'OK.' Gwen was wary. What was he going to confess to? Was he fresh out of prison for fraud? Embroiled in some kind of scandal? He had a risk-taking energy that promised things would never be dull.

He paused for a moment, steeling himself. There was a slight tic under his eye, perhaps from nerves. His veneer was thin, thought Gwen, but not through weakness of character. She could sense suffering.

'My wife died three years ago,' he said eventually, his voice thick with emotion. 'Ellen was a bloody angel, smart and funny and never took any crap from me. It was very sudden and very unpleasant and I don't want to talk about it much...'

'Of course not,' said Gwen. 'But I'm very sorry.'

He gave a nod.

'Anyway, me being the fool that I am, I lost the plot. Drank myself into oblivion. I'd have lost my business if my two daughters hadn't stepped in. They effectively sacked me. To save me from myself. They are chips off the old block. Their mum, I mean.' He managed a proud smile. 'So I sold our house and looked around for somewhere that had no memories of her. Somewhere

I wouldn't see her out of the corner of my eye, or hear her laugh, or smell her scent.' He took a deep breath. 'I'd never been here in my life before I viewed this flat. I bought it the same day. I am starting again.'

He punctuated his last few words with determination.

Gwen took a sip of coffee as she surveyed him. She could see a man who was barely keeping it together. A man who had been tough on himself. A man who was struggling to survive every minute of the day. A man with a thick carapace of bravado.

She put down her cup.

'Thank you for trusting me,' she said. 'And I know there's not much I can do to help. It's going to take time. But I am always here if you want a shoulder. Or a chat. Or a coffee. And I hope Tawcombe will bring you peace.'

She wanted to hug him, because that was her instinctive response to anyone in pain, but she could see he was willing her not to. That he would probably crumble at her touch and make a fool of himself, and she didn't want to humiliate him. He had been very brave and he deserved dignity.

He gave her a smile as if to indicate that the conversation was closed.

'What about you?' he asked. 'What's your story? Your flat certainly hints at a colourful past.'

Gwen did a double take at his candour. His eyes glinted with mischief, and Gwen saw a glimpse of the former Boyd, the Boyd not weighed down by grief and tragedy.

'Oh,' she said, flapping a hand. 'I'm deathly dull. I don't have a story. No skeletons, no drama. Just me and a load of bloody rubbish I've collected that I should get rid of. But no baggage. No baggage at all.'

26

Mick was in the yard, creosoting the fence that led to the exercise paddock, when his phone went. He didn't recognise the chirrup of his ring tone at first for he hardly ever used his phone. But the ringing persisted and eventually he pulled it out of his fleece pocket, wiping a few crumbled dog treats and some grass seed off the screen.

It was Geoffrey Minard. He remembered he'd told him not to call Hawksworthy.

'I don't want to get Sheila's hopes up just yet,' he'd explained.

It was a week since he'd been to see him at his office in Tawcombe, and he'd sort of assumed no news meant, well, no news.

But Geoffrey told him the film director had perked up no end when he described Hawksworthy to him.

'He's very interested,' he said. 'I showed him an aerial photograph, and the ordnance survey map showing the boundaries. He wants to come and have a proper look. I told him you're only thinking about it, but he seemed very keen. His wife's jumping up and down because they haven't found anywhere suitable yet.'

'Did you mention a price?'

'I did.' Geoffrey sounded pleased with himself. 'I stuck

another couple of hundred grand on to what we talked about. He didn't seem phased.'

'Get on!' said Mick with a chuckle.

'Of course, come the day he'll negotiate. But like I said, you can go down, but you can't go up.'

'Well,' said Mick. 'I'd better talk to Sheila then.'

'He was wondering about the weekend after next? For a viewing?'

Mick ran through his mental calendar.

'That's the weekend before the wedding. But I don't see why not.'

'Shall we say Saturday lunchtime? I'll show him around. You don't have to get involved.'

'Yep. Sounds good. Saturday week unless you hear otherwise.' Mick knew it was important to strike while the iron was hot. He didn't want his potential buyer to fall in love with somewhere else. You had to be cute with the DFLs – Down From London, it stood for. They assumed everyone who lived in the country was a gormless yokel, but you didn't keep a farm going for generations without being shrewd. And they always underestimated how much hard work it was, managing land.

He stood for a moment in the yard outside the farmhouse, the April breeze ruffling his hair like an affectionate great aunt. It smelled of fresh grass and spring flowers with a hint of sea. He felt a surge of hope and excitement at the chance for a new beginning. An adventure for him and Sheila. Relief from generations of duty and responsibility. It would be hard to leave, but he suspected it would be harder to stay. For both of them, and eventually for their children. The thought of burdening Robyn and Clover with the decision of when to sell the farm, if he and Sheila became elderly and infirm, was repugnant.

He had spent a long time thinking this through, but Sheila was a long way off thinking about selling. She threw herself into keeping everything going, and he was so proud of the success she had made of the kennels and the training school. He could see her now, in the far paddock, working with a client and his cocker spaniel puppy. It was, she always said, a question of training the owner rather than the dog.

She would be resistant to the proposal. Sheila liked change even less than Mick did. If she had her way, every day would be the same. Breakfast with her family around her, a hard day's work, dinner with her family around her, a good night's sleep. With one day off revolving around Sunday lunch. With her family around her.

He was going to have to find a way to sell it to her. He picked up his phone and dialled Rocky's number.

'Could I come and have a poke round one of your houses?' he asked. He wasn't one for small talk, or for beating around the bush.

Rocky was surprised. Mick had always shown polite interest in his enterprises, but never more than that.

'Of course. They're only shells at the moment. You'll need your imagination. But come on over.'

Rocky's latest development was two miles inland from Everdene on the edge of a small hamlet with a tiny church and a small local pub and a village shop. That might suit them well enough. He didn't want hustle and bustle and he didn't think Sheila would either. It certainly wouldn't do any harm to have a look.

*

Half an hour later, Mick pulled his car into the new development. Rocky came out to greet him. He was hard at work plastering, dressed in khaki shorts and a sweatshirt.

'Welcome to Dandelion Court,' he said, rolling his eyes at the whimsical name. But people liked to think they were buying into nature, and the brochure looked good: pale grey with white dandelion clocks.

'Don't want to interrupt you,' said Mick.

'No worries. The lads will crack on. Come on, I'll show you the biggest. The prime spot on the end.' He led Mick across the mud.

There were four houses built in a rough square around a small copse of ancient trees that had a preservation order on them. Built of local stone, each one was slightly different. Anthracite grey windows and guttering; an oak front door. Bi-folds at the back and a balcony leading out from the master bedroom looking out over the garden. In time there would be three en-suite bathrooms; a luxury kitchen and utility room; plenty of fitted cupboards and a garage.

And Rocky had made each one individual. The one he was showing Mick had a little turret on the side, which made it look very grand.

They would be warm. And dry. There would be no windy draughts coming down the inglenook. No slates falling off the roof. No smell of damp in the passages. No cellar to flood. And even though the sea was two miles away he could still smell the salt in the air and feel the kiss of the Atlantic on his skin. The house had a decent sized garden, too, and over the fence were fields and woods with plenty of footpaths, so they could take Mouse out for a good run without having to get in the car.

He could tell Rocky was curious about why he was

here. He thought a lot of Rocky. A hard worker who'd looked after his two boys, bringing them up on his own after his divorce. That took some doing. Mick couldn't imagine coping with all the trials of parenthood alone, although presumably Jake's mum Tina had some kind of input when they were younger. None of them had met her. She kept herself to herself up country. Presumably she would come to the wedding though . . .

Anyway, Mick thought Rocky would understand his dilemma. He was a man of the world. A realist. Practical.

'I've had a little nibble,' he said. 'Someone's after Hawksworthy. Wants to come and view.'

Rocky made an interested face. 'Do you know who?'

'I dunno, exactly. It's through Geoffrey Minard.'

'Ah.' Rocky knew Geoffrey. Lots of the people who bought his houses were selling their own through him, so he'd dealt with him on many an occasion.

'Some film bloke. He wants a holiday place for his horse-mad wife and kids. He's interested.'

'It would be quite some holiday place.' Rocky grinned ruefully. 'I trust he's got deep pockets?'

Mick shrugged. 'Deeper than mine. Which wouldn't be hard.'

He checked himself. As ever, he didn't want to sound bitter. Rocky nodded, nevertheless. He must know what it took to run a place like Hawksworthy.

'Is it a good offer?'

'I've named my price. No guarantee he'll pay it, of course.'

'But if you don't try . . .'

'Exactly.'

'Are you going to go for it? If he offers?'

Mick shrugged. 'I don't know. I'm the fourth genera-
tion to farm at Hawksworthy. Only I can't make it work.
It's bloody impossible without the cash to invest in a new
venture. Sheila works her fingers to the bone but we're
running just to stand still.' He paused, realising everything was coming out in a big torrent. He wasn't usually
this forthcoming. 'I think Sheila deserves better. It's not
her family farm. It's not in her blood. So why should she
have to bust a gut trying to make it work?' He looked
around the breeze-block walls, the thick grey electric wires
poking out. 'Maybe we need a change? Maybe this would
suit us? Easy to run, no responsibility, cash in the bank.'

'When you put it like that . . .' Rocky laughed. 'Listen,
I'm not going to do you the big sell. I'll get rid of these
as soon as I put them on the market. But you've got a
ten-year guarantee. And the re-sell is watertight.'

'I feel as if the answer is right here in front of me, but
I'm too scared to take it.'

'Mate, that's life. Sometimes you've got to make a
change.'

'Yeah, I know.' He shrugged. 'But I'd never be able to
buy Hawksworthy back. Once it's gone, it's gone.'

'Along with all your money worries.'

'Fair point.'

'Look, I made a massive change fifteen years ago. Jacked
it all in to move down here. It was the best decision I ever
made for me, but there were sacrifices. My marriage, for
a start.' He shrugged. 'Maybe that would have crumbled
anyway and moving just made it happen quicker. And I'm
not proud of that. It was tough for the kids. But by putting myself first, I changed things. Otherwise we would
have just limped on with everything staying the same and

drowning in frustration and bitterness and resentment.'
He paused for a moment. 'My wife would tell you I was
a selfish bastard, but I wouldn't have made her happy by
moving back to Essex. And the boys had a much better
life down here. I know they did. And it was bloody hard,
being a single dad, everyone thinking I'd taken them away
from their mum just because I wanted to go surfing every
morning...' He was starting to get a bit choked. 'Yeah,
I wanted to go surfing but not as much as I wanted the
best for them and me. And I tried to do my best for Tina,
but she didn't want the same things.' He shrugged. 'I
guess what I'm saying is sometimes you have to be selfish,
because everyone loses if you're not.'

Mick wasn't used to conversations where people un-
packed their emotional history.

'Right,' he nodded, not sure what to say.

'And,' Rocky was in full flow now. 'The definition of
insanity is doing the same thing over and over and expecting a different result. You have to pull out the Jenga block,
bring everything tumbling down, then build it up again.'

'Well,' said Mick. 'That's given me food for thought.
Thank you.'

Rocky came over and clapped him on the shoulder.
'Sorry. I think I've confused you even more. But if you want
one of these, give me the heads up.' He pressed a brochure
into his hand. 'All the specs are in here, along with artist's
impressions. I'm putting them on the market in June, when
we've got guaranteed sunshine. But I can put your name on
one. If you tell me early enough you can choose your own
kitchen tiles.' He grinned. 'Just say the word.'

If it was up to him, thought Mick, he'd sign on the
dotted line right now.

27

'I look awful! Like Worzel Gummidge in a dress. Look at my hair!'

Sheila stood in front of the mirror and plucked at her wayward fringe, desperately trying to smooth it into place.

'Mum, it's not the right dress, that's all.' Clover tried to soothe her. 'It's not doing anything for you. And I don't think you should wear a dress, anyway. It's a beach wedding. It's casual. Let's go back and look at those kaftans. They're really cool.'

'I don't want to look like Nana Mouskouri.'

Clover and Robyn looked at each other.

'Who?' mouthed Clover.

Robyn shrugged. She was trying not to laugh. Not in a mean way, as she didn't want to upset Sheila – clothes shopping always made her a bit hysterical.

'Let's go and have cake,' she suggested.

'Are you all right?' said Sheila, immediately alarmed. 'Are you feeling giddy?'

'No,' said Robyn. 'I just fancy cake, that's all. I'm fine, Mum.'

Sheila had turned into a helicopter mum ever since Robyn had announced she was pregnant, checking up on her several times a day. It was sweet, really, for Sheila wasn't usually the kind of mother that hovered. But as she had told Robyn, after everything she had been through herself, pregnancy in anyone else made her anxious. It was wearing, though. If Robyn yawned, or decided to sit down, or gave any hint of something not being quite right, Sheila panicked.

Robyn and Clover had persuaded her to take the day off for them all to go wedding shopping in Exeter. Clover had put herself in charge of styling them both. Robyn had been thrilled to bits with the outfit Clover had sourced for her. She'd researched it in advance on-line and reserved it in two sizes. Robyn had tried it on, nervous at first, for it wasn't what she would have chosen, but it suited her perfectly, and there was even room in case she suddenly put on weight. It was folded up in tissue paper in a paper carrier bag with rope handles, and she felt relieved to have got her wedding outfit out of the way.

It was proving more tricky with Sheila.

'How about this?' Clover picked up some wide-legged white linen pants and teamed it with a navy blazer. 'You can go blazer for the registry office then swap it out for a sweater on the beach. It's chic. And the nautical look fits in.'

'I can't wear white,' said Sheila, horrified at this flaunting of protocol.

'Mum, you can wear white. I don't mind at all. I'm wearing green.' Robyn pointed out.

'Yes, well.' Sheila looked disapproving. 'You know what they say about marrying in green. It's the fairies' colour. It's bad luck.'

'You always say if you drink tea someone else has poured, you'll have ginger twins,' Robyn laughed. 'Which would mean the world would be full of them. I'm not superstitious.'

'Come on, Mum.' Clover waved the outfit at her.

'OK, I'll try it.'

She disappeared back into the changing room.

'I'm exhausted,' said Clover. 'I was thinking about becoming a stylist but not now. It's a nightmare.'

'Don't be silly. You're going to become a high-court judge.'

'Oh yeah,' Clover hit her head as if she'd forgotten. 'And wear six-inch Louboutins.'

Robyn smiled. She could picture Clover in a wig and gown and towering heels. Her little sister was going to take over the world, she was sure of it.

Sheila emerged from the changing room looking uncertain. Both girls burst into spontaneous applause. Clover was right. The outfit was flattering and chic and made Sheila look far younger than any of the dresses she'd tried on.

'It's perfect,' said Clover. 'You can get some thick-soled white canvas sneakers. And I'll do your hair on the morning.'

Sheila admired herself in the mirror, surprised at the effect, turning from side to side.

'We just need to get something decent for your dad now.'

'I'm going to pick him up a navy polo shirt and chinos from M and S.' Clover had already worked out what she could persuade Mick into. 'You'll look like a Hamptons power couple.'

Sheila had no idea what Clover was talking about, but she was happy as she paid for her outfit. 'One less thing to worry about. I've just got to get baking tins from Lakeland. I'm still not sure about naked, though.'

'Naked?' Clover frowned.

'The cake. It's the fashion. I like a thick layer of icing myself, but Robyn's insisting.'

'She's such a control freak.' Clover rolled her eyes.

Robyn smiled, knowing they were teasing. She could not be less demanding. She was leaving everything to everyone else, pretty much. Mostly Gwen. And Rocky. Sometimes she felt guilty about it, but everyone was being so generous with their time.

Ten minutes later, they were in the department store café having shortbread and coffee. Robyn checked her emails automatically, then froze.

There it was. An email to say her birth mother was on the register and would like to make contact. Her details were there in black and white.

Emily Silver was only a click away.

She put her phone back in her bag hastily. The conversation carried on around her but Robyn couldn't hear anything. She was stunned. Even though she had thought endlessly about the possibility of this happening, she hadn't realised how very much she wanted it to.

Her birth mother wanted to make contact.

She might actually get the chance to meet her.

The woman who had carried her, just as she was carrying her own baby right now.

She wanted to cry, with happiness and relief and wonder, but she couldn't. Now was not the time.

'Everything OK?' Sheila detected a change in her, ever on high alert.

'Yes. Just a client chasing a quote. No such thing as a day off,' Robyn joked.

'To my mind, you shouldn't be working at all.' Sheila passed Robyn a hunk of shortbread, just in case she starved.

'Mum, stop worrying. Everyone works right up until the last minute these days.'

'Well, you needn't think you're going to. I'm already worried about you heaving things about.'

'I absolutely promise you: Jake isn't letting me lift anything heavier than a pot of lavender.'

It was true. She wasn't even allowed to push a wheelbarrow. She felt as if she was slowing things down at the hotel, but Jake had assured her she wasn't. They were on track to finish today, apart from the final planting, which she would do next week, giving her the week after to get ready for the wedding. Not that she would have much to do. The invitations had gone out and Gwen had sent her a list of menu suggestions for approval and seemed to have everything under control.

Thank goodness. Robyn didn't think she would be able to put her mind to anything now. All she could think about was the email on her phone, buried deep in her handbag. It was like a hand grenade. As soon as she pulled the pin, there would be consequences.

'I know what we should do now,' said Sheila. 'Go and look at baby things.'

'What?' Robyn said. 'It's way too early.'

'It's never too early to look,' said Sheila. 'This is my first grandchild. I want to make sure it has the very best.'

Robyn looked at her smiling face and her heart quailed. Would there ever be a good time to broach the subject?

Perhaps it would be best to wait until after the wedding? Everyone was slightly hyper and feeling the pressure, she could sense that. Even though it was a nice kind of pressure, there was an invisible clock ticking. They were all running around doing their bit to make her wedding day perfect for her.

If she told everyone now, she risked the chance of ruining the big day. She wasn't so worried about herself, but she certainly didn't want to spoil it for Jake, who was working all the hours he could. Or Sheila and Mick, who were beaming with pride. Or Rocky, who was putting his heart and soul into renovating the Shedquarters.

An emotional bombshell would be incredibly selfish.

'Come on,' said Sheila. 'I want to look at cots.'

'Isn't my old one in the attic?' asked Clover.

'They've changed all the rules since then. The bars have to be closer together.' Sheila was sweeping up her bags.

Clover looked at Robyn. 'She wants to buy a new one,' they chorused, and collapsed laughing.

Her family was perfect, thought Robyn as she followed her mother and sister to the baby department. Was she jeopardising everything she had, just because there was a need, deep inside her that she couldn't ignore?

28

'What do you think?'

Standing in the middle of the kitchen, Sheila held her wedding outfit aloft for Mick's approval.

'Very nice.' Which was exactly what she knew he'd say. Even if she'd held up a dress made out of sticky-back plastic and safety pins, he would say 'Very nice.'

'And Clover picked this out for you.' She pulled the navy polo shirt and chinos out of the bag. 'You just need to get yourself some decent shoes.'

Mick surveyed the outfit that had been chosen for him. 'I can always wear my wellies,' he replied, deadpan.

Sheila cuffed him round the head playfully. 'You,' she said, and folded up the clothes. 'I can't believe it's only two weekends away.'

'We're not having to worry about too much, are we?'

'The cake!' Sheila put her hands on her hips. 'I've got to worry about the cake.'

'You can do that in your sleep.'

Mick had every faith in his wife's baking skills. She sat down at the table with a sigh.

'I'm proper tired after all that shopping. Robyn insisted on going to the pub with Jake. She should be having an early night. She does too much.'

'Leave her be.'

'I know, but I can't help worrying.' Sheila's face was crumpled with concern. 'I know she's past the twelve-week hurdle but you know...' She took in a deep breath. 'It can happen any time. Can't it?'

She turned to look at him. There were tears in her eyes suddenly. Mick strode across the room and put a large hand on her shoulder.

'Now stop that. There's no reason why it might go wrong.'

'I know. But I'm still so scared. I can't ever forget. How awful it was. I don't think I could cope if it happened to Robyn.'

'Come here, now. You're being silly.' Mick folded her into his arms. It upset him when she remembered. He found the memories agony too, but not as painful as his wife's distress.

Sheila wiped her eyes.

'I know I'm being silly. It's not as if it's going to run in the family. She's not my real daughter.'

'She is your real daughter.' Mick was fierce. 'She's your real daughter as much as makes no difference. I won't have you talking like that.'

'I just worry. It's all too much. How am I going to find the time to help her when the baby's here? It was all I could do to get today off to go shopping.' She smiled at Mick. 'And thank you.'

He'd held the fort for her, dealing with the drop-offs and pick-ups, which she knew he hated. He didn't like talking to clients and handling money. He was much happier cutting hedges and creosoting fences.

'I'd do anything for you. You know that.'

He walked over to the dresser and picked up a slim folder.

'There is something I want to talk to you about. Which might affect the future.'

Sheila looked alarmed. 'You're not ill?'

It was her default to assume the worst, and Mick cursed himself for not being more subtle.

'No. No, course not. It's a good thing. Well, it could be a good thing.' He put the folder on the table.

Sheila stared at it. 'Dandelion Court?' She shook her head. 'Oh no. We always said we wouldn't do a conversion.'

It had always been an option, to convert the outbuildings that went with the farm, like so many other farmers did. But they'd never wanted strangers on their doorstep.

'Not a conversion. Geoffrey Minard got in touch with me. Says he's got a bloke wanting a place like ours on the coast.' He knew he was equivocating slightly about the order of events, but he didn't want to distract Sheila. 'He's willing to pay quite a bit. More than I ever thought the place was worth.'

'You want to sell?' Sheila sat down in her chair, the one nearest the range. 'You're selling Hawksworthy behind my back?'

'No. This will be our decision. In fact, it's more your decision than mine.'

'Even though you've been planning it?'

'I wanted to look at the options. What it would mean to us. I could have just told him no. Straight. But I reckon it could be good.'

'But this place is our life. It's everything.'

'It takes over our life.' Mick corrected her. 'I love this

land more than anyone, but every month my heart sinks when I look at the figures. And you're working all the hours God gives and more. It's not right.'

'I don't mind.'

'No. But things are changing for us. Robyn's moving out. Clover will be gone at the end of the summer.' He tapped the brochure. 'If we got roughly what this bloke might offer, we could get one of these. And have money left over that we could invest. You wouldn't have to work again.'

'But I love my work.' Sheila picked up the brochure and started leafing through. 'Not the kennels so much. But I love the satisfaction of turning a dog around.'

'You could carry on. You could go to people's houses, or hire a village hall. You don't need all this land. We're working just to keep my birthright. We don't need it, Sheila.'

She held up the picture of the house Mick had looked at.

'Underfloor heating. Power showers. The water would never turn cold halfway through in a place like this.'

'It would be bloody luxury, maid.'

'You'd really give all of this up?'

'My heart's not been in it since we lost the cattle. You know that.'

'I know,' said Sheila softly, as her eyes misted over. 'Triple-glazing. Built-in wardrobes.'

Mick smiled. 'He wants to come and look at it next weekend.'

'That doesn't give us much time to tidy up.'

'We don't have to. I've told Geoffrey it's sold as seen.'

'You mean they'd probably knock the place down.'

'He can do what he likes, if he gives me that kind of money.'

Sheila looked again at the drawings.

'We wouldn't be next door to Robyn and Jake.'

'Maybe it would be a good thing, to give them some space?' Mick was shrewd. He could foresee Sheila wanting to get too involved if they were on the doorstep. Driving Robyn and Jake mad. 'The little one would still have a field to run around in. And the sea at the end of the garden. And we'd only be two miles away. I reckon that's just about perfect.'

Sheila's eyes were drawn back to the picture of Dandelion Court.

She was already imagining them in the kitchen, with its silent integral dishwasher and the pyrolytic oven. She wasn't sure what that was, but she was sure it was better than an ancient range that always had a hissy fit on Christmas morning and cost two hundred quid every time the repairman came out.

'I reckon I'd like to have a look at it,' she said with a smile. 'I reckon it might do us very nicely. Maybe the time's right for a new start?'

29

That evening, Jake texted Robyn a row of palm trees and emojis with sunglasses on.

Mission accomplished! Meet you in the Ship Aground? Xx

That meant he'd managed to get the last of the tiles down and the pool area was finished, but for the last of the plants. Robyn knew he'd be relieved to get the money in. Jake worried more than she did about cash flow. He'd had a couple of bad debts before they worked together, and he still didn't trust people to pay, although he knew Bruno was good for the money. It took the pressure off them a bit.

They weren't having their usual beach-hut barbecue this Friday as Rocky had dismantled everything and there was wet paint everywhere, plus he'd taken the loo out to replace it.

'I was going to replace the lid, and the cistern, and the wonky handle and then I thought I might as well do the whole thing.'

'This wedding's going to end up costing a fortune. The idea is to keep the budget down, Dad,' laughed Jake.

'It's an investment,' Rocky reassured him. 'And the toilet's on me. Never say I'm not generous.'

Everyone was being so kind. This was the sort of wedding everyone should have, thought Robyn, where everyone mucked in and did what they were best at.

She pulled up outside the pub and parked. The Ship Aground had been part of her life as long as she could remember, and although it would never win a Michelin star, the grub was plentiful and good value and their knickerbocker glories were legendary. Though she wasn't sure she was quite in the mood for its upbeat vibe this evening. There was always loud music and lots of people. All she really wanted was a long bath and an early night so she could get up early and go and help Jake at the Linhay.

But Jake wanted to wind down and have a few beers with his friends, and rightly so after what he'd achieved. Robyn still felt guilty about taking the day off to go shopping, but Jake insisted that her mum needed the trip as much as anyone, and it had been good to be all together, giggling in John Lewis. Though she'd had a struggle to stop her mum buying the whole of the baby department.

'Let's wait until we've chosen the colours for the nursery,' Robyn suggested, and Sheila had made do with piles of leaflets.

Nurseries. Babies. Mothers.

Robyn rummaged in her bag and pulled out her phone to look at the email again. She had never been as near to her birth mother as she was now. They were one step closer to making a connection. As the adopted one, it was up to her; those were the rules. She would have to make the first move; Emily wouldn't have been given her contact details.

Warning bells were going off in Robyn's head. Now she knew her mother wanted to make contact, surely she should take some time to work through the implications? Perhaps she should have some counselling? To prepare her for an emotionally challenging experience. To manage her expectations. To steel herself for disappointment.

There was no time for that. Now they were connected, Robyn felt an urgent need to get this all over before she was married and the baby was born. If she didn't do it now, she would never do it. It felt very private, and intimate. And at the moment, the only person she wanted to share this journey with was Emily. Every time she felt tempted to tell someone else, she was terrified of the fallout. Everyone had their own worries and problems. She owed it to them to sort this out by herself.

She sighed. She should be in the pub by now. Jake would be wondering where she was. She pulled up a blank form on her email and began to compose a message. It needed to be brief and yet say so much. She was very mindful that it might be a shock, and to make it a tentative reaching out. Even then, she was going to have to be patient. It might take Emily time to respond. She might not respond at all.

She read through her words.

Dear Emily,
I'm writing to you via the register who have given me your details. I was very glad to know you might want to get in touch but I shall leave it up to you.
    With my very best wishes
    Robyn

Emily would know who she was from her signature: Mick and Sheila had kept her birth name and its unusual spelling. She kept the message deliberately brief and vague, in case the email got into the wrong hands, or Emily had changed her mind.

She looked out of the window for a moment. Darkness was falling and a mist was coming in off the sea. She shivered. Was she taking a huge risk, getting in touch with a total stranger?

Except she wasn't a stranger. She was her mum.

Before she could talk herself out of it, she pressed send, then got out of the car. The mist hit her in the face, wrapping itself around her.

'What have you done?' it seemed to say. 'What have you done?'

She hurried through it, wiping the droplets of sea from her hair and her face, and pushed open the door. Inside, the pub was heaving. She could smell sweat and beer and salty skin and chips. A classic Friday night at the Ship Aground. Thin Lizzy was blaring out. The Everdene boys were definitely back in town tonight. They were a tangle of sun-bleached locks, six o'clock shadows and tattoos, with Jake in the middle of them.

They all jumped up when she arrived, and there were kisses and congratulations, both for the baby and the wedding. It was the first time Jake had been out with them all since he'd proposed: his college buddies, his surf buddies, the guys who'd seen him through his teens and his twenties. Robyn felt a ripple of affection for them all. They'd made him the man he was today.

'You're going to kill me,' said Ethan, who was coming back from the bar with a tray of pints.

'Why?' said Robyn, wary. Ethan was wilder than Jake, much more headstrong.

'This lot want a stag do.' He nodded his head and half a dozen hopeful faces beamed back at her. 'We want to do that zip-wire thing in Exeter. Next weekend.'

Robyn made a fake throwing up face. 'I can't think of anything worse.'

'I've made a provisional booking. And I've found an Airbnb so we can stay over and have a few beers.'

'And?'

'We just need your permission.'

Robyn looked over at Jake who was squirming. 'Sorry,' he mouthed at her, and shrugged, tipping his head towards all his friends with a sheepish grin.

She raised an eyebrow. 'My permission?'

'He didn't want to go ahead and say yes without your say-so.'

Was she supposed to say no? Of course not. The weekend would be Jake's idea of heaven, galumphing about with his mates doing dangerous things.

'Well, yes, of course he can go. Because once the baby's here he won't be allowed out again. Not for a few years, anyway.'

Six faces looked at her. She nodded at them, keeping her face serious.

'So it will be his last night of freedom, really.' She smiled brightly.

They all looked a bit shifty, awkward at what she was saying.

'So he better make the most of it,' she finished.

They all nodded earnestly. She burst out laughing.

They'd truly believed what she'd said, as if she owned Jake in some way, and was going to lay down the law.

'Course he can go! Jake never has to ask my permission for what he wants to do.' She held up a finger. 'But if he falls off and breaks something, I will kill you all. And that's a promise.'

There was a burst of clapping and cheering. She sat in the middle of them while Ethan went to the bar to get her a lime and soda, singing along with them all to the retro tunes on the sound system, roaring out 'Roxanne' and 'Born to be Wild' and 'Stuck in the Middle with You', Jake's broad arm around her. Everyone she knew seemed to be in the pub that evening. She felt safe, and happy, and excited about the future. The Linhay. The wedding. The baby.

Until she stepped back out into the cold night air and remembered what she had done.

30

1988

The baby was two weeks late. Everyone was worried. There was a heatwave, and the air was stifling. Emily had swollen up until she was unrecognisable and barely able to walk. She couldn't sleep or breathe easily. They took her in to induce her, and she lay in a hospital bed while the hours ticked by painfully slowly, pessary after pessary doing nothing.

She saw other women lumbering past her cubicle, sweaty and inelegant. Some had been here for months on bedrest. She couldn't imagine how anyone could bear it. It was worse than prison. The *Neighbours* theme tune drove her mad. Everyone was glued to it.

In the end, she was put on a drip and filled with a hormone that brought on labour almost instantly. The pain was like being hit by a train. One epidural and fourteen hours later and the baby was still nowhere to be seen. She could sense the staff getting anxious, and so was her mother. Vivian was supposed to be her birthing partner, but she hated seeing Emily in pain. She wondered if she should have asked Olivia Bembridge, imagining her cool, calm presence.

'What's the matter?' she asked, as a midwife looked at the graph on the heart monitor.

'I think we should consider a section,' she replied, paging the consultant.

'Section?' asked Emily, wondering for a moment if they were locking her up in a madhouse. Then she realised. A Caesarean.

The baby was in distress. The atmosphere changed suddenly, a sense of urgency in the air, a swiftly choreographed ballet coming into play: a surgeon, an anaesthetist, theatre sisters... Emily was afraid, but not for herself, as her bed was whooshed into the theatre and a dark green screen placed over her stomach. She lay helpless, a peculiar tugging sensation inside her as they worked. There was tension, concentration, bright light and then suddenly... A small bundle held aloft with triumph. Smiles. Relief.

'A little girl,' the nurse told her with a smile. 'We'll get her weighed and cleaned and you can hold her. Have you got a name?'

Emily hesitated. It felt odd, giving the baby a name she might not keep. But she'd had one in mind all along: a name that she thought was pretty but strong.

'Robyn,' she said, when the nurse came back a few minutes later with the baby wrapped up in a blanket. She looked at her daughter's pink puckered lips and tiny seashell ears and the wisps of dark hair on her head that matched her perfectly arched eyebrows and she knew, in that moment, that they belonged together and that no matter how wonderful the farm in Devon was, no matter how many ponies her prospective parents could give her, no matter how little she had, she could not give her up.

She didn't say anything at first. There was too much

going on. They were stitching her up, then she was taken to a private room with baby Robyn next to her in a plastic see-through crib. She couldn't sit up yet as the epidural hadn't begun to wear off. Her mother came in, anxious.

'It'll be time to hand her over soon, darling.' She stroked Robyn's hand gently, trying to smother her own distress.

The plan was for the baby to go to foster carers who specialised in newborns. But Emily didn't think they could possibly know what her baby needed. Already Robyn would only settle when she was in her mother's arms; when Emily asked for her to be plucked out of her little bassinet.

'I'm not handing her over,' she told Deirdre matter-of-factly when the social worker came to see her.

She could feel the consternation between Deidre and her mother. She knew they couldn't force her to give the baby up.

'Darling, I know it's upsetting but we have agreed it's for the best.'

'We also agreed I could change my mind if I wanted. Remember?'

It had been made clear all along that it was her decision.

Emily felt determined. And strong. Everything that had been so confusing was now quite clear. Robyn had given her the clarity she needed.

Vivian hesitated, the dilemmas circling in her mind. Was it best to take the baby away regardless and make a clean break? Or give in to Emily and let her come home with Robyn? She knew, in her heart of hearts, that if

Neal saw the baby he couldn't turn it away. He wasn't a monster.

Vivian turned to Deirdre. 'This is awful. I can't have anything to do with this. It was easy to make a decision when it wasn't a real baby.'

Deirdre nodded. This was always a traumatic part of the process. It was vital to be empathetic, but firm.

'Let's see how Emily feels after a good night's sleep. Her hormones are everywhere, don't forget.'

But after a night's sleep, Emily felt even more determined not to relinquish Robyn. They were as one. She had never felt so strongly about anything or anyone. Except maybe Jonathan. Robyn was a little piece of him. The closest she would ever get to him. How could she possibly let that go?

Two more days went by. She wasn't recovering very quickly from the Caesarean: she found it very painful to walk and pick up the baby, and feeding was difficult. Her breasts were swollen and rock hard and Robyn could hardly latch on, which meant she got hungry. Emily began to feel more and more anxious, especially when a midwife offered to take Robyn off and give her a bottle. She refused. She wouldn't let Robyn out of her sight, more and more convinced there was a plot afoot, and that they were going to trick her into giving Robyn up somehow. She had to be careful. Ever watchful. Every soft tread, every concerned voice, every helpful pair of hands was a threat. When she did sleep, she had terrible dreams the baby had been taken away and she woke up screaming, which wasn't what they wanted on the ward.

'I want to leave the hospital,' she told her mother when she was still in after nearly a week. 'I want to go home.'

Her parents reluctantly agreed that she and the baby could come back to Manor Close while they talked things over.

'I can't force the decision on her,' said Neal, distraught for his daughter, praying she would see sense.

'I know,' sighed Vivian, agonised by the complexity of the situation.

And so it was that Emily found herself back in her bedroom, a Moses basket on a stand underneath her favourite poster of Robert Plant. The bookshelf containing her Lord of the Rings trilogy had been cleared for nappies.

It was surreal. Her body coursed with a mixture of pain, love and milk. Her scar felt as if she had been branded whenever she got up to walk. But it was a small price to pay for the bundle that was Robyn. Every time she looked at her dear little face, she melted.

'We're so worried about you,' said her mother, when she found Emily lying on her bed with the baby on her chest, sobbing uncontrollably. She felt overwhelmed. With love, but also the responsibility of doing what was right, even down to whether she'd done her nappy up too tightly. 'The health visitor says baby blues are quite normal, especially after a Caesarean, but they shouldn't go on too long.'

She went to lift the baby but Emily held onto her. She didn't want anyone else touching her. She was a tigress: possessive, protective.

'Emily, darling, you need to rest. She'll be all right with me.'

'No.'

She clung on. She felt as if her parents had her under surveillance; that the kindness they were showing her was just a front to lull her into a false sense of security. She wouldn't let them help. She wouldn't even let her mother take the baby for a walk while she got some much-needed rest. She got agitated when the health visitor came round, and even more so when Deirdre came to talk to her about her decision to keep the baby and whether it was really the right decision. She felt as if she was looking for signs of inadequacy, so she put up even more of a pretence, which then exhausted her.

Her love for Robyn fed her determination to keep her safe. Vivian's own words came back to her, when she'd first told her she was pregnant. 'I'm your mother. It's my job to look after you.'

The baby was thriving, but Emily became less and less able to cope. She barely slept, always on high alert, watching for signs of intervention. She became increasingly paranoid. She was nervy and jumpy, thinner than ever. Getting washed and dressed was overwhelming; something she could barely manage. Her room became a squalid mess and she wouldn't let her mother in to help tidy.

Her friends from school came to see her, but the visits exhausted her and she spent the whole time they were there fussing over Robyn, not allowing any of them to hold her. Emily could see them looking at each other in concern and she worried they would tell her mother, so she chivvied them out of the house before Vivian came back.

When they'd gone, she sobbed her heart out, looking at the sweet gifts they had brought – velour all-in-ones and cuddly animals and brightly coloured toys for Robyn to play with.

She heard her mother on the phone to the social worker, creeping along the landing and straining her ears to catch her whispers.

'I'm worried sick. She's not herself at all. She's really not fit to look after her, but she won't let us help.'

Emily's mouth was dry. This was serious. The authorities were going to step in any moment and separate them. She knew it.

'The thing is, she's not all that stable. There was the incident with the girl, last year. I worry she's a danger. To herself. And the baby. I'm worried she might do something unpredictable.'

Emily's heart turned over as she heard her treacherous mother betray her. She was doing everything in her power to get the baby taken away. Twisting things. Making things up. Making the staircase incident seem pre-meditated. Using it as proof of her instability.

She crept away, glad she had eavesdropped for now she knew what her mother's plan was. She was cleverer than she was, though.

She sat on the bed, looking at Robyn while she slept. And it dawned on her that there was one person in the world who would help them. Who would care about the baby as much as she did, once he saw her. She was his double, after all, with her wise eyes and her dark curls. To Emily, Robyn was like a mini-shadow of Jonathan — there was as much of him in her as there was her, and the love she felt reminded her of the feelings she'd had for him. It consumed her. And it completed her, for the baby seemed to be compensation for losing him. She had poured all that unused love she had for Jonathan straight into Robyn.

Once he knew the truth she was sure Jonathan would come to their rescue. Her heart melted at the thought of Robyn in her daddy's arms, him looking down at his daughter proudly. He was bound to fall in love with her like Emily had. She would be more important to him than his music.

She began to plan. She didn't have long. She needed to get away before they all closed in on her. Her parents had become more watchful, no doubt under instruction from a higher power. Emily began to eat, both to fool them and to give herself some strength. She was going to need all the strength she could get. She only slept when she was certain they were sleeping; when the floorboards in the room next door had stopped creaking. They didn't know she knew their plan. Didn't know she'd seen through their fake concern and cloying attentiveness. That her sharp ears, tuned to detect the slightest change in pitch, had picked up their every whisper, every murmured conversation, every muffled phone call. There was a conspiracy, she was sure of it.

She feigned slumber, limbs splayed out, concentrating on making her breathing heavy. It fooled them and it gave her the chance to eavesdrop and to prepare, for they dropped their guard while they thought she was sleeping. They never left her alone in the house, though, so she couldn't use the phone. So there was always a high level of risk.

They left the house one afternoon, when Robyn was sleeping soundly and Emily pretended she was going to have a lie-down too. Vivian thought they were safely slumbering, and shut her own eyes on the sofa, so it was easy to slip out of the back door. They didn't have much with them. The baby's changing bag, of course, with nappies, wipes, bottles and the little cartons of milk Emily had trained her to drink cold. No need for boiling kettles and mixing up formula. And another bag with babygros and cardigans for Robyn and leggings, pants and jumpers for Emily. And wash stuff. And a few toys.

Emily was exhausted from carrying the baby by the time they got to the B & B. She'd passed it often enough on her way to school, and it was perfect. It was tucked away behind a monkey puzzle tree so no one could see inside from the road, and running alongside it was a footpath that led to a cluster of shops – a mini-market, a chemist, a video store and a charity shop. Emily would be able to access them and get what she needed without too much fear of being seen, for it was a part of town her parents wouldn't frequent. There were always rooms available. It was only in the height of summer that she had seen the red NO sign slipped in front of VACANCIES in the bottom left-hand window.

The room they were given was in the basement, the walls running wet with damp, even in early summer. What else could they expect for twelve pounds a night? The only good thing about it was Emily knew the landlady wouldn't care who they were or why they were there. That was the whole point of places like 11 Mowbray Walk. Emily thought it was clever, to go to ground nearby at first, as no one would think they would stay around Worcester. They would be looking further afield. They were hidden in plain sight.

Nevertheless, she knew once they got there they had to

move on as quickly as they could, or she would drown in the freezing damp that bit at her lungs as she drew breath. At night she slept with Robyn pulled right into her. She wasn't going to let a single sliver of cold touch her skin. They stayed there for two nights, only half a mile from the place that pretended to be their home. Emily wanted her parents to lose hope. To imagine them on a ferry or a plane. She pictured their frustration and annoyance and it gave her strength.

On the third day, they left the B & B at lunchtime and walked the half mile to the station. She'd bought a buggy from the second-hand shop, and scrubbed it down with bleach in the B & B bedroom, removing any traces of mould and dirt and the encrusted rusks from someone else's baby. It was filthy, but she needed it and she had no choice. She didn't have the strength to carry Robyn everywhere.

It was funny, walking up the road she'd walked along so many times to school, singing and swapping jokes and chewing gum with her friends, admiring each other's shoes and haircuts, bemoaning homework and deifying the boys from the grammar school who were out of their reach, with their rugby shoulders and sailing tans. Never in her wildest dreams would Emily have imagined herself pushing a baby along that road. She hadn't spoken to any of her friends since they'd dropped round. She didn't trust anyone. It was Emily and Robyn against everyone else and she didn't want any chink in her armour.

She slid the buggy across the train platform. There was a light mizzle, which meant she could huddle up inside her raincoat to hide her face – the only upside, because she felt as if she would never get warm again. It might be June, but the damp and the rain seemed to have got inside her bones, and she couldn't stop shivering. That could have been nerves as well. She was twitchy about being recognised. This was the most dangerous part of their escape.

The station announcer woke the baby up, his voice crackling and echoing along the empty platform. Robyn lay wide-eyed as he announced the next train, so alert, as if she was listening out for their station to be mentioned.

The train is now approaching Platform 2 . . .

EMILY

~~Robyn~~ decided to stand in the corridor for the journey to Birmingham New Street. It seemed easier than folding up the buggy and getting settled, only to unfold it all again. She couldn't believe they were on their way to York, but she wouldn't relax until they had changed trains and were properly on their way, though they were still going to have to change again at Nottingham. Her coat was wet through, and she was starting to shiver, but it wasn't long before they got to Birmingham. Here, she felt completely anonymous. The station was swarming with people who had no interest in a young girl with a baby.

She found the right platform and when the train arrived they climbed on board and found a spare seat. Somehow she managed to fold up the buggy with Robyn under her arm before sitting down. The woman opposite offered to help, but she didn't want to draw attention to herself.

'I'm fine. Thank you.' She pushed their bags into the overhead rack and took off her wet raincoat. She wished she had a spare jumper or coat. Robyn was nice and warm, all snuggled up in her all-in-one with feet and a yellow cardigan.

'How old?' smiled the woman as she got out a bottle and began to feed the baby.

'Three months,' she lied, thinking if there had been anything on the news about them running away that would fox her.

'She's lovely. What's her name?'

'Actually, he's a boy. He's called William.'

'Oh.' The woman blushed. 'Sorry.'

She didn't ask any more questions. Robyn finished her bottle and began to get a bit grumbly, which she sometimes did after feeding. Emily stood up and pulled her cassette player out of the bag. It was the one thing she was worried about bringing as it was heavy, but it was important to her. She pressed down on the play button and the cassette started to whir, groaning a little as it always did, before the tune began.

The *Liebestraum*. The Love Dream. She could feel Jonathan in every note as they drifted up to her. She shut her eyes. The carriage was warm now and it was going to be all right. Her baby was pressed against her, making her feel very hot and sweaty, but she didn't want to move her. They were as one. But soon, they would be three. She thought about Jonathan's face when he saw Robyn, how his eyes would light up, how he would see himself in her and fall in love in an instant and they would be safe.

They both fell asleep. Emily started awake as the train stopped and the doors banged. She huddled herself around the baby so she wouldn't wake. Leicester, she saw out of the window. They were at Leicester. She racked her brain, wishing she had paid more attention in geography, but she couldn't place it on a map. They must be halfway, she thought.

And then she saw them. In the next carriage. One behind the other, stony-faced and determined, in their uniforms. The woman opposite couldn't meet her eye. Emily realised she was her betrayer. What had she seen that gave them away? She had been so careful to look matter of fact and capable; not fearful.

Emily got up, casual, because the woman couldn't see the police yet. 'Would you keep an eye on my stuff for a minute?' she asked her, and she nodded with a weak smile. Emily wanted to roll her eyes at her terrible acting, but instead she smiled her appreciation. 'Won't be a tick.'

She left their things so as not to arouse suspicion. She walked to the end of the carriage, slid the door open, slipped through. There was no one in the corridor. Anyone who was going to get off already had. She turned to the left as if she was going into the toilet. She wasn't going to make the mistake of turning right onto the platform, in full view of everyone. Instead, she opened the door on the other side and looked down. It wasn't too far to jump onto the track, and there was no one on the opposite platform to see their escape and raise the alarm.

She hadn't time to deliberate. She held Robyn tightly and jumped. The ground jarred her and she fell, holding the baby still. She scrambled to her feet but it was hard without the aid of her hands to push herself up. She was going to run the length of the train to the back end, because it wouldn't leave the station while those men were still looking for her. She hugged the side so the passengers by the window wouldn't see her. She didn't want any of them raising an alarm.

She hadn't been able to shut the door of the train, so she'd only got a short time until somebody noticed, or her betrayer said something. She was almost at the rear, where the platform sloped down onto the track. She was about to cross behind the train and then get into the undergrowth.

Then she heard a shout. One of the men had jumped out of the door she'd left open. He was pounding down the track after her.

'Emily!' she heard him shout. 'It's all right. We just want to make you safe.'

It was the same story. The same story her parents had told her over and over. The story she wasn't stupid enough to swallow. They didn't want to make them safe. They wanted to take the baby away. For her own good. She'd overheard every single argument.

'She can't look after a baby.'

'She's not well.'

'It's not fair on her.'

'The baby could have a proper family. A good start. A better life.'

'What is she going to live on?'

'How is she going to manage?'

'We know it seems harsh. But it's for the best.'

How could separating them be for the best? They belonged together. Emily put her head down and carried on running.

The policeman didn't grab her. He enfolded her. He pulled her into his arms, and for a moment Emily leaned against him, relishing the warmth, wanting so badly to be able to trust him.

'It's all right, love.' His voice was gruff and gravelly. And so kind it brought the pinprick of tears to her eyes. 'You'll be all right.'

She wouldn't be, of course. But she hoped Robyn would be. *Oh God, please let them look after you,* she thought. *None of this is your fault. You with your sixpence eyes and your prawn fingers and your hot little tummy. I am not good enough for you, that much I know, so perhaps this really is for the best.*

The other policeman arrived, out of breath.

'Emily Silver?' he puffed, and for a moment Emily wondered about denying it. Telling them they'd got the wrong person. But she felt her legs going from underneath her, and she didn't have the strength to lie.

31

On Saturday morning, Boyd was just coming in through the front door when Gwen went down to see if she had any post. He was in a big cuddly grey hoodie and shorts and trainers. Good legs, she thought.

'Morning!' She saw he had a paper under his arm – it was rare to see someone with a real newspaper these days – and a fresh pint of milk. 'Have you settled in nicely?'

He looked at her with a Jack Nicholson eyebrow. She laughed, realising how patronising the question sounded.

'No,' he replied. 'Since you ask. I haven't settled at all.'

'Oh.' She was a little taken aback by his candour.

He sighed. 'I've done my best. But it doesn't feel right. It doesn't feel like home.'

'I guess that comes with time.'

'No. I felt at home in your flat straight away. Mine feels all wrong.' He seemed very puzzled and put out. 'Maybe you could come and have a look? Give me some advice?'

He flashed her a look of such charm, she blushed. She couldn't resist.

'Of course,' she found herself saying.

She followed him inside his flat. It was the same footprint as hers, only the kitchen had been knocked through so it was all open plan. She could see what he meant immediately. Everything had been painted bright white and looked magazine perfect. It was the archetypal bachelor pad – architectural prints and movie posters on the walls, the leather sofa at a jaunty angle, the trendy desk by the window, a sleek television. But it was too cool to be welcoming. It felt a bit stiff and staged, and the down-lighters bleached everything out.

'What do you think?' he asked, anxious. 'Do you see what I mean? It doesn't feel lived in. I mean, I know it hasn't been. But I don't want to be here. It makes me feel . . . homesick.' He looked around the walls. 'I thought, you know, a new beginning. But I think I've made a terrible mistake.'

'It's early days. It's bound to feel strange. And you've been through a lot. You can't just flip into a new mindset because you've moved house.'

He sighed. 'I don't want to be here, though.'

Gwen walked around the room, getting a feel for his personality and taste. She tapped a finger to her lips, thoughtful. 'It needs some homely touches. I'm going to the home store on the industrial estate to get some things for the wedding I'm organising. Why don't you come with me? I could do with a hand, and you could pick up some bits and pieces.'

He gave a wary grin. 'That sounds expensive.'

'It needn't be.'

'Famous last words. I've got two daughters, remember. I've been tricked more times than I like to think.' But he was laughing.

'We can take my car. We won't get all the stuff in yours.'

'Do you mean now?' He was astonished by her spontaneity.

'Yes! Why not? I don't like to think of you feeling miserable. The sooner we fluff it up, the sooner you can feel at home.'

He looked a bit taken aback that she should care.

'OK. Let me go and get some proper clothes on.'

Ten minutes later they were heading for the big industrial park in Bamford fifteen miles away.

As they drove, Gwen made a mental shopping list. She knew exactly what he needed to breathe life into his surroundings. She felt excited. This was the kind of challenge she loved. There was something vulnerable about Boyd, despite his prickliness. He needed looking after.

She pulled up outside her favourite cut-price homeware store. Between them, she would get everything they needed. None of it would be top quality, but he could replace the items with more considered purchases in time. He needed a quick fix.

She was pretty sure she could work her magic and make him feel more settled. A house move was always daunting, but even more so if you were on your own. Especially if you were still struggling with bereavement. She could feel the unresolved grief rolling off him. The love that had nowhere to go.

It was his wife that was missing. The sound of her footsteps, her laugh. The scent of her hair. Her indentation in the sofa; the warmth of her side of the bed. Her heart ached for him. She couldn't bring Ellen back for him, but she could bring some life into the flat.

'Come on,' she instructed him.

He followed her around in something of a daze.

Occasionally she would ask him to make a choice about a size or a colour.

'Right,' she said when his trolley was full. 'Go and pay for that lot and I'll get the wedding stuff.'

She'd made a comprehensive list so she knew exactly what she was looking for. Fringed picnic rugs, lanterns, trays, wooden boxes, cushions, colourful serving plates – she had a shrewd eye and kept adding in things that appealed because everything was such a bargain. She was probably going to go wildly over the budget Robyn had given her, but it didn't matter. She would underwrite it. All that mattered to her is that it was perfect.

By the time they left, the car boot was bulging, as well as the back seat. They lugged everything back to their respective flats. Then Gwen came down to Boyd's.

'Right,' she said. 'I want you to go out for an hour. I don't care what you do. But don't come back until six o'clock.'

'I know exactly what I'm going to do,' he said. 'I'm going to the supermarket. I'm going to cook dinner for you. To say thank you.'

'Deal,' she said, delighted that he already seemed a little more purposeful.

'Any likes or dislikes?'

'I'm not keen on offal or goat's cheese.'

'Damn,' he said with a straight face. 'That's my liver and goat's cheese soufflé off the menu.'

Gwen laughed. 'Off you go.' She shooed him out of the door.

As soon as he'd gone, she nipped up to her flat for a hammer and nails and a paintbrush and set to work. She was completely absorbed in what she was doing and was just standing back to admire her handiwork when she realised he was standing in the doorway, his mouth open, a carrier bag in each hand.

'It looks like a different place,' he said.

He walked in and put the two bags of shopping on the kitchen counter, then looked around in admiration.

'It's just a few little tweaks,' said Gwen. 'But I hope you like it.'

'It's incredible. It feels cosy and warm and inviting and like somewhere I want to be.'

Gwen had to admit she had done herself proud. She'd speed-painted the chimney breast in a dark forest green, then when it was touch dry she hung a sunburst mirror over the mantelpiece and lined up a row of orange Penguin classics. Two tall, leafy plants stood like sentries either side of the fireplace. There was a textured rug in front of the sofa, a scattering of squashy cushions and a fleecy throw over one arm. Table lamps spilled pools of warm light into the darker corners. A scented candle filled the air with a citrusy scent spiked with ginger. The radio was tuned to a jazz station.

She had brought the room to life.

She looked at Boyd. He was blinking very hard, and she realised he was trying not to cry.

'Hey,' she said softly. 'This wasn't supposed to upset you.'

'You don't know what this means.' His voice was gruff.

This time she had the courage to step forward and put her arms around him. She felt him melt into her as he rested his head on her shoulder. He was sobbing quietly.

'Shhhh,' she patted him. 'It's OK. It's OK.'

Eventually, he stopped, stepping away from her, wiping

his eyes. He strode towards the kitchen area and started unpacking the bags. He pulled out a bottle of Barolo and held it out to her.

'Corkscrew in the drawer; glasses in the cupboard,' he said as he carried on unpacking.

She opened the bottle and poured them each a glass and sat on a bar stool while he cooked.

'We're having spaghetti cacio e pepe,' he told her, heating up a cast iron frying pan, then toasting a handful of black peppercorns.

Fifteen minutes later they sat with brimming bowls and a second glass of wine, digging their forks into the pasta coated in creamy pepper and parmesan and pecorino.

'The trick,' he said, 'is adding in a ladle of the cooking water when you add the cheese. It makes it cling to the pasta. It's taken me years to perfect this.'

'It's wonderful,' said Gwen, twirling her spaghetti round her fork.

I like him, she thought. I like his scratchy outside and his vulnerable inside. I like that he is both capable and helpless. I like how he knows what he wants yet somehow doesn't. I like how he can make a simple meal taste like a million dollars.

She reached for her glass and took a gulp of wine. She mustn't fall for him. Not her neighbour. And not a man who was obviously not over the death of his wife. It would be a disaster.

Anyway, she didn't do falling in love, she reminded herself. It never ended well.

32

Robyn was sitting on the floor of the nursery looking at colour charts. The plaster in the Linhay had nearly all dried and, being impatient, she had fast-forwarded to planning the decorating, even though the skirting still had to be put on, and the lights fitted. She was frustrated as there wasn't much else she could do. No one would let her lift a finger to do anything. She'd been relegated to choosing things. She was hoping they would get bored with the novelty of her pregnancy and she could start being useful – before she actually did get too big.

Next door in the master bedroom she could hear Rocky and Jake trying to plumb in the Japanese tub. There was a lot of banging and swearing but that was how they always worked.

'Hey.' Jake appeared in the doorway, making her jump. 'What have you decided on? Mermaid's Buttock? Oyster Vomit?'

He was teasing her. The paint chart she'd been choosing from had taken ridiculous names to the next level, inspired by the ocean.

'Mermaids don't have buttocks,' she told him. 'I'm thinking Sea Foam. With the woodwork picked out in Clamshell.'

'Green and white, then.'

'No. Very, very pale turquoise and a shimmery silvery cream.'

'Green and white,' Jake repeated, and she threw her shoe at him, laughing.

'How's the tub?'

'We nearly threw it out of the window, but it's almost plumbed in.' He grinned. 'Fancy giving it a try later? When Dad's gone, obviously.'

'Do you think it will take my weight? I've put on a few pounds already, I think.'

Jake pretended to look doubtful. 'We could risk it. I think the floor will take it.'

'Cheek!' she said, and he bent down to ruffle her curls with a grin.

She watched after him as he headed back to finish the job. Then she reached for her handbag to check her phone for the millionth time.

After nearly forty-eight hours since she had first made direct contact, she had almost given up hope of her mother replying. She reminded herself that Emily would need time to take in her message and think carefully about what to say. It wasn't something that invited an immediate response, like a party invitation. Besides, Emily might have had a change of heart, now Robyn had become a reality rather than a fantasy.

In some ways, she was rather relieved not to have a reply. It did mean she still had lots of unanswered questions, but it would make the run-up to the wedding so much easier, not having the burden of keeping it all to herself any longer, or the worry of when to let people in on her secret. Who to tell first, and when. She felt duplicitous, as if she was lying to those she loved. But, she told herself, it was to protect, rather than deceive them.

So when she saw Emily's name in her inbox, she felt her heart turn over.

She had a message. A message from her mother. She felt her past whooshing in; a blizzard of thoughts and fears. In a few moments, she would be nearer to knowing the truth.

She leaned her back against the wall, drew her knees in, took a deep breath and opened the email.

Dear Robyn,
Receiving your email meant the world. So hello. It's wonderful to hear from you.

I understand that this must be as momentous for you as it is for me.

I think it's important for us to take our time and not rush into anything.

I would like, if I may, to send you a letter. I wrote it a little while ago, but it explains everything that happened leading up to your adoption. I think they call them Life Letters now. They weren't really a thing when you were born, but I wrote it on the advice of someone very wise and very special. For me and for you, if we should ever be in touch.

Once you have read it, we can decide what to do. Whether to speak on the phone, or to meet. I don't want you to feel any obligation. Although I understand there must be things you'd like to know.

I'm sorry if this letter sounds formal. It's taken me a long time to write it. I feel very emotional but I don't want to overwhelm you. I hope very much that you have been, and still are, very happy.

Please let me know where to send the letter if you would like to read it.

With my warmest wishes,
Emily

Robyn read the words over and over. She couldn't have asked for a more wonderful reply. It was warm and kind and thoughtful. She could sense from it how much her getting in touch meant to Emily, yet her response hadn't been overwhelming or gushy. It was just right.

She looked up at the ceiling, her eyes swimming with tears. She wanted to run from the house right now and go and find her. She knew that would be foolish, but the feeling came from deep down inside. The yearning for her mother's arms.

She needed to think about her reply. She knew Emily would now be in as much agony as she had been over the past two days, waiting for her to get back to her. But she had to think carefully about the consequences of getting involved. She felt anxious again, having almost come to terms with the thought she wasn't going to hear anything.

It was such a mixture of longing, fear, joy and uncertainty.

For a moment she was tempted to run next door and tell Jake. But she knew he would be alarmed, and overprotective, and might think she should tell Sheila and Mick. She wasn't ready for that yet. This was something intensely private: a fragile bond between two women who'd been torn apart for reasons she didn't know yet. When she knew her better, she would decide what happened next.

Emily was right. It was important not to rush things, or place too much value on their relationship at an early

242

stage. They needed to be gentle with each other. Patient. And mindful. They would each have questions. Hopes. Expectations.

And wounds. Emily in particular would have wounds, she thought. She hoped they'd had a chance to heal over the years, but if Robyn could do anything to reassure her and help her make peace with what had happened, she would.

She shivered. The sun was going down and the temperature was dropping as dusk approached. She started to compose a reply, writing and rewriting, until at last she was ready to send it.

Dear Emily,
Thank you so much for your thoughtful email. You are right that we shouldn't rush things. I've had a very, very happy life and am about to marry a wonderful man, which was my reason for getting in touch. It seemed important before I got married to know more about who I was. So I would love to read your letter – my address is below. And if there is anything you want to ask me in the meantime, please do. I hope this hasn't come as too much of a shock.

I thought you'd like to know a little bit about me. I'm a landscape gardener, and I love my job. I don't know if I got my green fingers from you! But they have served me well.

Robyn

She gave her address as the Linhay, wondering for a moment if it was wise to reveal her whereabouts. But she didn't want the letter to go to Hawksworthy Farm, and

Emily's email didn't have the feel of a potential stalker. She had read stories of reunions that had backfired, expectations not being lived up to, a newfound love turning sour. She must tread carefully, and not invest too much. She hadn't mentioned the baby either. It seemed tactless, at this point, and might be too much for Emily to take in, the news that she was to be a grandmother.

She tried to conjure up an image of her in her imagination, but all she could see was a middle-aged version of herself. What are you like, Emily Silver? she wondered, Will we come to love each other, in time? Or is it too late?

'What are you doing, sitting here in the dark?' Jake was in the doorway.

'Sorry – I was daydreaming.' Robyn started to get to her feet. Jake came over to give her a hand up. She was suddenly starting to feel less agile; a little thicker round the waist, even though the awful tiredness of the first three months was fading.

'We couldn't quite get the waste pipe in place. So we'll have to do the tub another night.'

'That's fine. Anyway, it's going to be pitch-black soon.'

'The electrician's coming to fit the rest of the lights later this week. And Dad's offered to take us to the Ship Aground for something to eat.'

As if he hadn't done enough, helping with the Linhay and the Shedquarters. Robyn felt a burst of gratitude for her soon-to-be father-in-law. But she wanted to be alone with her thoughts this evening. She didn't have the energy for the Ship. She felt a little giddy with the shock of it all, but didn't want anyone suspecting that anything was wrong.

'Actually, I feel wiped out. I think I'll get an early night, if your dad doesn't mind.'

'Course he won't. I'll probably go, though. If you want to be on your own.'

Jake held her arm as they went down the stairs. She felt a bit wobbly. Strange shadows were casting themselves on the walls as the light began to fade. She shivered. She must have been sitting too long on the floor in a draught. Rocky appeared out of the gloom at the bottom of the stairs, making her jump.

She burst into tears. It was all too overwhelming. She had dreamed about this moment for so long. She was thrilled and scared and bewildered, all at once.

'Robyn! What's the matter?' Jake turned her to face him, peering at her, concerned. Rocky rushed over too, hovering behind Jake.

'It's nothing. It's just ... everything.' She gestured around her. 'All of this. The wedding. The baby. Everyone being so kind.'

She buried her face in Jake's chest and he put his arms around her. She could sense the two men looking at each other over the top of her head. She started to laugh through her tears.

'I'm really sorry. It must be my stupid hormones.'

They seemed to accept her explanation. Thank goodness for pregnancy. It seemed to excuse any kind of unusual behaviour. Robyn breathed in Jake's familiar smell – the salt from the sea that never quite left his skin, the sweat from his exertion. She would tell him when the time was right. When she felt ready. When she knew what she was doing and how she felt and what it all meant. When she had made sense of it all in her head. She was sure he would understand. She was sure he would forgive her.

33

'Do you know what your mum's plans are yet? For the wedding, I mean?'

'No idea.' Jake put a dollop of tartare sauce next to his scampi then squeezed ketchup all over his chips. 'I've told her I can book her into the Mariscombe for as long as she likes. Bruno will do me a deal.'

The Ship Aground was buzzing. It had been another beautiful spring day and Everdene was starting to fill up, especially in the early evenings when people fancied a walk on the beach and perhaps a bite to eat or a glass of wine. Jake and Rocky had managed to get their favourite table, nevertheless, in a corner by the huge window that overlooked the sea.

'I was thinking maybe I should go up and see her.' Rocky inspected his steak with the tip of his knife to make sure it was just as he liked it. Perfect. They served beautiful Ruby Red Devon beef in the Ship – he wouldn't have steak unless he knew exactly where it was from.

Jake put the ketchup bottle back on the table and frowned. 'Why?'

'I don't want any atmosphere. I mean, we haven't seen each other for, what, ten years?'

It still seemed odd, to be estranged from someone he

had once loved. The mother of his children. But Tina never came to Everdene, and Rocky hadn't been back to Enfield since his father's funeral. His close friends came to visit him, and there was a hardcore of them who went on a golfing holiday in Portugal if he wanted to catch up. They were much more fun in the Algarve than on their home turf.

'Dad, she'll be fine. She's pretty chilled these days. She won't cause any trouble.'

'I suppose so.' Rocky chewed thoughtfully. 'Has she got anyone else?'

Jake shrugged. 'No one serious as far as I know. Though there's usually someone in the background sending her flowers. You know Mum.'

'Yeah.'

Rocky smiled wryly. Tina was the kind of woman Interflora had been invented for. The reason shops like Tiffany existed. She was old-school glamorous. She made men lose their heads. He'd been proud to have her on his arm all those years. In the beginning, he'd questioned what he'd done to deserve her.

Not enough, in the end. Not enough. Flowers had been the giveaway. She had tried to pretend she'd bought them for herself, but he'd found the card in the bin. She hadn't even pushed it to the bottom. There it was, staring at him, when he went to throw away the tin of dog food. *Can't stop thinking about you . . .* At the time, he had wondered what kind of a man would have the nerve to do that, send flowers to his lover's house, under her husband's nose, even though it was no secret they were having difficulties.

He pushed the memory away. It was ancient history now, and he didn't want to lay any more anxiety at Jake's door. The last thing he wanted was to taint the wedding with any hostility, but Jake was right. Tina probably didn't give him another thought from one day to the next and would be totally laid-back. There would be no accusing glares or icy stares or barbed remarks. It had been so wearing. He had always battled so hard to say or do the right thing, which had invariably turned out to be wrong.

Yet again he wondered how things would have been if he hadn't been so naïve and dreamed of an idyllic seaside life for them all. He supposed they'd be in a bigger house in a better bit of North London struggling to keep up with everyone else, running to stand still. He'd be richer than he was now, on paper, because property there was worth five times what it was down here.

He knew he would be miserable, though. It had been exhausting, maintaining the lifestyle of the circle they moved in: the affluent self-employed who outdid each other with the cars, the holidays, the possessions you needed to keep your place. And business was cut-throat. You had to schmooze the right people. People whose values Rocky didn't share. He was continually gazumped. His staff were poached. If your face didn't fit, you were frozen out. If you didn't play the game, you lost anyway. At the end of the day, he wasn't tough enough. He was a grafter, but not a game-player.

Tina was tougher than him. She'd been brought up there, whereas he'd moved there from the countryside when he was sixteen, and had known a gentler way of life, which he came to crave. He'd seen Everdene as an opportunity for a happier existence. Somewhere he could flex his entrepreneurial muscles and take some business risks without being shafted. And it had worked, for him. He'd done some bread-and-butter renovations, building up until he could afford bigger projects, until he was now able to take on challenges like Dandelion Court.

He still loved every day that he woke up here. He was fit, solvent and knew how to enjoy life. He had a soul. What more could he ask?

After dinner, Jake went off to the Shedquarters and Rocky made his way back up the winding hill out of Everdene to his coastguard's cottage. The lights had come on while he was out, and the windows glowed a warm welcome. He opened the door and slipped inside. The evening was chilly, and the heating had come on too, just to take the edge off. The cottage might look quaint, but it had all the mod cons.

He flopped down on the steel grey velvet sofa that took up most of the lounge area. His son was so wise, he thought fondly. He shouldn't worry about his ex-wife, or let it cloud the day. He shouldn't worry about how he would feel if she turned up with someone. There was absolutely no reason why she shouldn't attend the wedding with a partner, if she had one. Though Jake seemed to think not. Funny, how they were both still single after all that time. Perhaps it wasn't surprising, after all the acrimony?

But he was tired of being on his own. It had been great to have dinner with Jake tonight, but he wasn't going to be around to hang out with much longer, especially once the baby was here, and it was a bit sad, to rely on your sons for entertainment. He had mates, loads of them, but that took organising and what he wanted was to *not* have to organise. To potter about and open a bottle of wine and throw something together in the kitchen and chat and then loll on the sofa in front of the telly *with* someone.

He looked around the cottage. He had it just as he wanted: rough oak flooring, bare stone walls, inglenook fireplace with a wood-burner, industrial lighting, hidden speakers. Cosy but high tech. All that was missing was a human presence. He had Lara for company, but although they worshipped each other, she couldn't speak back when he talked to her.

He thought back to his disastrous date with Melissa and her follow up. Could he see her here? He thought he could imagine her on the sofa with her legs tucked up underneath her and a glass of red in her hand. Maybe he should text her. Give her another chance. He'd been enjoying her company until she bolted.

He picked up his phone and called up their thread on WhatsApp.

Just wondered if you fancied getting together next weekend? Maybe a walk and something to eat at the pub?

He pressed send before he could think twice. And he felt better for being proactive. There was nothing worse than sitting around feeling sorry for yourself. His dream woman wasn't going to come knocking on his door on the off chance, after all.

Five minutes later he had a reply.

Sounds good. I'll get my walking boots ready!

He felt pleased. He thought about where to go. Heddon's Mouth was a spectacular beauty spot further along the coast, and the Hunter's Inn was perfect for lunch. Maybe it would be the most middle-aged date he'd ever been on but – he was middle-aged!

Great, he texted back. See you Saturday. How about Heddon's Mouth followed by the Hunter's Inn?

Perfect, came the reply. Then an xx a moment later. People scattered kisses everywhere in their texts these days, but nevertheless, it made him feel warm.

For an idle moment, he wondered about asking her to the wedding, if their date went well. But that would be crass. What was he even thinking? He didn't have to prove himself to Tina. There was absolutely nothing wrong with being single.

'Come on, Lara.' Lara jumped up to follow him up the stairs. He had got into the bad habit of letting her sleep on the bed. He probably should train her to sleep downstairs in her basket. Just in case.

Steady on, he laughed at himself. You're moving a bit fast. One thing at a time.

34

Robyn went over to check the post at the Linhay every day after her email exchange with Emily. She wanted to be on her own when the letter arrived, so she dropped in after lunch, once the postman had been. It was starting to look like a home. Sunlight flooded in through the windows and lit up the empty rooms. It was a glorious, light-filled space, and the view was spectacular: the sea ever-changing in the distance, morphing from teal to petrol to darkest black when night fell. Another six weeks and it would be finished, Jake reckoned. She could hardly wait.

She imagined them waking up together as the sun came up, husband and wife. Making coffee and wandering outside to the little patio they were going to lay outside the kitchen, and looking out over the sea while the gulls wheeled overhead. They would have to make the most of that freedom this summer, for eventually they would be woken not by the sun, but a little voice coming from the room next door. She imagined jumping out of bed and going into the nursery to see a warm bundle gazing up at her. It was still hard to imagine, especially when they didn't know if it was a boy or a girl. She didn't mind either way.

Every day she checked the tin box they had left for the postman. It was always stuffed with catalogues. Robyn had become slightly obsessed with sending off for samples and brochures for sofas and lights and carpets. Swatches of velvet and linen were taped to the windows; there were daubs of paint everywhere as she examined each colour in different lights. Jake teased her, but she loved this part of the process and didn't want to miss out on anything.

Today, she sifted through several bulky packages to find a thick white square envelope with a smudged postmark and careful handwriting addressed to Robyn Moss. Her heart thumping, she opened it up. Inside was a William Morris card: the Strawberry Thief, with its tangle of berries and birds and flowers. And inside that was tucked a sheaf of lined paper, several pages of A4, neatly folded.

She opened the card. The writing was small, the words dense, covering both sides on the inside and the back.

My dear,

I can't tell you what it means to be writing this to you. I have dreamed of this moment for so long. Thank you, for being brave. I know it must have taken a lot of courage, and I'm so grateful.

I wrote down our story some years ago, both for me and for you, on the advice of someone very wise, because I didn't want to forget a single detail if ever you were to ask. And it has helped me to put everything down in black and white, because it made me realise that it wasn't black and white. That there were no victims and no villains, just a lot of people who were very afraid. And that what is right for one person is wrong for

*another, and how do you decide whose future is the most
important?*

*Of course yours was the most important. I have spent
the whole of my life praying that what happened in
the end was the best thing for you, and now I know my
prayers were answered.*

*Please read this with forgiveness in your heart and
know that I have never forgotten, or stopped loving, you.*

Emily

Robyn gulped, tears stinging her eyes. Her lungs felt
tight as she reread every word, imagining the turmoil
and distress Emily must have been through. There was
something very elegant and considered about the way she
wrote, which somehow made it more touching.

She picked up the notepaper. There were pages and
pages of precise black ink, very neat. Had she written it
all in one go, or done a page at a time, or had she done
a rough copy and then copied it out for best?

Robyn knew it was going to make painful reading.
She wasn't sure if she had the courage to read it on her
own. But she didn't want to take it home. She didn't
want Sheila to find her a sobbing mess. Or worse, Clover.
And she certainly didn't want to take it to work and cry
in front of Jake. He would only be anxious about her
well-being, and she didn't want him worrying.

She was supposed to be doing a quote for a client this
morning. Breaking down the prices for a massive garden
makeover including an outdoor kitchen space. There was
no way she could concentrate on that while she had the

letter in her hand. But she didn't feel strong enough to read it on her own, out here.

She picked up her phone and called Gwen.

'I've had a letter,' she said. 'From my mother. With our story in it. I don't know what to do.' She hesitated. 'I'm scared.'

Gwen caught her breath. 'Oh darling. Of course you are. I totally understand. Would you like to come here?'

'Would you mind?' Robyn longed to have someone with her who knew the situation, and Gwen would be perfect. She wouldn't interfere, or judge, or ask too many questions. And she wouldn't mind if Robyn cried. The card alone had been an emotional punch to the gut. She was surprised how daunted she felt by the prospect of finding out her past and discovering more about Emily. Would the revelations be painful? Giving up a baby must be unbearable, even if it was the right thing to do.

'Of course I don't mind. I'll stand by with tissues.'

'Can I come over now?'

'I'm right here. I'll be waiting.'

A sudden squall came in from the sea as she drove to Tawcombe, and it was gloomy when she arrived. The damp air from the harbour curled itself around her and she shivered. It added to her apprehension, for she was fearful of what she might discover in the pages. Just looking at them made her heart twist.

As she approached Gwen's flat she saw a light on in the ground-floor flat.

'Someone's moved in?' she said as Gwen came down to answer the front door.

'Shhh.' Gwen twinkled and put her finger to her lips.

'Yes. He's interesting. To put it mildly. A widower. Little bit younger than me. Boyd.'

'Boyd?' Robyn looked at her friend, intrigued. Gwen seemed to sparkle a bit when she mentioned him.

'I'll introduce you next time, but not now.' Gwen ushered her into the flat. 'Let's have a look?'

Robyn showed her the card, and the accompanying letter. Gwen's face softened as she read Emily's introductory words. She couldn't speak for a moment when she'd finished.

'Can you imagine,' she said. 'How it must feel? You getting in touch, after all this time? She must be over the moon.' She was blinking away tears, moved by Emily's words. 'You snuggle up on the sofa and I'll bring you a cup of tea. I'll just potter about – I'm here if you need me.'

Robyn was grateful for her kindness. She loved Gwen for her understanding and the way she automatically knew what you needed. She made her way over to the sofa by the window and sank into the comfort of its duck-feather cushions. She opened the papers and smoothed out the first page. So many words, so many thoughts, so many emotions. She took in a breath and began to read.

She read about a funny little girl who didn't quite fit in, who loved Tolkien and playing the cello and had hair she could nearly sit on.

She read of a summer filled with music and passion for a boy with wild curls and kind eyes and a gift that took your breath away. And then heartbreak, and hurt, and shock.

And then . . . a realisation.

Her heart buckled as she read on. Emily's descriptions were unflinchingly honest and raw but never mawkish as she described her discovery, her parents' reaction, their agonising decision, the birth, her illness, her escape, her bid for freedom on the train to York. Her capture.

And finally, the day she gave up her baby.

Tears were pouring down Robyn's cheeks as she read the final words.

It turned out I was very ill. The woman on the train had been worried about me. I'd been shivering, feverish, slightly delirious and she had gone to the guard, who had called the transport police. I was rushed to hospital, where I was treated for pneumonia, exhaustion and diagnosed with severe post-natal depression.

By the time I came home, I didn't believe in myself any more. Running away had proved I was a danger to myself and to you. Even I could see how you would be better off without me. I had no fight left in me. I was broken. I was not good enough for you. You deserved better. A proper mum and dad. A farmhouse. A pony.

The social worker was almost unbearably kind. I sometimes feel it would have been easier if they'd not given me a choice, and just taken you away from me. But everything was explained. Nothing was arranged until I understood what everything meant. You were going to be fostered while the adoption process went through. I could still change my mind up until the last minute. But I knew I wouldn't. I wanted the best for you. Two loving parents with the means to give you a wonderful life. Not a strange, scared little girl who didn't have a clue.

Those last few days we had together were

extraordinary. I was in a complex tangle of joy and fear, committing every little bit of you to memory so I would never forget so much as an eyelash; a fingernail. My love – our love – was so pure and fierce, but it was tangled up with terror and anxiety. I had tried to rescue us, find a place of safety, but I hadn't succeeded. I was still in pain – a lot of pain – and I was too afraid to sleep. Although you weren't. You were good at sleeping right from the start, content and oblivious. If my love for you helped us in any way, it was to make you feel that you would always be safe.

You held my finger throughout that last night. I don't know how I managed to sleep, but you didn't let it go.

I can't write much about the day I said goodbye to you. I handed over the box I had prepared, with your favourite cuddly piglet, and the tape, and a photograph we'd taken of you. No one knew what to do or say to me. My mother was pale and red-eyed; my father mute with distress. Despite everything, it was a huge loss to them too. Who couldn't love you? But they firmly believed it was the best thing for both of us.

I stayed in my room when the social worker took you. The doctor gave me something that took me down into velvety blackness. I emerged, several days later, into a bleak, empty world, not knowing how I would be able to live without you.

But I did. Though not a day has gone by when I haven't thought about you, and imagined you running through those green fields, arms outstretched and a wide smile on your face. And if you are reading this, it's because my prayers have been answered.

This is our story. Now we have the chance to write a better ending, and I can give you all the love I've been keeping in my heart.

Emily

So there it was. In black and white. The story of how Robyn had come into the world. The revelation of a host of new people who were connected to her, who she hadn't known about until this afternoon. Her mother, just a young girl. Her father Jonathan, just as young. Her grandparents, Vivian and Neal . . . she had never really given much thought to them until now, but they were an integral part of how she had come to be on this planet.

And what of them all now?

She wiped away her tears as she thought about the boy who had fathered her, with his beautiful hands and his musical soul and his kind eyes, who didn't know of her existence. Where was he now?

And her grandparents. Were they still alive?

Did she have brothers and sisters? Half-brothers and sisters? Or nieces and nephews? How far did her family tree reach? And did it even matter? After all, she had a family. Did she need another? Did she need to go raking about in the fragile cobweb of her past?

She was finding it hard to think. Opening the letter answered some questions, but asked many others. Was she selfish for being curious? Did other people's feelings matter more than hers? Mick and Sheila's? Did they even need to know she was looking? Could she keep all of this a secret, or should she share it? If so, when?

Maybe it was time to tell Jake, she thought. But she

didn't feel ready quite yet. She needed to figure out how to manage what happened next. It felt very private, a pact between her and Emily. Reading her words made her feel closer to her. They needed some time alone, to forge a new relationship, and decide how they fitted into each other's lives, without any influence from other people. For other people would feel strongly about what to do, she was sure of that. Jake would be protective, perhaps overprotective. He would only care about her.

And she was determined to respect Emily's role in all of this. Relinquishing her baby had probably affected her whole life. She deserved to have control over what happened next, and decide who was drawn into the next chapter. Robyn wanted to handle it with a gentle touch. But she felt daunted, nevertheless.

Robyn had been the lucky one. She had been placed in the arms of two loving people who had dedicated their lives to keeping her safe and happy. But had Emily ever got over her heartbreak? She desperately hoped the rest of her story had ended happily.

She looked over at Gwen, furiously tapping away on her iPad, engrossed. Gwen would give her good advice.

'I need you to read this,' said Robyn. 'And tell me what you think I should do.'

Gwen looked at her over the top of her glasses.

'Are you sure?' Gwen came over and sat next to her. Robyn handed her the letter. Gwen held it for a moment.

'Are you OK?' she asked her.

'Yeah,' said Robyn, wiping the last of her tears away with the heel of her hand. 'I'm going to get some fresh air. I'll be back in a bit.'

She went and sat on the harbour wall. In the water,

the boats rose and fell with the swell of the incoming tide. Like the rocking motion of a crib, thought Robyn, pulling her coat more tightly around her, going back over everything she had read, the words flittering around her head. She had been part of that story, yet she had no memory of it. Her heart felt bruised. She could actually feel it aching.

She thought of Emily at the same age as Clover was now. And the pressure she had been under. She turned it all over in her mind. If Clover came home and announced she was expecting a baby, things would be very different. People were much more accepting of single mothers and unplanned pregnancies nowadays. There was no stigma. Everyone would pull together. Mick and Sheila would just get on with it. Plans would be made, compromises, sacrifices. Never in a million years would Clover be expected to give up her baby if she didn't want to.

But the times had been different then, even though it was only thirty years ago. There might not have been the shame of days gone by, when an illegitimate child was seen as a disgrace, but it would still have been tough for a young girl on her own.

And although it must have been heartbreaking, Robyn couldn't picture a different outcome. She couldn't begin to imagine a life without Sheila and Mick. And she would never have met Jake, her rock, her partner-in-crime, her soulmate.

She stood up and walked back across the road, realising she would have to ring the bell for Gwen to let her in, but just as she approached the door, it opened and a man emerged. He was wearing jeans, a stone-washed sweatshirt and a baseball cap.

Robyn pointed at the door before he could shut it.

'Would you mind letting me in? I'm just on my way to see Gwen.'

'Sure.' He grinned and held the door even wider for her. 'I've just moved in downstairs. I'm Boyd.'

'Hi.' Robyn smiled. The new neighbour. He was nice-looking. Twinkly. 'I'm Robyn.'

'Ah. The blushing bride.'

'Yes. Gwen's organising the wedding for me.'

'Well, if the menu's all wrong, you can blame me. She keeps asking my opinion.'

Robyn laughed. 'Oh dear. Sorry. You're probably not very interested.'

'Actually, it's kind of fun. And Gwen's very creative.'

'She is. I'm so grateful to her.'

'Where would we be without her?' He was joking, but Robyn could see he was already under Gwen's spell.

There was a little pause.

'Right, well, I'm off to see a man about a boat.' He nodded his head towards the harbour. 'When in Rome.' He put his fingers to his lips. 'Don't tell Gwen. I want to surprise her.'

Robyn watched after him as he headed off into the mizzle. She was intrigued. He seemed lovely. There was definitely something in the air, she thought. How nice it would be for her friend to have someone in her life. Gwen was so resolutely independent. For as long as she'd known her, she'd been on her own. It didn't have to be wedding bells, but a like-minded person to share things with would be a good thing.

When she got up to the flat, Gwen answered the door.

'Oh, Robyn.' Gwen's face was streaked with tears. 'Poor Emily. Poor little you.'

The two women stood in each other's arms, weeping at what they had just read.

'Do you think I should meet her?' asked Robyn eventually, disentangling herself and walking into the room. She could see the letter laid out on the coffee table. Her past; her history.

Gwen didn't answer for a moment.

'Imagine,' she said. 'Imagine having a baby. A dear little baby that was the centre of your world. And having that baby taken away from you. It would haunt you for the rest of your life. You would never wake up without her being the first thing you thought about. You would never go to sleep without wondering how she was.' She wiped a torrent of tears from her cheek. 'Of course you should go and see her.'

Robyn walked over to the window. In the distance, she could see Boyd talking to a man on the pontoon. They were pointing over at a boat moored in the middle of the harbour: a high-powered RIB. She smiled to herself. That was one secret she would happily keep.

'I'll contact her,' she said to Gwen. 'I want to meet her first, on my own. And then I'll tell everyone else.'

35

'I'm going to nip to Bath today,' Robyn told Sheila over breakfast on Saturday. She was resting her bare feet on Mouse, who was lying under the table. 'I'll go on the train. I still need some wedding shoes. Turns out nice but comfy is almost impossible. I've tried everywhere else round here.'

'Oh, damn,' said Sheila, sticking some more bread in the toaster. She was in her tartan pyjamas and the sheepskin slippers Robyn had got her for Christmas. 'I've got a client this afternoon, otherwise I'd have come with you.'

She came over and sat down, pouring herself a mug of tea.

'That's a shame,' said Robyn, feeling guilty at the glibness of her lies. 'But I'll probably be better on my own anyway. I've got a list. Some new foundation. And a decent bra.'

More equivocation. Don't overelaborate, she told herself, as she spread Marmite onto her toast. She'd better eat properly before she set off. Sometimes she didn't bother and ended up feeling giddy.

'Well, have a lovely day and don't overdo it.'

'That's why I'm taking the train. I can have a nap.'

'Text me when you get there. I worry you do too much.'

'Mum. I'll be fine. Honestly. It's a bit of light shopping.'

'If you see a nice pair of clip-on earrings that would go with my outfit, would you pick them up?'

Robyn hesitated. 'Yes, of course.'

'I'd ask Clover only she'd make me get something over the top. Just something small but smart to set it all off.'

Robyn's heart buckled. Her mum was secretly excited about what she was wearing, she could see that. If she didn't have time to get some in Bath, she could pick her up a pair during the week, or order some online.

'I'll see what I can find,' she promised.

'Are you sure I can't poach you an egg?' Sheila eyed the remnants of Robyn's breakfast, clearly not convinced she'd eaten enough. 'I'm doing one for your dad.'

'No, thanks.' Robyn wrinkled her nose. 'I've gone off egg. And meat. And about a million other things.'

'I couldn't touch fish with Clover,' Sheila admitted. 'Or liver. Oh! Speak of the devil.'

Clover appeared, dressed in a Dalmatian onesie and carrying a Lidl bag stuffed with overnight things.

'You should go with your sister to Bath,' said Sheila.

'I would, but she doesn't want a hen-do. So I'm going on the stag-do instead,' Clover said. 'Ethan said it was OK.'

'You could have got dressed.' Sheila looked disapproving.

'This is my outfit. And trust me, this is low-key compared to what some of them are wearing.'

'Come on, then,' said Robyn. 'You don't want to miss the minibus.'

She hurried her sister out of the house before the guilt overwhelmed her completely.

Sheila watched the two of them go then she cleared away the rest of the breakfast things. She felt guilty lying to Robyn about having a client. Should she have told her what was happening today? Mick had said not to say anything unless they had a bite.

'We can have a family chat when we know what's what. There's no point in worrying the girls yet.'

She sat down for a moment and poured the last of the tea from the pot. She was anxious about Robyn going to Bath all on her own. It was only an hour on the train but it was a long drive to the station. Maybe she should have gone with her? She wasn't really needed here – Geoffrey would show the film director around. But he might have questions, and Sheila was better at fielding questions than Mick, who wouldn't know the best way to answer – he'd just be brutally honest, and that wasn't always a good thing. Sheila knew there was a knack to selling houses, but wasn't sure Mick had the guile to tell a prospective buyer what they wanted to hear.

Not that there was anything to hide at Hawksworthy. You got what you saw. Acres of pasture on the edge of clifftop; raw, natural beauty and surely the greatest view in the land. On a clear day you could see Wales. As for the farmhouse and outbuildings, they would win no prizes as they were, but there was potential if you had the pockets. Look at what had been done to the Linhay. No one would have thanked you for it in its former state, but it was shaping up to be more than any of them had dreamed of. Perhaps the film director would have the same vision as Robyn and Jake.

It was out of her hands.

Sheila relished the silence in the kitchen for a rare moment. There was too much to think about at the moment. The baby, the house sale, the wedding – it was like a washing-machine cycle, the coloured stuff in with the whites, everything whirling round and the colours bleeding into each other. She was finding it hard to focus.

Breathe, she told herself. What was the important thing?

All of it! It was all important. Making sure the baby was safe. That the Linhay was finished in time. That the wedding was perfect. That their financial future was sorted. And she wasn't in control of any of it. Mick was always telling her to let go. That she didn't need to be in charge. But she hated that feeling. The only thing she was in control of these days was the dogs she trained. She could make them do exactly what she wanted. Everything else – not a chance.

Let it all go, Sheila, she told herself. Let everyone do what they want and look after themselves. What will be will be.

On the drive to Everdene, Robyn wondered about telling Clover where she was going. Her little sister would be furious with her if she didn't. But you could never tell how Clover would react. She might want to come with her, or she'd spill the beans to Jake, or she might even berate Robyn for not telling Sheila and Mick and insist they turn around.

So she said nothing, but listened while Clover burbled on giving her strict instructions about what to buy.

'You want a dewy foundation, not too matte, very light coverage. And shoes – nothing too clumpy. A wedged espadrille would be nice. And if there's an eyebrow bar anywhere . . .'

'What's wrong with my eyebrows?'

'A good brow can be better than a facelift.'

'I'm not touching them. And nor is anyone else.' Robyn laughed.

'I should be coming with you,' sighed Clover.

'I'll be fine,' Robyn reassured her.

At the Ship Aground, a minibus was waiting for a motley crew to get on board. Three of Jake's mates were dressed as traffic cones. There was a giant baby, and another one was dressed as a *Baywatch* lifeguard in a skimpy red swimming costume and a blond wig. Robyn couldn't stop laughing.

'You're all mad,' she said, and then her eyes widened as Jake appeared. He seemed to be having a piggy-back ride on a garden gnome. It was only when he got closer she realised the gnome was strapped to him and the legs hanging from the gnome's shoulders were fake.

'What are you like?' she said.

'Never say that I'm not on-brand,' he said with a grin.

'Please don't break anything,' she pleaded as she gave him a hug goodbye. 'You've got far too many things to finish, and I don't want you in plaster for the wedding photos.'

He kissed her amid cheers and clapping before getting into the back of the minivan with the others.

'All aboard!' called Ethan, who was driving and wearing an inflatable T-Rex suit.

'Looking good, Eth,' Robyn teased him, and he gave her a thumbs up.

'Always,' he said.

'Bring him back safely,' she said, peering in at Jake settling in at the back.

Right until the last minute she'd been tempted to tell Jake what she was doing today. But he needed this trip. He'd been working so hard, on the hotel and on the Linhay, and he needed some time with his mates to unwind and let his hair down. If he got any inkling of her plan, he would be overconcerned, overprotective, and would probably insist on coming with her. Which she loved him for, but she needed a clear mind.

Clover was racing out of the one-stop shop with a bag full of freshly baked doughnuts.

'Look after her too,' Robyn said to Ethan as Clover climbed into the van and settled into her seat, handing out her wares to the hungry stags.

'She can look after herself,' he grinned.

The minivan set off for Exeter, and Robyn headed to the station. Emily had told her Bath was frantic on a Saturday and parking was difficult so it was best to come by train. It was weird, corresponding with the mother she had never met about something as prosaic as travel arrangements.

The train journey to Bath seemed endless. The carriage was overcrowded and some of the seats had been double-booked, which meant every time they stopped at a station there were arguments. Robyn didn't dare leave her seat to get a drink or go to the loo in case someone pinched it.

She longed for silence so she could think, but there was a group of young girls drinking mini bottles of prosecco and shrieking with laughter, as well as a young boy watching cartoons on his iPad with the volume turned up, and the sound seeped in through her earphones no matter how high she turned up the music.

She promised herself that once this meeting was over, with Emily's blessing, she would tell everyone the truth. She didn't think she'd ever lied about her whereabouts to anyone before. She'd never needed to. Although this lie was to protect someone else, not herself.

She'd had some time to digest Emily's story. To come to terms with how she had come into the world, and then found her way to Hawksworthy Farm, a human pass-the-parcel, going from her birth mother to a social worker to foster carers and finally to Mick and Sheila. She had questions, of course she did, but her overriding concern was to know that Emily was all right, had somehow managed to survive the trauma and had gone on to lead a happy life.

And that meeting Robyn might bring her some added peace.

She checked herself in her phone camera again. She'd twisted her curls into a side-ponytail, had on a smudge of eyeliner and mascara to give her face a little definition. She was wearing a pale pink linen shirt with cropped jeggings and white sneakers – nothing too smart because she didn't really do smart anyway. She just wanted to be herself. She didn't look pregnant yet. Maybe a little fuller – she'd succumbed to the jeggings because they were so much comfier than jeans – but as Emily didn't know her usual size, she wouldn't notice.

At last, they drew into the station at Bath. It was only a few hundred yards from the station to the café, and as the weather was fine it would be nice to stretch her legs after being cooped up on the train. She looped her rucksack over her shoulder and got swept up in the streams of passengers leaving the train.

They were mostly groups of youngsters here for a weekend on the town, dressed to the nines even at eleven o'clock in the morning: boys with sharp haircuts in jackets over jeans and pristine trainers, girls in leopard-skin dresses with tanned legs, spidery eyelashes and elaborate up-dos. Robyn wasn't used to this level of grooming. She'd thought she'd made an effort, but she was dowdy next to these crowds of peacocks. She marched along, wishing she was one of them, having a day out, enjoying the thrill of a new city, pottering off for a cream tea. When she remembered why she was here, her stomach jittered.

But then she thought about how Emily must be feeling. There was probably guilt and remorse and distress and trauma; Robyn had none of that. She was simply apprehensive about whether she was doing the right thing, and a little nervous, which was understandable.

She stood in the shadow of the abbey for a few minutes of reflection, staring up at its golden façade, admiring the towers and the arched windows and the stained glass glittering in the sun. It was a rather reassuring presence. She wondered how many people had walked through its doors over the centuries seeking comfort. She wasn't religious, but she could see how you could be tempted in times of uncertainty to search for guidance within its ancient walls.

As a clock struck quarter past the hour, ringing out across the crowds, she realised she was going to be late.

She got her bearings and hurried down a road adjacent to the abbey, then into a little square lined with shops and cafés around a cluster of trees until she reached the one where they were meeting. She paused for a moment, wondering if Emily was inside already, watching the door.

The café was buzzing with people having elevenses at mismatched tables. The air was filled with the scent of baking and fresh coffee. She searched the faces, but couldn't see anyone sitting on their own looking expectant. She must be the first to arrive.

'Table for one?' asked a waitress.

'Two, please. I'm meeting someone.'

She followed the girl through to a table towards the back of the café, going past a glass counter filled with tempting cakes she couldn't face, for her stomach was upside down. She slid into the seat that faced the entrance.

'Just a cup of tea, please. I'll order properly when . . .'

She couldn't quite say *when my mother gets here*. The words didn't sit easily yet.

She fiddled nervously with the menu, looking up every time the door opened. But no one who came in looked as if they might be Emily. Her tea arrived and she drank it. Fifteen minutes went by. She checked her phone to see if there had been a message, but there was nothing.

She wasn't going to come.

She felt overwhelmed by her disappointment. She had been so sure they would meet. Emily hadn't given any indication that she was in any doubt, but she supposed it would have been a huge ordeal for her. She must have had second thoughts.

Tears sprang into Robyn's eyes. She bent down to

burrow in her bag for her purse, so she could pay for her tea and leave. She didn't trust herself not to burst out crying. She couldn't believe she felt so let down.

It doesn't matter, she told herself. She had got through thirty years of her life without knowing her real mother. She didn't need her: she had Sheila and Mick and Jake. And Clover. And... well, lots of people.

And at least now she didn't have to be disappointed. The chances of Emily being the perfect fantasy mother were pretty remote. What if they'd had absolutely nothing in common? What if they'd disliked each other on sight?

What if Emily had already caught sight of her and decided she didn't like what she saw? Mortified by the possibility, Robyn rummaged for the money she needed. She'd leave it on the table and go. She couldn't face asking for the bill.

Maybe she'd go and look around the baths? Or take a trip along the river? Or go and have tea at the famous Pump Rooms? She could take something back for Jake: a Bath bun in a little box. Maybe she should have been honest with him from the start. It would be nice to go home and have someone to share the disappointment with, instead of having to ask herself endless questions and wonder why Emily had chosen not to come. But Jake wasn't at home. She would be all by herself.

She put down the coins with a sigh. It would have meant a lot to have made a connection. To have looked into the face of the woman who had given birth to her, and to have searched for similarities. When she looked at Clover, she could see Sheila in the curl of her eyelashes and the arch of her eyebrow and the fullness of her lips. And Mick in the line of her jaw and the freckles on her skin. She had never seen any of her own features in someone else—

'Robyn?'

A deep voice startled her, and she looked up. Standing over her was a man, a tall man in a grey mac, his hands in his pockets, silver curls almost to his collar. And in that moment, she saw herself reflected in his grey eyes, saw her smile on his face, heard the timbre of her voice in his.

'Yes,' she whispered, half standing, her heart pounding, for she knew what he was going to say before he said it.

'Jonathan,' he said, holding out his hand. 'I'm Jonathan.' For a moment she thought he was going to cry, even though he was smiling. 'I'm your father.'

36

1987

'You know, deep down, that I'm right.' His mother's voice cooed in his ear. Jonathan was getting to the point where he could no longer bear to listen to her tireless encouragement. He had lived with it day in day out for so long now, from her getting him up first thing in the morning to sending him off to bed so he got a full night's sleep. She managed every moment of his life. It was exhausting.

Admittedly, there was plenty of praise and adulation in between the chivvying. But that was starting to wear thin. How many times a day could you be told about your gift and your talent and your genius before it became meaningless? Or you became an egotistical monster? He hoped he wasn't that, and managed to keep a modicum of self-awareness, but it was difficult.

He was good-natured, though, and perhaps that was part of the problem. If he'd been less tolerant of her, he might have nipped it in the bud. But he was well and truly under her thumb, and of course he was beholden to her now. All the sacrifices she'd made. The school fees, the piano lessons, the endless shuttling from audition to rehearsal to concert. Being his mother was, he knew, a full-time job.

He sighed. He was being harsh because he was tired. And because it was Saturday, and he didn't want to get on a bus and go to his piano lesson on the other side of the city. She meant well, and he loved her for it, and he knew she had to keep on top of him, because he was a lolloping, lazy teenage boy who would stay in bed all day if he could.

And, of course, they shared the same dream. That was the whole reason for her managing behaviour. And it was so close he could reach out and touch it. His teacher was confident. He was too, for he had been putting the practice in, hours and hours every day. It was only a few weeks until the audition for the Royal College, and then they would know.

Only after the summer, he knew he was slightly off his stride. A little distracted. He was constantly daydreaming and finding his thoughts ambling off somewhere else, away from Chopin and Debussy, away from scherzos and études and sonatas.

To Emily.

He'd always found girls easy company. And he'd had his fair share of admirers. But Emily had found her way straight into his heart. Thinking about her gave him a warm feeling, a Ready-Brek glow. His mind constantly strayed to her grave little face, her earnest expression, her mischievous little smile when something amused her. He did not know what to do.

His mother had sensed his disquiet. She had given him three pep talks in the past week about dedication and focus. She was right, of course – if he wanted to get into the Royal College, he had to practise every day without fail.

'Being good isn't enough,' she told him, again and again. 'Being talented isn't enough.'

And this morning, she had found Emily's Snoopy card where he'd left it on the side in the kitchen after reading it.

'I'm worried about this, darling.'

'Why?' Jonathan looked puzzled. 'It's Snoopy. When did he ever do anyone any harm?'

'Not Snoopy. Emily. You seem very distracted by her.'

'Not really.'

'You are. You drift off. I've seen you daydreaming.'

Jonathan shrugged. He didn't want to talk about Emily. He just wanted to think about her.

'You mustn't sacrifice your future,' his mother said gently.

He stared at her. 'You don't understand, Mum. She's a good thing.'

She shook her head. 'I don't think she's what you need at the moment. Mr Poynter says you've been under par the past couple of weeks.'

'Have you been spying on me?' Jonathan felt a ripple of panic. This was news to him. His teacher had always been nothing other than full of praise. Was he really having doubts?

'Not spying. Caring.' Maureen's lips tightened as if someone had pulled an invisible drawstring. He had noticed that about her lately, the stress she carried in her face. He felt a tug of pity. Her laughter lines seemed to have vanished altogether to be replaced by worry lines, even deeper than the ones she got when his father died.

He looked over at the photograph of his dad on the piano. He was doing this for him too. Trying to make a man whose memory was beginning to fade proud of him. It somehow took the sting out of his death.

It had been his dad who'd seen his promise when he was small and started him on lessons. His dad who took him to the music shop and bought him fresh sheet music on a Saturday, which he would have nailed by Sunday. His dad who put records on the turntable and made him listen, really listen, to each note, to each pause.

Fourteen-year-old Jonathan had played Rachmaninov's Piano Concerto number 2 at his father's funeral. Not brilliantly, but he got through it, the entire congregation holding their breath and each other's hands until he reached the final note.

Maureen had buried herself in Jonathan's musical career to cushion herself from her husband's sudden death, telling herself he would live on in Jonathan's success. Jonathan was grateful for her support. He did, after all, love his music with a passion, and had ambition for himself. But it was so relentless. So intense. Maureen had nothing else in her life. With Emily, Jonathan had seen a glimpse of something else.

But the time wasn't right. His audition loomed. All those years of dedication would go to waste if he didn't focus. And he didn't want to let his father down.

'I'm just very concerned, love,' his mum was saying. 'You've known her less than a month, but she could destroy your entire future. Cut her off now, and all will be well.' She put a piece of notepaper and a pen in front of him on the breakfast table. 'Write to her. You don't have to be cruel. And if she has any notion of what your future means to you, she'll understand.'

Jonathan put his head in his arms on the table. There wasn't much point in arguing with her about them being soulmates. Or about the wonder of what they'd done in bed – he definitely didn't want to discuss that. And his mum was right. He wasn't devoting himself to his music, and he had to, or everything they had worked towards would disappear.

'If you truly mean something to her, she'll wait. You can get back in touch once you've got in.'

He looked up at her, standing over him in her pale pink quilted dressing gown. He felt a flash of hope. That was a good compromise. He would send Emily a letter now, explaining about the Royal College. Then when he was in his mother's good books, he could get back in touch. Hopefully, she wouldn't meet anyone else in the meantime. She was at a girls' school, so she probably wouldn't get much access to other boys.

He picked up the pen and started to write. His mother patted him on the shoulder approvingly and went off to make his breakfast. So he wrote as nice a letter as he could manage.

Maureen picked it up and read it. She nodded, folded the sheet up and put it in a brown envelope.

'Pop her address on. I'm going to get dressed.'

She swept out of the room. For a moment, Jonathan was tempted to take the letter out and write something else, then seal the flap down, hoping to fool his mother. But he couldn't. He scrawled out Emily's address. He wavered halfway through, thinking about how she would

279

feel when she got the letter, then looked at the piece he'd been practising propped up on the piano.

He sealed the envelope, tossed it on the breakfast table and strode over to the piano. He banged out Prokofiev's War Sonatas, bashing at the keys, letting his frustration vent itself through the notes as they got choppier and angrier, hoping that his mother understood the message he was sending her up through the floorboards.

She came back downstairs, dressed in a maroon jumper and flared grey skirt, her feet tucked into brown lace-ups. She stood in the doorway listening for a moment, nodding in approval. Then walked across the room and picked up the envelope.

'I'm just popping out to the post office. Tea and a custard cream when we get back? Then I'll give you a lift to your lesson if you like.'

His fingers crashed down on the keys as she closed the door behind her. He hated custard creams. How could she not know that? She had just made him turn his back on the best thing that had happened to him, but she couldn't remember his favourite biscuit?

He forgave her, though, when she came back from the post office with a packet of chocolate Hobnobs.

'To cheer you up,' she said, slicing through the packet with a sharp knife. 'I know it's horrid, but it will be worth it.'

Two months later, the day of the audition boasted a cheerful blue sky as he navigated his way from the Tube along the Kensington pavements to the Royal College and ran up the wide stone steps at the front. He had done a trial run of the journey the week before to get his bearings. He wasn't going to let anything scupper his chances.

Inside, a white marble staircase with a black decorative edge led upwards to his fate. He had the manuscript bag his father had given him for his thirteenth birthday. Inside were his audition pieces: Beethoven's *Appassionata*, Chopin's Scherzo number 3 and Liszt's *Gnomenreigen*. They were all technically challenging, but not impossible, and he had perfected them at a speed he felt comfortable with. He felt as confident of his ability as he could.

He had refused to let his mother accompany him. It was the first time he had really stood up to her.

'You'll make me nervous. You'll put me off,' he told her, and she didn't argue. She had been more gentle with him of late. He wondered if she felt guilty about Emily. He felt a rush of warmth at the thought of her. He would send her a postcard when he knew he'd got in.

When his turn came, he sat in front of the piano and settled his music on the holder. The panel had welcomed him, politely and warmly. He'd had a chance to warm up in a separate room. This was it, he thought. The moment he had been working towards for the past four years since his father had died. It was almost a memorial to him. He thought he could hear his dad's voice encouraging him and he smiled. He was ready. He lifted his hands and looked at the notes in front of him.

And he froze. He shut his eyes and clenched his fists for a moment. Of course he was nervous. That was allowed.

'Take your time.' A voice floated towards him.

He wiped his hands on the trousers his mother had bought him for the audition. Slightly shiny black polyester. And a short-sleeved white shirt to go with it. She had put one of his father's ties on for him this morning. Tied it in a knot that was choking him now. He put his hand up to loosen it but it was getting tighter. He took in a breath but there wasn't any. He had no breath.

All he could see in his mind's eye was Emily opening the letter his mother had forced him to write, and her dear little face crumpling, and a single tear rolling down her cheek.

He couldn't do it. He didn't want to do it. This wasn't what he wanted at all. He had thought it was, but that was only because he'd been given no other choice.

He wanted to go out into the world and discover other things. Escape from the bars of music that had been his prison. He didn't want years of pressure and practice and pianissimo.

He stood up and picked up his sheet music.

'I'm sorry,' he said, and walked out of the room.

He didn't touch the piano at home again. It sat there, shunned, its lid firmly shut over the keys, gathering dust. The sight of it made him anxious.

'You must get back on the horse,' his mother said. 'All that money, all those lessons, gone to waste.' She had been beside herself when he'd turned up back at the house and told her he'd walked out. 'It's just stage fright. It's all in the mind.'

He ignored her, shutting down completely and withdrew into himself. It was all he could do to get to school. His teachers expressed concern and suggested he be taken to the doctor, who said he was burned out and had been pushed too far.

'When did you last have a day off? From practising?'

'I can't remember,' said Jonathan, who honestly couldn't.

'He hasn't touched the piano since the audition!' his mother protested, and the doctor raised an eyebrow, possibly the first person to recognise the pressure Jonathan had been put under.

He was diagnosed with nervous exhaustion. His mother was limp with remorse and regret, realising that she had pushed him too far. She had lost sight of what was normal in the throes of grief. She didn't want to lose her son too.

She booked them a holiday, to Normandy, and they both looked out at the grey, flat sea, poking cold frites into the buttery winey juice at the bottom of their moules.

'I'm so sorry,' she said. 'I just wanted . . .'

'I know,' he replied, because there was no point in making her feel guilty, because they both knew that if his father hadn't died everything would have turned out differently, and maybe he would be going to the Royal College and maybe he wouldn't, but they wouldn't have spent the past four years trying to focus on something to help them forget their pain.

It was five years before Jonathan found the courage to reach out to Emily.

In the end, he studied history at Bristol University. He never admitted to himself that he chose it because it was a long way from York, but that was certainly an advantage. And he loved it, grew in confidence and became more worldly wise and won pub quizzes and kissed girls and drank horrible warm beer. And decided, afterwards, that he would stay in Bristol, because he loved the warmth of the West Country accent and the maritime history and the suspension bridge. It suited him. It felt like an easier world. A world he could wear more lightly. He decided to train as a teacher. It was not as dull as it sounded, and he began work as a junior master in a large private school, teaching history and helping with the several orchestras.

And one day he walked past a pub in the centre of the city, a dodgy biker pub in a cobbled back street he never quite dared go into. Led Zeppelin and Golden Virginia trailed out of the door followed by a waft of stale bitter. The music stopped him in his tracks. He was whirled back in time to his room at the summer school, her lying in his arms.

'Where are you?' he thought.

The music gave him the courage. The pounding bass was a counterpoint to his heart as he hurried up the road back to his flat. Before he could stop himself he sat and wrote a letter. He could write nothing but the absolute truth.

Dear Em,

I walked past a pub today, and 'Kashmir' was playing. And I realised that you were right all along. It is the best track, by a mile. And I miss you. I live in Bristol. I can give you a guided tour. You haven't lived until you've had a half of scrumpy in the sunshine.

Jonathan

It said everything and nothing. It would either do the trick or not. He had nothing to lose, because he'd already lost everything – his dad, his music, her ... He remembered her address, of course, because you could hardly forget a two-line address when you could remember the whole of Beethoven's *Appassionata* – even if you had chosen not to play it at the most crucial moment in your life.

And off it went, with a commemorative first-class stamp depicting *The Kiss* by Rodin, which seemed perfectly appropriate, although he didn't care as long as it got there.

It was a week before he got a reply.

I'm not sure what to say, Jonathan. I miss you too. But you cut me off. I understand music school was important to you but that really hurt. You don't know what I went through afterwards. The most painful thing in my life.
Em

He could imagine her face as she was writing. The little frown of concentration. The intensity. The careful choice of words. He had expected her to be guarded after what he had done, but there was a weariness to her tone he hadn't expected. She couldn't be with someone else, though. If she was with someone else, surely she wouldn't have answered? He wasn't going to give up.

There was no point in holding back. This was his only chance. He had to spell it out to her, on paper. Make it clear it had been a mistake, how sorry he was, how much he wanted to see her again. Now he had seen her writing, her thoughts on a page, his memory of her was even more vivid. The way she stared at him before they kissed. Her hair spread out on his pillow. Her soft voice in his ear.

I don't blame you for being angry. I was an idiot.
And I didn't get in to the Royal College. I walked

out of the audition. So it was all for nothing and I still haven't forgiven myself. And I'm sorry for causing you so much pain. Please forgive me and give us a chance to try again, if only as friends. Because I haven't met anyone like you since. And I think of you every day. Every day, Em. I can see your face as if it was yesterday. I need you.

Was it too needy? He didn't care. He *did* need her. Her letter came back. Brief. To the point.

I'm not angry with you. You were not the cause of my pain. OK. Let's meet. But be gentle with me, Jonathan. I am not the girl I was.

He frowned. What did that mean? It sounded worrying. Not at all like the Emily he remembered, who wasn't a scaremonger. What had happened? Had someone hurt her? Acid fear flooded his gut at the thought of her coming to any harm.

If she had been hurt, he told himself, it was your fault. You should have looked after her.

He met her off the train a week later. She was standing on the platform, in a blue duffle coat and suede boots, her face a little thinner, her eyes a little larger, her hair cropped short. She saw him walking towards her and her face sort of crumpled and lit up at the same time and she stayed rooted to the spot until he was standing in front of her. The crowds milled around them as they hugged: proper hugging, of the kind where you pull the other person towards you so hard they nearly become you, and your hearts start to beat together.

She was crying, he realised. 'Don't cry, Em. This is a good thing.'

But she couldn't seem to stop and he didn't know what to do except hug her tighter.

'Hey, hey, it's OK. I'm here. I'm not letting you go. Come on.'

They got on a bus and went back up to Clifton, and he took her to his favourite pub that overlooked the suspension bridge. They had pasties, and scrumpy in the sunshine as he'd promised. She seemed quiet, and nervous, possibly even wary, but that wasn't surprising, after what had happened. He talked far too much, as usual, and she laughed quite a lot, eventually, but didn't tell him much.

And he could still feel the magic, but he wasn't sure if she could. There was something holding her back.

Afterwards, they went up to the suspension bridge and stood looking down at the gorge. It was spectacular, the deep ravine with the Georgian terraces looming over it. Jonathan felt a burst of pride at his new city, and was glad to have something to show off to her. He turned to look at her.

Emily was gazing down at the river, far, far below, and her expression was so grave, he felt afraid.

'Em?'

Her eyes were glassy. Was she about to cry?

'I need to tell you something.'

'Tell me.'

'Not here.' She looked around at the cars going over the bridge, the cyclists, the pedestrians. 'Somewhere quiet.'

He felt a terrible sense of foreboding. Was she going to tell him something he couldn't handle? Had someone hurt her? He felt a surge of protectiveness for this new, fragile Emily. He took her hand as they walked back to his flat, and she squeezed his fingers tightly, whether to reassure him or because she was in need of reassurance, he couldn't be sure, but it felt nice.

They arrived at his flat, on the first floor of a six-storey house in a sweeping crescent fronted by a wide pavement.

'Wow,' said Emily.

'Don't get too excited,' he grinned. 'It is, quite literally, a façade. The flat is classic bloke squalor.'

He opened his front door and they walked up the faded pink carpet of the stairs, then into the flat and into the living room, with its garish carpet and mismatched furniture, that he shared with two flatmates. None of them was particularly domesticated. But he was relieved that it was at least tidy – he had cleared out the mugs, glasses and takeaway cartons that morning, and even drawn the curtains.

'They're all out,' he said with confidence. 'We won't be interrupted.'

She sat on the faded chenille sofa. Her hands were twisting in her lap, her fringe across her eyes so he couldn't see the look in them. He was about to go and make a cup of tea when she said something.

'I had a baby.' Her voice was almost a whisper.

He stopped en route to the kitchen, startled, not sure he had heard right. 'What?'

'Your baby. Our baby. I had a baby.'

'Em . . .' He was aghast. 'Tell me you're joking?' He walked over and crouched in front of her, taking her hands. Was she telling the truth? She shut her eyes but tears were still rolling out from under her lids. Big round tears so solid he felt he could pick them off her cheeks and put them in his pocket.

She opened her eyes, looking straight into his, and he knew what she was saying was true.

'I couldn't keep her. They wouldn't let me. I had to give her up.'

He couldn't ask her the obvious. He couldn't say *why didn't you tell me?* Because of course she wouldn't have told him. He had chosen a future without her in it, let alone a baby.

'Her? It was a little girl?' he asked instead.

She nodded. 'I brought you a picture.' She leaned over the side of the sofa to open her bag and pulled out a photograph. 'That's her. Look at her. Our baby.' Her face crumpled again.

And so it was that Jonathan found himself looking at a photograph of the daughter he didn't know he had. A little girl in a white velour babygro, lying on a rug.

'I called her Robyn,' Emily's voice quavered.

'Oh, Em. That's a perfect name.' He was crying now himself.

'I don't even know if they let her keep it.'

She slumped forward onto him, and he took her in his arms, awkward, frightened, unsure of what he was supposed to do. But she seemed to take comfort from his embrace, as she told him everything, at times barely able to articulate what had happened. He kissed her head, pushing her hair back from her tearstained face.

'I'm so sorry,' he kept repeating. 'I'm so sorry. I should have been there. We could have...'

Could they? Two youngsters still at school, with no clue about the world or a baby's needs. He felt angry, with himself most of all, but also with his mother, for forcing them apart, and with Emily's parents, for not being brave enough to stick by her, for taking what seemed to be the easy option.

'What did you do?' he asked her. 'After the baby?'

She sighed. 'My dad got me a job in the housing department. I couldn't face going to university. Pretending to be normal and going to parties and having a good time when my heart was...' She searched for the word. 'Smashed. But I'm OK. I've got my own flat.' Her face brightened. 'When my mum forwarded your letter, it was like the sun coming through my letter box.'

'Oh, Em.' He gazed at her. The feelings were all still there. The Ready Brek glow. The sense of fitting together. Being with her was as right and perfect as well-worn slippers, as buttered crumpets, as a roaring log fire. 'I don't know what to do.'

She was gazing back at him. 'Hold me,' she said. 'Just hold me. That's all that I need.'

37

That Saturday morning, Jonathan came downstairs in his sweatpants and T-shirt all set to head to the shop for the bread run. He was surprised Emily was already up as she loved lounging in bed at the weekends and listening to Radio 4, the cats curled either side of her. He always brought her breakfast: coffee and fresh croissants and strawberry jam.

She was sitting on the sofa in her pyjamas, as white as a sheet.

'I can't do it,' she said.

Jonathan frowned. 'Can't do what?'

She began to cry. He hated it when she cried. He had dedicated his life to stopping her from crying. To making her laugh as much as he could. To immersing her in a world of joy: woodland walks and their silly fat cats and candlelit meals in tiny restaurants and labyrinthine bookshops and big bunches of tulips – there was a vase of them on the table; yolk yellow – and any number of the simple things in life that made you forget what you didn't want to remember.

But he knew he could never fully erase the trauma. It had been a trauma for him, too, when he had found out what happened. But he had never known the baby. It was just a story he'd been told. A story that had affected him, nonetheless, although he was more distressed by the impact it had on the woman he adored.

'I found her,' she was saying now. 'I found Robyn.'

'What?' He stood still, staring at her.

'She got in touch. She got in touch with me.'

Her face showed a jumble of emotions: both overjoyed and overwhelmed.

Jonathan knew she had put herself on a register some years ago, hoping Robyn might make contact. But he had always underplayed it, not wanting Emily to invest too much hope in it. It seemed like an added torture to him. He felt it was best to close the door and move on. But she always said to him she couldn't close the door, just in case.

'Like Wendy's mother in *Peter Pan*, keeping the window open for the children,' she told him, but he thought that life was not like a children's book, with a happy ending. But of course he didn't stop her. He just never mentioned it.

But it seemed he'd been wrong to be pessimistic.

'It was going to be a surprise. I wanted to bring her home for you. Our daughter.' She leaned back in her seat, defeated. 'But I'm scared. I'm supposed to be meeting her.'

'Today?'

Emily nodded. 'We've exchanged a couple of emails. And I wrote to her. I told her about how it all happened. Us meeting at summer school. Then breaking up. Then finding out I was pregnant.' She took in a juddering breath. 'I wanted her to understand why I couldn't keep her.'

She was weeping.

'Hey, hey.' He came to sit by her. 'This is amazing. But I don't want it to upset you. Maybe it's best if you don't meet yet? Give it a little bit more time. We can talk it over together.'

He didn't chastise her for not telling him earlier. He understood Emily. She would want to make everything perfect before she told him. But she had underestimated the emotional impact of meeting her daughter; forgotten how vulnerable she still was, after all this time.

She shook her head.

'She's getting married. Next weekend. She wanted to meet. Find out everything about her past before she...'

'I see,' said Jonathan.

Emily looked at the clock. 'She'll be on her way. It's too late to stop her.'

Jonathan paced around the living room. Emily was right. It would be cruel to renege on the meeting at this late stage. It would have taken courage to make contact, even more to come and meet the mother she had never known. But he wasn't going to force Emily. She wasn't strong enough.

'Would you like me to go and meet her?' asked Jonathan. 'I can talk to her for you. Then we can decide what to do. All of us. Together.'

Emily nodded. 'I'd love that,' she said, slumping with relief. 'There's just one other thing, though.'

Jonathan raised an eyebrow. 'What?'

Emily raked her fingers through Ron's ginger fur, biting her lip. Then she looked up at him.

'I haven't told her about you.'

*

Later that morning, Jonathan walked down the hill into the centre of Bath as if he was sleepwalking, unable to believe what was unfolding. That he was going to meet the daughter they'd never been allowed to love. The daughter they had often talked about. He had never allowed Emily to dwell too long, but he would paint beautiful pictures for her to imagine, of a happy little girl in a flower meadow, dancing in the sunshine. It was the only way they could get through the pain.

They had no more children. They had tried, for a short while, but every month Emily became riddled with anxiety as they waited to see if she was pregnant, and she seemed both disappointed when she wasn't, yet relieved too. It became a torturous cycle, of her both wanting to have a baby and yet fearing it. She was terrified the same thing would happen to her, that she would be plunged into a black world of post-natal despair and paranoia, despite endless reassurance from Jonathan that he would be there to catch her if she fell.

In the end, they decided to stop trying. The agony and the doubt proved too painful. Jonathan had to bury his anger that his wife had been so deeply affected, and search inside himself for an answer, a way of atoning and making up for the void. Though she assured him he was enough.

'I am so lucky to have you,' she said. 'You are all I need.'

And now, their reward had come. The daughter who had slipped through their fingers was back in their life. Jonathan knew that didn't necessarily mean happy ever after. It might be a rocky road. But at least they would know. They didn't have to imagine any more.

He wasn't sure, either, as he reached the centre of town

and began winding his way through the streets, dodging the Saturday shoppers, just how he should introduce himself. In the end, he decided he would do what he always did. Just be himself.

As soon as he walked into the café, he recognised her. The daughter he had never seen. Sitting at a table with her hands curled around a cup of tea, her dark hair coming loose from its ponytail, her skin ivory like her mother's, her profile perhaps more like his.

And as he said her name and she looked up at him with a smile, he felt a sense of peace wrapping itself around him, for now they would have answers, and they could give her answers too, for he saw a myriad of questions in her eyes.

For two hours they sat, barely pausing for breath. They had two coffees (Jonathan), two cups of Earl Grey (Emily) and a Bath bun each as Jonathan told Robyn the missing part of Emily's story, and she told him about life at Hawksworthy Farm.

Robyn was surprised at how at ease she felt with Jonathan. He was so calm and kind and candid. And so delighted to meet her, his eyes behind his glasses filling up with tears every now and then. He choked up when he spoke about Emily, and Robyn could see how much he adored her.

She didn't allow herself to think what might have happened if things had been different. That wasn't what this meeting was about. It was about the future, not the past. At least she hoped so.

'I wonder,' said Jonathan. 'If you would come to the house to meet Emily.' He fiddled with a packet of sugar, nervous. 'You've come all this way and I know it would mean the world. But I understand if it's too much to ask.'

Robyn was silent for a moment. They'd agreed neutral territory, but she understood how overwhelming this must be. It must be bringing back all the distress Emily had been through at the time. And it didn't make sense to come all this way and not see her.

'Or I could go back home and tell her that we've met,' Jonathan offered. 'And see if I can coax her out.'

'No,' said Robyn, standing up, decisive. 'I'd like to meet her.'

'We can get the bus. Or walk. It's quite a way up the hill.'

'I'm used to hills. I climb the dunes every day.'

'OK. I can show you Bath on the way.'

Jonathan insisted on picking up the bill and carrying her bag. They wandered through the streets, Jonathan pointing out the landmarks. They passed the Pump Rooms and the Roman Baths, then made their way up Milsom Street, lined with tempting shops, to the foot of Lansdown Hill.

'We love living here. We moved here from Bristol about ten years ago. It's big enough to be buzzy but small enough to be cosy and there's plenty going on. Em teaches the Alexander technique – posture and breathing; musicians use it a lot. And I teach history at a local senior school.'

'You never went back into music?'

'I did. Eventually. But only for pleasure. Em bought me a piano for my fortieth, so I bash away when the mood takes me. We go to a lot of concerts. It's still a big part of our life.'

They were quiet as they made their way up the hill,

lined with gracious Georgian buildings that peered down inquisitively at them. Eventually they turned into a narrow street, lined either side with small terraced houses in Bath stone.

'This is us,' said Jonathan, stopping outside. 'Are you ready?'

'I think so,' said Robyn. She had lost her earlier butterflies, as Jonathan had been such a kind and calming presence, but now she felt anxious for Emily. What a huge undertaking it must be, to come face to face with the baby you'd wondered about for so many years. 'I hope I'm not going to be a disappointment.'

'You,' said Jonathan, 'could not be further from that.'

He led her to the door, opened it and ushered her inside.

It led straight into an open-plan living/dining room, dominated by an enormous red tapestry sofa with a cat on either arm, one tortoiseshell, one ginger, tails curling like crochet hooks. It was the sort of room that had evolved and grown with its owners, and evidence of their interests was all around: open books, magazines, a half-done jigsaw, an open box of Lindor on a shelf. No television. Wonky shelves groaned under the weight of everything from Patrick O'Brien to Plato to PD James, and the walls were covered in pictures. There was a piano to one side – the birthday present Jonathan had mentioned – and a dining table with a laptop open on it: Robyn wondered if that was the spot where Emily had received her email, and how she had felt when it arrived.

And there, in the middle of the room, in a blue linen dress with big pockets on the front, was her mother.

Emily took in a deep breath and put both hands up to

her mouth as soon as she saw Robyn. She stood, frozen, her hands trembling slightly. One of the cats jumped off the sofa and stalked over to them, like a bouncer trying to fend off trouble outside a night club.

'Em,' said Jonathan. 'This is Robyn. This is our girl.'

Robyn smiled as Emily walked towards her. And the next thing Robyn knew, her arms were around her neck, her cheek was on hers, wet with their mingled tears, and they breathed each other in, mother and daughter.

'Oh,' was all Emily could say, her voice cracking with emotion. 'Oh.'

'I know,' said Robyn. 'I know.'

Emily released her for a moment, looking into her eyes. Robyn saw anxiety and fear, but also wonder and love.

'I couldn't come to the café,' said Emily, stepping back a little to look at her, but not letting go of her hands. 'I was too scared.'

'It's OK. It doesn't matter.'

'I was afraid you wouldn't come.' Emily looked over at Jonathan, her face lit up with joy. 'But she did. Look, Jonathan.'

'I know,' said Jonathan, with a kindly smile.

'Come and sit down.' Emily led Robyn over to the sofa. The cat followed them and jumped up onto the arm. 'This is Hermione.' She patted the remaining cat. 'And this is Ron, of course.' She sat, indicating the space next to her. 'Where do we start? Where do we begin? Are there rules? I don't know . . .'

'I don't either,' said Robyn, sitting down.

Now she was up close, Robyn could see Emily was older than she appeared. There were a few threads of silver in her hair, and some fine lines around her eyes. She was much slighter than Robyn, who had her father's height and strength.

She still couldn't believe it. A mother *and* a father. She'd presumed the young Jonathan she had read about in Emily's letter would have been lost, never seen again after that week at the summer school, relegated to a misty memory. But here he was, as large as life, as wonderful as Emily had described him. Older and wiser, probably, but kind and funny.

'We talked about trying to get you back,' said Emily, holding her hands. 'When we found each other again. But it seemed too cruel. You would have been settled with your new family. We just hoped that one day you might get in touch. And you did.'

'I'm sorry it took me so long.' Robyn felt a shoot of panic. She could have saved them years of wondering, if only she'd started her search sooner.

'You have to be ready,' said Emily. 'It's no good if you're not.'

'It suddenly became important to me when I knew I was getting married.'

'Tell me about him.' Emily's eyes were sparkling.

'Jake is . . .' Robyn searched for the right words. 'Wonderful. He's a landscape gardener, so he's pretty big and strong. He's crazy about surfing. He doesn't care much about money or clothes or any of that kind of thing. But he works really hard.' She pulled out her phone. 'I can show you pictures.' She started scrolling through her photos. 'There. That's him. Outside the house we're doing up. Well, it's a cattle-shed. But it's going to be beautiful.'

Emily peered at the picture of Jake standing outside

the Linhay in his work gear and wellies, pushing a wheel-barrow.

'He looks lovely.'

'I can't believe the wedding is next weekend.' Robyn laughed. 'We didn't see the point in stringing it out, and we only want a simple wedding. But my friend Gwen's organising it all. She loves that kind of thing, and I'm useless. We're having it at Jake's family beach hut. Just a chilled-out do – no fuss.'

'It sounds wonderful.'

Robyn put a hand over Emily's. 'Maybe you should come?' she said, impulsive, carried away with the moment.

'Oh.' Emily frowned. 'I don't think that would be right. It's lovely of you to ask, but I think it would be awkward for your parents. I don't want to overshadow things. We've got lots of time.'

Robyn gazed at her. How wise and thoughtful Emily was. Of course she was right. It would be too soon. The day belonged to her and Jake, and Mick and Sheila, and Rocky. There would be time for other celebrations in the future. Which reminded her that there was another piece of news she had to tell them. She felt the time was right. She knew the news would mean the world to them. She trusted them. They didn't feel like strangers.

'There is something else.'

Jonathan and Emily exchanged worried glances, as if her whole visit might have been a trick, and she was going to tell them she wasn't their daughter after all.

'It's a good thing,' she said, and paused for a moment to find the right words. 'I'm having a baby.' She smiled. 'It's due on the fifth of November.'

She would never forget the looks on their faces. Joy and disbelief in equal measure.

'Oh, Robyn,' said Emily. She was hesitant. She still wasn't sure of her role with her daughter, let alone a grandchild. 'I don't know what to say.'

'I think "congratulations" will do,' Jonathan said. He understood how delicate this new relationship was. How important it was to tread softly. He curled his arm around Emily as a fresh set of tears fell, but she laughed too, and soon all three of them were crying.

'This is more than I ever dreamed of,' said Emily.

And she took Robyn's hand in hers and held it to her heart.

38

Rocky was banging the mud off his walking boots from the last time he'd worn them, wishing he'd done it when he'd put them away, like he did every time. Half of the south-west coast path seemed to be stuck in the treads.

He was secretly glad that Jake and Ethan were away for the weekend while he went on his second date with Melissa. He hadn't asked them for any advice this time. He wanted to stay under the radar. The last thing he wanted was to be spotted out with her and for it to get back to everyone. News travelled fast in Everdene because not a lot happened, and there were spies everywhere. There would be smoke signals and tom toms and Morse code and the gossip would get back home before you did.

He checked his appearance once more, still fearing that there had been something about him that had made Melissa run the first time. Even if she was giving him a second chance. Faded jeans. Checked shirt over a blue T-shirt. A light parka to keep off any wind chill. He looked clean cut and outward bound. He'd sloshed on a little bit too much Aqua di Parma but hoped it had started to fade. There was nothing more off-putting than a man that reeked of too much aftershave.

He looked at the clock. Melissa was coming to pick him up, because she lived further away from Heddon's Mouth. There was still twenty minutes to wait. He looked around for something to do, but the house was immaculate. He'd tried to achieve a tidy-but-lived-in look, because he didn't want to look too uptight if she came in for... whatever.

There was white wine chilling in the fridge, and plenty of Fever Tree mixers, and a fresh bottle of Exmoor gin. And tubs of olives and some nice cheese and a loaf of sourdough.

A knock on the door made him jump. She was early. He smiled. He'd never dare do that to a woman. Fifteen minutes early would mean certain panic. But he was good to go. He picked up his boots, ready to put them on outside. He grabbed his house keys and headed for the door.

He blinked. She was standing there, in a black wrap dress and high suede boots, her hair in tousled waves. A drift of Coco by Chanel hit him, bringing back so many memories he almost couldn't breathe.

'Tina.'

She smiled. Shrugged. Laughed. Ran her fingers through that hair he'd run his own through so many times.

'I couldn't bear it,' she said. 'I wanted to clear the air between us. Before the wedding. I think it's important.' She looked at the boots in his hand. 'Are you going somewhere?'

'I was just about to take the dog for a walk,' he said, making his mind up in an instant. 'But I just need to make a quick phone call first. Come in.'

And he stood to one side as his ex-wife walked past

him. He pulled his phone out of his pocket and dialled Melissa, praying she wasn't out of signal, praying she wasn't about to come around the corner.

'Hi.' She answered, sounding upbeat. 'I'm just on my way.'

'I'm really sorry,' he said. 'I've got a family crisis on my hands. I've got to deal with it. It's really bad timing. I'm so sorry.'

He heard her sigh. 'No problem.'

'I promise you this isn't me dicking you around.'

'It's fine.' She sounded weary. 'I hope things turn out OK.'

'I'll be in touch.'

'Yeah, yeah.'

She rang off. He stared at the phone for a moment, feeling terrible. He hadn't lied. It wasn't his fault. He imagined her, all togged up in the female equivalent of his outfit but with make-up, feeling deflated, now facing an empty afternoon and evening. Not that he flattered himself he was such great company, but enforced solitariness was far more lonely than planned.

There was nothing he could do. Tina had obviously driven here all the way from Enfield. He'd better listen to what she had to say.

He walked back inside. Tina was looking around the cottage, gazing at the paintings on the wall.

'This is sweet,' she said.

The tiny cottage had been all he could afford after the split. A less tolerant man would have been rankled not to have been awarded more, given that he had ended up with the children, but all he had wanted at the time was to be settled and to have peace.

'It's tidier now the boys have gone.'

'I bet.' She smiled, and he thought she looked a little sad. He felt awkward with her here, after all the hard work he'd done to build himself a new life and a new space. He went into the cupboard under the stairs and found a pair of pink wellies one of Ethan's girlfriends had left behind.

'If we're going to talk,' he said. 'We'll do it while we're walking Lara.'

Lara was lying by the sofa, looking warily at Tina.

Tina grumbled a little bit, but relented, kicking off her suede boots and plunging her feet into the boots. 'These are way too big for me.'

'I'll get you some thick socks.'

'We better not go too far. Or I'll get blisters.'

Rocky smiled to himself. She hadn't changed. She was still a city girl through and through. But Lara needed her walk and he wasn't going to sacrifice it for Tina's sake. It would be better to talk in the open air. He didn't want the walls of his own house to ring with conflict.

They'd set off along the coast path that led up the hill and around the point to the lighthouse. The late afternoon sun was low in the sky, backlighting the silver clouds with coral, and the sea below was winding itself up into a fury as the tide came in. Everdene beach was behind them, the row of huts trailing off into the distance, the Shedquarters almost out of sight. Once, it had been the source of their antagonism.

What was she going to say?

'I want,' Tina began. 'To start by saying sorry. It was absolutely all my fault.'

'What?' Rocky was startled. He wasn't expecting that.

'I think I went a little bit mad when we moved here. I couldn't get my head around it. I really missed my friends and family and the bright lights and...' She laughed. 'Enfield. It's my home town. But that's no excuse for what I did.'

'Tina, it was over fifteen years ago.'

'No. I'm not talking about the affair. Fling. Thing. Whatever you want to call it.'

He flinched. It was still painful, the thought of it. However little it had meant to her, it had put the final nail in the coffin of their marriage.

'What was unforgivable of me,' she went on, 'was letting you take all the blame. You took what I did like a gentleman. You never let the kids know what I had done. You let everyone think it was your fault that we split up. That you had been selfish and forced me to move. When I didn't even try. I didn't make any effort. I made up my mind it wasn't for me and used it as an excuse to behave how I wanted.' Her hair was blowing in her face, and she swept it away, impatient. 'You're golden, Rocky. You took the bullet for me and saved my relationship with Jake and Ethan, even though I let you down. Even though I trod all over your dreams.'

They stood on the top of the cliff with the wind buffeting them.

'We're going to be grandparents.' He had to strain to hear her, she was speaking so softly. 'So I want a truce. I want us to be the very best of friends, so we can be the very best grandparents. I want us to be a family again. Support each other, and be kind to each other. Have each other's backs. But we can't do that unless you forgive me.'

He looked out to sea for a moment.

'Of course I forgive you,' he said. 'And thank you. For being big enough to say all of that. It means a lot.'

'What is it they say – you don't appreciate what you've got till it's gone?' She gave a rueful smile. 'It only took me fifteen years to figure it out.'

'Doesn't feel like fifteen years, if I'm honest.'

It certainly didn't feel like over thirty years since that chirpy Saturday girl had asked him out.

'You were a bloody diamond, Rocky. And I was a fool. I've never met a man to match up to you.'

He grinned at her. 'Have there been a lot, then?'

'Not as many as you might think.' She flashed him one of her killer smiles. 'Thing is, the nice ones are boring. And the bad ones are bastards.'

'Oh.' Rocky thought about that equation. 'Which one am I?'

She held his gaze.

'You're the one that got away, Rocky,' she said softly.

There wasn't much he could say to that. He wasn't going to take responsibility for her regret. But he did admire her for coming to see him. He had been a little nervous about how to handle her on the wedding day. It would be so much easier if they were all amicable. For pre-wedding meals, at the registry office, in photographs. And in the future, when the baby was here.

He held out his hand for her to take. 'Truce,' he said, and they shook hands, and he turned away, feeling emotional, whistling to Lara and walking on ahead so Tina wouldn't see *his* tears.

Maybe now he could move on properly, at last? Rid himself of any traces of guilt; any residue of bitterness. No one wanted to bring any of that to a new relationship.

He had still felt the shadow of his failed marriage when he had been out with Melissa. But with those few words from Tina, he felt as if his slate was clean.

Eventually he slowed to let Tina catch up, and they talked, swapping trivial details about their everyday lives, and chatting about Jake and Ethan. And, of course, the wedding. Tina was uncertain what to give them as a present, and Rocky made a few suggestions for the house. He offered to drive her over to the Linhay to see it, but they decided it would be nicer for Jake and Robyn to show her at a later date.

'I've taken the week off,' Tina told him. 'To get ready for the wedding.'

As they turned back from the lighthouse, Rocky felt lighter and freer. Any anxiety he'd had about the wedding day melted away with their reconciliation. It was good, to walk with Tina and feel like companions, years of resentment no longer between them.

He looked at his watch discreetly. If they got back in time, he could text Melissa, see if she'd like to meet for dinner instead. He would have some grovelling to do, but if he was lucky, she might still be free.

39

The sun was low in the sky as Robyn drove back from the train station to Hawksworthy Farm, willing the journey to come to an end. All she wanted was to fall into bed. She was exhausted from the travel and all the emotion. She longed to fall asleep and let her addled brain process everything that had happened. But she knew she had something to do before she had that luxury.

She had to tell Mick and Sheila straight away. She couldn't keep it from them a moment longer. Until today, meeting her mother had only been a dream. Now it was real.

She hoped they would be as overjoyed as she was. She couldn't wait to share with them how wonderful both Emily and Jonathan were, and how kind they had been, but of course she was mindful that this might not be welcome news. Not straight away, anyway. Perhaps they would need the time to digest the shock before she gave them any details.

If only Jake was here. She needed to tell him, too. Would he feel aggrieved that she hadn't trusted him?

Now she was heading down the drive to home, reality was closing in. Uncertainty nipped at her conscience. Her stomach churned with the anxiety. It rather dampened the euphoria she had felt on the train. She told herself to pull herself together. She had to be brave.

Sheila and Mick were sitting at the kitchen table when she came in. There were pieces of paper everywhere – they must be doing the accounts – surrounded by several empty mugs of tea. They looked up, startled, for she had come in quietly and Mouse, their alarm system, hadn't barked at her.

'Oh, love.' Sheila started putting the pieces of paper in a pile. 'How did it go? Show me what you got.' She looked up, eager to look at Robyn's spoils. 'Are your bags still in the car? Dad'll fetch them for you.'

Robyn sat down at the table. She couldn't waste time. If she didn't tell them straight away, she never would.

'I haven't got any bags. I've got something to tell you both.'

Sheila put a hand to her throat. 'Not the baby?'

Robyn realised how serious she must look. She tried to smile.

'Everything's fine. Honestly. It's nothing to worry about. It's just... in the past few weeks, I've been trying to trace my birth mother.'

Both of them stared at her. The clock on the wall ticked slowly. Outside, the evening breeze picked up and began to whump down the chimney.

'I didn't say anything until now. But we got in contact, and I went to Bath today to meet her.'

'You told me you were going shopping.' Sheila looked accusing. 'You said you needed *shoes*.'

'I know. I'm sorry.'

'I don't understand.' Sheila frowned. 'Surely you could have said something?'

'But it might have come to nothing. There was no point.'

'At least we would have known. That you wanted to know.'

'I didn't want to upset you.'

Sheila gave a short bark of laughter. 'So you lied instead?'

'Sheila, love.' Mick gave his wife a warning glance.

'We've always been open with each other. About everything. Haven't we?' Sheila looked stricken.

'You have, Mum. Yes. But when I started looking, I never thought I'd be able to find her. But I did. And it kind of escalated.'

'How long have you known?'

'We made contact about two weeks ago.'

'And you've been keeping it quiet all this time?'

'Because I wanted to wait for the right time. There's been so much going on. The baby. Now the wedding. The Linhay. I didn't want to cause any more stress for everyone.'

'Does Jake know?' Sheila looked accusing.

'Not yet. I didn't want to worry him. He's had so much on. No one else knows.' Except Gwen. And Robyn knew Gwen well enough to know she wouldn't tell anyone. She had needed that one confidante. 'I'll tell him as soon as he gets back.'

'I can't believe it.' Sheila sat back in her chair. She looked devastated. 'I should never have given you that box.'

'Yes, you should, Mum. It was my box. My history.'

'But I never expected you to go behind our backs.'

'It was something I needed to do for myself. It felt . . .

private. I had to figure it all out on my own. Surely you understand that?' Robyn's voice was getting higher.

'No,' said Sheila. 'I don't. Not really.'

'Hey, hey, that's enough now, you two.' Mick had been quiet until now. He turned to Robyn. 'It's all right, love. Maybe you could have warned us, that's all. Talked to us first.'

Robyn hadn't expected this reaction. She'd expected it to be delicate, but she thought her parents would understand. She put her hands up. 'I made a mistake. I'm sorry.'

'And why? Why now, suddenly? After all this time?' asked Sheila.

'Because of the wedding. And the baby. I just suddenly felt I needed to know where I came from.'

Sheila sighed. 'I thought this might happen. Didn't I, Mick? I said to you in the car, remember.'

Mick thought it was best not to say anything, so he gave a half nod, half shrug. Sheila turned back to Robyn.

'We could have done it together. We could have supported you. We've always been here for you.'

Robyn felt tearful. 'I'm sorry. I shouldn't have gone looking. I should have burned the bloody box.'

Sheila looked as if she was about to cry too. Robyn was mortified. She'd hardly ever seen her mum cry. Not even when the cows had gone. Sheila was tough. Not in a bad way, she just always confronted things head on. Her dad was far more vulnerable. She knew Sheila always had her eye on Mick, making sure he wasn't dwelling too much on what had happened. She kept him afloat. So it was strange to see her crumble.

'Mum.' She went over and put her arms around Sheila's

neck. 'I screwed up. I got it wrong. I thought I was doing the right thing. I'm really sorry.'

Sheila stood a while, then shrugged her off, nodding a curt acceptance of the apology.

'So,' said Sheila. 'What's she like then?'

'She's . . . very nice. Normal. Ordinary.' She swallowed. She had to tell them the rest. 'And . . . my dad. He was there too.'

There was silence. Robyn shut her eyes as she waited for the explosion. But there was no explosion.

'You met your real dad?' Mick managed at last, his face white.

Robyn sighed. 'Not my *real* dad, no. You're my real dad. I met my birth dad. They got together again. After you adopted me.'

'I can't believe this.' Sheila looked stunned. 'This is devastating.'

Mick put his head in his hands. Sheila went to his side and held his shoulder, glaring at Robyn.

'Have you any idea what this is doing to us?' she asked.

'But you both know how much you mean to me. You mean the world.' Robyn felt desperate. 'It was just something I wanted to do and now I can see I did it all wrong and I'm sorry.'

'It's all right, love.' Mick looked up, weary. 'It's just a shock, that's all.'

'I'm sorry,' said Sheila. 'I can't handle this, after everything else today.'

She choked back a sob as she left the room. Robyn felt overwhelmed. She was exhausted and confused, with no idea how to get out of the mess she had started.

'I tried to do the right thing. It's not fair. It was hard

for me, you know. I wanted to find her, but I didn't want to hurt anyone. How was I supposed to do it?'

'I understand, love. She'll come round, your mum. Give her a bit of time. You know she doesn't like surprises.'

'What did she mean, "after everything else"?' Robyn wiped away her tears angrily. She wanted to be calm and composed, but she could feel hysteria rising.

'We had somebody come and look round the farm.'

'You're selling Hawksworthy?'

Mick looked at her, his face bleak. 'I guess you're not the only one with secrets.'

Robyn flinched, and he regretted his harshness.

'I'm sorry. I didn't mean—'

'I'm sorry, Dad,' said Robyn. 'I need to go.'

And before he could stop her, she was out of the door. Mick stood in the kitchen, not knowing who to go after. His wife or his daughter.

His daughter, he decided. Robyn was pregnant. Jake was away. And although she'd upset them, she wasn't a malicious girl. She'd thought she was doing the right thing.

He sighed and picked up his coat. He hated conflict. Sheila didn't deal very well with not being in control. The film director hadn't given them any indication of whether he was interested after he'd been to look around earlier. Geoffrey Minard hadn't been able to give them any indication of whether he would put in an offer. And not knowing made Sheila very edgy.

Which was probably why she'd taken Robyn's news so badly. He was sure once she'd had a bit of time to think about it, she'd calm down.

He was about to go after Robyn when he turned to see Sheila in the doorway with tears streaming down her face.

'I'm sorry,' she sobbed. 'It's just . . . that's the thing I've been dreading since the day she arrived, and I don't know how to handle it.'

'Hey. Come here.' Mick held out his arms and let his wife step into his embrace. And as he held her, he thought of how many times he had comforted her in this very kitchen. After all the babies they'd lost. While they'd been waiting for news of adoption. The time that Robyn's mother had changed her mind after the baby was born, and they had thought they'd lost her.

The day they'd found out Robyn was coming to them after all.

If they could get through all of that, they could get through this.

40

Robyn ran over the fields behind Hawksworthy Farm and down the track, tears streaming down her face until she came to a halt in front of the Linhay. She looked at their future home in the evening light, the red roof glowing crimson and the glass front glittering as the last of the sun hit it. She could see the sea start to darken, and hear it whisper to her as it always had, a reassuring murmur. A sharp wind blew in from the east, slicing through her thin shirt without a moment's consideration. The very last of April, conflicted to the end, bringing both warmth with her sun then chilling you to the bone on a whim.

Just like today. A day of joy and surprise, and now despair. She'd messed everything up at what was probably the most important time of her life. When she needed everyone more than ever. She'd been insensitive, she realised now. She'd been so caught up in her own need to uncover her past, she'd underestimated their fragility. Especially Sheila's. Sheila who had always seemed so redoubtable and invincible but was as vulnerable as any of them. Of course she was.

What had she been thinking, going off to Bath like that without telling anyone? What kind of selfish little bubble had she been in? She'd thought the adoption was all about her, but of course it wasn't. Other people's feelings came into it too, but she hadn't considered them enough. Just scampered off with some romantic notion of ecstatic reunions and one big happy family.

She opened the front door of the Linhay. It was cold and silent, and she shivered a little as she crept up the stairs to the nursery. She pushed open the door and went over to the window. It was almost the same view as she'd always had in her attic bedroom. It should have comforted her, but all she could think about was what her parents must have been through before they had her. She was cruel to bring that memory back when all they had ever wanted was to make her safe. They'd cherished her. And she'd thrown it all back in their faces.

And then she remembered Emily's story too. The thought of having her own baby taken away from her didn't bear thinking about. She suddenly felt very afraid, as if what she had done might bring about some terrible retribution.

Stay calm, she told herself. But she couldn't. She needed Jake. She needed his strength, his voice of reason. His arms around her. She pulled her phone out of her pocket and dialled his number, praying he was in signal, praying he wasn't five pints down in a pub somewhere.

The phone rang out and went to voicemail. She gulped down a sob.

'Jake? It's me. I need you. I've really screwed up. I've upset Mum and Dad. And there's something I need to tell you. If you pick this up, can you phone me back?'

She hung up, her hands trembling. She was properly sobbing now, with the emotional ordeal of the day, and the distress of upsetting her parents. She tried some deep breathing, looking at the sun as it sank into the sea. The house was in darkness now. She felt a little calmer. She'd go back to the farmhouse. Try and talk it through with Sheila and Mick. They had always taught her not to go to bed on an argument. She would try and explain again, how she hadn't meant to hurt them.

She headed out into the hall, using her hand on the wall as a guide. It was almost pitch-black. She started towards the stairs and felt for her phone again. She'd better call Jake back. Leave a less hysterical message and tell him not to worry, that it was all a misunderstanding. She'd explain it all tomorrow when he got back.

It would be OK, she told herself, as she lifted the phone to her ear.

But as she stepped down onto the first stair, she lost her footing. She went to grab at the bannister but there wasn't one yet, just a smooth wall. She felt herself in freefall, the phone flying out of her hands and beating her to the bottom where it smashed on the limestone floor.

She landed there seconds later. She lay on her back, staring into the blackness, as a searing pain took the breath out of her, slicing through her. This was it, she thought. She had got what she deserved.

41

Emily and Jonathan were curled up together on the sofa. Once Robyn had gone, the house felt different. She had been there, their girl, in the four walls that had been their home for so long, and she had cast a spell over it. It had always been a haven for them, but now there was an overriding sense of peace and calm. A settling. Only the cats didn't sense it, sitting on their laps, jostling for pole position and clawing at their legs. But that was Ron and Hermione, endlessly needy and attention-seeking. They loved them for it.

'Tell me again,' said Emily, like a child who wanted the same bedtime story told over and over again. She still felt as if it had all been a dream.

'I walked into the café. And I saw her, at the back, and I knew straight away it was her. I didn't have to ask. She was *us*, Em.'

Emily put her head to one side, looking at the selfie they had taken of the three of them.

'I think she looks most like you.'

'Don't wish that on her, poor thing. She's you all over.'

'But she's got your hair. And your eyes.'

'She's got your sense of calm. And determination.'

'Your kindness.'

'Your laugh. Your laughs are identical.'

'I can't believe how lucky we are.'

Jonathan nodded. 'I'll be honest, I didn't think it would ever happen.'

'I never gave up hope. I used to wake up, every morning, wondering if this might be the day she got in touch.'

'You never told me that.'

'It wasn't a big thing. But it was always there. I learned to live with it.'

'Well, you don't have to worry any longer.'

'No. Even if we never see her again, at least I know that she's happy. That she's safe and secure.'

They sat for a moment, in silence, looking at the photo.

'I think,' said Emily finally, 'relief is one of the best feelings in the world. Especially the relief of finding something you've lost. You can keep going back to it, and it's still there, that warm glow.'

Jonathan ruffled her hair. 'I'm just happy for you. I didn't go through what you did. I'll never forgive myself for not being there.'

'You're here now. That's all that matters. We were only babies ourselves. We weren't in control of what happened.'

'Thank God,' said Jonathan, 'for Led Zeppelin. That's all I can say.'

Emily laughed. Jonathan always knew the moment to step back from introspection and bring levity. They'd had 'Thank You' as their wedding song, as a tribute to the band that had brought them together in the first place and then for a second time. It was *their* song, the one they agreed meant the most to them as a couple, when they'd finally tied the knot.

Jonathan got up and went to the turntable, tipping the

album out of its sleeve and slipping it onto the turntable. Then he turned and held out his arms. Emily stood up and walked over to him as the intro began, and they danced together, her head on his shoulder, both of them reflecting on their memories. That magical summer. The heartache that followed. Their reunion. Their wonderful wedding day, with her parents and his mother, for they had refused to let what had happened cast a shadow over their families. In their own ways, their parents had done what they thought was best for them, out of love.

The only other person at the wedding was Olivia Bembridge. Emily didn't think she would have got through it all without Olivia's support. She had carried on teaching her over the summer after the baby had been taken away, and the music had helped to heal Emily's broken heart and broken spirit. Her cello was still in the corner of the living room, always there for her when she wanted its comfort.

Later, Jonathan curled himself around Emily in bed. As he lay there with his arms around her, he realised it was the first time since they had found each other again that she had slept without disturbance. Usually, she was restless and wakeful. She would have little nightmares and cry out. Sometimes she would wake herself up sobbing, and she never knew what the matter was and he never knew what to do except hold her until she went back to sleep. But tonight she was sleeping sweetly and soundly, without waking once.

And he realised that at last, after thirty years, the nightmares were behind her and she was at peace.

42

Mick's phone was ringing. Mick didn't think it had rung so often in all the time he'd had it as this week. He wondered if it was Geoffrey to say the deal was on. Or off. He looked over at Sheila, who was more composed now. Should he leave the room to take the call?

Or maybe it was Robyn. He should go and find her. She'd been gone nearly half an hour, and it had grown dark in the meantime.

He looked at the screen. It was Jake. He was puzzled. He was off on his stag thing, surely? He'd dutifully asked Mick along, out of politeness, but he'd said no. It wasn't his sort of thing, and Rocky wasn't going either. But it was good of him to ask.

'Hello?'

'Mick.' Jake's voice was urgent. 'I'm calling you because I didn't want to worry Sheila. I had a call from Robyn. She left a message saying you had a row? But I can't get through on her phone.'

Mick thought carefully before replying. 'Oh dear. Yeah. We had a bit of a disagreement. Not a row, as such.'

'Can you see if she's all right? Let me know if I need to come back?'

'I'm not sure where she's gone, if I'm honest. I'll take a look.'

Sheila was looking at him, curious.

'Ring me back, would you?' asked Jake.

'Course.'

Mick rang off and put his phone in his pocket. He was going to try and play this down. He didn't want to put fuel on the fire.

'Robyn rang Jake. He missed her call but he can't get through to her. We'd better see if we can find her.'

Sheila rushed to the window.

'Her truck's still in the yard. So she can't be far. She must be over at the Linhay.' She looked anxious. 'What did she say to him? I feel so bad. I shouldn't have reacted like that—'

'Shush. We'll sort it. Come on.' Mick grabbed his torch from the hook beside the back door, and the two of them set off across the fields. The night, now it had come, was relentlessly black, as it always was here unless the moon was full, but it was behind clouds tonight. Their flashlight lit the way, and luckily the path was familiar. They reached the front door. It was open and they looked at each other anxiously.

'She can't still be in there. It's pitch dark.'

Mick pushed it open.

'Robyn?' he called.

'Dad?' came a tiny voice.

He pointed his flashlight into the hall and there they saw her. A crumpled figure at the foot of the stairs.

'Get an ambulance,' Sheila flew to her daughter's side.

'I fell.' Robyn tried to lift her head. 'I slipped and fell.'

'Don't move her, whatever you do,' said Mick, pulling out his phone, his face grim with fear.

'Where does it hurt, Robyn? Tell me.' Sheila began to run her hands over her daughter, looking for injury.

Robyn was as pale as skimmed milk. She looked up and held out her hand.

'Mum,' whispered Robyn. 'I'm sorry. I'm so, so sorry.'

As she spoke, she slumped back on the floor, her eyelids fluttering.

'Ambulance,' said Mick into the phone. 'My daughter's fallen down the stairs. She's pregnant.'

'Tell them to hurry,' said Sheila, and she began to pat Robyn's cheek. 'Robyn. Stay with us. It's OK. We're here. It's Mum and Dad. We've got you. We've got you, love. It's going to be all right...'

43

The main hospital in Bamford was over half an hour's drive from Hawksworthy, but there was usually an ambulance parked up outside Tawcombe, as they were often needed on a Saturday night. It still felt like hours until it arrived, although it was only fifteen minutes before Mick spotted the lights coming down the drive and went to wave them down.

Within minutes the ambulance was parked outside the Linhay and the driver and two paramedics disembarked in their high vis uniforms, carrying bags of kit.

'She's here,' said Sheila, trying to disguise her panic, ushering them through to the hall, where she had covered Robyn with a dust sheet she'd found.

'What have we got here, then?' said the driver. 'What have you been doing to yourself?'

The driver bent down next to Robyn. She had such an air of calm and matter-of-fact kindness that everyone felt at ease. Robyn tried to sit up.

'Don't worry about me. I'm fine. I'm just worried about the baby.'

'All right. Just lie back down. Let's take a look. How far along are you?'

'About sixteen weeks.'

'Any bleeding?'

'I don't think so.' Robyn's voice quavered.

Between them, the paramedics took Robyn's obs and examined her gently. There were no obvious injuries, but she was trembling, shaking with the shock.

'Ok. We'd better take her in and get a scan. I'll call the maternity unit,' said the driver. 'Does someone want to come with us?'

'Definitely,' said Sheila.

'All right. You can come in the ambulance. Your husband better follow in a car or you'll be stranded in Bamford. It's a hell of a taxi fare back to here.'

'Are you OK to drive, Mick?'

Mick nodded, tight-lipped with worry. 'I'll be right behind.'

'Have you phoned Jake?' asked Robyn.

'Yep. They've already left. If they step on it, they should get to Bamford about the same time as us.'

As the paramedics led Robyn out to the ambulance and settled her in, Sheila came over to Mick. They embraced for a moment, holding each other.

'I'll never forgive myself if she loses the baby,' said Sheila, tearful.

'It was an accident,' said Mick. 'It wasn't your fault.'

'It was,' said Sheila. 'We should have sat down and talked it out.'

'You were upset.'

'I was selfish. I was only thinking about myself.'

'It was a shock.'

Sheila shut her eyes, blocking out the memory. 'She's going to be all right, isn't she?'

'She is,' said Mick. 'I promise you. Now go on. They're ready to go.'

He watched his wife head into the back of the ambulance. His lips tightened. It was his job to protect his daughter. He'd sworn he always would, the day she had arrived. He'd failed. He should have gone straight after her, then this wouldn't have happened.

But it had, and now they had to hope against hope that she and the baby would both be all right.

He waited until they shut the doors then headed back to the farm. He would only be five minutes behind.

In the ambulance, Sheila sat in the little chair reserved for companions next to Robyn, who was strapped into the bed. The vehicle sped through the country lanes, the headlights picking out the overhanging trees and twisted trunks. The moon came out from behind the clouds as if to help guide them on their way. Sheila couldn't stop thinking – if Robyn hadn't phoned Jake, and he hadn't phoned Mick, Robyn could have lain there all night.

'I'm so sorry,' she whispered. 'I should never have gone over the top like that. You took me by surprise, that's all. We love you so much, me and your dad. But you had every right to find your mum.'

Robyn smiled and squeezed her hand.

'I love you, Mum. You and Dad. You know that. I didn't do it because—'

'Shhhh,' said Sheila. 'Not now.'

The paramedics around them worked quietly, checking her blood pressure and trying to keep her comfortable, phoning ahead to the maternity unit with details.

At last they arrived in Bamford, circling roundabout

after roundabout on the by-pass before arriving at the hospital. Sheila climbed out of the ambulance and hovered, waiting for Mick, who had parked the Land Rover before hurrying over.

'Is she all right?' he asked.

'So far.' Sheila shivered in the night air. She hadn't thought to put a coat on when they'd left.

'Here.' Mick took off his fleece to give to her.

'No, you're all right,' she protested, but he insisted on putting it on her, the only thing he could do to be helpful.

'We're going to take her up to the maternity unit,' said one of the team as they led a pale and shaken Robyn out of the ambulance.

'Can one of us come with her?' asked Sheila.

Robyn shut her eyes. She felt sick with tiredness. She just wanted to sleep. 'I want Jake.'

'He's on his way,' said Mick. 'He should be here any minute.'

Bamford was on the way to Exeter. They wouldn't be far off.

He'd filled Jake in on the details of what had happened on the journey over, putting his phone on loudspeaker. Jake was in the hire van while Ethan drove him.

'Robyn went to Bath to find her birth mother,' Mick told him. 'They contacted each other a week or so ago and arranged to meet.'

'What?' Jake was dumbfounded. 'Why didn't she tell me?'

'I suppose she wanted to sort it out for herself. You know Robyn.'

'But how did the accident happen?'

'Sheila didn't take it too well when Robyn told her

about finding her mum. She got a bit upset. Then Robyn got upset and went off to the Linhay . . .' Mick trailed off, remembering the commotion. He should have stepped in. He should have handled it better. 'She missed a step and fell down the stairs in the dark.'

'Shit.' Jake sighed. 'If I'd known, I'd have gone to Bath with her. What was she thinking?'

'Well, I don't know.'

'Anything could have happened. Do you know who this woman is? Her mother?'

'By all accounts, she was very nice.' Mick paused. 'And she's still with Robyn's dad. She met her dad too.'

There was a moment while Jake took in this revelation.

'I can't believe all this was going on while I was hanging off a bloody zip wire.' He didn't know whether to be cross or exasperated or just plain upset.

'We're all a bit upside down over it.'

'Yes,' said Jake, realising how much more distressing it must have been for Mick and Sheila. 'I'm sorry, it must have been a shock for you both.'

'We didn't handle it very well.'

Jake was silent for a moment. 'There's no point in blaming anyone.'

'No.' said Mick, grim. 'All that matters now is she's all right. What about Clover?'

'We've told her what's happened. She wanted to come with us, but we managed to persuade her not to.'

'We can't have too many people.'

'Course not. And the lads are looking after her.'

'OK. See you at the hospital.'

*

In the hire van, Jake hung up, grim faced.

'All right?' asked Ethan.

'I dunno. It's a bit crazy. Apparently Robyn went off to find her birth mother today. I had no idea. She never said anything to me about it.'

'Bloody hell.' Ethan made a face. 'I knew she was adopted. But that's a pretty big deal.'

'She found her dad too. They're still together. Her birth parents.'

'Wow.'

'Poor Mick and Sheila. They must have been gutted.'

'Pregnant women do crazy things sometimes, don't they?' Ethan told him. 'Although it's probably best not to say that . . .'

Jake shook his head. 'Why didn't she talk to me about it? I'd have gone with her. Anything could have happened!'

'Yeah, but you know Robyn. She won't have wanted to worry anyone. She'll have wanted to handle it herself.'

'Bloody strong-minded independent women,' said Jake, rueful.

They sat in silence for a moment as Ethan put his foot down on the quiet night road. He looked sideways at his brother.

'She'll be all right, buddy,' he said. 'Robyn's a tough one.'

And now, suddenly, Jake was there, striding up to the ambulance where they were all gathered, still in the clothes he'd been wearing for the zip wire, sweaty and dishevelled. He went straight over to Robyn and took her in his arms.

'What have you been doing?' he said, his voice strangled with emotion.

'I'm so sorry.' Robyn leant against him, weeping.

'Let's take you up to the ward,' said the nurse who'd been sent to meet them from the maternity unit. 'Are you the father?'

'Yeah.'

'I suppose we'll have to go?' said Sheila, her voice very small.

'I'll let you know as soon as we know anything,' Jake promised.

The small group were hurried inside, leaving Mick and Sheila standing in the cold night air, holding hands, watching after their daughter as she was led away.

Robyn and Jake were taken up to the maternity unit and taken to a bed at the end of the ward, a yellow curtain swished around them to hide them from curious eyes. Most of the patients had settled down for the night, but some of them had been on bed-rest for weeks, so a drama was of interest.

'Let's see if we can find that heartbeat,' said the nurse. Everyone had such an air of calm that Robyn felt re-assured as she was wired up to the foetal heart monitor. She clutched Jake's hand while they waited.

'It's going to be OK,' he said. 'That baby will be tough, like its mum.'

Robyn tried to smile, but she felt sick with tension. She shouldn't have done what she'd done. She should have left the box closed. She had always feared what was inside. Always worried that it was going to unleash something she couldn't control. And now the worst had happened. She should never have opened it—

'There!' The nurse smiled in satisfaction. They listened

as the whooshing sound made itself known. Their baby's heartbeat.

Two tears slid down Robyn's cheeks. Jake lifted her hand and pressed it to his mouth, his own heart pounding. He began to breathe again.

'We'll leave that on for a while. Try and relax. You'll be staying in overnight. And we'll get you to a scan as soon as we can.' The nurse left, pulling the curtain back round them.

'I'm so sorry,' said Robyn, as soon as they were alone.

'What were you thinking?' he whispered to her.

But he didn't chastise her. Every time he thought of her falling down those stairs he felt sick. If only they'd put the lights in earlier. If only he hadn't let Ethan talk him into a stag night. If only she'd trusted him enough to tell him about looking for her mother. That was what hurt him the most: that he thought they shared everything, yet she hadn't let him in on her secret.

Now was not the time to ask her why.

Later, at the scan, while the sonographer checked everything over thoroughly, they were able to see the baby on the screen again, moving around quite happily, and visibly larger than the last time.

'We'll keep an eye on you in the next month or so. And of course if you have any bleeding, come straight in. But as far as I can see, all is well,' the sonographer reassured them. 'Babies are surprisingly resilient. But be careful.'

As soon as they left the consulting room, Robyn called Mick and Sheila. They were in the kitchen, none of them wanting to go to bed until they had news. Sheila snatched up the phone in the kitchen on the first ring.

'It's all OK, Mum,' Robyn told her. 'They've done a scan and the baby's fine. Live and kicking.'

'Oh, thank God,' said Sheila, giving Mick the thumbs up.

'They've said I can go home in the morning.'

'Just one slight problem,' said Jake. 'I haven't got my car, remember.'

'We're stranded, Mum,' laughed Robyn shakily. 'We'll have to get a taxi.'

'Ethan will come and get us.' Jake told her.

'Don't be silly. Your dad'll come and get you. Let us know what time,' said Sheila. 'And I'd better phone your sister. She's been calling us non-stop for news.'

Robyn smiled.

'Send her my love.'

She hung up, and the emotion hit her. All those people worrying and caring about her. She leant against Jake, overcome with a wave of tiredness.

'Come on,' he said. 'You need to sleep. You and that baby of ours.'

They made their way back to the bed on the maternity ward. Jake was allowed to sleep in the chair next to her – there was no way he was leaving. He pulled the sheets and blankets over her to tuck her in.

'Promise me,' he said, 'you will never keep anything from me again. Ever.'

'I promise,' she said.

'We don't have secrets, Robyn. It's a deal-breaker.'

'I should have trusted you. I should have trusted Mum and Dad. I know that now.' She sighed. 'But I'm *glad* I found them. And if I hadn't done it now, I never would. And I think you're going to really like them.'

'I'm sure,' said Jake. 'But tread carefully. Your mum and dad are very special.'

Robyn was quiet for a moment. 'That's exactly what Mum said when she gave me the box,' she said eventually. 'And that's what I was trying to do. But there was never going to be a right way of doing it. Except keeping the box closed forever. And that wouldn't have been fair. On me, or Emily and Jonathan.'

She was gripping the edge of her bedsheet, her face pale, her hair wild around her.

'Hey,' said Jake. 'It's OK. We're going to work through this, all of us together. You didn't do anything wrong. You didn't mean any harm.'

Robyn gazed into the middle distance, thinking back over everything. 'No. I thought I was doing the right thing. I didn't mean to hurt Mum and Dad.'

Jake leaned forward, taking her hands. 'They understand. I *promise* you.'

And then she smiled. 'But I found her. I found my mother. And my dad too.' She struggled to sit up. 'Did they bring my bag?'

Jake put his finger to his lips, anxious not to wake anyone else on the ward.

'Shhhh,' he said. 'Lie down. Yes, your bag's here. Your mum brought it.'

'There's a letter inside. I want you to read it. It explains everything.'

He burrowed inside the bag until he found the envelope with Emily's letter inside. Robyn nodded.

'Read it. It tells you everything.' She lay back on the pillows, closing her eyes. She was so tired.

And so, in the dark quiet of the ward, Jake read the

letter by the light from his phone as Robyn slept. And as he reached the end, he wiped away a tear, reaching out for Robyn's hand. And he held it all night long, just as Robyn held Emily's finger on that last night before they were separated, never knowing if she would see her daughter again.

44

At six o'clock on the morning of her wedding, Robyn decided it was OK to get up. She'd been awake since five, relishing the excitement of the day ahead and the relief that the day had arrived, and all was well.

The sun was shining, although when she looked across the sea she could see dark clouds in the distance over Tawcombe. You could never tell what the weather would do here. It could change in an instant. It was an occupational hazard for her, wondering if it might rain. But she had no control over it, so she wasn't going to worry. After what had happened this week, all that mattered was that she was all right, and the baby was all right, and she had everyone she loved around her on her wedding day.

She pulled on a T-shirt and sweatpants and crept out of the house. She knew Mick and Sheila would be up any moment, for they were early risers, but she wanted a few moments of peace to herself. She slipped out of the back door and across the fields to the small copse between the farm and the Linhay.

She bent down and began picking the best blooms, still wet with dew. She didn't want an expensive bridal bouquet. A little bunch of bluebells from Hawksworthy felt much more meaningful. This was her favourite place at her favourite time of year, the magnificent carpet of flowers under the oak trees bright with spring optimism. They didn't pick them, usually, but she felt this was a special occasion and the bluebells wouldn't mind her borrowing just a few.

She ran back to the farmhouse and into the kitchen.

'There you are.' Sheila smiled. She was already peeling off bacon and putting it into a pan. 'Oh, those are lovely.'

'I thought I'd have them as a bouquet. I wasn't going to have one, but I thought of these when I woke up.'

Sheila nodded her approval.

'Give them here. I'll sort them for you. Tea's in the pot.'

'Thanks.' Robyn sat at the table and poured herself a cup while Sheila plunged the stems of the flowers into boiling water to sear them.

On the table stood a card that had arrived the day before. Robyn picked it up to read it again. Inside the words were simple.

To Robyn and Jake,
wishing you a life of happiness together,
with love from Jonathan and Emily

'They could have come, you know.' Sheila said, wrapping the stems in a white silk ribbon.

'No. They honestly didn't want to. It's far too soon. They didn't feel it was right – it's our day.'

Sheila nodded, snipping the ribbon ends at an angle and putting the flowers in a jug to stay fresh.

'But thank you,' said Robyn. 'For understanding.'

'When I read that letter, it nearly broke my heart,' said

Sheila, shaking her head. 'That poor girl.' She reached over and squeezed Robyn's hand. 'I'm glad you found her. For Emily's sake.'

'Me too.'

'And we'll sort out a day after the wedding. Get them over to meet us. I know it will be tough. But it's the right thing to do.'

'Thanks, Mum. I know how grateful she is to you and Dad. I know she'll want to thank you.'

Sheila nodded, at a loss for words. She still found the subject very difficult.

'Bacon sandwich?' she asked, for providing food for her loved ones was far preferable to discussing deep emotions. 'It'll be a long time before you get a chance to eat.'

'I would love one,' said Robyn. She looked around the kitchen, thinking how much she was going to miss it, the chaos and the cooking and the chatter. It had been such an important part of her life. And Clover's. She thought of all the birthdays and Christmas mornings; the first time she had brought Jake here for Sunday lunch.

Geoffrey Minard had phoned the day before to say the film director had made an offer.

'A hundred grand less than we asked,' he said triumphantly. 'But we'd stuck an extra two on, so win–win.'

Mick and Sheila had accepted his offer immediately, and put in a firm offer to Rocky for the house at Dandelion Court.

'You're sure about selling, Mum?' Robyn asked now. 'You're not just doing it because of Dad?'

'Not at all,' said Sheila. 'To be honest, I can't wait. To have a house that gets warm at the flip of a switch, with no overflowing gutters. And decent broadband.'

Sheila had a Netflix addiction and was constantly infuriated by the low download speed at Hawksworthy.

'You don't think you'll miss it here?'

'I'll miss the view. The sea. But I can come to you if I need to see that.'

'And the kennels? The dogs?'

'I love the dogs. You know that. But it's bloody hard work.' Sheila put two thick pieces of bacon between two slices of bread and cut it in half diagonally. 'I'm going to talk to the vets. They've been asking me for years to do puppy training classes for their clients. I've always been too busy. But I reckon now is the right time. It would just do me, along with a bit of freelance work. I can please myself.'

She put the sandwich on a plate and put it in front of Robyn.

'I'm proud of you, Mum. For not being afraid of change.'

Sheila shrugged. 'There won't be much change. It's people that matter, isn't it?'

Robyn chewed on her bacon sandwich. They would all be the same, all of them, whether they were at Hawksworthy, or the Linhay, or Dandelion Court. And they would still all come together at the Shedquarters, on a Friday, to share food, and what had happened to them that week. The little haven that brought all the strands of the family together, that was waiting for them today.

'Yes,' she said. 'You're right. It's people that matter.'

45

Every single work surface in Gwen's little kitchen was covered in cooling racks, Tupperware boxes, tins and baking trays. Downstairs, Boyd's was the same. He'd offered Gwen his kitchen as backup, when he could see the catering was getting out of control. He'd even taken some of the cooking off her hands, as he wasn't a bad chef. She'd trusted him with sausage rolls – followed to her exacting recipe, which involved onion marmalade and poppy seeds – and he'd made his speciality focaccia, with rosemary and sea salt.

'Blimey,' said Gwen when he offered her some to try. 'You're quite the chef.'

'I'm almost perfect,' said Boyd. 'It's very hard to live with.'

'Right, well, we'll have a dozen loaves for the wedding, in that case.'

'Consider it done.'

They'd become as thick as thieves after Gwen had done his makeover. They had so much in common. Not specific things – their tastes were quite different, though they enjoyed learning from each other – but they both loved exploring, eating out, cooking, burrowing about for antiques, listening to music. She had taken him to all her favourite local places. The little French restaurant you wouldn't know about unless you were in the know. The back-street auction rooms that were a treasure trove. Secret coves for picnics.

And he'd offered himself up as her assistant for the wedding.

'I've got nothing else to do. One board meeting a month, that's all I'm committed to now the girls have taken over. I'll only get into trouble if I don't occupy myself.'

'Right,' said Gwen. 'You don't know what you've let yourself in for.'

It turned out that Boyd was very handy and could create the wonderful things she had in mind out of a few old bits of wood and some sacking. All she had to do was show him a picture on Pinterest and off he would go in search of materials.

'A chef *and* a carpenter,' she said, admiring, when he created an archway made of reclaimed wood and muslin and strands of nautical rope, decorated with starfish, to use as a frame for taking photographs.

'I believe I'm what's known as a renaissance man,' he laughed, making no attempt at modesty.

The week before the wedding had been spent in a frenzy of cooking, shopping, decorating and list-making. And now it was the big day. They were up at five, cooking the things that could only be done at the last minute.

Gwen had taped a timetable to her kitchen wall. They had to be out of here by half past eight to get to the beach. They'd loaded up both cars last night and taken a load of stuff to the Shedquarters to be stored overnight.

Boyd was watching her ice a triple batch of biscuits she'd taken out of the oven at six. They were in the shape of beach huts, and she was decorating them with Robyn and Jake's initials in white. She wore a chambray shirt and rolled-up jeans and sneakers, a big blue apron wrapped round her, icing sugar in her hair and on her cheek.

He watched as she concentrated, the precise flick of her wrist executing the letters to perfection.

'You really care, don't you?'

Gwen looked sideways at him. 'Of course I do. This is so important to me. I love Robyn.'

He felt his heart flutter. He wanted to reach out and brush away the sugar from her cheek. She was incredible. He never thought he would feel like this about another woman after Ellen.

'I need to say something,' he said. He could feel a lump in his throat.

Gwen looked at him. 'Don't tell me I'm doing it all wrong.'

'No.' Boyd wasn't sure how to go on, now he'd started. 'I just want to say – you've turned my life around.'

'Oh.' She looked startled, but she was smiling, which gave him courage.

'When Ellen died, I thought that was it. That I would never feel happy again. That I would never *feel*. But you've . . . brought me to life. You've given me back my *joie de vivre*. You make me glad to wake up in the morning. You make me laugh. You make me want to do things. Big things. Little things. You've given me a purpose, Gwen.'

'Well,' she said, looking pleased. 'That's lovely. Thank you.'

There was silence for a moment as they looked at each other. Boyd couldn't tell by her face what she was thinking. Had he overstepped the mark? He didn't think he'd been too over the top. But perhaps she found it awkward? Maybe she did just find him a helpful pair of extra hands? Maybe she was longing for him to shut up so she could get on with what she was doing?

Gwen put down her icing bag. 'Shall we just get it out of the way?'

'What?' He looked alarmed.

'I can feel it,' she said, smiling, her eyes sparkling. 'And it's stopping me concentrating.'

'Feel what?' His heart was beating. Could it be she felt the same?

Before he knew it, she stepped forward, slid her arms around his neck and kissed him. A proper kiss, not just a peck.

'Oh,' he said, surprised.

She gave him a minxy grin. 'That's what's known in the trade as unfinished business. Come on, we've got work to do.'

46

'Will you please stop wriggling?' demanded Clover. 'I'm going to end up burning your ear and that is not a good look for a bride.'

'Hurry up, then.' Robyn was looking anxiously at the clock. They had only just over an hour before the ceremony, and it would take half an hour to get there, plus parking. And she didn't want to arrive red-faced and sweaty. She was still bruised from her fall and couldn't move as fast as she wanted to.

'OK. Last ringlet.' Clover drew the tongs through a final strand, then put them down and ran her fingers through Robyn's hair, giving it a very professional tussle. 'There.'

Robyn stared in the mirror in delight. Clover had done her an elaborate half-up half-down do, some of her hair caught up in a clip made from fine silver flowers and fresh-water pearls, the rest of it curling down to her shoulders.

'I didn't know my hair could even do this.'

'Right. Out of your dressing gown and into your outfit. Do you need a wee first? It'll be hours.'

'I had one just before you started my hair.'

'OK. Just let me help you if you need to get out again.'

Clover held out the column of sea green silk as Robyn slid herself in, then did up the zip.

'Shoes!'

Robyn put her feet out obediently and Clover buckled her into the low-heeled silk wedges Gwen had lent her, when time had run out for shoe shopping.

'Now,' said Clover. 'What do you think? Final chance. Do you think I should jack in any ideas about being a high-court judge and be a stylist?'

Robyn laughed. 'Yeah. Maybe.'

She couldn't believe her reflection. Clover had been right about choosing a jumpsuit over a dress: an inspired choice that suited Robyn down to the ground. It was in a floaty sea-green silk that shimmered when she walked. The legs were wide and flowing, the sleeves fluted. It was dreamy and elegant; it fitted her perfectly, with a sense of occasion that wasn't too obviously bridal and didn't make her feel hemmed in. It was far more suited to a beach wedding than any of the dresses they'd seen. It was perfect.

Clover had done her make-up too – glowing skin, sparkly eyes, glossy lips.

Robyn hugged her little sister. 'Thank you. Because you know if it was left to me I'd stomp up the aisle in my dungarees and Birkenstocks.'

'Oh, I know,' said Clover. 'Believe me, I know.'

But she held her sister tight. The accident had terrified her more than she liked to admit.

'I love you so much,' she murmured.

'What?' laughed Robyn. She was sure Clover had never admitted that before.

'Shut up. I love you, OK? And that baby of yours. I love it too.'

Robyn's heart buckled. Clover rarely admitted her true feelings.

'I'm going to miss you, when you go to uni,' she told her.

'It's all changing, isn't it? With Mum and Dad selling Hawksworthy. I don't know if that Dandelion Court place will feel like my home.' Clover's face clouded. 'Not that I'd ever stop them. And I know I'm probably going off to London. But I'll miss you and me, like this.'

'You can always come to the Linhay. I'll keep a room free for you.'

Clover scoffed. 'That place is going to be full of babies. There's not going to be any room for me.'

'There will always be room for you, Clover. I promise.'

In the kitchen, Sheila was putting the finishing touches to the cake, still in her dressing gown. Clover had already done her hair and make-up, and as soon as she finished she was going to get dressed. She stood back to admire her handiwork. Three layers of feather-light sponge, filled with buttercream and then just a scraping of icing on the outside so the cake showed through. It went against all her instincts, but once she had assembled it at the Shedquarters and added the clusters of frosted berries and edible flowers, it would look very pretty.

She stopped for a moment, blinking back tears, finding it hard to believe that here she was icing a wedding cake for that dear little baby that had arrived on a summer's day, a ray of sun that had never grown any dimmer.

She gasped as Robyn walked in.

'Oh!' she said.

'I know. I don't look much like me.' She held out her arms and did a twirl, a shimmer of green silk and dark curls. Sheila clapped her hands.

'You look perfect. Oh, she's clever, my girl.'

Robyn spotted the cake behind her. 'That looks amazing.'

'Clover's got to drive me while I hold it. Hopefully it will stay intact.' Sheila held up two lots of crossed fingers.

Clover bounced into the kitchen, looking as if she was off to Coachella. Never knowingly underdressed, she was in a saffron yellow maxi slashed to the thigh with possibly every item of jewellery she owned adorning her ears, her neck and her wrists.

'Come on, Mum. Stop faffing and let's get you sorted. It's nearly time to go.'

'I'm nearly finished.'

Robyn stood by the door, watching Sheila boxing up the cake layers and Clover getting more and more agitated, trying to get her to put her outfit on so she could finish her hair and make-up. She'd better leave them to it, she thought, smiling, and realised the next time she saw them would be at the registry office, about to get married. She slipped out of the door without saying goodbye. They were too wrapped up in their preparations to notice.

Outside in the yard, Mick was striding up and down beside the car, which he'd scrubbed inside and out to take Robyn to the registry office. She had asked him to drive her, and then take her into the ceremony on his arm. To give her away.

'You're sure?' he said, obviously secretly worried that now this was not his role.

She was never going to let him think he would play second fiddle to Jonathan. There would be a place for Jonathan in her life, but it wasn't at her side as she walked down the aisle.

'You're my dad,' she told him. 'Of course I'm sure.'

Now, she looked at him with pride, dapper in the outfit Clover had chosen for him which set off the softness of his eyes so perfectly.

'Here I am,' she said. 'As ready as I'll ever be.'

Mick gazed at her, slightly in awe, hardly recognising his daughter. 'Get on!' he said, his stock response when he was stuck for what to say.

'And you,' she said, 'look very handsome.'

'You don't think I should be wearing a tie?'

'No, Dad. I've never seen you in one before, so why now?'

'I reckon Rocky will be in one.'

'Rocky's Rocky. You're you. I don't want anyone to be anything other than themselves at my wedding. Let's go!'

She climbed into the front seat.

Mick drove the car as smoothly as he could along the drive. Robyn could see his gaze raking over the pasture either side, the hedgerows filled with froths of cow parsley, the air bosky with blossom. May was always the best time on the farm, when everything burst into flower and before the sun had got too relentless.

'You're not having second thoughts?'

'I am not,' said Mick. 'I'm made up. I feel free. Like a weight's lifted. I love this bloody farm but I haven't got what it needs. Time for someone else to take it on.'

'But won't you miss the land? I mean, you are a farmer.'

He chuckled. 'I've got a plan, don't you worry. I've got my eye on a piece of ground that's come up for sale. Just a few acres. Enough for a small herd of Jerseys.'

'You've kept that quiet!'

'It doesn't do to blabber. Don't want anyone else after it.'

Robyn sat back in her chair, grinning. That's why she loved her dad. He kept his counsel, but he wasn't afraid to get what he wanted, once he'd figured it out.

He looked sideways at her.

'Everything always sorts itself out in time,' he told her. 'Always remember that.'

47

At the beach, Gwen eyed the sky with anxiety. It had been a grey start in Tawcombe, the spiteful slate clouds taunting her, reminding her they could quite easily ruin her hard work at any moment they chose. But by nine o'clock they relented and slid away to torment someone else. Here, the sun was climbing ever higher in the sky, and Gwen worried about keeping the food fresh and the drinks cold. She had ordered vast quantities of ice to be delivered.

Rocky had done the Shedquarters proud. It stood, freshly painted in turquoise and white vertical stripes, with new ironmongery and shining windows. It had gone from being tatty and weather-beaten to the most immaculate beach hut on Everdene Sands. Inside, all the clutter had been cleared away and the surfaces were pristine. It was ready for the most important occasion it had ever been witness to.

'Right,' Gwen said, clapping her hands and calling her team together. She had organised a little team of helpers from the local youth club to carry everything down to the beach. She was giving them twenty quid each for a morning's work They all had their instructions, all to be executed under her watchful eye. And gradually, the transformation took place.

Boyd cordoned off the section of the beach they were using for the party with rope, to resemble a VIP area. Branches of driftwood were strewn around the edges, bound with pale green moss, dusty pink roses and amethyst sea holly. In front of the hut were three trestle tables covered in fine hessian, and on them were white enamel plates and pearl-handled cutlery, and platters of food for sharing: chicken and pistachio pie, spanakopita, cured meats, local soft-rind cheese, ripe fruits and baskets of Boyd's focaccia. There were white linen napkins tied with rough string and zinc buckets filled with bottles of sparkling rosé and recycled glasses with white ribbon tied around the stems.

And beyond the food, there were benches covered in sheepskins, picnic blankets scattered with Moroccan cushions and beanbags, and grey-and-cream striped deckchairs, so everyone could sit and eat just where they wanted and gaze out to sea.

The whole effect was of a dreamy bohemian beach banquet, all the colours very soft, as if faded by the sun and the salt.

For a moment Gwen's eyes filled with tears as she looked at her handiwork. She had begged and borrowed, even stolen if you counted hauling the wood for the food boards out of a skip. It felt wonderful, to have done this for two people whose love she believed in so fiercely.

She looked at her watch. The wedding ceremony would be starting about now. Robyn had invited her to the registry office, but it had been impossible, timing-wise, with everything she had to do, and it was family only, really.

She went into the hut to get changed before everyone arrived. She had found the perfect outfit – a vintage Paul Smith jacket and capri trousers, simply cut, elegant but eye-catching. It was rather bright compared to the understated look she had gone for with the wedding décor, but sometimes you needed to express your personality. It made her feel happy and it fitted like a glove. Outside the hut, she could see Boyd putting the finishing touches to the archway, fixing the starfish in place. He was, it seemed, more of a perfectionist than she was.

He looked up and saw her watching, then came over.

'You look stunning,' he told her. 'I'll be off now. But I'll see you later.'

She knew, that if she'd asked Robyn, she would have invited Boyd to the wedding. But it felt too early, and he felt awkward about it.

'I don't want to be a wedding crasher,' he'd said.

'You wouldn't be,' Gwen replied. 'But I understand. And I'd never have managed all this without you.'

'It's been a pleasure,' he said. And it had been. He'd loved hearing her ideas, and helping her make them come true. It really was going to be a dream wedding.

'Is everything organised for later?'

He winked at her.

'Don't worry. I won't let you down.'

And he kissed her on the cheek and headed off up the dunes.

Unfinished business, she thought, and smiled.

48

Jake was waiting on the steps of the registry office with Rocky and Ethan. It was quarter to twelve. Surely Robyn should be here by now?

'Chill, dude,' said Ethan, who could sense his brother's agitation.

'You don't think she's got cold feet?'

'Errrrr – no?' Ethan rolled his eyes, and jabbed Jake in the ribs with his elbow. 'Tell him, Dad.'

'She's not late yet,' said Rocky. 'This is not anyone's definition of late.'

'It's the bride's prerogative,' smiled Tina. 'I was ten minutes late, remember?'

Rocky nodded. 'She was. Nearly gave me a heart attack.'

Tina pulled out her phone and stood in front of the three of them.

'Right, come on, you three. I want a photo of you. I want to admire my handiwork. Line up on the steps.'

Rocky watched as his ex-wife chivvied them all. She looked incredibly glamorous herself, in a bright pink coat dress over silk cigarette trousers. After their rapprochement of the weekend before, she had spent the week helping them get ready, and they'd all gone off on a trip to Exeter when she found out Jake hadn't actually planned to buy anything new to wear.

'It's supposed to be casual!' he'd protested, but actually they had a brilliant day out, the four of them, shopping followed by lunch. And Rocky could see how much his boys appreciated the truce. They had been good-natured and long-suffering as she had chosen their outfits for them: tweed jackets, jeans and linen shirts, set off with floral silk ties.

Earlier in the week, Tina and Rocky had taken Jake and Robyn out for dinner, to break the ice, as Robyn had never really got to know her. Tina had exuded warmth as she congratulated Robyn on the baby.

'I can't believe how excited I am about being a grand-mother.'

'I can't believe you're going to be one – you look far too young.'

Robyn had been slightly in awe of Tina at first, but when she'd come to look around the Linhay, they had bonded over paint charts and light fittings, and Tina had bought the most beautiful kelim rug as a wedding present. And when she had seen the nursery she had actually cried. Tina was softer than any of them realised underneath the glamour and the drive.

Rocky felt a little stab of regret that they hadn't worked harder to fix things sooner, but maybe reconciliation came at its own pace. It couldn't be forced. But he had to admire Tina for having the courage to hold out an olive branch in the first place. It had made everything so much more relaxed.

There were cheers as Sheila and Clover arrived. Clover had worked her magic on her mum too: the blue jacket and white trousers had a nautical splendour, yet she didn't look uncomfortable. Just beaming with happiness.

'I don't know where they could be,' she said. 'They left ten minutes before we did.'

'Probably parked up waiting for us all to go in. Come on. Let's go.' Jake nodded his head towards the entrance.

The small crowd moved inside the building and walked down the corridor to the registry office, where the registrar was waiting to greet them. It was just a simple room, with a few rows of chairs lined up in front of the table where the signing of the register would take place.

'I'll sort the music,' said Ethan, and conferred with the registrar's assistant, fiddling with the Bluetooth speaker until he got his phone connected.

Everyone else arranged themselves in the chairs, only taking up the front row. Jake stood at the front, chatting to the registrar, his hands in his pockets, feeling for the box with the rings in it for the twentieth time.

And then the music began – Jack Johnson, 'Better When We're Together' – and he looked up, and there she was, walking in on Mick's arm, and Jake took a deep breath and put his shoulders back and smiled at her. She was in flowing pale green, a small posy of bluebells in her hand, her hair cascading around her.

His Robyn. The love of his life. His bride to be. He didn't think he had ever felt so proud.

The ceremony was short and simple. They stood facing each other, repeating the heartfelt words required of them, aware that this moment was the culmination of the love they felt for each other. At the given moment, Jake produced the two rings he had ordered from Marley that would match the engagement ring.

As the ring slid on to her finger, Robyn remembered his words of that night only four weeks ago. 'This vein leads straight to your heart'. She could feel it, the love shooting up her vein, and she could see he could feel it.

And with trembling hands, she put his on too, and they looked at each other.

'I love you,' she mouthed.

Next to him, Rocky heard Tina give a tremulous sigh of happiness. Sheila was dabbing at her eyes. Mick nodded in approval. Clover leaned against Ethan.

'Oh my God,' she breathed. 'I hope someone looks at me the way Jake's looking at her one day.'

Ethan put an arm around her. 'They will,' he assured her, and Clover actually blushed.

Robyn and Jake held each other's hands tightly as they drew in for their first kiss. And everyone applauded, as everyone always did at a good wedding.

And there they were, husband and wife.

49

It was two o'clock and the sun was high in the sky, aware that it had a very important job to do today and that everyone was counting on its performance. Beneath it the sea spangled, throwing out droplets of diamonds and sapphires. The sand glittered with gold-dust, warm beneath everyone's feet. Behind the tideline, a cluster of seagulls sat and watched as the guests arrived, one by one, two by two, dressed in finery unusual for this setting, and made their way to a beach hut almost at the end. The gulls ruffled their feathers in excitement, sensing an opportunity to scavenge. But not just yet. They knew to wait until the coast was clear. Something was afoot, and they would have to be patient.

Most of the guests had arrived and were wandering around with a Driftwood cocktail, made by Boyd with gin and elderflower and lemon. They revelled in the sunshine and the glorious view, Gwen's team of young waiters passing around canapés to keep hunger at bay: scallops wrapped in bacon and chicory leaves stuffed with crab mayonnaise.

And then suddenly, they were here, the bridal party, arriving to applause and laughter as they made their way down the dunes, led by Jake and Robyn, followed by Mick and Sheila, Rocky and Tina, and Clover and Ethan.

Gwen had never seen Robyn look so radiant or Jake look so proud. Her heart swelled with affection and pride and joy as she watched them greet their guests: Robyn's friends from school, Jake's mates from college, some of their favourite clients, Bruno Thorne and his wife, Marley and her wife, a few of their neighbours from the Shed-quarters. The guest list had grown sneakily. Of course it had, as all guest lists do.

And then Robyn spotted her and ran up, flinging her arms around her.

'Oh Gwen,' she cried. 'It's more wonderful than I could ever have imagined.'

Jake was at her side too. 'This is incredible,' he told her.

'Just enjoy your day,' said Gwen, who shied away from attention when it came down to it. 'And congratulations.'

'But I can't thank you enough,' said Robyn, moved to tears by the effort her friend had gone to. 'If it had been left to me, there'd have been a few sausage rolls and a bowl of sangria.'

'You can thank Boyd,' said Gwen. 'The poor man has been run ragged for the past week, following my instructions.'

'Boyd?' said Robyn, her eyes gleaming with interest. 'Is he here?'

'No,' said Gwen. 'He's gone home to have a rest, I think.'

'You could have invited him.'

Gwen hesitated. 'No. I mean, you don't really know him. This is only close friends.'

358

'Gwen,' said Robyn. 'He would have been welcome.'

There was a faint pink tinge to Gwen's cheek. 'There's plenty of time,' she smiled.

Before long, everyone was sitting or lying somewhere on the beach, diving into the food, opening bottles, passing around the platters. The afternoon passed in a blur of bliss, even Mouse and Lara in seventh heaven as they bounded around looking for scraps.

'I've been thinking,' said Tina to Rocky as they sat on a rug together. 'I might sell the business. The wear and tear is getting to me. I've already got RSI and I can't stand up all day any more. I just can't. I think Tomas would be keen to buy the business off me.'

'Well,' said Rocky. 'If you think you're ready for retirement?'

'No!' She looked horrified. 'Just semi. I could stay on as consultant and do one or two days a week for my oldest clients.'

'Can you afford to do that?'

It was great, he thought, that she trusted him enough to have a conversation like this.

'I can sell my house. It's far too big now. And get a flat. A nice one. But a lock-up and leave.'

'Leave?'

'Once the baby's here, I want to try and spend more time here. I want to be a hands-on granny. I don't want to miss out.' A shadow flittered across her face. 'I know you might think that after what I did, I don't deserve it.'

'No,' said Rocky. 'I don't think like that. You know I don't.'

'I might not have been the best mother to Jake and Ethan, but maybe I can make up for it.'

Rocky reached out and squeezed her hand. He didn't say anything, and she wasn't expecting total absolution, but she felt comforted. It would take time, but the wounds she had inflicted on her family were starting to heal already.

She wanted to do more at the refuge too. She would keep doing that until the day her fingers seized up altogether. It was the women there who had made her realise how lucky she had been. And how spoiled. How she had turned her back on something real and honest just because it hadn't quite suited her. Was it too late to atone?

'Don't rush into anything,' Rocky advised her. 'Find a way of winding down before you sell.'

She looked at him. He was so wise. She hoped that the woman he had started to see would appreciate him. He'd told her about Melissa, about how she'd run out on him after their first date. She was lucky he was giving her a second chance. But that was Rocky. Endlessly forgiving.

She sighed. She would never find another Rocky. But she was glad to have him back in her life, and for them to be a team as both parents and grandparents.

After everyone had eaten, Gwen brought out the cake and set it on a table for Robyn and Jake to cut. Sheila held her breath, convinced it was going to topple over, but it looked splendid, and everyone clapped as the pair of them cut down through the layers, both of their hands on the knife.

And then Robyn stepped forward to speak.

'We agreed on no long speeches, because we wanted to keep things informal. But I just want to say a big thank you to my mum Sheila for the cake, even though I shouldn't really eat it because it's soaked in rum. But thank you, Mum, for the most beautiful cake, but more importantly for being the best mum in all the world.'

She ran over and threw her arms around Sheila's neck, suddenly overwhelmed with love for her and wanting to be sure she knew exactly how important she was. She hugged her dad too.

'You're the best dad in the world, too,' she whispered to him, and Mick patted her. She didn't have to say it in front of everyone and embarrass him. He knew.

Jake went on to thank everyone else, especially Gwen, and everyone clapped and cheered as she took a curtsey, rather hating the attention. But the day had been just what she planned, right down to the last tiny detail. And the surprises weren't over yet.

As the sun began to go down, Gwen lit two fire-pits then handed around skewers loaded with plump marsh-mallows for everyone to toast. The flickering flames filled the air with a sweet smoke. Ethan came and sat cross-legged on the beach hut steps and began to strum his guitar. Clover went and sat next to him. They looked like something out of a video, all golden and tousled and glamorous, Ethan with his tie undone and his shirt untucked, and Clover with her hair tumbling down over her bare shoulders.

Robyn and Jake looked at each other, confused. 'What's going on?'

And Clover and Ethan began to sing, their two voices mingling in a duet, smiling at the lyrics as they batted the words back and forth to 'I Got You, Babe', Ethan's voice husky and rough, Clover's sweet as honey, both of them a little tentative at first, but as the audience cheered them on, they grew more confident. They had chemistry, and although it was raw, it was charming.

Jake held out his hand to his bride, and everyone gathered around as they started to dance, barefoot and starry-eyed. Jake, conscious of his two left feet, was slightly awkward at first but held his bride in his arms nevertheless, spinning her round and pulling her into him then bending her back to rapturous applause.

'I had no idea those guys could sing,' said Robyn.

'This is Ethan's gift to us,' laughed Jake. 'He's been training up your sister.'

'I love it!' Robyn threw her head back, laughing, and looked up at the sky. The sun was starting to drop, a ball of fiery coral throwing out burnt orange and hot pink over the horizon as the rest of the wedding party joined in the dancing.

And then suddenly there was the noise of an engine. She looked out to sea. A man in a white cap was driving a motorised inflatable boat towards them. It was long and sleek, and carved through the waves at high speed, flashing white and silver, before coming to a halt just off the shore.

'It's Boyd!' she said, recognising the boat he had been negotiating to buy the day she'd first met him.

'It's time for you to leave,' said Jake. 'It's been a long day. A long week. Come on.'

He bent down and scooped her up in his arms, just as he had that morning only a few weeks ago, when he'd dropped her in the sea. She put her arms around his neck out of instinct.

'But I need to say goodbye to everyone,' she protested.

'Nope. You'll be here all night if you do that.'

He stepped into the sea.

'Where are we going?'

'Wait and see.'

Jake was up to his thighs in water when they got to the side of the boat. Boyd, resplendent in a navy blazer with brass buttons, leaned over to greet them.

'Captain Boyd, at your service,' he said.

'Did Gwen put you up to this?' asked Robyn.

'Maybe,' he said with a grin, and reached out a hand to help her on board. She could sense there was no point in protesting, but sat down in her seat and buckled herself in. Jake clambered in and sat next to her.

'You knew about this too!' Robyn looked at him accusingly as Boyd revved up the engine and turned the boat around.

Jake grinned. 'She knew you'd be exhausted. And she knew you wouldn't leave unless you were forcibly kidnapped.'

The boat sped out towards the horizon, then veered left and headed out past the headland and into the next bay. Minutes later, Boyd pulled up alongside the pontoon outside the Mariscombe Hotel.

'What are we doing here?'

Jake jumped off onto the pontoon and held out her hand to help her off. Boyd saluted them both, then backed the boat up and turned it round, heading off into the sunset.

'We can't go in here. We're soaking wet. They'll kick us out.'

'Shush.'

Jake took her hand and led her through the grounds of the hotel, admiring their handiwork as the guests lolled by the side of the pool.

'We did a good job there,' he said, and Robyn agreed. With the sun about to melt into the sea in a puddle of pink gold, they could have been in Ibiza. Though why would you want to be anywhere other than here? she wondered.

Jake led her around the side of the hotel, up a winding path heavy with the scent of evening jasmine and through a set of French windows.

'Welcome to the honeymoon suite,' he said with a flourish.

Robyn looked in astonishment at the most beautiful white room, swathes of silk draped over an enormous bed covered in rose petals. At the foot of the bed, on a luggage rack, was an overnight bag with their things in it.

'Oh my God,' she said, falling onto the bed and lying on her back, spread out. 'Oh my goodness.'

'It's a present,' said Jake. 'From Bruno. To thank us for doing such a great job.'

'This is heaven,' said Robyn. 'I never want to leave.'

She lay for a moment, smiling up at the ceiling. 'How lucky are we, Jake?'

She realised how many people must have been in on the surprise. Everyone must have known but her. Her heart swelled with love.

'Very,' he said. 'But I have to say, it's been exhausting trying to keep all these secrets. The singing, the boat, the hotel room.'

'I thought we said no secrets?' she said, indignant.

'Good secrets are allowed.' He looked down at her. 'I better go and get out of these wet things. I don't want to ruin that duvet cover.'

He disappeared into the bathroom. Robyn lay back and closed her eyes, going over the events of the day, all the images of her friends and family floating in and out of her mind in a montage until she was nearly drifting off to sleep.

As Jake came back out of the bathroom, swathed in a plush white towelling robe, Robyn jumped, as if she had been pinched.

'Oh!' She put her hand on her stomach.

'What is it?' Jake was on high alert, alarmed by any sign of discomfort.

She lay still for a moment.

'The baby. I think I can feel the baby.' She waited and then smiled. 'I can feel it, Jake.'

She grabbed his hand and put it on her tummy. He shook his head.

'I think it's probably way too small for me to feel yet.'

She gasped again. 'It's like lots of little bubbles.' She laughed in delight. 'Hello, little one.'

'Are you sure?'

'Definitely. It's our baby, Jake.' She saw a tear slip from his eye and roll down his cheek, and she reached up to brush it away. He took her in his arms and pulled her in to kiss her.

'It's our baby, Jake,' she whispered, overwhelmed. 'This is the best wedding present of all.'

'I love you so much,' he murmured back, running his fingers through her hair, and she pulled him down towards her, her wonderful husband, the father of their baby, and the last of the sun disappeared into the sea behind them, slipping away discreetly to leave them in peace.

50

It was the first week in July, two months after the wedding, when Jake pulled the keys to the Linhay out of his pocket and opened the door with a flourish.

The door was double width, made of horizontal planks, with glass panels and fishing lamps hung either side. THE LINHAY was etched into the glass in block capitals. Behind him was the slate path he had laid, with millions of pinprick lights set into the stone. Robyn had planted agapanthus into the gravel on either side, their spiky green leaves and brilliant purple heads giving a splash of colour.

'Ta da!' he said to Robyn. Today was the day they were officially moving in, and they were celebrating with a special lunch. A special lunch with special guests, for Emily and Jonathan were coming to meet Mick and Sheila.

They had worked tirelessly over the past week to get it all finished, deliveries arriving several times a day: furniture, curtain poles, blinds. And finally, the day before, a delivery from the farm shop to fill the fridge.

They'd called it a day at midnight last night, having washed the dust off all the floors and windows, screwed in all the lightbulbs, hung the curtains and even put loo roll in the bathrooms. Everything was perfect.

The last thing Robyn had done was to lay the silk rose eiderdown from her bedroom at Hawksworthy onto their bed. It was symbolic, bringing a bit of her past into her future. And it suited the room perfectly, the colours of the ageing fabric soft in the sunlight from the window.

Today, they stepped over the threshold, eager to see what it was like in the light of day.

The ground floor was completely open plan, except for a utility area and cloakroom tucked next to the stairs. The open kitchen was at the back, and the rest was a massive living space with double height windows that looked out towards the sea. There were logs stacked up to the ceiling either side of the wood-burner, Tina's kelim rug covering the stone floor and a long table made from an ancient tree chopped down on the farm was ready to be laid for lunch, with benches either side.

And on one wall, blown up onto a huge long canvas, was a photograph of all of their wedding guests lined up in the sea, trousers rolled up and skirts tucked into knickers, a tribute to the joy of their day, taken not long after they'd cut the cake.

'Oh, Jake,' sighed Robyn. 'It feels as if we've lived here for ever. It feels like home already.'

Jake nodded in approval.

'I think we've done all right,' he said.

'We're so lucky,' whispered Robyn, sliding into his embrace and enjoying the comfort of his arms. Suddenly the chaos and drama of the last few months was starting to settle. She and Jake were married, their little home was finished, and today, her two sets of parents were meeting each other.

She prayed they would like each other; that they would

all get on, and could be part of her life. Their life. Their baby's life.

Sheila and Mick would be champing at the bit to help, now their own life was going to change so dramatically. Robyn knew neither of them would be at a loose end, because they were both do-ers, but it was going to be odd for them not to have the responsibility of Hawksworthy Farm weighing them down. It was going to be even more strange driving up the drive to the Linhay when Hawksworthy belonged to someone else, but Mick had been right. Why have a millstone when the money could be used to help everyone have the life they wanted?

And they would only be two miles away. Rocky estimated their house at Dandelion Court would be finished by October, so they were trying to dovetail the completion with the new owners. In the meantime, there was a lifetime of stuff to sort through and chuck away. And Clover would be off to university: her results were due the next month, but everyone was confident she would get the grades needed. Robyn felt a burst of pride at her little sister. For all her fizz and glitter, she was a hard worker.

New beginnings, thought Robyn. This was the next phase of their life. Taking responsibility not just for themselves but for others. Keeping the family together, all the disparate and disjointed parts of it. Today was an important part of that.

She looked at the clock. Only two hours before everyone got here.

'We better get the chicken in,' said Robyn. 'And start doing the vegetables. I hope Mum's remembered she promised a lemon meringue pie.'

'Has your mother ever forgotten a culinary promise?' Jake asked.

'Good point,' said Robyn, chucking him the potato peeler. 'You're on spud duty.'

They worked quietly in their new kitchen, getting to know how it worked. The induction hob took a bit of getting used to, beeping and blinking at them. Jake moved the bin three times before it was in a sensible place. Robyn couldn't get over the size of the fridge. Four doors *and* ready-made ice instead of fiddling about with ice trays.

Just before twelve, she began to get nervous. Jonathan and Emily would be here any minute. And then suddenly she saw their car, tootling along the drive. She dropped the knives and forks on the table she was about to lay and ran outside as they pulled up.

Emily got out of the passenger side, a little overwhelmed both by the occasion and the setting.

'Robyn,' she said. 'This is beautiful.'

She was wide-eyed with awe. Robyn hugged her tight and they stood and looked over the grass sweeping down to the cliff's edge, and the sea beyond.

'This is where I was brought up,' Robyn told her mother, pointing over to Hawksworthy. 'This was all my playground.'

'I wish I could have imagined this,' said Emily softly. 'When I wondered where you were all that time.'

Robyn squeezed her hand as Jonathan came to join them.

'Wow,' he said. 'I was expecting a view, but nothing this dramatic.'

'It can be pretty wild, in the depths of winter. We've been cut off a few times when it snows.'

Jake ventured out of the front door, holding his hand up in a tentative greeting. 'Welcome to the Linhay.'

'Hey!' Jonathan bore down on him and shook his hand. 'Robyn's told us so much about you. I'm Jonathan.'

There were more handshakes and greetings. Robyn saw that Jonathan, despite his bonhomie, was a little overwhelmed, as he stepped to one side and wiped away a surreptitious tear. It must be odd for him, only just getting used to having his daughter's presence in his life, and she wondered if he felt as protective of her as Mick did; if that paternal need to shield your offspring was present even if you barely knew them. She felt a pang for both Jonathan and Emily, and wondered if a day like today was hard for them. It must bring what they had missed home with acute poignancy. She was more determined than ever to make them feel welcome, and at home. And of course, they were thrilled about the baby.

'We never want to intrude,' Emily had told her the last time they had spoken. 'But we are always here for you.'

Emily rushed to the car and brought out a huge bunch of creamy lilies. She held them out to Robyn. 'I know this is probably coals to Newcastle, but they smell so gorgeous.'

'Honestly,' said Robyn. 'No one ever buys me flowers because they always think that. Thank you.' She looked at her. 'Come on. There's something I want to show you.'

Emily followed her, up the stairs, Robyn holding firmly on to the thick rope that went up the wall, not just because she didn't want to lose her footing, but because she was getting bigger by the day. And at the top of the stairs she led Emily to a door and pushed it open.

'Oh,' said Emily, putting her hands to her cheeks. 'Oh Robyn.'

She looked around in delight. The walls were a soothing pale sea green and the floor-length curtains were a similar colour with hand-drawn seagulls printed all over them. There was a brand-new cot, and an antique nursing chair re-upholstered in yellow velvet.

'Mum saw the cot in the sale and couldn't help herself,' laughed Robyn. 'If she had her way she'd have bought the whole of John Lewis baby department.'

'It's beautiful.' Emily walked over to the window and looked out at the view. 'This is going to be the luckiest baby in the world.'

She turned to Robyn, and the two women held each other, and Emily tried not to cry at the memories, but to be glad. She managed it until she saw the little piglet she had put in Robyn's box, perched on a little shelf over the cot.

'I wanted the baby to have it,' said Robyn, her voice choked with tears. 'Because it was locked in a box all those years, and it deserves to be loved.'

Emily nodded and held her even tighter. 'This means the world,' she managed to say. 'The absolute world.'

At half past twelve, Mick and Sheila's car pulled up behind Jonathan and Emily's. Robyn felt nervous. It was going to be a strange day for them, and the last thing she wanted was for them to feel threatened. She was conscious that Sheila might still feel on her back foot; Mick was more phlegmatic and far less likely to judge or take offence or overreact, but he could be withdrawn if he felt uncomfortable.

'Mum...' Robyn rushed forwards to greet Sheila as she came through the door, wielding a lemon meringue pie as big as a cartwheel. 'Let me take that off you. Mum, this is Emily.'

She watched as Emily and Sheila stared at each other for a moment. Both of them her mother; both in very different ways.

Emily broke the moment. She stepped forward and took Sheila's hand. 'I want to say thank you,' she said, her voice hoarse with emotion. 'I can't thank you enough, for looking after Robyn. For making her who she is. For giving her a wonderful life...'

She couldn't speak any more. Robyn waited, rooted to the spot, for Sheila's reaction. The woman who had been her mother since she was a tiny dot; who'd seen her through teething and potty training and primary school; who'd taught her to read, but also to plant flowers and bake bread. And to be patient, and kind, and get up in the morning even if you didn't want to.

'Thank *you*,' Sheila said eventually. 'For giving us our daughter. She's brought us joy every single day. Hasn't she, Mick?'

She turned to Mick, who was nodding in agreement but didn't want to voice his opinion just yet. He had always been shy next to Sheila. Or at least kept his counsel until he was certain of his position.

'She's a good girl,' he said eventually.

He turned away. For all his farmer's steadfastness, he was deeply moved. He'd often thought about Robyn's real parents, in a quiet moment, and now they were here in front of him he felt overcome with emotion. The protectiveness he had felt from the day he first saw her was still there, in full force. But he was generous enough of heart to be able to share her, now, even if it was difficult.

'I'm Jonathan,' said Jonathan, stepping forwards to shake Mick's hand. 'Thank you for being such a good father to her. I'm incredibly grateful, and in awe of what you've done.'

Mick nodded, but the look on his face showed he was touched by Jonathan's thoughtful words. He took his hand and shook it, holding it for a moment, then stepped away, gesturing that was enough.

There was silence as everyone took in the momentousness of the occasion, no one quite sure what to do or say next. It wasn't a hostile silence, just a gentle intake of breath while everyone adjusted to their new position and took in the reality of the people they had wondered about all of their lives. Everyone seemed a little overwhelmed by the story that had come full circle. The story that wasn't at an end, but had a new beginning. A story full of hope.

And then Clover burst in, Mouse at her heels, with a giant New Home balloon, and shattered the silence.

'Hey, guys,' she exclaimed. 'Surely we need a toast? What are you all waiting for? Hi!' She smiled at Jonathan and Emily. 'I'm Clover. The super-annoying little sister.'

She insisted on opening a bottle of prosecco and exploding it all over the kitchen, thereby living up to her description of herself, but no one minded as she'd broken the ice. Jonathan took it off her and filled all the glasses while Sheila mopped the floor, and Mick tied the balloon onto a beam in the middle of the room, and the timer went on the oven to say the chicken was done. Everything just fell into place, with everyone finding their role. It could have been stiff and awkward and uncomfortable, but everyone mucked in and chatted and made each other laugh. Mick carved and Jonathan poured the wine and Sheila made the gravy and Mouse tried to work out whose chair to sit under for the best chance of scraps.

'What should I call you?' Clover asked Jonathan, in her blunt, coquettish way. 'I mean, what are you to me?'

'Just Jonathan will be fine,' he replied amiably, not too startled by her.

By the time the chicken had been carved, Rocky and Ethan arrived. It had been agreed they would arrive a little later than everyone else, to give everyone a little bit of space to meet.

'Do you think the table's big enough?' Robyn asked Jake in a panic, wondering if everyone was going to be too squashed.

'Just wait till Christmas.'

'Oh,' said Robyn. 'Christmas.'

And she imagined a tree in the corner, twinkling with lights, and a flaming pudding being brought to the table. There'd be everyone who was here, and maybe Tina if she came down for Christmas once the baby arrived. Perhaps Melissa too – she and Rocky had been going steady for a month now. And Gwen and Boyd, if they could stay still in one place and weren't off on one of their endless adventures, drinking their way through Burgundy or getting the night train to Vienna. Her family, old and new, close and extended, and her friends, all pieced together to make a wonderful whole.

She looked at the table. She'd thought it was enormous, but now she was worried it wasn't going to be big enough for all the people she loved. There would be room for the highchair at the top. Mick had found her old one in the attic and had sanded it down and painted it.

'I can paint the name on when you know what you're going to call it,' he told her.

She gulped at the thought. They'd talked about names. Peony. Rose. Violet. Ezra. Lucas. Kit. Round and round they went, but in the end they concluded it was impossible to decide in advance.

'Thank, you, Dad,' she'd said, tears blurring the space where their final choice would be painted.

As they all gathered at the table, Jake stood at the head, holding up his glass and Robyn came to stand next to him. Sunlight blazed through the window lighting up the expectant faces. Sheila, smart in the wedding outfit she was now wearing at every opportunity. Mick, in his wedding polo shirt tucked into his usual jeans. Emily in a white linen dress; Jonathan in a pin-striped seersucker blazer. Clover and Ethan arguing over what to put on the sound system, heads bent over her iPhone. Rocky, handsome and tanned, his eyes raking over his handiwork, checking for glitches that weren't there, because it was perfect.

'I'd like to propose a toast,' Jake said. 'I want to welcome everyone to the Linhay. Jonathan and Emily, it's an honour to have you here. And Mick and Sheila, without you we wouldn't be here in this wonderful house. And Dad – your sweat is in these walls. Literally. I'm so grateful.'

'Yes,' said Robyn. 'It's taken a lot of hard work to get here. But we're so proud to have you all around the table. So our first toast is . . . to parents.'

Everyone raised their glasses.

'Secondly,' said Robyn. 'To brothers and sisters. Ethan and Clover, you guys are the greatest fun. You are going to be the best uncle and aunt we could wish for.'

Ethan and Clover looked at each other and whooped, banging the table.

'Which brings us neatly to the third toast,' Jake smiled. 'Because we had another scan yesterday. And we couldn't resist it this time. We had to ask.'

He looked at Robyn, and she nodded for him to go ahead.

'This time I want you to raise your glasses,' he went on. 'To mothers and daughters.'

And he held his glass up to Emily and Sheila and finally Robyn, and then held the glass in front of her tummy with an arched eyebrow.

'Oh my God,' said Sheila, clasping her hands in excitement, the penny dropping. 'It's a little girl.'

'To mothers and daughters,' everyone chorused, raising their glasses.

And Robyn caught Emily's eye and smiled.

Credits

Veronica Henry and Orion Fiction would like to thank everyone at Orion who worked on the publication of *A Wedding at the Beach Hut* in the UK.

Editorial
Harriet Bourton
Olivia Barber

Copy editor
Justine Taylor

Proof reader
Laetitia Grant

Audio
Paul Stark
Amber Bates

Contracts
Anne Goddard
Paul Bulos
Jake Alderson

Design
Rabab Adams
Joanna Ridley
Nick May
Helen Ewing

Editorial Management
Charlie Panayiotou
Jane Hughes
Alice Davis

Finance
Jasdip Nandra
Afeera Ahmed
Elizabeth Beaumont
Sue Baker

Marketing
Sarah Benton
Lynsey Sutherland

Amy Davies
Helena Fouracre

Production
Ruth Sharvell

Publicity
Maura Wilding
Alainna Hadjigeorgiou

Sales
Laura Fletcher

Esther Waters
Victoria Laws
Rachael Hum
Ellie Kyrke-Smith
Frances Doyle
Georgina Cutler

Operations
Jo Jacobs
Sharon Willis
Lisa Pryde
Lucy Brem

Discover Your Next Read from
VERONICA HENRY

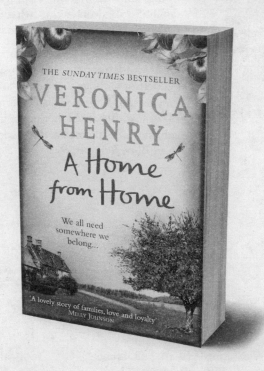

Sunshine, cider and family secrets…

Dragonfly Farm has been a home and a haven for generations of Melchiors
arch rivals to the Culbones, the wealthy family who live on the other side of
he river. Life there is dictated by the seasons and cider-making, and everyone
falls under its spell.

For cousins Tabitha and Georgia, it has always been a home from home.
When a tragedy befalls their beloved Great-Uncle Matthew, it seems the
place where they've always belonged might now belong to them…

But the will reveals that a third of the farm has also been left to a Culbone.
Gabriel has no idea why he's been included, or what his connection to the
arm – or the Melchiors – can be. As the first apples start to fall for the cider
harvest, will Dragonfly Farm begin to give up its secrets?

Everyone adores Christmas...

Especially Lizzy Kingham. But this year, she is feeling unloved and under-appreciated by her family. So she wonders . . . what would happen if she ran away and left them to it?

Lizzy heads to her favourite place: a beach hut on the golden sands of Everdene. But back at Pepperpot Cottage, her family are desperate to find her. For Christmas isn't Christmas without Lizzy. Can they track her down in time and convince her she means the world to them, every day of the year?

The perfect mix of family, friends and delicious food.

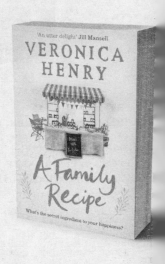

Laura Griffin is preparing for an empty nest. The thought of Number 11 Lark Hill falling silent – a home usually bustling with noise, people and the fragrant smells of something cooking on the Aga – seems impossible.

Feeling lost, Laura turns to her greatest comfort: her grandmother's recipe box, a treasured collection dating back to the Second World War. Inspired by a bit of the old Blitz spirit, Laura finds a new sense of purpose and her own exciting path to follow.

But even the bravest woman needs the people who love her. And now, they need her in return...

A gorgeous escapist read for anyone needing a hug in a book.

Hunter's Moon is the ultimate 'forever' house. Nestled by a river in the Peasebrook valley, it has been the Willoughbys' home for over fifty years, and now estate agent Belinda Baxter is determined to find the perfect family to live there. But the sale of the house unlocks decades of family secrets – and brings Belinda face to face with her own troubled past . . .

'A delight from start to finish' Jill Mansell

Everyone has a story . . . but will they get the happy ending they deserve?

Emilia has just returned to her idyllic Cotswold hometown to rescue the family business. Nightingale Books is a dream come true for book-lovers, but the best stories aren't just within the pages of the books she sells – Emilia's customers have their own tales to tell.

There's the lady of the manor who is hiding a secret close to her heart; the single dad looking for books to share with his son but who isn't quite what he seems; and the desperately shy chef trying to find the courage to talk to her crush . . .

And as for Emilia's story, can she keep the promise she made to her father and save Nightingale Books?

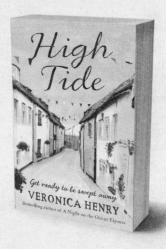

Pennfleet might be a small town, but there's never a dull moment in its narrow winding streets . . .

Kate has only planned a flying visit to clear out the family home after the death of her mother. When she finds an anonymous letter, she is drawn back into her own past.

Single dad Sam is juggling his deli and two lively teenagers, so romance is the last thing on his mind. Then Cupid fires an unexpected arrow – but what will his children think?

Nathan Fisher is happy with his lot, running picnic cruises up and down the river, but kissing the widow of the richest man in Pennfleet has disastrous consequences.

Vanessa knows what she has done is unseemly for a widow, but it's the most fun she's had for years. Must she always be on her best behaviour?

Return to Everdene Sands, setting for the *The Beach Hut*, and discover secrets, love, tragedy and dreams. It's going to be a summer to remember . . .

Summer appeared from nowhere that year in Everdene and for those lucky enough to own one of the beach huts, this was the summer of their dreams.

For Elodie, returning to Everdene means reawakening the memories of one summer fifty years ago. A summer when everything changed. But this summer is not all sunshine and surf – as secrets unfold, and some lives are changed for ever . . .

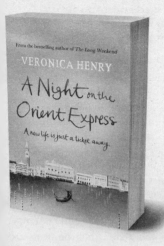

A new life is just a ticket away

The Orient Express. Luxury. Mystery. Romance.

For one group of passengers settling in to their seats and taking their first sips of champagne, the journey from London to Venice is more than the trip of a lifetime.

A mysterious errand; a promise made to a dying friend; an unexpected proposal; a secret reaching back a lifetime. As the train sweeps on, revelations, confessions and assignations unfold against the most romantic setting in the world.

A short break can become the holiday of a lifetime

In a gorgeous quay-side hotel in Cornwall, the long weekend is just beginning . . .

Claire Marlowe owns 'The Townhouse by the Sea' with Luca, the hotel's charismatic chef. She ensures everything runs smoothly – until an unexpected arrival checks in and turns her whole world upside down.

And the rest of the guests arrive with their own baggage…

Here are affairs of the heart, secrets, lies and scandal – all wrapped up in one long, hot weekend.

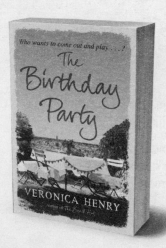

Secrets, rivalry, glamour – it's time for the party of the year . . .

Delilah has lived out her tempestuous marriage to hell-raiser Raf in the glare of the media spotlight. Now planning a milestone birthday, she has more on her mind than invitations.

Raf has been offered a part in a movie he can't refuse. But will he succumb to the temptations he's struggled to resist for the last ten years?

Delilah's three daughters are building careers of their own, only too aware that the press are waiting for them to slip up. For the Rafferty girls might look like angels, but they are only human.

It's the perfect recipe for a party like no other . . .

On Everdene Sands, a row of beach huts holds the secrets of the families who own them

'FOR SALE: a rare opportunity to purchase a beach hut on the spectacular Everdene Sands. "The Shack" has been in the family for fifty years, and was the first to be built on this renowned stretch of golden sand.'

Jane Milton doesn't want to sell her beloved beach hut, which has been the heart of so many family holidays and holds so many happy memories. But when her husband dies, leaving her with an overwhelming string of debts, she has no choice but to sell.

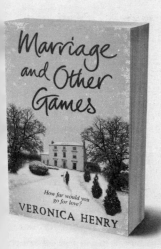

How far would you go for love: a white lie, a small deceit, full-scale fraud . . . ?

When Charlotte Briggs' husband Ed is sent down for fraud, she cannot find it in her heart to forgive him for what he has done. Ostracised from their social circle, she flees to the wilds of Exmoor to nurse her broken heart. But despite the slower pace of life, she soon finds that she is not the only person whose life is in turmoil.

t was the opportunity of a lifetime – a rundown hotel in Cornwall, just waiting o be brought back to life

When the rundown Rocks Hotel comes up for uction in Mariscombe, Lisa and her boyfriend George make a successful bid to escape and live he dream. But their dream quickly becomes nightmare. Their arch-rival, Bruno Thorne, wner of Mariscombe Hotel, seems intent on abotage.

Meanwhile, local chambermaid Molly is arbouring a secret that will blow the whole illage apart. Then an unexpected visitor urns up on the doorstep. It seems everyone in Mariscombe is sailing a little too close to the ocks . . .

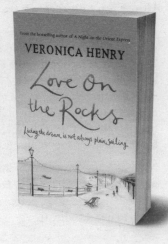

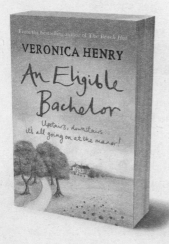

Upstairs, downstairs . . . it's all going on at the manor

When Guy wakes up with a terrible hangover and a new fiancée, he tries not to panic. After all, Richenda is beautiful, famous, successful . . . what reason could he have for doubts?

As news of the engagement between the heir of Eversleigh Manor and the darling of prime-time television spreads through the village, Guy wonders if he's made a rash decision. Especially when he meets Honor, a new employee of the Manor who has a habit of getting under his skin. But Honor has her own troubles – a son who's missing, and an ex-boyfriend who has made an unexpected reappearance . . .

Home isn't always where the heart is . . .

Jamie Wilding's return home is not quite going to plan. A lot has changed in the picturesque Shropshire village of Upper Faviell since she left after the death of her mother. Her father is broke and behaving like a teenager. Her best friend's marriage is slowly falling apart. And the man she lost her heart to years ago is trying to buy her beloved family home.

As Jamie attempts to fix the mess, she is forced to confront a long-standing family feud and the truth about her father, before she can finally listen to her own heart.

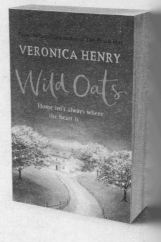

Welcome to Honeycote, and a Christmas no one will ever forget

As the nights draw in, garlands deck the halls and the carols ring out, there are secrets and lies, love and lust all waiting to be unwrapped. After all, it's the most wonderful time of the year…

'Veronica Henry writes like a dream'
Jill Mansell

Originally published as *Honeycote*

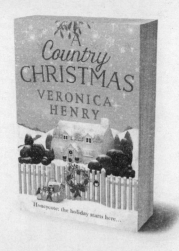

Will an escape to the country be their saving grace… or a recipe for trouble?

WANTED: Enthusiastic couple to breathe new life into a traditional village pub.

When Suzanne and Barney Blake take on the faded Honeycote Arms, it's a fresh start for both of them. But it seems the Blakes aren't the only new arrivals in the village looking for an escape…

Originally published as *Making Hay*

Return to Honeycote in this perfect comfort read, brimming with humour and heart

As the champagne goes on ice and the church bells ring out, it looks set to be a perfect day. But between the bride's clashes with her mother, the groom's cold feet, and a ghost from the past, it seems that trouble has arrived uninvited.

Everyone loves a wedding, don't they?

Originally published as *Just a Family Affair*

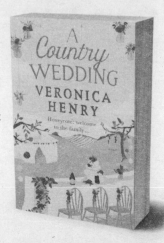